THE EXCALIBUR CODEX

15-11-16

Also by James Douglas

THE DOOMSDAY TESTAMENT
THE ISIS COVENANT

and published by Corgi Books

THE
EXCALIBUR
CODEX

James Douglas

CORGI BOOKS

TRANSWORLD PUBLISHERS
61–63 Uxbridge Road, London W5 5SA
A Random House Group Company
www.transworldbooks.co.uk

THE EXCALIBUR CODEX
A CORGI BOOK: 9780552167925

First publication in Great Britain
Corgi edition published 2013

A CIP catalogue record for this book
is available from the British Library.

Addresses for Random House Group Ltd companies outside the UK
can be found at: www.randomhouse.co.uk
The Random House Group Ltd Reg. No. 954009

The Random House Group Limited supports the Forest Stewardship
Council® (FSC®), the leading international forest-certification
organisation. Our books carrying the FSC label are printed on
FSC®-certified paper. FSC is the only forest-certification scheme
supported by the leading environmental organisations, including
Greenpeace. Our paper procurement policy can be found at
www.randomhouse.co.uk/environment

Typeset in 11/14pt Sabon by
Kestrel Data, Exeter, Devon.
Printed and bound by
CPI Group (UK) Ltd, Croydon, CR0 4YY.

2 4 6 8 10 9 7 5 3 1

MIX
Paper from
responsible sources
FSC® C016897
www.fsc.org

For Siobhan, Greg and Ruaridh

PROLOGUE
Britain, 1937

'Are we lost again, Neumann?'

'This is it, Wulf, I'm sure this time.'

'And the last three times.'

Neumann blushed. 'No, this time I'm certain,' he insisted. 'Look at the hills.' The younger boy pointed to a distinctive shape dominating the horizon and Wulf Ziegler's pulse quickened. He pulled a folded square of paper from the inside pocket of his brown uniform and opened it, comparing the silhouette to the one in front of his eyes. They were exactly as he'd been told they'd be and marked the place he sought as clearly as any signpost.

Wulf patted Neumann on the shoulder and remounted his bicycle. 'We'll ride for another hour and find somewhere to camp.' As the others set off, he looked again at the hills and let out a prolonged sigh. The most difficult part of the mission remained, but even so he experienced nothing but exhilaration. They were here.

Eight boys, aged between fourteen and sixteen, they'd set out from Dortmund on their bikes a month earlier with a hundred comrades. Wulf was the eldest, and the leader – *gefolgschaftsführer* – of the *Hitler Jugend* unit. At sixteen he was a six-year veteran of the organization, respected for his command ability and already marked for the *SS-Junkerschule* at Bad Tölz. He'd helped organize the 'cultural exchange' with members of a Boy Scout troop in Birmingham, but the Dortmunders had told their hosts they were keen to experience more of this fascinating country. With Baedeker guides in hand, the sub-units fanned out across Britain, through the industrial Midlands, and as far south as the hop fields of Kent, seeking out sights of interest. Wulf Ziegler's allotted region had been the north and he'd led his party first to the soot-stained factories and belching chimneys of Manchester, before crossing the mountainous spine of the country to Leeds and joining the road to Newcastle. The journey taxed even fit young men at home in the saddle, like his comrades, but they'd been welcomed wherever they went, offered campsites by ruddy-faced northern farmers, and cloudy lemonade and dry cake by the farmers' cheerful wives. On the way, they had seen many interesting historical sights, but, perhaps more important, great sprawling industrial plants, mills and vast dockyards, each carefully marked on the map Wulf carried. The previous day they'd camped on a windswept moor and been visited by soldiers from the armoured unit training there, eager to meet these unlikely exotic visitors and share their stories.

Today the chosen campsite was on the heather-clad shoulder of the northernmost hill, overlooking the broad loop of a river that twinkled like a silver ribbon two hundred metres below. As the other boys unpacked the tents and bedding and dug the latrine, Wulf climbed swiftly over treacherous pink-veined scree and through patches of green and gold gorse bushes to the summit of the peak. Here, he had a panoramic view of the entire valley through the twin lenses of the Zeiss birdwatching binoculars that had served him so well. He felt an uncharacteristic thrill of fear as he studied the curve of the river and the large house with the grey chimneys exactly where the aerial photographs said it would be. Fear of failure and fear of the consequences of failure. He went over it in his mind, as he'd done a hundred times since the endless rehearsals at the training range. Compared to this, the rest had just been little boys' games.

Tonight.

They would do it tonight.

I

'And the light drizzle will continue well into the afternoon . . .' Abeba Trelawney's hand flicked out and hit the radio switch, consigning the weather report to some distant corner of the ether. God, she hated driving in the rain. The little sports car was fine for nipping about town, but on a jam-packed M25 in a deluge it lost a helluva lot of its charm. She gritted her teeth as the intimidating bulk of an articulated truck surged up the outside lane, throwing a wall of spray that momentarily blinded her. 'What's your hurry?' she snapped at the passing behemoth. Three lanes of traffic moving intermittently between zero and forty miles an hour max; nobody was getting anywhere fast. That reminded her. She was going to be late. Should she call Jamie? Her hand groped for the mobile phone on the passenger seat.

'Damn.' The movement towards the handset distracted her and she almost missed the brake lights on the car in front.

She took a deep breath. No, it was illegal, and Abeba was a girl whose solicitor parents had brought her up to respect the law. She'd leave it for now and perhaps stop later at a service station to send him a text. The thought brought with it an electric surge of excitement from low in her belly. Should she tell him? She smiled to herself and decided not. This wasn't the kind of news you imparted in a text, or even in a phone call. It had to be face to face. The smile broadened as she thought of his reaction. Would he be pleased? Of course he'd be pleased. She caught sight of herself in the rear-view mirror: soulful brown eyes; long hair, black as a raven's wing, and a complexion the shade of pale honey. She looked like the cat who'd just been given a saucer of cream. Would he be pleased? Please, God, let him be pleased. I couldn't stand it if he wasn't pleased. Just one flinch and I'll burst into tears.

But Jamie wouldn't flinch. Not the Jamie Saintclair she knew and loved.

Now it was his face that swam into view. Thin-lipped, sardonic and maybe just a little tired, but with wide green eyes that sparkled with humour and crinkled at the edges. She loved the way his unruly dark hair flopped low over his brow and had been surprised at the lean, muscular hardness hidden behind the old-fashioned suits and assumed air of wholesome innocence. Time had taught her the world-weariness was a defence mechanism, a barrier imposed by his supposed failures with women in the past. She had had to fight to break it down. He was an easy man to like, but there were hidden shadows that made him harder to love, and wary of being in love. An art dealer – she smiled at the memory of their first meeting – not really her type, she'd thought, and maybe a little protective of his secrets, which intrigued and kind of irritated her, until she'd understood why. With patience she had drawn out the real man from behind the psychological suit of armour he wore. At first he had been restrained in bed, and she sensed he wanted to be led, but when she had persuaded him to make the running and allow his passions and desires to rule him, the results had been spectacular and most worthwhile. She gave a little unladylike snort at the images she'd conjured up. They hadn't seen each other for a week and he'd just come back from a trip to France to investigate a painting that might have been stolen by the Nazis during the Second World War. Perhaps later . . .

The outer lane was moving much faster than the others and she considered switching, but immediately thought better of it, even though the big truck was by now a hundred and fifty yards further ahead. Fortunately, the rain had begun to slacken and visibility was much clearer. As pointlessly as it had sped up, the outside lane slowed to a halt and she glanced right to see two wide eyes staring at her from a scarlet face. A furry arm rose to wave a greeting and she blinked. The TV puppet vanished as swiftly as it had appeared to be replaced by a grinning curly-haired urchin about the same age as the kids in the Year One class she taught. She smiled back and tried to concentrate on the road as the traffic picked up speed at last.

From the elevated cab of his truck, Rasul Mohammed had a view of all three lanes ahead. He could feel the adrenalin building in his system as his satellite navigation system told him he was getting closer to the mark. The rain and spray reduced his visibility, but he had no doubt he would know the place when he got there. He had driven this route ten times over the past few weeks and never missed it once. Closer. He nudged the accelerator pedal and moved up so he was almost bumper to bumper with the car in front, which in turn edged forward away from the intimidating presence of the forty-tonne monster. Rasul licked his dry lips. He'd performed the manoeuvre he was about to attempt often, but never in the rain and never in a fully laden truck. That had been for the movies. This was for real. The most important scene he'd ever shoot.

'Mark One.' The voice sounded unnaturally loud in his ears, but he didn't need the instruction. There it was, a white rag tied to a distinctive bush. Less than a quarter of a mile. He flicked the plastic indicator lever to signal that he wanted to move into the middle lane and began to edge his way across into the solid line of cars. In his passenger-side mirror he could see open mouths that would undoubtedly be cursing him for the thoughtless and potentially dangerous manoeuvre. He could almost feel their puzzlement and anger at the giant throwing his weight around like a prizefighter in a pub queue, but he ignored them. Concentrate. Not too far, his positioning had to be exactly right; half in one lane and half in the other, blocking both.

He could see the second mark a hundred yards ahead. Everything seemed so clear. His gaze darted across the dials. Speed: perfect. Weight distribution: perfect. Position: perfect. Even the rain might help, because it would give his tyres less traction.

Now.

'Now!' the voice in his ear echoed the shout in his brain, but his hands and feet were already working in sequence to put the command into operation. In one movement he hauled the wheel to the left and his foot hit the brake with just the right amount of pressure.

For a moment Abeba wondered if she was dreaming. Her consciousness was fixed on the car in front, but at its perimeter a surreal image formed of the articulated lorry swerving into the lanes ahead. The image was followed instantly by a terrible rending of metal and, as if in slow motion, the truck toppled to block the three-lane motorway. She hit the brakes and her scream of fright merged with the squeal of hundreds of tyres.

When the noise subsided, she sat with her head bowed, breathing as if she'd just run the hundred-metre sprint and still only half believing what she'd seen. That idiot . . . she could – would – be stuck here for hours. But natural concern quickly overcame anger.

What about the driver? And the people in the cars up ahead? There had to be casualties from an accident as bad as that. One of the lorry's tyres must have burst to cause the sudden change of direction. Or maybe the driver had had a heart attack? She reached for the door, but by the time she opened it she saw, in the narrow gap between the cars ahead, that dozens of people were already streaming towards the stricken vehicles. She hesitated before closing the door. For a few moments her fingers remained on the handle, but she was forced to acknowledge that apart from basic First Aid she didn't have any particular medical skills to contribute. There was no point in just getting in the way. In some ways it was a relief. The car was a warm metal cocoon that protected her from the realities of what was happening a few hundred yards ahead. She tried to call Jamie, but only reached his voicemail, so she left a short message outlining her situation and began backing it up with a text because she knew he often forgot to listen to voicemails.

Up ahead, Rasul lay stunned among the shattered glass and scattered detritus of his overturned cab, his mind waiting for the pain that would signal a broken bone or a torn muscle. Nothing. He almost choked on the surge of relief and exhilaration that flooded his body. It had worked. The lorry now filled most of the motorway and the carefully distributed cargo of gravel would have blocked the rest. He clawed frantically at the harness of his seat belt. His job was done. All that mattered now was to use the escape route that had been set up for him.

He'd just released the catch when a black-clad figure appeared in the upturned oblong of the shattered windscreen. The man was wearing a ski mask that covered his entire head apart from the eyes and the mouth. He carried a short-barrelled assault rifle as if he knew how to use it. Rasul's first reaction was fear at the unexpected sight of an armed man, but it quickly gave way to elation. They'd done it. His face broke into a smile. Now they would hold all these hundreds of people to ransom for the cause and he would disappear back into anonymous, but cheerfully wealthy, obscurity. The man with the rifle smiled back, but his eyes told a different story and suddenly Rasul Mohammed was screaming inside. The dark mouth of the rifle barrel lifted and the last thing he saw was a flicker of light before the bullets tore through his chest.

An unfamiliar sound froze Abeba's finger on the send button. A sort of flat stutter like the bolt removers you heard when you went to get a new tyre. But not. From quite far away she heard what sounded like panicked screams. Curious, she craned her head to look along the gap towards the overturned lorry in time to see men and women who'd gone to help the crash victims dropping to the ground like puppets with their strings cut. Puzzlement turned to a thrill of raw fear as a man ran desperately into the space a hundred yards ahead and she saw his head disappear in a haze of bright scarlet. Instinctively she drew back and hunched low behind the wheel. She fought to control her breathing, but her body seemed to have dissolved into its constituent parts and she had no authority over any of them. At the same time her mind struggled to assimilate what was happening with reality, but it wouldn't work. What she had seen was impossible. It *couldn't* be happening. More screams and the sound of shattering glass, all accompanied by the flat stutter she had heard originally. Without warning, a ball of red and gold flame erupted to her front left, followed instantly by the sharp crump of an explosion. A car's petrol tank. And much closer than the front ranks of the jam. Whatever *it* was, *it* was happening, and it was coming for her. She had to do something. Anything. Now.

She looked frantically to her right as a young man in a blue T-shirt opened the passenger door of the adjacent car and stood up to get a better view. Her mind screamed at him to get down, but too late. A volley of bullets punched holes in the metal with a drum roll of sledgehammer clatters and he was thrown backwards, half in and half out of the car. Abeba looked across the divide to see a woman's face frozen in horror and the curly-haired boy and a girl who must be his sister staring from the back seats with their mouths gaping. She wanted to shout to them, to reassure them that everything would be all right, but their father lay sprawled in front of them with his body ripped open and the life blood spewing in dark gouts from his open mouth. The screaming was constant now and all around, and she sensed that similar scenes were being played out among the cars and lorries packed tight into what must be a miles-long queue of traffic. It was only then that she realized she was screaming with the rest and she clamped her bottom lip between her teeth. She heard the metallic crunch of cars crashing into each other as drivers tried vainly to escape the trap. A few sped past on the hard shoulder, but a larger explosion followed by a second eruption of flame gave evidence of the futility of attempting that route. With a stricken glance at the shattered family three feet away, she crouched down in the cramped foot well and tried to think rationally. She had to get away. She'd thought she was brave, like her mother, who had survived civil war and famine, but here and now bravery didn't come into it. There was nothing she could do for the woman and children or anyone else trapped in the cars. Jamie's face swam into her vision again. She closed her eyes and her mind locked onto his aura of quiet calm like a drowning person clutching a lifebelt. That was it, she thought tearfully. It was imperative she get to Jamie and share what she knew and he did not. She risked a glance through the steering wheel and found herself staring into the eyes of a masked gunman less than twenty feet away. He was tall and slim and as she watched he raised his gun, a strange modern machine pistol that would be the last thing she would ever see. She flinched at three quick-fire flashes, but the burst must have been aimed at someone fleeing a car behind. With a last glance in her direction, the masked man turned away and she dropped her head. She realized with shame that she'd wet herself. A thought attempted to pierce her fear, something about the gunman, but she thrust it deep, the instinct for survival and waves of terror fighting for supremacy. Her hands shook uncontrollably. Somehow she managed to influence her fear, dragging panic-stricken breaths into her lungs between the sobs. She had to get out or the car would become her tomb. She must survive.

II

The figure in the black ski mask walked calmly among the dead and the dying, picking out targets and executing them with short, efficient bursts from the Heckler & Koch 416 rifle, or firing methodically into the trapped cars, turning the interiors into individual slaughter-houses. This weapon was the ultra-compact C variant favoured by US special forces, fitted with a suppressor and a thirty-round magazine. The suppressor didn't completely silence the weapon, but it was important for their purposes that there should be no general panic in the early stages of the operation. Of course, that wouldn't last. But by then it would be too late.

The three squads had been designated Leopard, Lion and Tiger and the commander, Leopard 1, was quietly satisfied at the way the plan had come together. Satisfied, not proud. Naturally one regretted the necessity for shedding so much blood. They had debated long and hard whether to spare the women or the children, but the outcome had never really been in doubt. There was no such thing as innocence in their world. A lesson must be taught and a lesson learned if their people were to have the future they deserved. One culture threatened all others on the planet and only by being as hard as the followers of that culture would they provoke the reaction they needed. Their mission was to create a compact killing zone one mile long and three lanes wide that Leopard 1's calculations estimated would contain upwards of one thousand vehicles and three thousand potential targets. Of course, some would escape, but the first instinct of most would be to stay with their cars. Each fighter carried eight spare thirty-round magazines in pouches fixed to his belt or a special harness. The extra weight affected their manoeuvrability, but it gave them an awesome killing power. Fifty feet away in the line of cars a passenger door opened and, as a young man stood up beside his car, Leopard 1 turned and fired, throwing him backwards in a welter of blood. Off in the distance the other two teams worked their way into the long lines of cars, vans and trucks. The trap was shut. Up ahead, a distinctive red sports car drew Leopard 1's attention just as three boiler-suited workers emerged from a white van beyond it. The rifle came up and half a magazine bowled them over like skittles. Leopard 1 replaced the magazine with a fresh one and was about to turn the gun on the red car, but a shout drew attention to a stream of people fleeing from a tourist coach towards the central reservation.

'Leopard 2. Targets at your ten o clock.'

The throat mike scrambled his commander's calm voice, but Leopard 2 received the order loud and clear. He reached into a pouch of his close-fitting black overalls and pulled out an oval of olive green metal. With practised movements he flicked the safety clip and removed the pin holding a metal spoon in place. Counting down the seconds until it was time to throw, he lobbed the fragmentation grenade in an arc that landed in the midst of the fugitives. Four or five were engulfed in an explosion that ignited the fuel tanks of three nearby cars, incinerating still more casualties. With a last curious glance at the sports car Leopard 1 moved away to finish off the survivors.

Abeba hauled herself across the gap between the seats, cursing as her belt caught the stub of the gear lever. The engine was still running and she reached for the electronic switch that lowered the window. Her instinct had been to open the door and run, but she had seen what happened to the man in the next car. The wing mirrors on the MX-5 were quite large and in the passenger one she could see what was happening among the cars to the rear. Teams of masked men had emerged from only God knew where to fire mercilessly into the trapped cars, taking no account of the age, sex or colour of the occupants, and to throw what must be grenades into the cabs of the lorries and coaches. The mirror was also big enough to allow her to poke her head from the window so she could look beyond it to what was happening ahead, but still remain at least partly concealed. It felt as if she was screaming at them to shoot her, but, despite her fear, she forced herself to stay in position long enough to make some sense of what was going on. The gunmen wove among the cars, picking their targets, and it could only be moments before they reached her. It seemed to her that they operated with a terrible detached professionalism and she was only grateful they weren't methodically working the lanes. Some targets, it seemed, were proving more attractive than others, and many people must have been attempting to flee the carnage. She had a chance if she could only retain the calm to pick her moment. She waited, counting the seconds, darting glances between the mirror and what was happening to her front, gauging the moments when no one was looking in her direction. One. Two. Oh, Christ. Three. She hauled herself through the open window and dropped to the ground, rattling her shoulder and tearing the knees of her jeans. Fortunately, the car opposite was a big off-road gas guzzler and she was slim enough to squirm beneath the chassis before she caught the attention of the men to left and right. Shaking with terror she lay on the wet Tarmac, with the stink of petrol in her nostrils and her fist in her mouth to stop the convulsive sobs that wracked her body. Her heart stopped as the windscreen of the MX-5 exploded and a pair of black jump boots topped by dark trousers appeared momentarily beside her head. She imagined the gunman staring into the car, wondering where its occupant had gone. All it would take was one look and she would be dead, but the killer had better things to do and the feet moved on. She wriggled sideways under the car towards the strip of hard shoulder that would take her to the grass verge, with its gorse bushes, and sanctuary. Her fingers touched something soft and she froze. Slowly she turned to check the obstruction . . . and bit back a scream. The body of a large man with half a head and a single staring eye blocked her escape. She fought for breath, trying to still the ever-rising terror. Perhaps it could help her. If she huddled up close to the dead body no one would see her. That was it. She would stay beneath the car and ride out the storm.

She closed her eyes and lay as close to the corpse as she dared. She could feel something wet soaking into her jeans and she knew it must be his blood. Oh, Jamie. Why wasn't he here to comfort her? But she knew if Jamie Saintclair had been in the car he would have already died trying to protect her. The questions started to come. The who and the why? The stutter of the machine guns was non-stop, punctuated by loud explosions. Al-Qaida was the only group capable of such murderous ruthlessness. This was an attack that made the 7/7 bombings of 2005 look like a pinprick. But surely the security services would have been watching them? How did they get the weapons into the country, and where did this frightening level of military organization come from? She realized she was analysing the attack to keep her mind off the dangers all around her; the unrelenting screams of people dying; the shrill plea from the woman she had left in the next car and the awful cries as the children were executed. Yet taking her mind off the danger was dangerous in itself. A particularly loud explosion somewhere close was followed by a blast of heat. Something flickered at the edge of her vision and a line of yellow-blue flame ran unerringly across the Tarmac towards her hiding place. Burning fuel. Even as she watched, it licked at the off-roader's rear tyre. If she didn't move soon she'd be incinerated.

She managed to wriggle round so that her head was level with the dead man's and pushed forward until she could see past him to left and right. Nothing. She had a chance. Four yards to the grass and another two up the bank and into the bushes. She tensed, checking again for the terrorists, but could see no sign of imminent danger. With a twist of her hips she wriggled clear and crouched beside the car, making one final check before throwing herself across the road and into the safety of the bushes. Heedless of the thorns that tore at her clothing, she squirmed deep into the prickly gorse and went to ground, attempting to make her body one with the damp earth. There was no question of going further because behind the bushes lay a fence, then open ground. She wouldn't get another five paces before she was gunned down.

From her elevated position she could see the entire motorway for almost a mile through a gap in the bushes.

Incredibly, on the far side, the occasional car still drove past, the occupants ghoulishly ogling the carnage until they realized how dangerous it was. In the far distance one group of black-clad terrorists worked their way through the traffic towards the overturned lorry, as a similar unit, presumably including the gunman she'd seen, moved towards them. In the centre, another team fired methodically into the trapped cars and threw grenades among the dead and the dying. There must be hundreds of casualties already, maybe even thousands. This wasn't 7/7, it was the British equivalent of 9/11— a mass slaughter that would never be forgotten – or forgiven. At the very heart of the cornered traffic the terrified driver of a large fuel tanker attempted to smash his way clear of the trap, crashing into the cars in front and behind as he tried to create room for manoeuvre. But, even as she watched, one of the terrorists lifted some sort of tube to his shoulder and a missile streaked out to hit the big lorry square in the centre. For a moment, nothing seemed to happen, then the tanker opened like a giant rose petal and with an enormous 'whoof' a fireball shot hundreds of feet into the air and a wave of burning fuel engulfed the lorry and everything around it. Car after car exploded to add their fiery death throes to the conflagration. Stunned by the blast and frozen with horror, Abeba prayed their occupants had all been killed outright, but she knew it was an impossible hope. In the centre of that orange and red inferno, individuals and families were burning alive; she would never hear their screams, but the memory of them would never leave her.

The rocket attack on the tanker must have been the signal to withdraw, because the terrorists began to funnel back through the cars to a central point on the motorway verge a hundred yards to her right. She was surprised how few they were, probably only a dozen; tall and lean in their dark clothing, faces covered by identical masks and carrying their weapons with the casual ease of people who handled them every day. Abeba bunched up in an attempt to make herself smaller as two of the killers walked by within feet of her – no, not walked; the way they moved, confident, arrogant, but always wary, made her think of films she had seen of hunting leopards. She felt a surge of relief as they disappeared from sight and fought the urge to vomit, making a tiny choking sound as they moved off.

A minute later she heard the sound of engines starting up. Her first instinct was to stay hidden, but curiosity and an odd feeling of guilt commanded her movements. She had survived. All those people in the burning cars had not. Their killers were about to escape to God knows where and she owed it to them to at least see which direction their murderers took.

She turned and wriggled through the bushes to the top of the bank. By the time she reached the summit, two or three powerful cross-country motorcycles were already gunning their way across the field and they were quickly followed by four more. The first bikes reached a fence, and she expected them to stop, but they rode on as if it didn't exist. Of course, they would have cut it to clear their escape route. Sirens in the distance. At last. How had it taken them so long? She glanced at her watch and was astonished to see that less than ten minutes had passed since the lorry overturned. Images flashed through her head; blood and flame and terrified young faces. And something else. To her surprise she was still clutching her mobile phone as if it was some kind of talisman, the message to Jamie still on screen. He'd hear about the attack on television. She needed to tell him she was safe. Her fingers fumbled for the correct buttons and she had time to form the words 'I'm OK' before she heard the rustling behind her. Somehow she managed to type in seven more characters and hit send before the shadow loomed over her. The sirens were increasing in volume and they'd been joined by the soft, rhythmic thud of a faraway helicopter, but she knew it was too late for her.

She looked up in mute appeal and the figure in the mask said something she didn't quite catch. The gun barrel rose. Abeba Trelawney's last conscious thought was that her killer had blue eyes.

'I'm sorry,' Leopard 1 repeated. 'You should have stayed quiet.'

The masked figure turned to join the others, but at the last moment noticed the mobile phone in the dead woman's hand and stooped to pick it up, staring at the screen. The 'whup, whup, whup' of the approaching helicopter precluded any further deliberations and the terrorist leader ran to where the three remaining Leopards waited on their trail bikes, pulled on a helmet and mounted the fourth machine.

'Let's go,' Leopard 1 shouted. 'Pull them into the middle of the field.'

'Jesus Christ, what the hell is happening down there?' The forward observer's words echoed what the pilot of the police surveillance helicopter was thinking, but he was too professional to broadcast his own feelings over the air. Besides, he knew exactly what he was witnessing as he flew through the pall of smoke that towered over the motorway. Unusually for a police pilot, he had flown choppers in combat, in Iraq, and the scene below reminded him of the road to Basra after American jets and attack helicopters had shot up a ten-mile convoy of fleeing Iraqis. He could see the burning cars and the great glowing pink flower that had once been some kind of petrol tanker. Among the jammed lines of traffic lay dozens of still figures, some of them so small they must be children. He hoped they were hiding, but knew they were not. The pilot was a parent himself and as the scale of the massacre became clear his initial shock turned to anger. He vowed that, if he had anything to do with it, the evil bastards who'd done this would spend the rest of their lives in jail.

'There! At six o'clock.'

The pilot felt his heart quicken as he spotted the little

knot of motorcycles speeding away across the fields. In the distance he could see several others making their way towards a large wood. For once anger overcame discipline. 'I wish this was a fucking Apache,' he said through clenched teeth. 'They wouldn't be so cocky with a couple of hundred rounds of three-hundred-mill and a Hydra up their arses.'

'Just stay on them.' The observer, operating the helicopter's video camera, liked his pilot well enough, but sometimes resented the fact that he thought the only heroes were in the military. In the rear, the aircraft's tactical commander relayed instructions to the ground units homing in on the attack. He grunted. 'Don't worry, we'll get the bastards.'

The pilot put the chopper into hover at three thousand feet, just to make certain the stabilized Wescam could get the best possible picture of the terrorists and the bikes they were riding.

'That's great, boss,' the observer announced. The camera's high-tech lens was picking up every little detail. 'Ah . . . ?'

'What?'

But the white spark the observer had spotted among the trees had turned into a streak and it was already halfway to the Eurocopter EC153. The pilot reacted with the speed of a veteran, but by the time his fingers twisted the cyclical control stick and his foot kicked the left anti-torque pedal to put the aircraft into a dive it was too late.

'Oh, fuck.'

The Stinger missile hadn't even reached its top speed of Mach 2 when it struck the helicopter a foot below the rotor blades. The tactical commander, seated just beneath the point of impact, died instantly as the three-kilogram warhead exploded, incinerated and dismembered in the same millisecond. A ragged-edged fragment of alloy engine block decapitated the pilot so that his still-helmeted head fell between his feet and his neck fountained blood to paint the windscreen scarlet. With no power and no one at the controls, the Eurocopter went into an uncontrollable spin. Trapped at the centre of the inferno, all the observer could do was scream and watch the earth rise to meet him in a whirling blur of speed, fire and light.

The terrorist leader watched the chopper flutter downwards like a butterfly with burning wings to crash with an enormous rending of metal. The main fuel tanks exploded on impact with a massive 'whump', finally ending the agony of what was left of the observer. Leopard 1 brought the big bike round and rode up to the wreck. The bike slid to a halt and its rider savoured the pungent scent of burning petrol, intrigued by the blackened, twisting form sitting upright in a pool of fire beside the wreckage.

'Here endeth the first lesson,' the helmeted figure whispered. *'Allahu Akbar.'*

III

Jamie Saintclair felt a curious sense of detachment as they lowered the oak coffin into the grave, as if it was someone else standing here in the soft drizzle watching the violated body of the woman he loved being placed in the earth. He closed his eyes. Maybe it was part exhaustion – sleep had been hard to come by – but he should feel more than *this*. His fists clenched, nails biting deep into the palms, and he flinched as a hand touched his shoulder. Abbie's brother Michael; he was the one who should have needed comforting. By the time Jamie opened his eyes the coffin had disappeared and the priest was muttering the last few words: *Ashes to ashes, dust to . . .* Oh Christ, why her? Why Abbie? His mind struggled to visualize what it had been like for her in those final moments and he had to force it to stop before his whole world disintegrated. A long silence trying not to think of anything.

Across the void her father stood, features as immobile

as if they'd been fixed in a steel vice. His expression betrayed a mix of anger and pain and grief, pale lips clamped in a razor line to cage the cry of anguish that welled up inside him like lava in a volcano. His eyes met Jamie's and the younger man knew Robert Trelawney was seeing a mirror image. He had his right arm around the shoulder of Abbie's mother, Meseret. Tall and slim, with the pale, golden skin and sculpted features of her daughter, Jamie had barely been able to look at her during the ceremony. The Trelawneys were believers and would take comfort from the priest's words, but Jamie had never been sure what to believe in. The only thing he knew was that it had nothing to do with stained-glass windows or a man on a cross. If the God these people worshipped existed, how could he have allowed it to happen? Abeba, the name was Amharic and meant flower, but it could just as well have been sunshine, because she had brought a light into his life that he'd never previously known. With Abbie every day seemed filled with smiles and laughter. Now she was gone, and the darkness inside him was a bottomless Stygian well. She had been on this earth for a paltry twenty-six years, three months and twenty-two days. And now all the joy and hope, goodness and energy that made her what she was, was lost for ever. His first reaction, after the initial shock, had been rage at the people who murdered her. He would have happily killed them all: the gunmen, the planners, the facilitators and the suppliers, right down to the contributor of the last penny to the blood money in their bank accounts. Then Bob Trelawney had told him about the doctor's letter and the baby, and anger had been displaced by a feeling of loss beyond bearing. Jamie had lost his mother and his grandfather, and never even known his father, but he had not truly understood what loss meant until Abbie and his child had been taken from him. Loss meant a gaping emptiness that had once been occupied by his soul and would never again be filled. It meant eyes that would no longer see the world with the same delight. A heart that would never know joy. He knew this was an exaggeration. Things would change. The hurt would fade. But nothing would alter the fact that they were gone.

The anger remained. He still wanted these people dead.

He must have shaken Michael's hand, because here was Bob Trelawney, solid as a west-country outhouse, thrusting a fist like a leg of lamb at him. He took the hand and shook it, neither man bothering with the traditional crushing match that had defined their relationship so far.

'Remember, you'll always be welcome, Jamie. Our house is your house.' The words came out in a choked rush. Jamie nodded, not daring to speak, ashamed that he couldn't articulate his thanks for what was an unlikely offer. Bob was replaced by Meseret, pinning him with Abbie's tear-filled, wondrous brown eyes, dabbing his cheek with Abbie's soft lips and filling his head with her perfume. He heard a whisper in his ear, or it might have been the breeze, and he held her close, only realizing he hadn't released her when she pulled his arms away from her body. She took a step back, her eyes never leaving his, nodded and was gone.

Jamie waited while the crowd moved away and he was completely alone, standing over the grave and staring down at the polished casket that contained the mortal remains of Abeba Trelawney. For a minute and more his mind fought for something to say, something that would make it right, but there came a moment, almost, of liberation when he sensed there was no need. The essence that had been Abbie was gone, to wherever such essences found peace. Part of her remained, not in the wooden coffin, but inside him, and she would always be there.

The council gravediggers stood patiently a few dozen yards away, talking together in low voices. They didn't look at him, but he knew they wanted to finish their job. With a last look into the grave, he reached into the pocket of his overcoat and pulled out two red roses. The rose had been Abbie's favourite flower. He'd joked that it was because it resembled her: a delicate thing of exquisite beauty that could be dangerous if not handled with care. She had enjoyed that. He dropped them on top of the coffin. One rose for a life extinguished on the very threshold of fulfilment. One for a tiny life that would never be lived. When he turned away the world was a blur.

As he walked towards the cemetery gates he felt a

presence at his side and an immaculately dressed man in his mid-forties took step beside him.

Jamie acknowledged Adam Steele with a polite nod. 'I didn't see you in the crowd, but thanks for coming along.' He wished the tone matched the sentiments, but the other man would understand. A friend since the Cambridge days when Steele had been one of his tutors – though friend was perhaps too strong a word for it – they'd had similar interests; art and languages. Jamie had eventually graduated with a First in Fine Arts, fluency in German and Spanish, and a working knowledge of Russian that was getting a little rusty. At first he'd found the antics of the public school set a bit overwhelming, but Steele gradually eased him into a group of acquaintances who'd been helpful since he'd set up his own art dealership and recovery business in a fourth-floor Old Bond Street office the size of a shoebox. Their paths diverged when the older man had inherited the better part of a substantial merchant bank and exchanged the leafy groves of academia for the dogfight of the City, but recently a shared hobby had brought them closer again.

Steele pushed his hands deeper into the pockets of his cashmere overcoat and hunched his neck against the raindrops dripping from the cherry trees lining the path. 'The notice said friends and family, so I thought I'd keep a low profile,' he said. 'She was a very special girl, and . . .' He shrugged. Yes, Jamie thought, since the massacre there had always been an 'and . . .' Two weeks after the horror on the M25 they still hadn't finalized the number of dead. At least Abbie's parents had been able to identify their daughter's body and the police were sufficiently satisfied with the cause of death to release Abbie for burial. They were the fortunate ones, if you could call it that. There had been whole coachloads of bodies, all mixed together in a great carbonized mass as they died fleeing the bombs and the bullets. Some of the people closest to the exploding petrol tanker had been more or less atomized. Burnt-out cars might contain the remains of one cremated body or four, only forensics would ever tell, and that would take time. Meanwhile, the families waited. He'd heard that just one body in four had been formally identified, leaving hundreds praying that their missing father, son or daughter was one of the still anonymous burns victims lying in a coma, or taken to a hospital so overwhelmed by the number of casualties that they couldn't keep up with the paperwork.

He stopped abruptly as they approached the gate, frozen by the flicker of dozens of camera flashes that had Abbie's distraught family trapped in their bright embrace. As he watched, Michael hustled his mother and father away from the pack of press photographers into the car that had carried Jamie to the funeral and it drove off.

'Vultures,' Steele muttered. Sensing Jamie's anger, he took him by the arm and steered him away. 'Why don't we take a walk? I like cemeteries. People are at peace here.' The gravel path led them to the older part of the graveyard, where the moss-covered stones didn't hold the same threat to mortality as the gleaming marble they'd passed. Here there were no carefully tended plots, or mini gardens with plastic flowers and gnomes, no children's toys or gold embossed epitaphs, only time-worn inscriptions to men and women long gone, and well on the way to being forgotten.

'She liked to take me dancing.' Jamie gave a short, bitter laugh when he saw the startled look on Adam Steele's well-fed features at the unlikely suggestion. Quite suddenly he felt the need to unburden himself in a way that hadn't seemed possible in the past few days and the words poured out. 'Nightclubs. Up the West End. Three in the morning and still going strong. She didn't even drink. Could go all night on two glasses of tonic water.' He shook his head at the memory. 'Liberating, she called it. "Here," she said, "we can be whoever we want to be." At first I didn't want to be there, all thumping base and techno-whatever, but gradually she got me to relax and I enjoyed it. Not exactly what I'd call music, but it was hypnotic.'

'You've never struck me as someone who needed to *search* for himself, Jamie,' Steele murmured. 'I'd say you always knew exactly who you were.'

'Actually, I was just happy to be with her,' Jamie continued, as if the other man hadn't spoken. 'She was so full of life, you see. Bursting with it. I can still see her now, tall and beautiful, waving her hands in the air, and so elegant; like one of those graceful African antelopes you see on safari. Aloof, you might have said – life seemed to flow around her – but I've never met anyone who *cared* more.'

'And the bastards killed her.'

Jamie's head whipped round and Adam Steele recoiled from the violence in his eyes. He'd heard stories, just whispers, about certain events surrounding the discovery of a Raphael painting, the provenance of which was still being verified. And more recently something concerning an art-loving Russian billionaire who'd become the victim of a now-deceased serial killer. For the first time he saw a hardness, verging on savagery, in Jamie Saintclair, that convinced him those whispers might be true. As quickly as it appeared, the flame died, leaving just the glowing embers. 'Yes, they killed her.'

'Al-Qaida.'

'Or one of their spin-offs.' Jamie's voice held an almost visceral loathing. 'According to the news they used the correct code word when they *claimed responsibility*.'

'Gloated, you mean.'

The eyes flared again, and the tone matched them. 'They butchered her in cold blood. Stood over her and pumped three bullets into . . .' Jamie shook his head as if he was fighting a knife deep in his guts, '. . . into her face. She was so beautiful. Why would they do that?'

'Because they despise beauty,' Adam Steele said. 'Because they're savages.'

'Abbie wouldn't have believed that, even if she'd known what they did to her. She wasn't like that. She always thought the best of people.'

'And you, Jamie?'

'Me?' Now the green eyes went as cold as an Arctic ice field. 'If it was up to me I'd kill every last one of the bastards and consign their rotten souls to Hell.'

They continued on for a while and Jamie was surprised to find they were back at the gate. The photographers and the funeral cars were gone, and the only vehicle in sight was a sleek black Aston Martin sports car.

'Looks like they've abandoned you.' Adam glanced at his watch, 'Can I give you a lift to the hotel?'

'No thanks, I've made my excuses. It will be mostly Abbie's relatives and her workmates. Warm tea, cold sausage rolls and copious amounts of sympathy. I'm not quite ready for that.'

'Home? Office?' Steele persisted. 'Sure?'

Jamie shook his head. 'I need a bit of time to myself. I'll walk to the station, it's not far.'

The older man held out his hand and Jamie took it. 'Look, old son,' Steele said, 'take this for what it's worth. I'm no psychiatrist, just someone who does a little business, enjoys life and collects baubles with sharp edges. Sometimes, though, it's better to get straight back into the saddle. Give the mind something else to dwell on. When you feel up to it, come round to the flat. I might have something for you. Something that will definitely interest you, I promise.'

Jamie gave him a look, and Steele laughed as he opened the Aston's door. 'Don't tell me you're too bloody busy?'

Jamie watched the big car roar away, the powerful engine kicking through the gears. No, he wasn't too busy. Saintclair Fine Arts was walking its usual perilous tightrope between solvency and the other thing. Truth was, he needed either a change or a rest, but something told him a rest would only invite the ghosts of the past back into his life. There had been something in the way Steele made his suggestion, a certain electric charge in his voice, that made Jamie Saintclair think he might well take up that offer.

But not now. Now, he needed a bottle of malt to numb the pain, some music to remember her by, and a lonely bed where he could dream of vengeance.

IV

Bang. Bang. Bang. His mind threatened to explode as he smashed his fists against the coffin lid. Bang. Bang. Bang. It wouldn't budge, not even the tiniest fraction, and he knew that even if it did he would still be buried beneath six feet of damp, black earth that would pour into his mouth and suffocate him. His throat constricted at the thought and the level of panic rose, so he would have screamed if he had been able. Bang. Bang. Bang. Jamie Saintclair came bolt upright in the bed, the breath wheezing in his throat and cold sweat running down his back. The coffin had been a nightmare, but the banging was real. He rolled over and stood up on shaking legs, dragging on the black silk robe Abbie had given to him on his last birthday. The sound came from the front door of the Kensington High Street flat and he staggered through, wishing to Christ he hadn't had the last of the Macallan and with half a dozen horrible scenarios fighting a nuclear war in his aching head.

Bang. He ripped back the bolt and opened the door.

'Mr Saintclair.'

'Ugh?'

'Perhaps there might be a better time, sir?'

Through a half-opened eye the blur became a uniformed sergeant of Her Majesty's Metropolitan Police. He shook his head. 'Wha' can I do f'r you?' God, something had made a nest in his mouth and he sounded as if it was still in residence on his tongue. He licked his cracked lips. 'No, um, time like the present, Officer.'

'I just wondered if I might ask you a few questions, sir, and return this.' The policeman held out a clear plastic evidence bag containing a mobile phone that Jamie vaguely recognized as his own. 'And perhaps I might make you a cup of coffee to apologize again for the bad timing of my visit. Though I'm sure you, more than anyone, understand the urgency of the situation?'

Five minutes later they were seated at the kitchen table. Jamie had thrown on a few clothes and he sucked at the life-giving nectar that was milky Nescafé with three sugars, though he usually took neither sugar nor milk. 'Good.' He raised the cup in salute.

The grey-haired sergeant gave the tight smile of a man who'd administered many such life-giving revivers and took out his notebook to signal that the interview had entered its more formal phase. He placed the evidence bag on the table in front of Jamie.

'You volunteered your mobile phone as evidence on,' he checked his notebook, 'the twelfth of February, three days after the unfortunate events out by Gerard's Cross. Can you just confirm that this is the evidence in question?' Jamie nodded, but made no attempt to pick up the phone. 'Good. Then I formally return this evidence to your possession. If you could just sign here, sir.' He produced a form and Jamie accepted a cheap plastic ballpoint and signed with a shaking hand. The sergeant smiled, relieved to have the difficult part of the proceedings out of the way. He picked up the bag and carefully dropped the phone into his palm. 'Now, sir,' he handed Jamie the slim oblong of black plastic, 'if I could ask you to switch it on – I think the battery should still be charged – and, er,' his face twisted in a way that said he wasn't entirely comfortable, 'bring up the final message you received from the, ah, late Miss Trelawney. I hope this isn't too painful for you, sir. As I say, I can come back another time.'

'No, that's all right. If it's important?'

'The latest count is four hundred and forty-five dead, sir. Everything is important.'

Jamie grimaced. 'Yes, sorry. It says. "Caught in traffic, going to be late. I'm OK." Then a space, then: "febluis".' He shook his head. 'She . . . Abbie . . . was obviously trying to reassure me that everything was all right. It must have been sent before the attack.'

'Well, that's the thing that's slightly bothering our people, sir. According to the timings on the phone, and the data from the service providers, this message was transmitted in the latter stages of the assault on the motorway traffic. In fact, it was sent only two minutes before our surveillance helicopter was shot down, at a time the cameras we recovered from the chopper show the first terrorists already making their escape.'

Jamie tried to force his drink-fuzzed mind to analyse the significance of the information. 'I . . .'

'That's right, sir. It appears that Miss Abeba Trelawney survived the first phase of the attack and was killed while the terrorists were making their withdrawal.'

'Shit.' The breath turned to mud in Jamie's lungs and he struggled to breathe. 'She . . .'

'I'm sorry, Mr Saintclair, but there's no easy way to say it. Your young lady was among the last, if not *the* last, to die on that day. Which makes this text enormously significant. The main part of the message seems perfectly normal. What I need to know is if "febluis" means anything special to you. Is it some kind of special shorthand between you? A coded message only Miss Trelawney and you would understand?'

'It doesn't mean anything. I mean . . . *febluis* . . . what could it mean?'

'That's what we're . . . I'm, asking you, sir. Our best people have turned it upside down and inside out. She'd have been frightened and confused.' Jamie flinched at the image of Abbie terrified amongst the burning cars and trucks, trying to send her last message, the petrol smoke thick in her nostrils and her murderers prowling all around, and that final moment . . . 'They've checked out all the ways she might have missed the keys she was aiming for, but they haven't been able to come up with anything. We're looking at whether it could be a name, or a word in a foreign language. I'm told Miss Trelawney is part-Eritrean? To be honest, you're our last resort.'

'I'm sorry, Sergeant.' Jamie shook his head. 'I can't help you. How . . . how are the investigations going? Are you any closer to catching these animals?'

'I couldn't say, sir. You'll understand that this is far and away this country's biggest murder inquiry. I'm just a superannuated delivery boy, really, and with bad knees at that. I read in the papers that several suspects are being held and we are "following a number of lines of inquiry". You know what, sir?'

'Yes?'

'You'll have seen *Casablanca*, with Bogey and Claude Raines?'

'Of course.'

'Well, strictly between you and me, from what I hear, this is a case of: Round up the usual suspects.'

'What do we have?'

The Director General of the Security Service chewed his lip. 'Well, Minister, we are using all our resources and we're following a number of lines of inquiry—'

'Don't give me that bullshit,' the Home Secretary exploded. 'Keep it for the bloody newspapers. I want facts. The Prime Minister is breathing down my neck and the papers are talking as if I'm already fucking history.'

The refined Home Counties accent made the profanity all the more shocking. An aide whispered something to her and she took a deep breath and visibly calmed. 'I apologize. Please, strike that from the record.' She took a sip of water from the glass in front of her. 'Mosques are burning in Leeds and Bradford and there have been race riots on the streets of the capital. Parliament is demanding to know why we had no forewarning of an attack that has cost the lives of at least four hundred and fifty men, women and children and thus far I have not been able to give them any answers. Hundreds more are injured or still missing. This is why you exist, gentlemen. A failure on this scale means that unless we apprehend these murderers very quickly there will be a root-and-branch reform of the security services of this country. That decision will come later, but for the moment I prefer to concentrate on what we are achieving.'

The MI5 chief had been thinking about his rose garden, and that dealing with politicians who had no sense of scale or perspective, and no idea how the real world worked, was one of the great burdens of his job. He could have trotted out the old chestnut about the terrorists only having to get it right once, which was entirely true, but he doubted the minister would appreciate that. The words *root-and-branch reform* sent a worrying chill through him.

'Nick.' He nodded to one of his assistants.

The young man in the dark suit and heavy-rimmed spectacles looked up from his notes. 'We are going through the process of putting every intelligence asset, agent in place and informant on our books through the proverbial wringer for any information about the attack, unusual movement of people or provisions, odd changes in behaviour or large financial transactions. We're also talking to the Islamic community's religious leaders. Many of the radicals have been shocked by the scale of this atrocity and we're assured they'll do anything they can to avoid the inevitable backlash against their people. Acting on our instructions, Special Branch have pulled in every name on the Black List known or suspected to have visited militant training camps in Pakistan or the Horn of Africa over the past decade.' He removed his glasses for a moment, focusing his thoughts as his eyes drifted towards the window and the restricted view through the security grilles to the red-brick buildings on the other side of Marsham Street. 'This was a highly skilled, well-disciplined operation; whoever carried it out had undergone intensive training and had knowledge of weapons, logistics and tactics. Given our past experience, it's likely the attack was planned and coordinated from Pakistan. We have our own sources there, but obviously the Pakistanis have more and better. We've asked for priority access to their intelligence, but the ISI is being its usual cooperative self: all smiles and assurances and weasel words. We might have to ask the Cousins to pull some strings, but that will take time.'

'And the results of all this activity are?' the Home Secretary demanded.

'Nothing.'

'Nothing?' The word emerged almost as a groan.

'All indications are that there was no apparent abnormal behaviour from any of our known or suspected threats. To all intents and purposes, the people who carried out this attack are ghosts.'

'Don't be melodramatic,' the minister snapped.

The DG frowned. 'Could they have been brought in for a one-off job?'

'It's possible,' Nick acknowledged carefully, knowing his boss was as aware of the answer as he was. 'But it would be risky to bring the personnel *and* the weaponry through customs. We have a good record of hampering or stopping the movement of terrorist suspects, whether by air or by sea. They'd have to be very good, but then I suppose they've proved they are.'

The Home Secretary drew in a long breath through her nose and Nick was reminded of a bull about to charge. 'So what *do* we have?'

The MI5 man snapped open a green folder on the desk in front of him. 'From forensic analysis of the ammunition fired during the attack we know that the weapons they used were Heckler and Koch 416C assault rifles, a very effective automatic weapon popular with special forces troops both here and in the United States. Further analysis and liaison with our friends in the CIA have confirmed that these particular guns came from a batch that went missing en route from the States to Afghanistan, while they were going through a supply depot in Peshawar, Pakistan. The word on the ground at the time was that they'd probably bring someone a nice profit in the weapons bazaars up north. It turns out the word was wrong. The terrorists also had the use of Soviet-era RPG-7 missiles of unknown origin, and at least one Stinger missile, ditto.' His voice turned apologetic at the disturbing list of intelligence failures, but this wasn't his first high-level meeting and his eyes met the minister's accusing gaze without flinching. 'As you'll know, Stingers are not commonly available on the arms market, and that may give us our best route into the terrorist supply chain. From the surveillance film recovered from the downed helicopter we know that there were twelve attackers, physically fit, weapons trained, with faces masked to conceal their identity, as you would expect. The ammunition was generally delivered in clinical three-round bursts, which is very professional and, in its own way, quite surprising. Our Islamic brethren have a tendency to get excited and blow the hell out of everything in sight.' He saw his boss's icy glance at this detour into subjectivity and returned swiftly to his brief. 'The perpetrators escaped on twelve off-road trail bikes and we can track their movement across the fields, but once they reached the road they appear to have split up and rendezvoused with other getaway vehicles – again, type and origin unknown, but they must have been large enough to accommodate bikes and riders.' He paused and took a sip from the bone-china cup in front of him, his face wrinkling with distaste when he realized the tea was stone cold. 'We believe we have discovered the remains of five of the bikes at sites across the Midlands and southern England, all burned out and with any serial numbers filed or etched off with acid. It's possible we can restore the numbers, but the likelihood is that the bikes were stolen to order. Still, if we can track down the previous owners it might provide us with a concrete avenue of inquiry. Finally, we come to the lorry that caused the traffic jam. It was definitely stolen, two weeks prior to the attack, from an overnight truck stop outside Leicester. The owner/driver was sleeping in the motel and didn't know anything about the theft until he woke in the morning. By the time it was driven on the day of the attack, the number plates had been changed and it had been given an expert paint job. That means it must have been kept in a garage or a warehouse for up to fourteen days. The police have several teams across the Midlands and the south attempting to locate that warehouse, but I'm sure you can imagine the scale of the task. We're also pretty certain the terrorists must have made at least one dry run, so we're studying film from traffic cameras along the route. Again, that will take time. More than a million people use the M25 every day, so it's like looking for a needle in a field of haystacks.'

'Gerald.' The Director General nodded to a second aide. 'You're our special ops expert.'

'My instinct is that these people are home grown.' Gerald's pale eyes roamed the table, daring anyone to challenge his opinion. His long fingers worked at a pencil with an intensity that made his junior colleague wonder that it didn't break. Nick had joined Five straight from university and, if he was being honest, the former SAS officer sometimes intimidated him. 'An operation of this complexity and scale and carried out with such precision would require months of preparation and training. They knew the terrain, how the traffic would be affected by an accident of a certain type, and the reaction time to the second of the police helicopter. They would have reconnoitred the target and the escape routes in minute detail. Their leader would have run them through the mission a hundred times, practising for every eventuality, timing their getaway and familiarizing them with their weapons.' He rapped the table top with the pencil. 'That means somewhere remote and outdoors. I have our people checking every out-of-bounds school, adventure-training facility and large-scale paintball course in the country. Their choice of weaponry was designed to fit the scenario exactly as it happened. It would have been simple enough to smuggle in the assault weapons, grenades and RPGs in a batch of engineering equipment – we know they have the covert backing of some very powerful business people.' He shrugged. 'The Stinger would have taken a little more doing, but these people are professionals. Personally, I have my doubts whether the supply chain will give us anything.'

'You're telling me we have got precisely nowhere.' The minister had her head in her hands.

Gerald and his chief exchanged glances, while Nick studied his notes before answering.

'Oh, I wouldn't say that, ma'am. There are several avenues of inquiry open to us, and we're still hoping to get a lead from GCHQ about the type and method of communications they used. The NSA is helping with that. There's also satellite surveillance. The Americans say their birds don't cover the United Kingdom, but we know that to be a little white lie and we're pushing for a look at anything they've got. And we have identified the driver of the lorry.'

The blond head rose and the minister fixed him with a predator's eyes.

'His name is – rather, was – Rasul Mohammed. British-born of Pakistani origin. Age thirty-four. He was a karting champion – that would be racing go-karts, ma'am – at age fourteen, wanted to get into Formula One, but his career stalled in one of the lower Formulas. He looked for other ways to carve out a career as a driver, and stumbled on truck racing, where the big money is in America. By all accounts he made a decent living and was known for the tricks he could do with a forty-tonner. That led him to part-time work as a stunt driver for film companies.'

'Al-Qaida?'

'No radical links, as far as we can tell, at least not until recently. A month ago his bank account received a major payment well above anything he'd ever been given for appearing on a film set. The payment has been traced back to a dormant account in the Cayman Islands, known to have been used by Al-Qaida in the past.'

'So Al-Qaida.' The Home Secretary's voice took on a note of command. 'We bring in his wife, his family and his friends and we squeeze them until the pips squeak.'

The chief of SIS ran a lazy eye over his political master. 'If he was mainstream Al-Qaida, Minister, I suspect he would be out there with them and not left dangling like a bullet-riddled piece of bait to tempt us in the opposite direction from that which we—'

'I'm perfectly aware of that,' the Home Secretary huffed.

'The reason he was killed is precisely because he was not Al-Qaida and therefore could not be trusted to keep his mouth shut,' the Director General continued remorselessly. 'He was probably paid half in advance with half due on completion. Instead, his accomplices delivered the second part of the payment at a muzzle speed of about four thousand feet per second which, I presume, was much less welcome.'

'So what do we do? I must have something to take back to the Prime Minister.'

'Do? We follow the leads we have, which are mainly connected with the transport. Twelve men on motor-cycles transferring to some other form of vehicle. Someone must have seen something. We have the co-operation of many in the Islamic community. These men all have mothers, fathers, brothers, sisters and lovers.

All it takes is one whisper and we'll have them all. Oh, and we pray.'

'Pray?'

It was Gerald who answered. 'Yes, Minister. We pray that they've gone into deep cover and they're not already planning their next spectacular.'

The images flickered across the screen of the television in the sparsely furnished room at the secure compound in the far north of Pakistan. The watcher frowned, taking in for the fourth time the smoke billowing from the burning petrol tanker and the lines of trapped cars filled with the dead and the dying. He signalled to the young man standing politely by the doorway to approach.

'We must discover who is spilling the blood of the infidels in my name.'

'Of course, al-Amir,' the younger man agreed.

He studied the screen again, this time the picture was a close-up of the wreckage of a downed helicopter. The scale of the atrocity was impressive. Much more impressive than the organization's Jihadis had achieved in their attack on the London transport system in July 2005. It spoke of excellent planning and coordination and was a great blow against the hated British, yet it perplexed him. 'He who rides the tiger must always be in control of it, lest it devour him.'

'Our friend in Washington has sent word that some of the equipment used in the attack has been traced back to one of our cells.'

The watcher nodded. The friend in Washington had made himself useful – keeping him one step ahead of the unmanned drones that had proved so deadly against his less well-informed rivals. Of course, he was much more secure now; as secure as any man who lived his lifestyle could be. He no longer used the satellite phones that the CIA had somehow used to track him in the past, and hard experience and heavy losses had taught him the folly of passing information on the Internet. No matter how sophisticated the technology, the Americans were always one step ahead, as the shameful execution of The Leader had proved. The infidel Americans and British believed the death of The Leader was the end. He intended to prove to them that it was only the beginning, may God strike them down.

Now he maintained contact with his organization through a single courier, a man who had been with himself and The Leader in the caves in Tora Bora and had served him well ever since. If the watcher trusted anyone, it was Jamal al Hamza. From this remote compound he controlled the mainstream Al-Qaida network through that single strand, and by proxy spread his will across a web of fellow travellers throughout the world. It was sometimes a frustratingly slow method of communication, as now, when he would have liked to unleash his wolves against the imitators who shamed him by acting without his consent. But his safety and security were paramount, and it must suffice. Still, he would do what he could.

'Activate the security team.'

The young man, who was his son, and would be his successor, bowed and went to encode the message the courier would carry to Islamabad, where it would find its way to England.

Abu Ayoub al-Iraqi returned to his task of planning his great coup against the enemy. He dreamed of a dark mushroom cloud against a clear blue sky and a white house in ruins.

V

Jamie would have been quicker taking the Tube, but on some mornings he woke with a distinct aversion to train travel, brought on by an unfortunate experience when he'd made a closer acquaintance with the underside of the 12.20 to Euston than was good for a man. So today he boarded the No. 10 bus from Kensington High Street to Hyde Park Corner. From there it was just a short walk to the Mayfair mansion off Berkeley Square that Adam Steele laughingly called 'the flat'. The elderly man in the next seat disembarked at the Albert Hall and Jamie absently picked up the newspaper he'd left behind. The date on it surprised him. He didn't really do dates any more. His calendar was the number of days since Abbie's death and today was number thirty-five.

For many, the initial anger and grief that had followed the M25 massacre had condensed into a bitter, festering hatred. The main picture on the front page was of a burning mosque with masked white youths dancing in front of it. There'd been another running battle between whites and Asians, in East Ham. It was the same in Manchester, where BNP supporters had stormed through a Pakistani market, beating up customers and overturning stalls. Labour MPs in the House of Commons were demanding to know what progress had been made in finding the attackers and what guarantees the Government could give that there wouldn't be another. The Prime Minister was even under attack from his own backbenchers. The headline across two pages read: 'An act of extreme violence demands extreme measures' and the accompanying news story had right-wingers calling for the mass round-up and detention without trial of anyone considered a threat to the nation's security. Jamie struggled to rationalize his feelings as he read the paper. Six months or a year ago he would have said he'd never had a racist thought or knowingly uttered a racist word. He had black friends. His lawyer was an Asian. Once or twice he'd had to defend Abbie against bigots from both sides of the divide: young British men for whom all people of colour didn't belong and young black men who despised her for being with a white man. Now he looked at the pictures and couldn't find any sympathy for the dark-eyed, bearded men and veiled women looking so despondent outside their looted shops. Logic said *they* had nothing to do with Abbie's murder. But logic couldn't compete with the anger burning inside him, and that anger declared *them* at least partly responsible for what had happened. It was *their* community who harboured the men who had pulled the trigger. How could *they* have let that happen if they professed to be part of the same society he did? Yet even as the thoughts formed he could hear Abbie shouting at him to be the man she knew he was. This was not her way. Hatred and blame were not part of her world.

He closed his eyes and resolved to fight the corrosive rage that ate at him. But when he opened them again a young dark-skinned man in a turban had taken the seat opposite. Their eyes met, the other man's dark and unfathomable. Jamie's heart thundered and his mind went blank and before he knew what was happening he was walking towards the stairs. When he got off at the next stop the only loathing he felt was for himself. Christ, the man had been a Sikh, not a bloody Muslim, and the reaction was triggered purely by the colour of his skin.

By the time he rang the doorbell at Adam Steele's mansion house he'd almost recovered his composure and his chest was filled with restless anticipation. A tall, chestnut-maned girl with a languid smile opened the door and welcomed him with a silky handshake, introducing herself as Charlotte Wellesley, the banker's PA. Her greeting had the easy self-confidence that comes with the best public schooling, and beneath the black silk suit she had the kind of angular, rangy figure that reminded Jamie of an American detective of his acquaintance.

'He's upstairs in the play room,' she whispered. 'He was expecting you, but you know what he's like.'

He smiled his thanks. Why had he come? Partly boredom. There'd seemed no reason to go into the office after Abbie's death, but, when he worked from home, he found he couldn't concentrate on the catalogue research that normally fascinated him. Gradually it became clear that grief had taken up permanent residence and was eating him away on the inside. He was drinking too much. He missed out on meals. He'd stare out of the window of his Kensington flat and before he knew it three hours had passed and it was dark. When Steele had sent a text message reminding Jamie of his offer it had felt like someone opening the door of his cell. He needed a change. He needed a life. At some point he needed to forget.

An enormous gilt-framed mirror dominated one side of the broad hallway, while the other wall held an astonishing display of curved cavalry sabres and scabbards, arrayed in a circular formation that must have been almost eight feet in diameter. The hilts were highly polished, but the blades had the dull bluish sheen and pitting that marked them as well-cared-for antiques and not cheap modern replicas. Other more exotic swords held individual pride of place in glass cases, some of them with jewelled hilts and great curved blades inlaid with gold and silver.

Charlotte led him past numerous oak-panelled doors to the carpeted stairway. 'You know the way.' The smile faded and she reached out to touch his arm. 'I was so sorry to hear about your friend.'

What she called the 'play room' was actually a large gym that filled most of the top floor of the house and before he reached it, Jamie could clearly hear excited shouts and the clash of metal on metal. He felt his blood begin to rise as he walked through the doorway and almost smiled. There was something about a battle of wills that brought out the best and the worst in him. Two anonymous figures faced each other on a narrow mat that ran virtually the full length of the twenty-five-yard-long room, sharply lit by the sunlight that filled the white-walled space. Each wore a mesh mask that covered the face and neck and a smooth white jacket with padding to protect the chest. As he watched, the man on the right advanced warily, a long narrow sword held aggressively in front of him, forcing the fighter on the left to retreat step by step. The button tip of the sword made slight threatening movements and it seemed certain the attacker had the advantage. So fast the eye could barely register it, the defender's sword flicked out, forcing the attacker to parry and retreat in his turn, and following up with a whirlwind series of attacks that lasted only a fraction of a second. The swordsman on the left attempted another desperate parry and followed it up with an attack, but the point of his opponent's sword made a solid hit on his chest and the blade bent into an arc.

'My match.' The victor's muffled voice sounded hollow

and alien as the two men stepped back, allowing their blades to drop and removing their masks one-handed. Adam Steele's face glowed pink with exertion and his breath came in short gasps, but his eyes shone with an almost messianic light. Steele's opponent was short and compact, with narrow, suspicious features, cropped sandy hair and a mouth set in a sardonic smile. For a fleeting second, Jamie thought he noticed a hint of anger before the face dissolved into a wry grin. 'Fair and square, boss.'

Steele smiled and introduced Jamie to the stranger. His voice was still fuelled by the adrenalin coursing through his body, the words emerging in machine-gun bursts. 'Jamie Saintclair. Gault. Don't ask. Just Gault. He does bits and pieces for me. Ex-squaddie, Special Forces type, sort of intelligence officer. Doesn't like getting beat. Can be bloody wearing, but makes for a good contest. Fancy a crack? I'm just getting warmed up and there'll be a vest to fit you. Nothing too strenuous. Best of five hits?'

Jamie murmured something about time being short. He knew Steele to be a fierce competitor, who would make the bouts last and who wouldn't be satisfied if he didn't win. They'd met by chance for the first time since Cambridge at a south London fencing club a year after Jamie had taken up the sport. Steele had been by far the more experienced, with a passion for the sport, but Jamie proved to have the speed, coordination and downright bloody-mindedness to give him a contest, with the result that they practised often together. He hadn't lifted a blade since Abbie's death and really didn't feel like it today. Yet Adam Steele persisted, and there was a challenge on the man Gault's face that was almost a sneer.

He shrugged. 'All right then, but just five hits.'

He slipped out of his jacket and Gault brought him a mask and a vest that fitted. The shoes weren't ideal, but they'd have to do. He pulled a fencing glove over his right hand and picked up the rapier-like foil. It was an old-fashioned weapon, with a bone hilt, what they called an Italian grip, and not one of the new high-tech versions with the pistol grip they used in competition these days. He tried a couple of cuts to test it for balance and to flex his wrist.

'We'll make the first one a warm-up, shall we?' Steele suggested. 'Not fair to fight without letting you loosen up.'

Jamie took his stance, right foot forward and foil at the ready.

'Fence,' Gault snapped.

Jamie danced forward, his eyes never leaving the point of Adam Steele's sword but his mind constantly calculating the position of his opponent's body and the movement of his feet, always seeking a route to attack, but equally ready to defend if necessary. Steele allowed him to come, then feinted an attack that made Jamie step back in his turn.

They kept up the minuet for fifteen seconds, a lifetime

in a fencing bout, and Jamie knew that Steele was either playing with him or allowing him to loosen his muscles. At this stage of the contest, with his opponent's mind already in battle mode, he understood he was at a double disadvantage. Still he managed to give almost as good as he got until Steele's point hit him below the heart.

'Good,' the other man said. 'Now let's do it for real.'

They resumed the *en garde* position and waited for the word. This time it was Steele who attacked, forcing Jamie to parry, but allowing him no time to counter-attack before the point probed his defences again. Jamie was faster, but the other man the more experienced, and his blade created a bewildering whirlwind of bright steel. Somehow Jamie managed to force the point left so the touch was on his upper arm, an off-target hit that meant the bout had to be restarted. Now it was Jamie's turn to go on the offensive, he felt a surge of adrenalin as he saw his opening and landed a good hit on his opponent's chest, taking a simultaneous touch on his own body.

'Your point.' Steele acknowledged Jamie had been the original attacker and had priority, one of a dozen rules that made fencing so much more complex and interesting than it looked to an outsider. In the next ten seconds Jamie took one hit and gave another. One more and he'd be the victor. He went on the offensive, driving his opponent back and forcing him to parry frantically. But he had underestimated Adam Steele's determination. Steele let him come, giving him an opening, then manufactured a compound riposte that allowed him to slip inside the point to make a touch from an almost impossible angle. Two each.

'Let's make it interesting, shall we?'

Jamie frowned as Steele removed his face mask. 'You're crazy. You'll lose an eye.'

The other man smiled. 'I've always rather wished I'd lived in the age of the duellists, when you looked another man in the eye as you fought him. I'm pretty certain I can trust you not to spoil my good looks. The question is, do you trust me?'

The tone was jokingly self-mocking, but something in the air told Jamie his friend was being deadly serious. He glanced at Gault, but the former soldier only shrugged. Jamie's first instinct was to lay down his sword and walk away. People fought in masks for a reason. Six inches of the finest Italian steel through the brain could seriously spoil your day. But to refuse would mean the whole foundation of their relationship would change, and he didn't think he wanted that. *Do you trust me?* He pulled off the mask.

Steele visibly relaxed and Jamie realized he had passed some kind of test. Just what kind he would no doubt discover later. But first he had a fight to win.

Being able to see the other man's eyes entirely changed the dynamic of a fencing bout. Against a masked man the point of the foil and the little hints betrayed by the body were the key. Now it was all in the eyes. The eyes measured the distance between sword and target. They calculated the angle of attack. The signals they gave were fractional, at best, but if you could read those signals you had an edge. Jamie had been trained in the art of knife fighting by Royal Marine unarmed combat instructors. Not that long ago he had battled for his life against a man determined to skin him alive. Steele fought with his usual cold resolve, but he found his every movement anticipated; try as he might, he couldn't break down Jamie's guard. Jamie knew all he had to do was bide his time for the right moment. It came with a move born of Adam Steele's frustration. The *flèche*. Steele executed a running lunge off the front foot designed to batter through the ring of steel that protected his opponent, and delivered with such force that it would have snapped the blade had it been on target. Jamie recognized the moment of decision and was already moving when the foil darted towards his chest, a dancing check step that took him inside the point. In the same instant his arm extended and his point hit Adam Steele in the centre of the chest. Steele's eyes widened as if he could feel the cold metal in his heart and he stumbled off the mat.

The sound of a slow hand clap punctuated the stunned silence. 'As neat an *intagliata* as I've seen.' Gault grinned. 'You'll bear watching, Mr Saintclair, so you will.'

Steele gave him the kind of look that would strip paint, but his face split in a smile. 'Neat? A combination of dumb luck and an opponent who moves with all the speed and grace of a hippopotamus, eh, Jamie?'

Jamie knew being beaten had annoyed his host, so he kept his tone equally light. 'Not my fault if you send a postcard every time you attack, old chum.' They pulled off the fencing gear and by the time Jamie had replaced his jacket, Steele was already bounding for the door.

'Time for a drink, I think. Charlotte?' he roared. 'Two bottles of the good stuff and three glasses in the library.' Jamie exchanged a glance with Gault as they followed in his wake. 'And I mean now, darling, not when you've powdered your bloody nose.'

Charlotte was walking towards the kitchens when they reached the stair. 'Why do I put up with him?' she whispered.

'Because, despite my many faults, you can't get enough of me in bed?'

She rolled her startling sapphire-blue eyes. 'Ears like a bat and a mind like a sewer.'

True to its name, three walls of the library were lined with books on shelves that rose to almost twice the height of a man. Unlike books in some large houses of Jamie's acquaintance, many of these looked as though they had actually been read. On the fourth wall, a gilt-framed canvas of some unfortunate Peninsular War general expiring as his red-coated soldiers looked admiringly on hung above the massive fireplace, surrounded by a display of individually mounted swords, each different, but an object of beauty in its own way. Some of them were in their scabbards, others with the blades glinting dangerously. A window looked out on to the gardens and Adam Steele took his place beside it, staring appreciatively across the damp lawns until Charlotte appeared carrying a tray with two dust-coated wine bottles and three bulbous glasses. She picked up a cork-screw.

'Gault will take care of that.' Steele reached for the curtains. 'Switch on the light on your way out.'

The girl hesitated.

'Please.' The tone and the word seemed curiously at odds and Charlotte frowned. She shrugged and, as the light flicked on, Steele drew the velvet drapes together, cutting them off from the outside world. He met Jamie's puzzled glance. *You'll see.*

Gault handed Jamie a glass and Adam Steele picked up another, breathing deeply at the tawny liquid within. 'The 'eighty-six. Should probably decant it and let it breathe, but life's too fucking short, eh? Not a bad year, if you like your tannins. All old boot leather and cow manure,' he said appreciatively.

Jamie sipped his wine and waited.

With all the flamboyance of a Shakespearean actor taking the stage, Steele marched to the wall and swept one of the swords – a French cavalry officer's personal weapon, individually crafted for the owner – from its scabbard.

'When this was made it was the supreme example of the metalworker's art. It had to be, because the care that went into creating it could mean the difference between life and death to the man who wielded it.' He tilted his head and studied the heavy, curved blade. 'It is beautiful, but beauty is not its primary function. Killing is. That has been the story of the sword for at least four millennia, but it's not why I collect them. Likewise, the reason I collect these beautiful objects is nothing to do with aesthetics. It has to do with magic. A sword is the child of earth, air and fire.' He paused and lovingly resumed his study of the curving bar of glittering steel. 'Look closely at this blade and you can see the ghosts of the tree roots that bind the earth to the Otherworld. The craftsmen who smelted the metal and forged the first swords from bronze were thought to be sorcerers or wizards and the blades they created became creatures of myth and legend; things of rare power to be passed down through the ages, or given as gifts to the gods. Sometimes the swordsmith came close to being a god himself. Think of Wayland, whose name has been passed down through English legend for more than two thousand years, or Murumasa, in Japan, whose blades are said to be endowed with supernatural powers.'

Jamie waited, wondering if Steele expected a reply to the refrain he'd heard any number of times, but the other man was only gathering his thoughts.

'Yet throughout history there have been swords that have transcended even the swords of the masters, because they *were* the swords of the gods: the swords that won kingdoms, that created champions, or swords with the power to change the world in which they existed. These are the swords men have followed. The swords men have died for. Show him.'

Gault marched to the fireplace and pulled the painting away from the wall to reveal a small safe. Quite suddenly the room seemed to go very cold. Jamie stared at Adam Steele as realization dawned. This was a step further than hospitality, or even friendship. It was an initiation.

Gault dialled the combination and drew out a slim file. He handed it to Jamie with a knowing smile.

The bland, grey exterior gave no hint of the contents, but he would swear there was a tremor in the hands that held it, though they seemed steady enough as he opened it and read the first line. His mind instantly made the conversion from English to German.

Meine Zeit naht, aber ich kann nicht weitergehen, ohne preiszugeben was ich gesehen und gehört habe, und vielleicht als Wiedergutmachung für das, was ich getan habe . . .'

VI

My time is close, but I cannot pass without revealing what I saw and heard and, perhaps, making amends for what I have done . . .

Steele's voice cut through Jamie's concentration. 'I could have had it translated, but your German is as good as mine and I wanted you to see the original. As you can see, it forms part of a legal document. The main section is the last will and testament of an elderly gentleman who died in the city of Dortmund a year ago. It is of no interest to us apart from helping identify him. This was a codex added in his final hours. It has only just come into my possession.'

Jamie leafed through the contents, taking in the distinctive German typeface and archaic language until he came to a single word that made him feel as if the breath had been sucked from his body. He didn't know whether to laugh or shake the other man's hand. 'Is this a joke?'

'As far as we know the document is genuine and Wulf Ziegler believed what he wrote. Of course, that doesn't necessarily make it true, but it does make it worth following up.'

'But this is impossible, I—'

'You're the man who found a hundred-million-pound painting that had been hanging in a lost Nazi bunker for sixty years,' Steele pointed out. 'Would you have believed that if someone had told you a couple of years ago?'

Jamie shook his head. 'That was different. There was evidence, clues in my grandfather's diary.'

'And what is this if not evidence?' the other man demanded. 'Every quest has to start somewhere, Jamie.'

Jamie noted the use of the word 'quest' and knew Adam Steele had used it deliberately. 'I don't know.'

Steele nodded slowly. 'I understand your scepticism. I felt exactly the same the first time I saw the codex. Look, we'll leave you alone for a while.' He went to the door, smiling at Jamie's obvious confusion. 'Read the document and then tell me Wulf Ziegler is lying or deranged.'

Gault followed him out, leaving Jamie to wonder whether the whole world had gone mad or if it were only him. Drawing a deep breath he turned back to the codex. With every word he read the room increasingly took on the stillness of the grave and he was drawn ever further into the past.

My time is close, but I cannot pass without revealing what I saw and heard and, perhaps, making amends for what I have done in the name of the Führer and the Third Reich. There are two parts to my story. The first begins in the year of 1937 when I was gefolgschaftsführer of my Hitler Youth unit in Dortmund, a prestigious position that would reward me with a place at an SS-Junkerschule and a future full of promise. Among many other things of military value, we were trained in intelligence gathering and reconnaissance. In April of that year we were visited by a senior Hitler Jugend commander from Berlin and briefed for a reconnaissance mission to England to gather information on industrial, naval and military sites. Before the officer left, I was surprised when he drew me aside and offered me the opportunity to carry out a highly secret assignment on the personal orders of Heinrich Himmler. I was warned the mission could be dangerous and that I must not fail. He told me: 'There is no pressure on you to agree, but you would have the thanks of the Reichsführer and your part in this would be remembered.' Of course I accepted. That summer we sailed to England and spread out across the country. My eight-man section cycled east from Manchester and then north up the spine of the country. After just over a week we reached a range of low, bleak hills where seldom a tree grew. We camped with an armoured unit under training in the area and they made us welcome, almost treating us as comrades. They appeared to have no suspicion of the war we knew was coming and for which we had trained. We thought them pleasant fellows, but very naive and not at all professional. For most of the journey, the sun shone and it was more like a holiday than an intelligence mission, but I knew we would soon be close to our objective and demanded rigorous discipline from my comrades. Our target was a small schloss by a river that lay to the north of a distinctive hill formation. At midday, following our night with the tankers, we passed through a small town with an impressive ruin, which was another of my landmarks. A little later we breasted a rise in the rolling countryside and my heart almost stopped when I saw what lay before me. There it was, exactly as I had been told, and on the far side would be the house I was looking for. You may imagine my excitement as I looked down from the upper slopes on the broad silver ribbon of the river below and focused my binoculars on a large grey building with tall chimneys. I felt an enormous pride because only I knew the true purpose of our mission and the responsibility was mine and mine alone. That evening we made a detailed reconnaissance of the area, and as darkness fell I led Gunther, Neumann and Berndt down a narrow road that brought us close to our objective. I had studied detailed plans until the terrain and the approach were etched upon my brain. Leaving Berndt, who was youngest, but among the most reliable, with the bicycles, we crept through the undergrowth until we reached the walls of a formal garden. Thanks to our training we were as at home in the darkness as in daylight, though the trees cast grotesque, intimidating moonlit shadows on the ground around us. We followed the walls until we came to a gate, which took the work of only a few moments to open. The schloss lay on the far side of a broad, cropped lawn and I left Neumann by the gate to act as look-out while Gunther and I ran forward over the grass. We were halfway when Gunther froze and gave a little mew of terror. My heart stopped and I scanned the darkness for the threat. There! A solitary figure almost directly in front of us. Gunther turned and I could see the panic flashing in his wide eyes. I made a calming motion and he backed towards me.

'What do we do?'

'Wait,' I whispered. I studied the crouching figure blocking our way to the house. If we had seen him, surely he would have seen us. Maybe he had his back to us. The minutes ticked by and still he didn't make his move.

'Scheisse.'

'What is it?'

I walked forward and touched the figure on his unyielding shoulder. He was a boy of around our own age, but dressed in archaic clothing, kneeling with his hands together in supplication in front of him. He

could do us no harm, because he was carved from
stone.
  'Come. We're wasting time.'

Jamie had to pause because his mouth was so dry. True
or false, the tension of Wulf Zeigler's memoir spanned
the decades. It took a long draught of Adam Steele's
Burgundy before he was ready to continue in the footsteps of the *Hitler Jugend* leader. He continued reading.

The house loomed over us, massive and threatening,
the moonlight painting the stones silver. I shivered
as I moved into its shadow. It was a place of myth
and legend. The man who had built it was long
dead, but it was as if his presence was all around us.
I knew I must quickly thrust this foolishness from
my mind. From this moment on we were on a war
footing. We had trained often using a building of
similar proportions on the outskirts of Dortmund,
and Gunther followed as I dropped to the ground
and slipped round the corner, keeping my silhouette
to a minimum. We squirmed through what must be a
rose garden – and by the scent, one which had been
recently manured – ignoring the thorns that clawed
at our flesh and clothing. Eventually we reached the
base of a thick stem of ancient ivy that had attached
itself to the house. I grasped hold of the stem and
Gunther made a back so that I was able to boost
myself the first two metres or so with comparative

ease, before hauling myself into the thick foliage where I would be hidden from anyone below. When he saw I was safely in position, Gunther withdrew to his place beside Neumann, leaving me alone. One of the reasons I had been chosen for the assignment was my slight frame. It was obvious by now that the way here had been paved for me and I wondered as I climbed why whoever had been my pathfinder could not have carried out the mission in my stead. Only in later years did I realize my guide must have been a highly placed agent too important to risk on such an unlikely mission. High to my right, and just above the level of the foliage, lay a darkened window barely large enough to allow a child access. Everything depended on whether the ivy stems to which I clung were strong enough to hold my weight. If not, I had an alternative, but much more perilous, route. I held my breath as I inched my way towards the window, as if the act would somehow reduce my weight. I could feel the stems beneath my feet narrowing and becoming more fragile and I was struck by – and grateful for – the strength of the tiny hairs that held the plant to the flaking stone in an elemental death grip. By now I was six metres up and a single slip would send me plunging to the garden below, to certain injury if not death. I used the stems as a ladder, climbing until I was just below the window. This was where my training proved invaluable. Clinging with one hand and with the toes of my boots only having the slightest purchase, I used my free hand to unloop the short length of rope that hung from my shoulder. My comrades called me 'Monkey' because of my climbing abilities, but even my simian namesake would have struggled to make the leap from ivy to ledge. Fortunately, my controllers had considered every eventuality. With a single rotation I swung the rope so that the specially designed metal claw caught hold on the window's sandstone sill. It made a distinct clatter that froze me in place for a few moments, but when there was no apparent reaction from inside the house or out, I tested it with my free hand. This was the moment of truth. I closed my eyes and switched my right hand from ivy stem to rope and swung outward, allowing the thin cord to take my full weight. The sound of metal scraping on stone above made my heart stop and I dropped slightly before the hooks held fast. Terrified, I hung for a moment, twisting in the air, before hauling myself hand over hand until I reached the sill. It provided just enough room for me to crouch with my back wedged against one pillar and my shoulder against the other, while I reached down to check the bottom of the window. A narrow gap allowed me to insert my fingers and pull it upwards. At first I thought the information I had been given was wrong or that the faulty catch I had been told to expect had been repaired. In my cramped position I found it difficult to exert much pressure, but I shifted a little to my right, gritted my teeth and pulled till my muscles were on fire. It came up with a shriek like a strangled cat and a jerk that almost threw me from my perch. Somehow I managed to hold on and wriggled through the narrow space. Sweating with relief, I dropped into a cramped water closet with a toilet bowl and a tiny sink. The entrance was at the far end and I felt for the handle, praying no one had heard the din as the window opened. With enormous care, I opened the door a few centimetres. In the gloom beyond I could just make out a passageway with a polished wood floor and a strip of carpet down the centre. I waited another few seconds to ensure I was still alone and then slipped out into the corridor. It was full dark, but I knew the layout of the house as well as I knew my own home and I was able to make my way to a broad stairway, imagining the disapproving eyes that followed me from the paintings lining the wall. The stairs led down to the main level of the house and I descended one step at a time, testing each as I went. The carpet would deaden the sound of my feet, but a creaking board had betrayed many a burglar before me and I knew not to take any risks. I counted the steps and when I reached the bottom I could picture the wood-panelled hall in the pictures I'd been shown. Turn sharp right and twenty paces ahead would be the armoury. Large windows allowed in something that might be called light and I became aware of the displays lining the wall: full suits of armour, breastplates, daggers, swords and long spears, ancient flintlock pistols and muskets. Something that could only be a Napoleonic regiment's eagle. The smell of floor polish was familiar enough, but there was another, musty odour that tickled my nose; the scent of great antiquity. A marble bust on a pedestal depicted the house's former owner, a severe man with receding hair, a long nose and fleshy features. Behind it hung a painting of the same man with a fine dog, a wolfhound of some sort, at his side. This proof that I was a few steps from my goal made my heart beat faster, if that were possible, and I hurried towards the far end of the room. Here the panelled wall was decorated with a much larger display of very fine swords, formed in a circle, their blades shining dully in the gloom. I walked towards the swords and turned left, down a narrow, concealed passageway that led to a windowless room. When I reached it, I closed the door behind me and risked flicking on my torch, blinking as the thin beam cut through an almost Stygian blackness. The room was entirely empty. Bare stone walls and grey flagstones, but a worn step in the centre of the far wall indicated the existence of a long filled-in doorway. My legs shook as I crossed the last few paces. I laid the torch aside so that I could use both hands as I knelt before the step. It seemed massive, utterly immovable, but I had been instructed what to do. I ran my hands over the block until my fingers found a narrow crevice on the right, between the step and the wall. I pulled with all my strength using my own weight to exert more power. To my astonishment the great stone slid back, pivoting away from the wall on some sort of hidden mechanism. For a few moments I couldn't move, paralysed by the enormity of what I had achieved. A thousand voices roared out the 'Fahnenlied' in my head. I lifted the torch and shone it into the cavity I had exposed.

VII

'What do you think?'

Jamie was so engrossed in what he was reading that he hadn't heard Steele returning to the library. He looked up in annoyance at the banker's interruption. 'I don't know what to think,' he said sharply. 'Where was this house?'

'My people are working on it. Probably in the north of England, we believe. We've confirmed that MI5 suspected the Hitler Youth of sending out spying missions just like Ziegler's, under the guise of a cultural exchange. They were also worried that the Boy Scouts who went to Germany were being indoctrinated.' He smiled. 'Apparently Baden Powell was very keen on Adolf Hitler.'

'Have you considered that this might be another Hitler Diaries hoax? What better way to lure you into paying a fortune for some expensive forgery.' The Hitler Diaries had been one of the great scandals of the nineteen eighties, after the German magazine *Stern* claimed to have bought sixty-two handwritten volumes of memoirs written personally by Adolf Hitler and recovered from a crashed plane at the end of the war. Reputations and careers had been destroyed when the diaries were authenticated, only to turn out to be crude fakes written by a small-time Stuttgart art dealer called Konrad Kujau.

Steele nodded solemnly. 'Yes, that was the first thing I considered. But unlike *Stern* and *The Times*, I've already had the papers scientifically analysed by some of the country's top experts. The Hitler Diaries were an enormous fraud; this is a simple account that can be easily verified. Wulf Ziegler is a real person. He exists, or at least existed, and his family still live in the centre of Dortmund.' Passion made his voice quiver. 'The codex is the key that opens the first door into what could be a straightforward journey, or a bloody complicated quest, Jamie. Can we afford not to turn that key?'

Jamie wasn't convinced. 'I still think it's impossible.'

'That may be so, but what if you're wrong?' Steele demanded, the over-bright eyes daring his guest to argue. 'We are talking about creating history. The greatest sword ever created. Excalibur. There, I've said it even if you won't. The sword of Arthur, lost for a hundred generations. Proof positive that the man who wielded it truly existed. And I want *you* to find it. Take up my offer and the name Jamie Saintclair could be mentioned in the same breath as Howard Carter and the Earl of Carnarvon. I want to know, Jamie, and I'm willing to commit a million pounds to find out, and a lot more to get hold of it if it does exist.'

The audacity of it took Jamie's breath away and for a moment he was tempted to laugh off the offer as a joke. Did Adam Steele really believe finding Excalibur would rank alongside the discovery of the Valley of the Kings and the golden treasure of Tutankhamun? 'You forgot to mention Schliemann,' he said mischievously.

But Steele was deadly serious. 'Schliemann was a crook,' he snorted. 'A fantasist who discovered Troy by mistake and destroyed his reputation by stealing the treasure for himself. This will be different, Jamie. All above board. I'm in it for the glory, not the money. The most famous sword in history. A collector's dream. But I won't keep it for myself. It will go on display in the British Museum with my name beside it, but it will be for the people of Great Britain.'

'Then why don't you go looking for it yourself? Then the name Adam Steele will be mentioned in the same breath as Carter and Carnarvon.'

Steele looked up sharply with a dangerous glint in his eye, but the threat quickly subsided. 'Because you're the man with the skills, Jamie. You know how to unlock the doors the Excalibur codex leads to. Besides, I have a bank to run.'

Jamie stared at him. It was too soon. Abbie was barely cold in her grave. He couldn't leave her now. But what would Abbie have said if she was here? He remembered the plans they'd made. The great adventures they were going to have. Machu Picchu. The Great Wall. Swimming with sharks and walking with lions. And always it had been Abbie who made the running. Abbie seeking out something new and exciting. Suddenly it all became clear.

'When do you want me to start?'

Adam Steele gave a loud roaring laugh as if he'd just won the final of a fencing competition and Jamie found himself clasped in a pair of incredibly powerful arms. Eventually the banker loosened his grip. He grinned. 'Now is as good a time as any. Take as long as you like. I'll pay you twenty thousand pounds a month, plus expenses. First class all the way. I'll also provide you with a little insurance.'

He pressed a button on the desk and Gault reappeared a moment later. 'Don't be deceived by the grey hairs – Mr Gault isn't quite ready for his pipe and slippers yet. He speaks pretty good German and I think you'll find him a very handy man to have around.'

Gault held Jamie's eyes and dared him to say no. 'Where will we start?'

Jamie looked from one man to the other, taking in the raw excitement in Steele's eyes and something he couldn't quite read in the former soldier's. 'Dortmund, I think. Let's see what other secrets your Herr Ziegler has been keeping up his sleeve. In the meantime, if you'll excuse me, I have some reading to catch up on.'

The second part of my story opens on the Oder front, in mid April 1945, south of the village of Seelow. I had recently been promoted to the rank of SS-Unterscharführer and transferred from Third SS Totenkopf Division to command a company of Hitler Jugend holding a strategic crossroads near Dolgelin. My unit consisted of eighty-four boys aged between fourteen and sixteen and armed with Panzerfaust anti-tank rockets and First World War rifles they barely had the strength to carry. Facing us were veterans of Katukov's First Guards Tank Army and Chuikov's Eighth Guards Army who had fought their way to the Oder from Stalingrad, via Kursk and the Vistula. We were dug in with other units on the height overlooking the river, defending Reichstrasse One, which stretched away behind us like a dagger into the very heart of Berlin. By now I was worn thin by war and death and constant terror; when I looked in the mirror I saw the face of a decaying corpse, eyes sunk into dark pits and bones fighting to free themselves from the flesh. My heart was no longer my own. My soul, if it had ever existed, was buried somewhere out on the Russian steppe with the bodies of a thousand kameraden. I had seen things and done things that would haunt me for ever. More important, perhaps, I no longer believed, but to even think it was to risk a bullet from the chain dogs of the Feldgendarmerie. Tomorrow would be my twenty-fourth birthday.

On the night of 15 April I inspected our position and whispered words of encouragement to my 'men'. The boys stared at me from beneath over-large helmets that wobbled on their heads, wrapped in greatcoats that enveloped their thin bodies. Their frightened eyes seemed too big for faces pinched and narrow from constant hunger. More than half were orphans, or believed they were; their parents casualties of one front or another, or buried in the rubble of bombed-out homes in Berlin. They had known nothing but war, or the preparations for war, so that this, lying in the damp earth at the very heart of Dante's inferno, with the smell of roasted flesh in their nostrils and the star shells lighting up the sky all around, could be reckoned normal. As I went I passed out boiled sweets, and they smiled shyly as they accepted them, like children at a school prize-giving.

'When will they come?' It was a lad called Werner, one of the youngest, but eager to prove himself; still bright-eyed and unknowing.

'Soon enough.' I managed a grin. 'Get some sleep, junge!' I hoped that, in their innocence, they would all sleep well, for tomorrow we would die.

The bombardment began before dawn, the shells from a thousand artillery pieces marching across the flood plain and up the hill like an unstoppable army; an inferno of fire and steel that struck terror into every man who endured it. Horrified, we watched the monster approach, devouring everything in its path, hurling trees and houses and men into the air, where they hung or disintegrated as was the beast's pleasure, dropping back to bury the dead and wounded alike.

'Down,' I screamed. 'Get in the bottom of your holes and stay there.'

The ground shook as if it were a living thing and the beast closed on us with the wind of its coming gusting across the top of our pits and trenches like the precursor of a storm. I tried to make myself part of the earth, but no matter how hard I dug it rejected my living flesh. An instant later we were at the centre of an apocalypse of heat and light and noise, the air torn from our lungs and our ear drums bursting with the hellish percussion of the devil's orchestra of shells and rockets.

As quickly as it had arrived, it was gone, and in the relative silence the only sound was of sobbing, and the distant screams of someone who had only seconds to live.

'Please, sir,' the shrill voice seemed unnaturally loud, 'I think Werner's hurt.'

He lay on his back, his dark eyes like bruises against the marble white of his flesh. He was still alive and when I placed a sweet between his lips they turned up in a smile that he would wear for ever. The boy in the next rifle pit had been wounded and Werner had run to his aid like a brave little Hitler Jugend. He was fortunate. He never even felt the enormous shell splinter that cut him in half at the waist.

The sound of the barrage subsided into the distance, replaced by the rumble of engines and the sharp cry of whistles, punctuated by incessant bursts of heavy machine-gun and rifle fire.

'Tanks!' The warning was unnecessary because as the smoke lifted we could see them crossing the flood plain below like a plague of giant beetles, swarms of brown-clad tommy-gunners running among them, urged on by their political commissars. Occasionally, one of the machines would turn into a bright matchhead of flame as a faust or a shell hit its mark, and the little figures around it would shrivel up or drop to the ground. The engine note changed to a deep growl as the machines hit the steep slope of the Seelow Heights and began the climb towards us. I called out to check the position of the faust teams and gripped the MG-42 more tightly. Manfred, my loader, a fifteen-year-old baker's son from Bielefeld, crouched beside me, his face serious and determined, eyes narrowed behind thick, round spectacles.

'Steady,' I called. 'Wait until they're right on top of us.'

The firing came closer and fleeing men began to spill back towards us over the brow of the hills.

'Hold your fire, they're ours.'

'Cowards!' A high-pitched voice called from the far end of the line.

'Shut up!' Where was our artillery? Of course, the slope wouldn't allow them to see their targets yet.

A man staggered into sight, using his rifle as a crutch. He was making for the sanctuary of one of the front trenches and the men occupying them shouted encouragement. At first, it seemed he would make it, but without warning a massive shape mounted the crest and bore down on the fleeing soldier. He looked back and desperately tried to speed up, but the T-34 kept pace with him like a cat playing with a mouse. The game went on for a few moments before the commander became bored, the tank accelerated and with a terrible shriek the landser went down under the tracks to be crushed flat by the twenty-six-tonne monster.

His terrible death brought a retaliatory fusillade of fire from the front trenches. The infantry around the tanks went down as if a scythe had cut the feet from under them, but the tank, now accompanied by three more, came on, undeterred even by a Panzerfaust strike. When the machines reached the trenches a few men ran, to be chopped down in their turn by the T-34's machine guns. We were trained to stay in our trenches. Every two men were issued with a magnetic anti-tank mine. Once the tank passed over the trench you emerged to clamp the mine to the weaker armour at the rear and blow the beast to kingdom come. Of course, the covering infantry were likely to kill you before you had the chance to *celebrate your victory, but the sacrifice would be deemed worthwhile. But these Russian tankers knew their business and I heard my boys gasp as the T-34s settled over the trench before dancing on their axis, crushing everything below them to a pulp.*

'Steady.'

Somewhere along the line a quiet voice was praying, a practice not encouraged in the Hitler Jugend. For once no one seemed to care.

I clamped my teeth shut to stop them chattering. Our turn. Somewhere, someone was growling like a dog and it wasn't until I saw Manfred's look of puzzlement that I realized it was me. I had fought tanks before, but familiarity made it no easier on the nerves or the bowels. They seemed to grow before the eyes as they advanced over the rough ground. Machine-gun fire sprayed across the top of the trench and I heard a frightened yelp from not far away.

'Keep your fucking heads down. Steady. Faust teams one and two take the tank on the left. Three and four, the one in the centre.'

Fifty paces. The infantry had returned, thick as wasps around rotting fruit and seeking out targets with their tommy guns. I aimed at a group to the left of the centre tank. The MG-42 bucked in my hands, spewing out twenty rounds a second in a series of short buzz-saw rasps and, as the men fell, the MG was joined by the crack of rifles and the familiar raw thump of the Fausts. I looked up expecting to see the tanks burning, but they kept coming on and it was only then I noticed the spring mattresses tied to their fronts and sides; a crude but effective protection against our single-shot rockets.

Shit. 'Aim for the tracks,' I screamed, but I knew it was too late. In horror I watched the rifle pits ahead of me obliterated. I tried spraying the driver's eye slits, but knew I had as much chance of stopping them as I had of surviving the war. I exchanged a desperate glance with Manfred. Should we take our chances in the open? Anything was better than being turned into mincemeat by those tracks. I was reaching for the rear of the trench when an incredible flat crack tore the air above my head, followed instantly by the enormous clang of a giant bell being struck. The next time I looked, black smoke was boiling from the tank and the first crewman was struggling to escape from the turret.

'Kill the bastards.' Bullets shredded the tanker and whether the remaining Ivan was too injured or too terrified to emerge, we heard his screams as he burned alive inside. As my head cleared I became aware of more T-34s being hit as our 88mm guns finally found their range. We continued firing until the last of the infantry disappeared or were lying dead on the ground.

A single wounded Russian rose from the prone figures, calling out, 'Kamerad. Stalin kaput.' I nodded to Manfred and the boy raised his rifle, frowned with concentration and shot the Ivan through the body. The soldier collapsed, groaning and clawing at his guts. Manfred walked over to him and pointed the barrel at his head. I pushed the rifle aside. 'He's finished. Don't waste a bullet. You should have done it properly the first time.'

I checked our casualties as an SS runner came up with orders to hand over the trenches to his company and regroup on Reichsstrasse One. Despite our success in holding the centre, it seemed the Ivans had broken through to the south. We had no time to bury the dead. The enemy would undoubtedly be preparing for the next attack. Already the shells were beginning to fall, targeting the artillery positions to our rear. I could hear the terrifying shriek of the Stalin Organs, Katyusha multiple rocket launchers, and to the south the enormous hammer blow of a strike seemed to chew up an acre of ground, destroying everything within.

I formed up the exhausted boys, some of them snivelling at the loss of comrades, and marched them through the reinforcing SS men. They stared as we passed and the contrast between the jackbooted veterans weighed down with grenades, knives and machine pistols and the kids in their over-sized helmets and uniforms seemed almost surreal. One of them sneered and I felt like punching his yellow teeth down his throat. We had stood. We would see if they did.

We had marched a hundred metres before I heard an inhuman howl and the whole world turned red.

When I woke, it was in a charnel house with the smell of torn bowels filling my nostrils and the ground all round strewn with gobbets of torn flesh and larger pieces recognizable as limbs and torsos. A lance of pain speared my left leg and my mind reeled as I felt my body for the terrible injury I knew I must have suffered, but the leg was still there, only broken. Shouting for a medic, I looked around for help, only to find myself staring into a familiar face with sightless eyes already turning opaque. Manfred: I wondered idly what had happened to the rest of him. A few shell-shocked survivors wept among the remains of their comrades. Two of them helped me to the rear where a doctor checked me over before two orderlies threw me unceremoniously into the back of an ambulance.

As we drove off, someone shoved a canteen in my hand and I guzzled down the contents, not realizing how thirsty I had been and still trying to come to terms with my good fortune. I had survived again.

'You might need that later, soldier.'

When I looked up, two startling blue eyes studied me from the other side of the ambulance and I froze beneath their gaze. They belonged to an SS-Gruppenführer, a general no less, and even more surprisingly one prepared to share his transport with a Schutztruppen like me. He had his right arm in a sling and the blood from a shoulder wound seeped through his bandages. His face was pale, but he was still alert enough, for he said: 'Don't I know you?'

He would be in his mid twenties then, barely a couple of years older than I; a handsome man, with strong intelligent features and dark hair swept back from a broad forehead. Since I had seen him last all those years ago, he had clawed his way to the highest echelons of the party, using the bodies of his rivals as hand- and footholds as he rose to Hitler's inner circle.

'The sword,' he whispered. 'You gave me the sword.' Then he fell back and closed his eyes.

When I next woke, I found him watching me and drinking from a brown glass bottle, which he immediately offered. I reached across, wincing at the pain in my leg, and took a swig, choking as the raw heat of the brandy scoured my throat and exploded in my chest.

'Good stuff, eh?' He grinned, the brightness of his eyes and the slurring in his voice testament to the inroads he had made into the bottle. I nodded and handed it back, eyeing him warily. He studied the Iron Cross on my breast. 'You've seen some hard fighting, I'd guess? Where did you serve?'

I shrugged. 'Poland. France. The Ostfront; Kiev, Kharkov, Tula, all the way to the gates of Moscow.'

'And back.' He grinned again.

'We would have won if the Wehrmacht had fought as hard as the SS,' I said defensively.

The lorry lurched and I felt the bones grinding together in my thigh. Everything turned hazy, but before I lapsed into unconsciousness I was sure I heard him whisper: 'We should have won.'

Some time later a hand shook my shoulder and I discovered that we had been evacuated from the ambulance to a clearing by the side of the road.

'Jabos,' my Gruppenführer explained. 'Sturmovik ground-attack fighters.' From somewhere he had found another bottle and he drank freely from it as we lay together, he propped against a tree and I on my back with my leg in a splint. He was beyond drunk now, on some euphoric plane where blood loss and alcohol had taken him out of reach of the pain from his shattered arm. He spoke in a hoarse whisper, but every word pierced my brain like the point of an SS dagger. 'You deserve to know. You of all people deserve to know. The man who made it possible.'

The treasure I had brought back from Britain, he said, had been taken first to a sacred place where it had been joined with other such treasures. Each was a thing of power, and it was believed that, together, they could call on a great force for good. They had been gathered on the direct orders of the Reichsführer for a ceremony his advisers assured him would change the world. Himmler's was the vision, but it *was Heydrich who had tracked them down, one by one.*

Yet the time and the place must be right. The Reichsführer had argued for their immediate use, here, in this holy of holies he had created, but the High Priests of the Ahnenerbe cautioned otherwise. When Poland capitulated, the treasures had been taken east, because it was from the east that history tells us the greatest threat will come. There, in April 1941, in a place not far from where the Führer charted the course of the Thousand Year Reich, an ancient rite would be re-enacted and the spirit of Europe's greatest warriors would emerge to aid the righteous in their battle against the forces of darkness.

He grabbed my arm. 'I was there, you know. I felt its power. The cloaked and masked figures. The words from the book. Beneath the Knight's Cross, one round table, five swords formed in the shape of a pentagram, twelve Knights of the Black Order – and one other element of which I will not speak. Joyeuse, the sword of Charlemagne; Durendal, the sword of Roland; Gotteswerkzeug, the sword of Werner von Orseln, defier of the Eastern hordes; Zerstorer, the sword of Barbarossa; and your sword, the gift of the Lady in the Lake, the sword of Arthur: Excalibur.'

VIII

Excalibur. Even on the second reading the word hit him with the impact of a twelve-pound hammer. It was madness. Beyond madness. The Sword in the Stone was nothing but a story, stolen from Old Welsh and combined with a dozen other tales by a medieval charlatan before being embellished by a French-speaking knight fallen on hard times. A few minutes before he had been thinking of it as a pointless, if intriguing and potentially lucrative, game – an opportunity to take his mind off Abbie's death, nothing more. Yet when he began to consider the facts set out in the codex, he found himself beginning to take it seriously.

Jamie knew all about Heinrich Himmler's obsession with the occult, none better. And Himmler had been fascinated by the tales of King Arthur, enough to incorporate them into his most ambitious project. *'Here, in this holy of holies he had created . . .'* could only mean one place. Jamie had stood beside the Black Sun in Wewelsburg Castle's *Obergruppenführershalle* with its twelve niches for the busts of the *Reichsführer*'s favourites. Twelve places for his twelve Knights of the Round Table, the men who ran the state within a state that was the SS. Himmler had created the *Ahnenerbe*, the SS ancestral research and teaching society, supposedly to search for the roots of German culture. In reality its members combed the world for clues to the whereabouts of the lost city of Atlantis, and the Vril, the ancient civilization of superhumans the Nazis believed were the forerunners to the Aryan race. The *Ahnenerbe* had sent expeditions to Tibet and Mongolia, was it really so fanciful that they might have attempted to bring together the great swords of Europe for some hocus-pocus ritual? And another of those blades stirred a distant memory. The hunt for the Crown of Isis had brought him closer to Himmler's dark knights than he was comfortable with, but in one conversation he was sure there had been a mention of Charlemagne's sword.

One element that certainly held the ring of truth was Ziegler's horror story about the sacrifice on the Seelow Heights. As their front-line divisions had disappeared into the meat grinder of the Eastern Front, the Nazis had increasingly called on the young and the old to continue their fight to the death. Most had ended up in the *Volkssturm*, a kind of German Dad's Army who had died in their tens of thousands in the ruins of Berlin, but Hitler Youth units had been incorporated en masse into the SS. An entire *Hitler Jugend* Division had even fought in Normandy and at the Battle of the Bulge. It made sense that the Hitler Youth would be involved in the defence of the Fatherland and should be simple enough to confirm if he could discover the identity of Ziegler's unit. The only thing that *didn't* seem to fit was the chance meeting in the ambulance with the man to whom he had handed over the sword stolen in Britain. The chances of that must be millions to one. Yet coincidences did happen, especially in wartime. He'd heard of brothers who hadn't seen each other for years literally bumping into each other on the battlefield.

He cleared his head and tried to take stock. All right. Let's say he believed Wulf Ziegler. A unit of Hitler Youth boy spies had broken into an English country house in 1937 and stolen a sword of some kind on the instructions of, from what Ziegler's informant had hinted, one Reinhard Heydrich. He looked around the bookshelves for volumes about the Second World War. They seemed to be mostly fiction or ancient texts on weaponry and metallurgy, apart from a few books about King Arthur scattered artlessly over a table in the corner. For a moment, he was tempted, but he decided they could wait. He pushed the button Adam Steele had used to summon Gault, and a few moments later Charlotte appeared in the doorway.

'You wouldn't happen to have a laptop with an Internet connection I could borrow?'

'Of course.' She smiled. 'I'll just fetch it.'

She returned a moment later and placed what was

obviously one of the latest machines, feather light and as slim as a demand from the taxman, on the table in front of him. 'Would you like me to stay and help?' He hesitated, uncertain just how informed she was about Steele's plans. She sensed his confusion and smiled. 'I'm very good at research – among other things.'

What the hell, was she flirting with him? Still, another pair of eyes couldn't do any harm.

'I'm interested in a man called Reinhard Heydrich. He was a top Nazi before and during the Second World War.'

She pulled up a chair and flipped open the lid of the laptop, instantly bringing it to life. He watched as her fingers fluttered over the keyboard and within a few seconds she turned to him with a puzzled look. 'Wikipedia or the United States Holocaust Museum archive are the top hits.'

'Let's try the Holocaust Museum. It's unlikely to be very complimentary, but potentially more accurate.'

'Is this going to be unpleasant?'

'Probably,' he admitted. 'Say hello to the Devil's Disciple. Heydrich was a bureaucrat, but one with blood on his hands. He's the man who came up with the phrase "Final Solution", and he helped make it happen by creating something called the *einsatzgruppen*, essentially murder squads who followed the *Wehrmacht* into Russia and wiped out every Jew, gypsy and Communist they could lay their hands on. If I remember correctly, they butchered two million men, women and children.'

Charlotte flinched at the steel in his voice and he instantly regretted being quite so brutal. Six weeks ago it wouldn't have happened, but he was a different person now. 'Sorry.' He smiled ruefully. 'I didn't mean it to come out like that.'

She gave him a long, appraising stare. For a moment he wondered if she was going to walk out, then her expression changed. 'It seems you already know quite a lot about him?'

'I know the basics,' he agreed. 'But I'm especially interested in what he was doing in the summer of nineteen thirty-seven.'

She nodded and hit a few more keys. 'Hmmm. Missed being called up for the First World War by a couple of years, but his family was impoverished in the aftermath. Joined the German navy in nineteen twenty-two, forced to resign in disgrace over a woman in April, 'thirty-one. He must have had something going for him, because he joined the SS in August of that year. Helped form something called the *Sicherheitsdienst*?'

'They were the Nazi secret service. A bit like the Gestapo, but without the leather coats.'

'In nineteen thirty-three he became deputy commander of the Bavarian police political detective force under Heinrich Himmler. Took part in something called the Night of the Long Knives, which doesn't sound too pleasant. Appointed overall head of the Nazi security operation, including the Gestapo, in nineteen thirty-six, and continued in that role into the early years of the war. Nothing specific about 'thirty-seven, I'm afraid.' She kept scrolling and her hand went to her mouth. 'My God.'

'Yes, he really was a complete and utter bastard. His colleagues called him "The Hangman", and with good reason—'

'What the fuck is going on?'

Jamie looked up to see Adam Steele's substantial frame filling the door, his face twisted with fury. Charlotte turned pale. She opened her mouth to explain. 'I—'

'I wasn't asking you. Get out. Go and paint your fucking nails or something.'

Steele marched across to Jamie, brushing past his assistant as she fled the room. 'Are you out of your mind? I've been searching my whole life for an opportunity like this and the first thing you do is blab about it to the hired help?'

'She's your PA, Adam. The last time I checked PA meant Personal Assistant, personal, as in keeper of secrets.' Jamie refrained from pointing out that he could also be counted among the hired help. 'And just so we're clear about this, old chum, I was always taught that a gentleman treated women with a certain amount of respect. Maybe I was wrong about you. Maybe I was wrong about this whole thing . . .'

Adam Steele met his gaze for a moment, chewing his lip, before he released a long sigh. 'What can I say?' He opened his hands in a gesture of defeat. 'That was completely out of order. I can be a moody bastard sometimes and things haven't been going too well with the bank. Shareholders all over my backside like a rash. Sometimes Charlotte has to put up with more than she should. I'll make it up to her. That okay with you?' Jamie let the silence lengthen and he saw something unexpected in Steele's eyes, before the banker blinked and it was gone. 'You have to understand that this has taken a long time and a great deal of hard work to put together,' Steele continued, grinning ruefully. 'For a man with my – let's face it – my obsession, this could be a defining moment. I can't do it without you, Jamie. Don't make any rash decisions. Please.'

'I didn't mention anything about the codex.' Jamie turned the computer so Steele could see the screen. 'As far as Charlotte is concerned, we were doing some research on old Nazis.'

The banker's eyebrows rose as he recognized the figure in the dark uniform. 'Heydrich, eh? Well, next time you need a helping hand with your research let me know. Maybe I was too hasty about Charlotte? If there's going to be a lot of this kind of technical stuff perhaps there's a place for her on the team. Gault knows his stuff, but her German is better than his. I'll think about it. The main thing is did you find anything?' He waved a hand at the computer.

'Only that Heydrich was kept busy locking people up in Dachau, rounding up Jews in Austria and blackening the name of his rivals at the time Wulf Ziegler hints he was involved in the Excalibur affair. Not that that necessarily means anything. He was Hitler's handyman. If it needed doing Heydrich would get it done.'

Adam Steele produced an almost beatific smile. 'That wasn't all he was good at.' Jamie waited expectantly. 'He was also a very expert swordsman, who could have taken both of us on and we wouldn't have got a touch.' He grinned at the younger man's confusion. 'If any man in Nazi Germany knew his swords, it was Reinhard Tristan Eugen Heydrich.'

'You rang, boss?' Gault appeared in the doorway.

'Mr Saintclair needs some help with his research.'

Gault raised an eyebrow and Jamie smiled and threw him a book from the table. 'You've got until dinner tonight to learn everything there is to know about King Arthur and Excalibur. I'll be taking questions after pudding.'

IX

'So what do we have?'

Casually dressed in a pink open-necked shirt and mustard-coloured corduroy trousers, Adam Steele sat back in his chair at the head of the long oak table after his butler had cleared away the dishes and decanted another bottle of wine. Charlotte cast a nervous glance into the dining room a few minutes later and asked if they needed anything else. She looked surprised when Steele gestured to her to take a seat. Gault rose and checked the door.

'All clear, boss.'

'This is all a bit cloak and dagger, isn't it?' Jamie laughed.

Steele sipped his wine. 'When it's your million quid, you can do it your way, Jamie, but as long as it's my hard-earned cash we do it mine, and that means tight security. Christ knows what would happen if another collector got wind of this, or, God help us, the bloody newspapers. No, we keep it within the family for now. Charlotte?' He produced a wry smile. 'I apologize for my behaviour earlier. You shouldn't have to put up with that and I'll make it up to you. You have a little catching-up to do, so you might want to get out your notebook.'

Charlotte exchanged glances with Jamie and he nodded.

'So,' Steele said. 'What do we have so far?'

Jamie shrugged. 'Between us Gault and I have checked every major source we could find for the Arthur legend and every reference to Excalibur in your books or on the Internet, and nothing changes my opinion that you're wasting your money. The earliest mentions of an Arthur are in a Welsh poem, *The Gododdin*, about a group of British warriors riding to the aid of a southern king facing annihilation by the Saxons. The Gododdin are all but wiped out, but when he's listing the heroes who made the trip, the writer, a poet called Aneirin, says of one of them 'he was no Arthur'. This was supposedly written in the sixth century, but there must have been a parallel oral tradition. There's no mention of a sword in the poem, yet it appears a couple of hundred years later as *Caledfwlch,* which apparently means "notched by battle", and the man who wields it is called Arthur.'

Adam Steele nodded, and Jamie realized he was only telling the businessman what he already knew. He paused, pondering where to take the story next. Gault had the look of someone who'd walked into the wrong meeting and his bored eyes wandered restlessly over the paintings of the banker's uniformly stern, bewigged ancestors lining the wood-panelled walls. Charlotte sat hunched over her notebook with a frown of intense concentration.

'The twelfth-century chronicler Geoffrey of Monmouth, who may or may not have been Welsh, latinized the name of the sword to *Caliburnus* in his *Historia Regum Britanniae,* a hotchpotch of tales from the island's settlement by descendants of the Trojans, through the Roman invasions to Arthur and beyond. He claimed the book was a translation of an earlier British work, but it's more likely to have been put together from Welsh poems, Bede's earlier history, the writings of a Northumbrian monk called Gildas, and his own fertile imagination. When it was published he was accused of making up the sections that mentioned Arthur . . .' From the bay window came the faint sound of a siren somewhere down towards Piccadilly and Jamie faltered, his mind immediately jumping to the chaos of lights and sirens on the TV the day Abbie died.

'You all right, Jamie old boy?' Steele asked eventually.

Jamie blinked and his vision cleared. 'Sorry, just got a little lost.' He licked his lips and discovered that they were the texture of sandpaper. 'Anyway, a couple of hundred years later the *Historia* must have been picked up by an impoverished knight called Thomas Malory, because an embellished version of the Arthur sections of Geoffrey appear in a book called *Le Morte d'Arthur,* apparently written while the author was in jail, only now Arthur's sword is called Excalibur. The Sword in the Stone first appears in a French poem that is actually about Merlin, who as far as we can tell doesn't appear in the early sources and shouldn't have anything to do with Arthur at all. That poem is also the source of the Grail legends and the Lady in the Lake. *Le Morte d'Arthur* picked up and embellished both these stories and is the basis for every unlikely myth, legend and work of fiction that follows.' Now all their eyes were on him and he met their gaze with a rueful smile. 'Everybody wants a piece of the Arthur action. He's linked to most of Wales, Tintagel in Cornwall, Glastonbury, and anywhere that begins with Cam in England, as well as a couple of places in France. There's even a historian who claims Arthur is Scottish, but they claim that about most things, I find.'

In the long silence that followed Jamie could hear the sound of some ancient clock ticking the seconds away. Adam Steele took his time before venturing an opinion. 'Yet Wulf Ziegler believes he stole a sword later identified as Excalibur for Reinhard Heydrich, who wasn't a man prone to mistakes?'

'True,' Jamie conceded. 'But Heydrich was a man known to indulge in smoke and mirrors from time to time.'

Steele pursed his lips as if he'd sucked on a lemon. This wasn't what he wanted to hear. 'My instinct is that Ziegler is telling the truth as he saw it. You'd agree?' Jamie nodded, he'd made his point. They both knew that even if the sword was genuine and it had been where Ziegler's informant claimed in 1941, there was no guarantee they'd be able to track down its present whereabouts. A lot of things had vanished during the Second World War and stayed vanished. *If* it existed, the chances were that it was in a steel box at the bottom of the Elbe or rusting away in some Bavarian salt mine. One thing was certain, Reinhard Heydrich wasn't telling. Himmler's mastermind of the Final Solution had died in Prague in the spring of 1942 from a bad case of the after-effects of hand grenade fragments in the lower intestine. But Adam Steele's confidence wasn't to be dented by a little problem like a sixty-odd-year time lapse and a room full of dead witnesses. There had never been any doubt about the decision. He grinned. 'Then we proceed on the assumption that he found what he believed he found. You still think Dortmund is the place to start?'

Jamie nodded. 'Whether you believe him or not, Ziegler left a lot of unanswered questions. Why didn't he give us a description of the sword? He must have seen it. If we knew what it looked like, it would at least give us a hint whether it was worth chasing after. If Excalibur exists it isn't a medieval sword, but much earlier. We need to know one way or the other. We have only the slightest hint where the ritual took place—'

'Wewelsburg, surely?' Steele interrupted, telling Jamie he hadn't read the codex as carefully as he might have. 'Himmler's Camelot.'

'Wewelsburg is the holy of holies Ziegler refers to earlier.' Gault's head came up sharply as the art dealer corrected his boss. 'It's in northern Germany, not the east. And then there's the cryptic reference to Adolf Hitler – *in a place not far from where the Führer charted the course of the Thousand Year Reich* – once we work that out we'll have a clue, but we need more information. He mentions the Polish invasion, so it's likely to be somewhere in Poland, but inside the German zone after the country was carved up in nineteen thirty-nine. Which takes us to who took part? Heydrich, almost certainly – it was his party. The others were all of the rank of *Obergruppenführer* in nineteen forty-one and members of Himmler's SS inner circle, so we should be able to track down their identities. I have some ideas about that. Ziegler's informant was a *Gruppenführer,* an SS general, but not one of the chosen few and he must have been several ranks lower in the early part of nineteen forty-one. That means there were others involved in the ritual, perhaps observers or helpers.'

'How does that help?' Charlotte asked.

'The men who played the key roles would all have been in their forties and will almost certainly be dead, if not in the war, then of old age. According to Ziegler, the *Gruppenführer* was in his mid twenties, so there's at least a chance he might still be alive. The first step is to talk to Ziegler's family. If he made a will he must have left his worldly goods to someone. Maybe they'll give us more clues.'

Steele rose from the table and stalked the length of the dining room, his voice shaking with passion.

'Can you imagine what it would be like to hold the sword of Arthur?' The legend says he's sleeping in a cave waiting for the call to save Britain in its time of need. I find that comforting, although I can't quite bring myself to believe it. But, make no mistake, this is our time of need.'

The banker stopped abruptly and his dark eyes challenged anyone in the room to deny it. He fixed on Jamie. 'The attack that killed your Abbie was just the start. Britain looks for strong leadership. The forces of darkness aren't just gathering, they're upon us. What if a man could stand up holding Excalibur high for all to see and offer that leadership? What could that man not achieve?'

Jamie felt a tightening in his chest at the throwaway use of Abbie's name, but he managed a smile. 'I hope you're not thinking of going into politics, Adam?'

Steele's expression didn't alter. 'Find it for me, Jamie.'

X

Charlotte walked into the office as Jamie and Gault were going over their technical equipment. The former SBS man barely spared her a glance as she sat down at the table. He handed Jamie a mobile phone that looked as if it had come straight from the box. 'Satellite phone for secure encrypted calls between you and the boss only. Press two and it will speed dial his number and connect from anywhere in the world. The encryption code changes with every call, so theoretically it's impossible to break into. This phone,' he held up a slim Nokia, 'is for everyday use if you want to contact either of us.'

'*Us?*' Jamie asked.

Charlotte grinned like a schoolgirl preparing for her first class trip overseas. 'Adam decided my research skills might come in useful after all. I'll be organizing our travel and accommodation.'

'The boss thought it would be more natural having Her Ladyship along,' Gault said. 'Provide a nice bit of natural colour while we run around on our wild-goose chase.' He grinned at Charlotte and she glared back at him.

There were clearly tensions here that Jamie didn't understand, and he wondered if the pair had some kind of history. 'You don't believe in the sword,' he asked the soldier, 'so why agree to come along?'

Gault shrugged. 'Because the boss is the boss, and traipsing around Europe babysitting you is better than doing real work. Now, if we can get back to business?' He drew a laptop from a padded case. 'Like the phone, this is state-of-the-art kit with the best security available. Any searches you do on the Internet, files you create or e-mails you send should be safe.'

'You say *should*? You're not certain?'

'This is the stuff the CIA uses, which means it's been tested until it squealed for mercy. Who knows what they know and we don't? For the same reasons the Russians, the Chinese and maybe even the Iranians will have their best people trying to get into it. You should have one of these already?' The last was to Charlotte, who nodded.

'Well, you might as well get started,' Jamie said. 'We'll need three flights to Dortmund tomorrow and two nights' hotel with an option to extend. Oh, and we'll need a car.'

She jotted the requests in a notebook. 'Anything else?'

'While you're at it, see if you can track down some reading material for the plane. What I'm looking for are the names and a short profile of all the candidates who might have taken part in the Excalibur ritual.' He saw the shadow of dismay cross her face. 'Don't worry,' he smiled, 'there weren't all that many *SS-Obergruppenführer* in the early days and we only need Himmler's allies: the men he thought of as his Knights of the Round Table; men who were available to attend the meeting in April nineteen forty-one.'

The next direct flight to Dortmund was with a budget airline and left from Luton at an unearthly hour, so Steele's 'First Class all the way' would have to wait for another day. Fortunately, it had the advantage of being less than half full and they were able to choose their seats and even have a little privacy. Charlotte handed out the sheets she had made up on the possible participants in the Excalibur ritual and Jamie was impressed by the cast list she'd put together in such a short time, some of them with photographs.

Jamie studied the first two familiar faces on the list. There didn't seem to be anyone within eavesdropping distance, but he kept his voice low just in case and the others huddled close to hear him. 'I think we can rule out Martin Bormann and Rudolf Hess, because Himmler regarded them both as rivals and their SS rank was more or less honorary. The meeting was also less than a month before Hess made his crazy flight to Scotland to try to stop the war, so he may have had other things on his mind. Any initial thoughts?'

'Some of the things I read almost made me sick,'

Charlotte said. 'It seems obscene even to think of these men as Knights of the Round Table.'

'Every one a bastard,' Gault confirmed. 'Only some are bigger bastards than others.'

Jamie had to agree. 'I thought Heydrich was the biggest bastard of them all, but even though he was Himmler's right-hand man, created the *einsatzgruppen* and is responsible for more deaths than the Black Plague, he's just a pen-pusher compared to some of these butchers.'

'Friedrich Jeckeln . . .' Charlotte paused as a steward approached offering snacks and hot drinks from a trolley. When he was out of earshot, she continued: 'After the invasion of Russia Himmler gave him command of all *einsatzgruppen* – why don't we call them what they were, murder squads? – in the east. He was an educated man,' she shook her head as if decent schooling should be a barrier to mass murder, 'an engineer, but regular firing squads weren't efficient enough for him because the victims would sprawl all over the place and fill up the mass graves too quickly. Jeckeln developed a method he called "sardine packing" where the people to be killed lay down in rows on top of the already dead before they were shot in the back of the head. Anyone who didn't die immediately was just buried alive. Jeckeln was hanged by the Russians in nineteen forty-six, but it's surprising how many of these people survived the war.'

'Udo von Woyrsch.' Gault pointed to an image of a hard-eyed man with a nose like an executioner's axe and identified by the collar tabs of an SS general. 'Death squad commander and a personal friend of Himmler. His unit were so brutal in southern Poland that the *Wehrmacht* petitioned the Gestapo to have them removed from the area. He only served ten years and lived till he was eighty-three.'

'Gottlob Berger is the only man I've actually been able to confirm was among Himmler's chosen few,' Charlotte continued. 'His biography states quite openly that he was one of the *Reichsführer*'s Twelve Apostles. Subordinates called him "The Almighty Gottlob", as in Almighty Gott/God? Himmler put him in charge of the Eastern Territories in nineteen forty, so if what we know about our ritual is true, he's almost certain to have been involved. He was captured, did a few years in jail and died in nineteen seventy-five.'

As the flight continued, Jamie ran through the rest of the candidates for places at the Round Table. Kurt Daluege, notorious for wiping out the village of Lidice in Czechoslovakia after Heydrich's assassination in Prague, hanged 1946; Erwin Rösener, who had encouraged terror and massacre in Slovenia, where his *Domobranci* anti-Partisan units' favoured method of execution was by woodsman's axe, also finished up on the end of a rope; Karl Wolff, Himmler's one-time adjutant, who would later become Heydrich's rival and notorious for his part in the massacre of Italian partisans late in the war; Karl von Eberstein, who brought Himmler and Heydrich together, and was later responsible for Dachau concentration camp, served just three years and died peacefully in 1979; Sepp Dietrich, a soldier-thug and unlikely occultist who served in every theatre of the war, and who would find infamy as the instigator of the Malmedy Massacre when American prisoners were shot in cold blood during the Ardennes offensive in 1944; Erich von dem Bach-Zelewski, destroyer of Warsaw and responsible for the deaths of hundreds of thousands, somehow escaped the rope to die in prison; Oswald Pohl, overseer of a ruthless slave empire based on the concentration camps exploiting his victims for their gold teeth, their hair and their every belonging before consigning them to the ovens. And the two who interested him most: Darré and Hildebrandt, architects of the *Ahnenerbe* and encouragers of Himmler's obsession with the occult.

He saw Gault frowning. 'You have a problem with this?'

'Only that for all their very obvious faults these were practical men. They don't seem the types to have been taken in by Himmler's mumbo-jumbo. I can see them cheerfully slaughtering Russians and Slavs and Jews because they thought they were racially superior, but not standing around in the dark in hoods and cloaks muttering incantations over a set of old cutlery.'

Jamie allowed himself a smile. 'Practical, maybe, but every man on our list was in Himmler's thrall. By nineteen forty-one they'd spent twelve years steeped in a culture of his creation, and the SS culture was defined by ritual and theatre. They wore Death's Head rings and carried Death's Head daggers. The SS leaders, his twelve Apostles, were each allocated their own coat of arms and on their deaths those arms would be burned and their ashes kept in his Camelot at Wewelsburg, along with the *Totenkopf* ring of every SS man who fell in battle. Himmler based the organizational structure of the SS on the Jesuit order, but in reality they were more like medieval Templars, or the Knights of St John. He wanted the SS to be cloaked in mysticism and fear, and he succeeded. Worship of the past was bred deep and his enthusiasm for the occult directly linked to his obsession to make contact with the great figures of history, whether it was through seance, ritual or some kind of object, like the Spear of Destiny that was used to kill Christ . . .'

'Or Excalibur,' Charlotte whispered.

'Yes,' Jamie said, 'or Excalibur. The point is that Himmler *believed* in an ancient race of Aryan supermen capable of using mind-control on their enemies, and he *believed* they could provide him with the weapons for world domination. He *believed* that the Spear of Destiny would bring with it a power that the Nazis could use. In their hearts, these practical men may not have believed with the same fervour, but what really mattered was that where Himmler led they were prepared to follow. They proved that by doing things that no rational human being would have done and that left them with the blood of countless millions of people on their hands.'

Jamie settled back and turned his attention to the

window and the spotless white carpet of cloud below. Far away to the west a tiny replica of their own jet slid smoothly across a pristine sky of eggshell blue. He could feel Charlotte's warm presence and smell the sweetness of her perfume. The scent brought with it a wave of nostalgia that threatened to overwhelm him. Abbie would have been fast asleep now, with her head on his shoulder. She loved to travel, but always slept the moment the plane took off. What would she make of this strange quest? He decided she would approve. The romantic in her would have seen Excalibur as a symbol of justice and good. Maybe Adam Steele was right and Britain needed a new Arthur, but it was too late for Abbie. What was clear now was that whether he found the sword or not, he would have to wade through the most degrading filth and pestilence of war to reach his goal. Because the twelve men who attended the Excalibur ritual had been the men who had enforced Heinrich Himmler's writ in the East. Not his Knights of the Round Table.

His Angels of Death.

XI

Dorstfeld, where the Ziegler family lived, lay on the west side of the city of Dortmund, the opposite from the airport, and they checked into their hotel before Jamie called the number he had been given. The phone was answered with a grunt and in a thick Westphalian accent that his brain took a few moments to decipher.

'Herr Ziegler? Herr Rolf Ziegler?'

'Wait. Old man? It's for you.'

Jamie heard the rustle of feet across a carpeted floor and a hard voice confirmed: 'Ziegler.'

He sensed the reluctance at the other end of the line as he explained that he wanted to ask a few questions about the will of the late Wulf Ziegler. 'We will only take up a few moments of your time, Herr Ziegler,' he assured the man at the other end of the phone, 'and of course, we'll be happy to pay you for your trouble.' He saw Gault's eyebrows rise and shrugged. It was Steele's money.

'How much?'

'Shall we say two hundred and fifty euros?'

A short pause. 'Where are you staying?'

'The Park Inn.'

'I don't know it.'

'It's in the city centre on . . .' He grabbed for a piece of the hotel's headed notepaper. 'Olpe?'

'Sure. You got a car it will take you ten minutes. Drive out to the fifty-four at Sudwall and turn right. Keep going until you hit Rheinischestrasse – you'll know when you see the old Union Brewery building up ahead – then follow it until you cross the bridge. When you can see the steel works you're there.'

'The steel works?'

'You can't miss it. It'll be on your right. We're on Joachimstrasse, directly across the road from the old offices. Look for the blue block. Number thirty-four on the second floor. Okay? Opposite Aldi.' Jamie repeated the instructions and Charlotte took them down on her notepad. 'When you gonna be here? We're just about to eat.'

Jamie looked at his watch: just gone six. 'Can we say eight o'clock?'

With what might have been a grunt of acknowledgement the line went dead.

They had a light meal in the hotel restaurant and Jamie managed to prise a little history from the soft-spoken Gault, who it turned out had served in Iraq and Afghanistan and a few other places he was even less eager to discuss. 'I wouldn't have thought there was much call for the web-footed persuasion in Afghanistan, given that there's very little water there,' Jamie teased.

'You had to be there.' Gault grinned, taking no offence at the land-based soldiers' derogatory label for the amphibious variety. 'Admittedly, it was drier than you'd like up in the Shahi-Kot Valley and Tora Bora wasn't exactly tourist territory, but the one that took the school prize was Qala-i-Jangi Fort. Six hundred Terry Taliban prisoners and their Al-Qaida mates bust into the armoury and were about to break out into open country, armed and dangerous, when we got there. Eight of us. We kept them pinned down with an MG till the Northern Alliance arrived and a few of us even snuck into the jail and tried to rescue a CIA bod, who'd got himself captured. The Yanks wanted to give my boss on that mission the Congressional Medal of Honor, but some bastard politician at Westminster vetoed it.' Jamie found himself the focus of what might be called a significant look. 'One of the reasons I hate bastard politicians. Time we had a few military men running the country, eh?' Jamie didn't rise to the suggestion and Gault shook his head. 'Anyway, what I'm saying is it's not only the SAS that can crawl around in the dark, Mr Saintclair. Though I guess you wouldn't know that, what with your less than glorious military record.'

Jamie let the jibe at his two short weeks at Sandhurst slide by like a straight right in the boxing ring. 'Not everybody's cut out for soldiering, old boy. Taking orders turned out to be not my cup of tea. If you liked it so much, why didn't you stay in? You're not that old.'

'I didn't have any choice, old boy.'

Before Jamie could ask the obvious question, Charlotte, who seemed to have appointed herself his minder, interrupted sweetly. 'Isn't it time we were going?'

The evening light was fading as they drove out of the hotel car park in the hired black Audi. The street lights showed a Dortmund of steel, brick and glass, with hardly a piece of dressed stone in sight. Jamie reckoned it must be one of the most modern centres he'd ever been in. A city born in the nineteen fifties, and still to mature fully. He mentioned it to Gault and the SBS man, who was at the wheel, laughed.

'If we'd been here sixty odd years ago, there'd have been nothing but rubble for miles around. This is the industrial heart of Germany. Dortmund was right in the middle of Bomber Harris's Battle of the Ruhr. In the summer of nineteen forty-three the RAF visited Dortmund about once a week with four or five hundred Lancasters. By the time they'd finished you'd be lucky if there was one stone standing on top of another.' He drove out onto a wide highway and followed the line of the rebuilt city ramparts northwards until they reached an intersection marked by a brick tower topped by a huge spotlit letter U. 'Left here, I think,' Charlotte said.

Jamie heard Gault mutter something under his breath about 'not being fucking blind'.

To their right, running like a broad river through the centre of the city, was a floodlit expanse of rail tracks, which split a couple of hundred yards later to create a concrete peninsula that Gault reached via an iron bridge. 'Jesus, what a fucking shithole,' the former SBS man said as an enormous industrial building that must be the Union steelworks reared up to fill the skyline ahead. They continued on until they reached the first actual old building Jamie had seen since their plane landed, a four-storey block of red brick and sandstone decorated with enormous Romanesque pillars. Gault took the first street on the left and turned into the almost empty car park of the supermarket, choosing a space to the rear away from the lights.

They studied their surroundings. The back wall of the shop was to their right, with the usual collection of bins and a cage full of discarded cardboard just visible in the shadows. Ahead, a row of modern, brightly painted tenements blocked the view. Jamie's eyes were drawn to the block in the centre, a sickly duck-egg blue, with lights shining on every floor.

'Okay,' Jamie said eventually. 'We play this just as we discussed. Gault and I will go in and talk to the son. Charlotte will stay with the car, in the driver's seat with the engine running.'

'Isn't that a little over-cautious?'

'You're not in Hampstead now, Charlotte,' Jamie said evenly. 'And that's not a Waitrose. Strange things happen in Germany, or at least they happen to me. Better safe than sorry. Right, Gault?'

Gault nodded. 'And you don't go for a drive to look at the sights and you don't nip into the supermarket to see what you can pick up for tonight's supper.'

From the back seat came the sound of a wounded snarl as the rear door opened. 'I wish you'd stop treating me as if I'm some kind of idiot. I'm Adam's PA, not his bloody bimbo.' The two men exited the car and Charlotte threw herself into the driver's seat, refusing to look at either of them. They heard the door slam shut and engine start as they walked warily across the almost empty car park towards the bright lights of Wulf Ziegler's home.

XII

'Herr Ziegler? Jamie Saintclair, and this is Mr Gault.'

Rolf Ziegler studied them in the doorway without inviting them inside. Lank grey hair hung across his forehead to combine with a pair of eyebrows that seemed about to take flight. He must have been close to sixty, with suspicious, deep-set eyes in a worn-out, pinched face, but the muscles beneath his T-shirt were threaded with whipcord tendons, and the thick fingers of his workers' hands were tipped with black crescents under the nails and looked capable of tearing telephone directories in half. 'You said something about money?'

Gault counted off five ten-euro notes. 'That's a down payment,' he said in his featureless military school German. 'You get the other two hundred when we're satisfied.'

The German's glance flicked from the money in his

hand to Gault, but saw nothing there to give him hope that he could extract any more for now. He stepped aside. 'You'd better come in.'

Jamie almost gagged on the thick scent of curry that filled the apartment, but Gault grinned appreciatively at their host. 'I do like a nice hot bhuna.'

Ziegler ushered them through to a small lounge dominated by a large and plainly very new flat-screen television that stood to the right of an open stairway. A thin, worn-out woman in cardigan and jeans looked up warily from the magazine she was reading, before rising to push her way past a sturdy youth of about seventeen into the kitchen. Rolf made a movement with his head that told the boy to leave them alone, but the teenager glared and stood his ground. He wore his dark hair cropped short and his father's features were just recognizable in a puffy, slightly overweight face. Jamie felt a shiver of anticipation as he realized where the opposition in this house would come from. Everything about the kid said: *I don't want you here and I don't give a shit who knows it.*

'My son Otto.' Rolf shrugged a parent's resignation that there was sometimes no point in pushing it and ushered them to one of a pair of matching cloth sofas. 'You want coffee?'

'Thank you.'

Ziegler relayed an order to his wife and waited until she appeared with three large cups. The coffee was thick, black and strong enough that you could stand a spoon in it. Jamie drank appreciatively and Gault took a tentative sip.

'You said this was something about my father's will?'

Jamie hesitated, but they'd already decided there was no mileage in trying to deceive Rolf Ziegler if they wanted his cooperation. At the first sign he was being used he would clam up and they'd be as well walking out of the door. 'We are more interested in the . . . ah, codex, than the will itself.'

'So you're here about the old man's crazy sword story, huh?' Rolf glanced at the TV and smiled for the first time. 'Maybe two hundred and fifty isn't enough.'

'I told you we should have sold the thing ourselves instead of getting that lawyer to do it.' Otto layered every word with contempt for his father, the visitors and his life in general.

'Shut it, boy,' his father snarled.

'We've got the copy and—'

'I said shut it.' This time the voice was like the crack of a bullwhip and Otto sullenly resumed his place against the doorframe, his mouth twitching with anger.

Jamie watched the exchange with interest. It told him two things. First, that whoever had made the offer on Adam Steele's behalf to buy the codex had betrayed something of its true value and Rolf Ziegler had come to the correct conclusion that that value had something to do with the mention of Excalibur. Second, that father and son, for their own separate reasons, were keen to cash in further on any opportunity for potential profit.

That didn't really matter as long as they'd kept it to themselves, but if word spread . . .

Gault saw it too, and immediately stepped in to close one avenue. 'I believe part of the agreement with your lawyer was a clause binding all parties to secrecy,' he said in a bored voice. 'Perhaps it would be better if I had the copy,' he aimed the words at the father. 'It might save you a lot of money in the long run.'

Rolf Ziegler glared at his son and shook his head in disgust. He got to his feet, extracted a file from a cabinet in the corner of the room and handed it to the former soldier. 'All right, what do you want?'

Jamie allowed his eyes to wander round the room, taking in the peeling wallpaper and threadbare carpet. When he eventually spoke, he did his best to sound like a lawyer and as if this was just a simple legal quest for more information. 'I'll ask you questions about the codex and your father, and depending on the quality of your answer we may consider offering some kind of bonus payment above the agreed sum. Of course, we'll already *know* some of the answers so be careful what you say. Agreed?'

The German nodded.

'I think, firstly,' Jamie pulled a small black diary and a pen from the inside pocket of his jacket and opened it ready to take notes, 'we need to know what state of mind your father was in when he dictated the codex. He did dictate it, I understand, not write it himself.'

132

'He was dying of cancer,' Rolf's head dropped between his shoulders, 'what sort of state of mind do you think he was in? He wanted to make his peace with God.'

Jamie frowned. 'Had he always been a church-goer?'

'Mama said he turned to the Lord for help when he came back from the war. Never missed a Sunday mass at St Anna's along the road. He helped rebuild the steel-works after you English knocked it down with your bastard bombs, then he got a job on the production line. Worked every hour he could get for his family, just like me. She used a word I didn't know then: atonement. Sometimes I heard them whispering together and he would be crying, saying he was ashamed of what he'd done.'

'He was a hero. He fought for the Fatherland.'

The Englishman ignored the voice from the kitchen doorway. 'Did he say what he had done to be ashamed of?'

'He was in the SS and he served in the East. Do you want me to draw you a picture?' Rolf's lips were a pale line and the words were forced through clenched teeth. 'He joined the *Deutsches Jungvolk* on the day of his tenth birthday and the *Hitler Jugend* on his fourteenth. When he received orders for the *SS-Junkerschule* he wrote his mother that it was the best day of his life. He worshipped Adolf Hitler; would have done anything for him—'

'*Heil* Hitler!' Jamie looked up to find Otto Ziegler grinning at him, with his right arm raised in the Hitler salute. He felt Gault tense, but laid a hand on the former SBS man's arm and he sat back on the sofa.

'Why don't you go and play with your toys?' Rolf said wearily.

'At your orders, Father,' Otto laughed.

Mrs Ziegler's concerned eyes followed her son up the stairs. When Otto was gone, she exchanged an anguished glance with Rolf. He shook his head and she closed the door.

'I'm sorry,' Jamie said.

'Kids, eh?' The German's expression reminded Jamie of a smile on a corpse. 'What can you do if they get in with the wrong crowd? They're still your kids.' He closed his eyes. 'Let's get this over, then I don't want to hear another fucking word about this thing ever again.'

'After your father dictated the codex, did he ever talk about what he'd written? I'm thinking of any information that might be relevant, but that he didn't include. Did he say what the sword looked like? Where the meeting was?'

Rolf shrugged, 'Sometimes he'd talk about the spying trip to England. A happy time, playing at soldiers, but not being in any danger. You have to understand that by now the morphine ruled him. One day he'd be lucid, the next . . . well, you never knew what to believe. I thought the swords only existed in his imagination, but he said he wished now he'd looked at the English sword. The only reason he didn't was because he had orders to deliver what was in the hole exactly as he found it, and he found it in some kind of leather bag. One time he laughed when he told me they smuggled it back in a sack full of poles for an old bell tent and the English never even searched them. I'm certain he never said where the meeting was.'

'What about the *Gruppenführer* he met in the ambulance? Did he ever mention his name?'

'Not his full name, no, but I know what his first name was,' Rolf's smile was surprising and almost friendly, 'because my father named me for the man who saved his life. Any other SS general would have kicked him out of that ambulance. If he hadn't got on he would be old bones now on the Seelow Heights, along with the rest of them, he'd say. If I'm Rolf, so is he. Does that help?'

It was a step forward, but not the detailed information Jamie had hoped for. He bit back his disappointment and smiled his thanks as the German went back to the drawer where he'd picked up the copy of the codex, and pulled out a brown envelope.

'This is my father on his wedding day in nineteen forty-nine.' He showed them a monochrome picture of a slimmer version of Otto in a light-coloured suit standing proudly beside a pretty blonde girl in a white dress. 'The suit was borrowed and the dress was made of Yankee parachute silk saved from the war. Dortmund was like that then. Ach . . .' He sighed and slipped the picture back in the envelope.

'Hey, English, you want to see a better picture of my Grandpa, the hero?' Otto stood grinning at the top of the stairs where he must have been watching them. Rolf

Ziegler went deathly pale and the envelope shook in his hands as he slumped into the chair.

'No, Otto, please . . .'

'You not proud of your old man, Father? Come on, English, it's the only picture you'll ever see of Wulf Ziegler in uniform, huh. Don't worry, my bedroom's not so much of a shithole today.'

Jamie looked to Rolf for permission, but the other man wouldn't meet his eyes. Gault was already on the stairs and Otto was laughing. Jamie followed.

By the time they reached the top of the stairs where Otto waited by a painted door, puffed up and officious, taller and more threatening now that you were standing close to him. He had his hand outstretched ushering them inside. As they entered Jamie stopped dead on the threshold and he heard a growl of outrage from Gault. He hoped the former SBS man wouldn't do anything silly, the kind of thing only an enormous amount of willpower was stopping Jamie from doing himself.

The room was a shrine to an age of infamy. A Nazi flag adorned one wall, beside a framed picture of Adolf Hitler. A coal-scuttle helmet with SS lightning flashes sat on a dresser beside an iPod dock. Pictures of marching formations of bright-eyed automatons vied with battle scenes showing hard-faced young men, festooned with stick grenades and machine pistols. But pride of place went to a single picture above the bed. On it, a gaunt figure in trousers and shirtsleeves sat on the edge of a large pit. His face showed no fear, only a weary resignation, but there was something terrible in his eyes, a raw emotion that no one would ever read. Behind him, to his right, stood a row of laughing men in grey uniforms and forage caps. On his left, the grinning figure with one arm outstretched holding the pistol that was about to put a bullet in his head.

'My grandpa, the hero. What do you think now, English? I wish he was here so we could do the same thing to the stinking fucking Turks. Take your time. Enjoy.' His mocking voice faded as he vanished downstairs. 'Otto's got something to celebrate.'

Gault would have gone after him, but Jamie held him back. He would have liked to tear the room apart, but Abbie's face appeared in his head and suddenly he felt as resigned as the man in the picture and he relaxed. Gault looked at him with wild eyes. 'Don't ever do that to me again. I would have ripped his fucking guts out and strangled him with them.'

'That's what I was afraid of.'

When they returned to the lounge Rolf Ziegler's wife hovered protectively over him, but he shrugged her aside.

'So now you know.' Ziegler's voice was made brittle by anguish. 'My father served with the *einsatzgruppen*. The photograph was taken at Minsk. I don't even know where Otto found it. My son lives a lie, Herr Saintclair. Everything he believes in is wrong, yet nothing I can do or say will undermine his certainty that he is right and everyone else is wrong. He even lies about the picture. Father is not the one pulling the trigger. He's among the men in the background. But it is enough that he is there. You asked what he had to atone for. Well, that is part of it.'

Jamie knew there was nothing he could say that would help. They had everything they were going to get; there was no point in staying.

Gault handed over a wad of notes that was far in excess of the two hundred euros Rolf was owed. The German looked at the money for a moment, his jaw working, before he dropped it to the ground as if it had burned his hand. He accompanied them from the room while his wife gathered up the fallen notes.

When they reached the door, Jamie stopped. 'You said *that is part of it*?'

For a moment Rolf Ziegler looked as if he had been punched. His face crumpled like a burst football and Jamie had never witnessed such a terrible combination of despair and defeat.

'My father was twenty-two years old when he came home from Russia on leave in September of nineteen forty-three. It took him a week to discover that his parents were feeding an old Jew who had set up home in the basement of a bombed-out factory. To them it was an act of Christian charity. To him it was an act of treason against his beloved Führer. What could a good Nazi do, but denounce them? My grandfather and grandmother, Hans and Martha Ziegler, were guillotined in Dortmund prison on the same Christmas Eve.'

XIII

'Christ, that was—'

Gault didn't get the chance to finish his sentence. They came out of the shadows in a screaming mob when he and Jamie were halfway across the car park. Jamie's first glance took in dark clothing and faces masked by black scarves, a couple of pool cues and baseball bats at the head of the pack and the rest coming up fast behind. He counted eight before being forced to duck under a swinging cue and managed to land a straight right in his attacker's middle, doubling him up and disabling him for the moment. Gault was similarly engaged, disarming his man with a twist of the wrist and throwing him with some kind of ju-jitsu move that left him with the baseball bat just as two more thugs arrived to batter him to the ground, their fists pumping like steam hammers. With bewildering speed Jamie found himself facing three wild-eyed young men jockeying for position, but too wary to rush him. He didn't have time to wonder who their attackers were, but he had his suspicions. He ducked and weaved, using all the skills that had almost won him a boxing Blue at Cambridge, but was unable to avoid a lashing boot that sent a lightning bolt of pain through his thigh. The problem was keeping them all in his line of sight, because there was always one on the periphery of his vision. A scream of agony proved they weren't having it all their own way with Gault and Jamie used the momentary diversion to dance forward and ram his fist into the centre man's face, feeling a satisfying crunch of breaking cartilage as it landed plumb on the thug's nose. All the time his mind had been screaming at him that the greatest danger wasn't to his front. Where was the eighth man? The one with the second baseball bat. 'Jamie!' The only thing that saved him was the high-pitched scream. He ducked and turned in the same movement, the bat ruffling his hair as it missed his skull by a millimetre. Only one chance. He went in low, aiming his shoulder at the batsman's midriff and keeping his legs pumping as he drove forward in a textbook rugby tackle. But the instant they were down the boots started to come in and he felt a savage blow and a lance of agony in his side that felt like someone had stove in a rib. 'Fuck you, English.' Someone gripped his hair and pulled his head up. The last thing he saw was a hand holding some kind of can, before his eyes caught fire and he could feel his eyelids melting. The men who were intent on maiming him were forgotten. All he could think about was saving his eyes. In the same instant, he'd inhaled some kind of gas that stopped the breath in his throat and made him choke, his whole body reacting to what was happening by having some kind of seizure.

His last conscious thought was: *Please put me out of my bloody misery.*

'Pepper spray.' The voice was Gault's, but the hand applying something soothing and cool to his eyes wasn't. 'All you can do is let it pass.'

The hand moved away and Jamie protested, a sort of mooing sound in his throat. He tried to open his eyes, but it was like being underwater, a blur of light and shade that didn't mean anything until one piece of shade moved.

'Just lie back, Jamie,' Charlotte said, and the soothing coolness returned. It didn't help the pain so much as make him feel mothered, which was unusual and quite pleasant, because he hadn't been mothered even when he had a mother.

Everything faded rapidly and he disappeared into a pain-filled, gasping half-sleep. When he opened his eyes again he could finally see, which was an improvement. He was lying on the soft sheets of the bed in his hotel room and he could hear voices murmuring not far away. The downside was that his lungs felt as if they had been scoured by acid, and when he tried to move someone stabbed him in the side with a skewer. He let out a groan of agony.

'Stay still, we think one of your ribs might be broken.'

Charlotte's head appeared on the right and Gault on the left.

'Probably only popped cartilage. More painful, but it'll heal quicker,' the former soldier gave his opinion.

'What happened?'

'That little bastard Otto and some of his pals jumped us.'

'Why the Christ would he do that?'

'For fun? He seemed the type. But it appears he's not the only one around here who'd like to see a Fourth Reich. According to the hotel manager, there are certain areas where groups of young Nazis can more or less get away with anything, and Dortsfeld where we were is one of them. They break up Turkish businesses and throw bricks through restaurant windows and the cops won't touch them.'

Memories of the attack came flooding back and Jamie felt a cold sweat as he remembered the moment when the spray hit his eyes. 'I thought I'd had it.'

'You would have done. They were all set to put your lights out and I had my hands full when Charlie here . . .'

'Charlie?' Charlotte shrugged and Gault grinned.

'Charlie came to the rescue. She rushes them, scream-ing, and Otto turns to take her out with a baseball bat. Next thing you know the Kick-Boxing Queen here . . .'

'Tae kwon do, actually.'

'. . . pivots and her size-six Jimmy Choo takes

Otto right in the chops and his teeth are all over the Tarmac. Never seen it done better. With the head boy out of action and their casualties mounting – your man with the broken nose didn't look too chipper – they decided they'd had enough fun and legged it, shouting compliments as they went. And that was that.'

'Apart from you lying there clawing at your face and gasping your lungs out.' Concern made Charlotte's voice ragged. 'I thought someone had thrown acid in your face, but Mr Gault, who knows a suspicious amount of detail about such things, diagnosed pepper spray, and said that there was no point in taking you to hospital, because the effects would fade eventually.'

'That was very good of Mr Gault.' Jamie was fairly certain that he'd read somewhere that pepper spray had killed several dozen people in the States when used to excess by law enforcement agencies. Still, he'd survived. Just.

'A pity we didn't get anything from Ziegler,' Gault complained. 'Apart from the fact that his father was a murdering thug – and that was only because of his Nazi bastard of a son. It makes the whole trip a bit of a waste.'

'We didn't get any closer to the castle or the sword,' Jamie admitted, 'but we didn't come away with nothing. Ziegler said he was named after the man who saved his father's life on the Seelow Heights. I'm pretty certain there will only be one or two SS *Gruppenführers* called Rolf. So that's your next job, Charlotte – track them down and cross reference them until you find one with links to the Hitler Youth, who was on the Seelow Heights and has some sort of connection to one of our twelve Angels of Death.' Charlotte nodded. 'And Charlotte?'

'Yes, Jamie?'

'I really appreciate you saving me, but I was just wondering why you didn't drive the car at our Nazi *kameraden* with the lights blazing and the horn blowing, which would probably have been enough to scare them off?'

'Oh, I wasn't in the car. I was in the shop. You can't leave a girl on her own for two hours in the cold and not expect her to go for a wee.'

Charlotte came off the phone the next morning with a look of what could only be called conspiratorial smugness. 'Just the one match: Rolf Lauterbacher; born Halle, nineteen twenty. Adam's having the details checked at the Berlin Document Centre where they hold all the captured SS personnel records, but he seems to fit. Joined the Hitler Youth when he was of age, and the Nazi party a few years later. By the time he was nineteen he was something called high area leader of the Hitler Youth West, which I'm told would have taken in Wulf Ziegler's Dortmund unit. He was also close to Reinhard Heydrich, who took an interest in his career because the two families were friends. He didn't join the SS until the start of the war, but by nineteen forty he was already a *Sturmbannführer* and on the staff of . . . guess?'

Gault looked as if he wanted to take her by the throat and shake her and Jamie thought he'd better play along if violence were to be avoided.

'One of the chosen few?'

'Correct.' She grinned. 'Josef "Sepp" Dietrich, then commander of the *Liebstandarte SS Adolf Hitler*. If Dietrich attended the Excalibur rite in nineteen forty-one, then it's very likely Lauterbacher would have accompanied him. He must have risen rapidly through the ranks because by nineteen forty-five he's a *Gruppenführer* in command of an *SS Panzergrenadier* division that suffered severe casualties on the Seelow Heights. He was seriously wounded in the fighting there. I don't have any information on his post-war life. Adam's people are working on that, too, and they've promised to send me anything that seems relevant.'

'Tell them everything is relevant and that we need it today.'

She nodded and opened her laptop. 'I'll e-mail them.'

By lunchtime Jamie had made a sufficient recovery to be able to think about food and they went to a restaurant close to the hotel where they had steaks washed down with Hövels beer. When they returned to Jamie's room Charlotte's e-mail reply had arrived, complete with a downloaded report.

Her eyes widened as she read the contents and Jamie moved in beside her so he could see what was on the screen.

'Don't bloody hold out on me, woman,' Gault growled.

Jamie read from the computer file. 'Our *Gruppenführer* has had an interesting life. After the surrender, Rolf Lauterbacher was tried for war crimes. The Americans accused him of murdering Allied prisoners of war and the crew of a shot-down bomber. The court acquitted him, but he was still wanted in Poland, where he would almost certainly have faced the death sentence. In nineteen fifty he turned up in Buenos Aires, where he's suspected of providing an escort for one Adolf Eichmann, who arrived around the same time. A few years later the CIA, would you believe, sent him to Egypt where he trained anti-Israeli guerrillas. By nineteen fifty-six he's back in Germany, in Munich, but he disappeared again when the authorities began sniffing about. The suggestion is that he was being protected by the Gehlen Organization.'

'Gehlen?' Charlotte's voice mirrored her confusion.

'It was an independent spy service set up by the Americans under a tame former *Wehrmacht* general at the start of the Cold War. They used Nazi intelligence experts who still had contacts behind the Iron Curtain. Lauterbacher must have somehow fitted the bill. He didn't resurface until the mid-seventies when he was an adviser to the Omani ministry of youth. Last known living the life of a recluse in Madrid, Spain.'

'He's still alive?' Gault demanded.

'There's nothing here that says otherwise,' Jamie frowned. 'But he must be in his eighties now.'

Charlotte reached for her laptop. 'Then we'd better get there quickly.'

XIV

Twenty men sat round the table in what had once been the wood-panelled ballroom of a large mansion house in the London suburb of Hampstead. They knew they could speak freely because it had been swept for listening devices or any of the other nefarious intelligence-gathering apparatus the security services had at their disposal these days. Each man had come here separately and by a route and a means of transport designed to either lose any follower or, at the very least, make them show themselves. Strategically placed watchers had confirmed each of the arrivals had been 'clean', which was a relief to the organizer – the alternative would have meant further complications in what was an already complicated scenario. They were powerful men – politicians, industrialists, businessmen, at least one high-ranking military officer, and a relatively minor member of the Royal family – all with a devoted following of other powerful men, who commanded the loyalty of still more. As a group, they had a net worth of many billions, but the influence they wielded made them worth several times their mere monetary value.

'So we are agreed, gentlemen?' The chairman's voice carried a gravity and an authority that even these men of power could not ignore. 'In the light of the latest outrage and the likelihood of future even more costly atrocities, the time has come to take strong action against those in our society who pose a threat to this country. Our United Kingdom has not been in greater danger since the darkest hours of the Second World War, and it is only by invoking the spirit of those times that this nation will prevail. The man who led us from the darkness into the light never shirked from taking difficult decisions, no matter the hardship it caused.' He paused, allowing the abrasive bulldog figure of their hero to fill their heads. 'Let there be no doubt in your minds, gentlemen, we are as much at war now as we were then, only the enemy is not at the gates, he is already in our midst.' Another decisive pause to make his point, and he had to make a mental effort to stop himself imitating the gruff wasp-chewing voice that filled his head as he continued. 'It is a different type of war, but one that will require even greater courage to fight. Our present leader must prove he has the moral fibre to take the necessary decisions, or he does not deserve our support.' A murmur of approval rippled around the table. One of the politicians – a man whose presence was unfortunate, but necessary – opened his mouth to say something, but the chairman resumed before he could speak. 'This meeting triggers a four-stage programme to make our Government see sense. In the first instance, we will use our collective influence to place pressure on the Prime Minister to act with the kind of courage required in our current situation.'

He waited, meeting each man in the eye so they understood it was not only the Prime Minister who required courage to do what must be done. When he resumed, he counted off each priority on his slim fingers as he gave voice to it. 'First he must reinstate the death penalty for terrorist-related murder. Second, he must order the immediate arrest and detention of all suspected Islamic extremists, their funders and the radical imams who trumpet their acts as though they were some kind of triumph. Third, he must order the closure of all mosques linked to these persons. Fourth, he must put in place a registration scheme for all immigrants, up to and including the fifth generation of their line, and create selection centres where they can be thoroughly screened. And finally he must agree to the expulsion of all those with the slightest taint of a threat, plus their immediate family, to their country of racial origin.'

He looked round the room and saw that he had them: the electronics factory owner wondering where his next defence contract was coming from; the billionaire property developer unsure whether the 'incentives' he'd provided would ever bear fruit under the current administration; the not quite so well-connected industrialist who'd lost his market and needed government intervention to create another. The knowledge gave him the confidence to take the next step.

'If terrorist atrocities continue even under these restrictions, he must put in place a strategy to create quarantine zones where the divisive elements in our society can be held in isolation until the danger is past. No opposition can be tolerated if it threatens public order and our ability to hunt down the terrorists. It is our fervent hope that the Prime Minister will respond to these reasonable suggestions. However, should he not, we will move to Stage Two.' He deliberately kept his tone to a dull monotone now, as if this was just another board meeting, because he knew any sign of passion might frighten some of the more intuitively conservative among them. 'We will rally our all-party support in Parliament and the Lords to campaign for a free vote on the above matters; a vote that in the current climate we would expect to result in a resounding victory.' He allowed another long pause to let them contemplate the righteousness of their cause. The politician was too busy nodding sagely to speak. 'Obviously, we would expect any rational person to agree to what is a perfectly reasonable and democratic request, however,' he saw a few heads come up, concern in the eyes, even fear, the usual suspects, there would always be one or two; the cause might be just, but certain risks were involved and not everyone could be a hero, 'if our legitimate demands are thwarted by the intransigence and timidity of our so-called leaders, then it may be necessary to rouse up our supporters, to take our protest to the streets if that is the only way to make our voices heard.' Naturally none of the men in this room would be marching, but their financial contributions and the climate of fear engendered by the M25 massacre would ensure there would be no shortage of support.

'And finally,' now he allowed his voice to become grave, 'there is Stage Four. I will not go into detail, because you are all aware of the particulars and the part you have in them should the unthinkable happen and our leaders betray us. Suffice to say that it is a last resort, but this country *must* have strong leadership or the society we all know and cherish and which has served our United Kingdom so well will be destroyed, perhaps for ever, by the aliens we have allowed, nay, invited, into our lives and who have abused our hospitality with bloody intent. It is a time for strong men to stand up and be counted.' His eyes met the Duke's and he saw a mask of resolve that was only mildly blighted by the several brandies he had consumed and the air of privileged conceit that hovered over him like some over-officious servant. 'I know I can count on all of you.'

A few nods, a 'hear, hear' and a slap on the table from the politician, but the faces were uniformly grim, as they always were when the question of Stage Four came up. And it was only right, considering what the men who were now filing from the room had invested, and, more pertinently, what they had to lose, when – when, not if – Stage Four was implemented.

He waited until the murmurs faded and the house had been silent for more than a minute before he pushed the button below the table. A tall figure in a dark suit emerged from a concealed door in the panelling. Pale eyes the colour of old ashes swept the room and he carried himself with a wary alertness that always reminded the chairman of a presidential bodyguard, which was appropriate enough. The man poured himself a drink from one of the decanters on the table before taking a seat.

'What did you think?'

'They're solid,' the tall man acknowledged. 'We'd know soon enough if anyone stepped out of line and the arrangements are in hand for that contingency.' The chairman's smile set rigid and the tall man suppressed a smile of his own. Odd that someone who had done what he'd done and contemplated what he did should be so squeamish about his friends. 'My only real concern is Franklin. He's a little too erratic for my liking.'

'Franklin is a politician.' The chairman's voice took on a note of contempt. 'He clawed his way to within reach of the ultimate prize and then his greed brought him down. The thought of being back at the top table excites him but, more importantly, the rest think he'll bring his party's backbenchers with him. Of all the people who sat in this room, he is the most venal, arrogant and self-obsessed, which is something of an achievement. Fortunately, there will come a time when he's expendable.'

The other man nodded. Only the inner circle, five out of the twenty, those the chairman deemed most reliable, were aware of the true extent of the plan. A new Britain. A Greater Britain that would no longer be a figure of fun on the world stage, kowtowing to earnest Harvard graduates and bossy German hausfraus. There would be no stages two or three. If the Prime Minister turned down the group's demands, the next atrocity would take them immediately to Stage Four and nothing anyone could do would stop it. They were ready. Only one other element was required. Their eyes met as they simultaneously pondered the weakest link in the plan.

'The Duke?'

'He has his limitations, but we need a figurehead.'

'We've discussed it before, but—'

'I know,' the chairman growled. 'The figurehead needs a symbol to show the people he has been chosen by God.'

'We must have the sword.' The tall man's features turned hard and his expression sent a shiver through the chairman. It was the face of a fanatic, the kind of man who could command a firing squad and then joke about it with his friends in the mess afterwards. 'Whatever it takes . . .'

'We will. If anyone can find it, Saintclair can.'

*

Three hundred and twenty miles east of the London mansion, a young man braked to a halt beside a parking bay in the city of Cologne and manoeuvred his dark BMW saloon into the space. He had no idea why he'd been told to use this particular space, only that he was doing a favour for a 'friend of a friend'. Neither was he aware that in the locked boot of the BMW a hundred pounds of high explosive had been carefully packed, linked to a detonator wired to a cheap mobile phone and surrounded by drums of rusty nails. In fact, the site had been chosen because it was close to a bar popular with the local police and a shopping mall where hundreds of schoolchildren from the nearby *Hauptschule* liked to gather when they finished their lessons in the early afternoon. If things went to plan the bomb was due to detonate at around two p.m. when this assembly was at its height, with young people of all ages packing the entrance hall directly opposite the epicentre. The timing didn't need to be exact. The shockwave from the blast, travelling at a thousand feet a second, would throw a wall of shattered glass ahead of it, devastating and eviscerating everything caught in its path; the incredibly high temperature would carbonize flesh and ignite combustible material including school uniforms. Anything that survived the initial millisecond of the blast would suffer severe trauma injuries and soft-tissue damage from the lethal hail of nails propelled in the immediate wake of the shockwave. It was calculated the bomb would inflict several hundred casualties, including many deaths, and cause maximum outrage due to the arbitrary nature of the event and the number of 'innocents' killed.

The young man dutifully purchased a parking ticket and displayed it on the inside of the windscreen. When he locked the BMW's door a motorcyclist drew up beside him and handed him a spare helmet, before driving him north out of the city. The time was 1.45 p.m. Fifteen minutes later, the young man was given notice of the other critical gap in his knowledge when the helmeted biker shot him in the back of the head with a 9mm round from a Ruger semi-automatic pistol as he walked to his car on waste ground near the river. The young man's name was Mohammed, and he was named for the Prophet, but wasn't particularly religious, a fact that annoyed his younger brother, a supporter of the radical imam Abu Hamza.

XV

The only flights to Madrid from Dortmund were via Palma in Majorca, with a lengthy stopover, but Charlotte discovered they could fly direct from Dusseldorf, less than fifty miles to the west. When they were a few miles from the airport Gault turned to Jamie.

'I almost forgot, the boss asked if you could call him and give him an update at two.'

It seemed odd that Gault had overlooked an important instruction from Adam Steele, but Jamie shrugged the thought aside, switched on the satellite phone and pressed 2. It rang out after five rings and he was forced to redial the call. This time it was answered immediately.

'Steele.'

'Gault says you're looking for a progress report, but I'm not sure I can add much to what he's already told you.'

'I just want to hear that you're convinced the Excalibur

codex is genuine.' Jamie could hear the smile in the other man's voice. 'No more talk of the Hitler Diaries?'

'I'm convinced Wulf Ziegler stole some kind of object from an English country house in nineteen thirty-seven and I'm convinced he's faithfully recorded what he *thinks* he heard in the back of an ambulance on the Seelow Heights. But Ziegler never saw the sword, he'd just been blown up by Katyusha rockets and according to his account the *Gruppenführer* had a hole in him the size of a soup plate. That's not the most solid foundation for an accurate report of the proceedings.'

'The *Gruppenführer*, not Rolf Lauterbacher?'

'All the evidence points to Rolf Lauterbacher being the soldier Ziegler met,' Jamie admitted. 'The records confirm that, but records have been known to be wrong, fabricated or just misplaced, especially in the final years of the war. We know many of the top SS men altered or wiped their records at the end of the war and simply became someone else. If the hints about Lauterbacher's involvement in the Gehlen Organization are correct he would have been perfectly placed to disappear for good. With a death sentence hanging over him I wonder why he didn't. Our best hope is that he can describe the sword to us and give us a location for the ceremony. Once we have that I'll let you know what our next move is. But we won't know until we reach Madrid.'

The address they'd been given for Lauterbacher was in an upmarket residential area close to the Plaza Salamanca, to the north of the verdant green island of Retiro Park. Germany had still been in the last fragile grip of winter, but here the trees were in bud and the air contained a subtle, softly pleasant and very welcome warmth. The broad streets and their tall, elegant buildings were the product of an earlier, more sophisticated age, but they hadn't come here to admire the architecture. As they discussed their plan of approach Jamie decided that, even in his eighties, Lauterbacher, the old army officer, would identify Gault as one of his own kind the minute he laid eyes on him.

'You stay with the car. I'll take Charlotte and she can charm the old Nazi.'

Charlotte reached for her handbag, but Gault frowned. 'You're not leaving me behind. The boss said I was to cover your arse and I can't cover your arse from the car. What if you walk into another trap?'

Jamie shook his head. 'We'll be safe enough. This is midday in sunny Madrid,' he said reasonably. 'Not midnight in darkest Dortmund. Our man stays on the ground floor of that block over there, so we'll never be more than a hundred feet away. And he's in his eighties, so unless he still has a machine pistol tucked away, I reckon Charlotte could probably take care of him on her own.'

'I still think I should go with you. Who's to say he isn't armed? A lot of old soldiers hang on to their guns.'

'And what would you do if he was?' A little worm of suspicion wriggled naughtily at the base of Jamie's skull.

'Unless you happen to be packing yourself all you'd do is give him another target.'

'At least call Steele.'

'Look, Gault, you may be my babysitter, but Adam hired me to find the sword and as long as he still wants me to do that, what I say goes. Understand? So unless you want this to end right here and now you stay with the car.'

The former SBS man glared at him. 'All right, your lordship; have it your own way. But if you get into trouble don't expect Gault to come running and change your nappy. And that goes for you, too.'

'Well, I'm so glad we got *that* cleared up,' Charlotte breathed. 'We really should go, Jamie. I do believe that policeman is considering giving us a parking ticket.'

She took Jamie's arm as they crossed the road and the sensation of human contact after so long gave him a glow that was nothing to do with the physical warmth she exuded.

'Gault really is a lout,' she whispered. 'No breeding at all. The first time I met him he tried to pinch my bottom.'

Jamie smiled. 'Well, if he tries it again, just let me know and I'll have a word with him.'

'Oh, it's not a problem. I told him very sweetly that if he did it again I'd tear off his arm and beat him to death with the wet end.'

Jamie was still laughing as they approached the door. He reached for the bell with a mixture of anticipation and excitement. But in the shadowy depths of his mind another emotion stirred: a sense of foreboding as he wondered if he was about to take another step into Nazi Germany's heart of darkness. He placed his finger on the little brass button and they heard a prolonged ring from inside. There was no immediate reply, so he tried again.

'*Buenas tardes*?' The voice came from their right where a grey-haired woman in a shapeless dark work dress and wearing neon-yellow rubber gloves appeared from round the side of the house.

Jamie responded to the greeting with a smile that wasn't reciprocated by the washed-out blue eyes or the small, bitter mouth. She would be in her sixties, he guessed, and something about her said the world had not been kind. A soul corroded by anger.

'We are seeking Senor Lauterbacher, Senor Rolf Lauterbacher?' He spoke in Spanish, but she surprised him by replying in perfect German.

'My father is dead, sir, and good riddance.'

Charlotte froze and Jamie felt as if all the breath had been knocked out of him. He winced as the pain from his damaged ribs returned with a vengeance.

'Our condolences, Frau . . . ?' It wasn't exactly appropriate given her sentiments of a few seconds earlier, but what else do you say if someone tells you their father has just died? At least her manner indicated Lauterbacher's death had been recent. But just how recent?

'Fräulein Inge Lauterbacher.'

'Would it be possible to talk with you about your father, Fräulein?'

She snorted dismissively and he saw irritation flash across her face. More people to get in the way of her work. As if she hadn't more important things to do. 'I am just disposing of some of his rubbish . . .'

For the first time Jamie became aware of the scent of smoke on the woman's clothes. Christ, if that meant . . .

'Perhaps if I . . .' He reached into his pocket but before his fingers reached the wad of euros Gault had placed at his disposal, Charlotte laid her hand on his arm.

'We would be ever so grateful,' she said with a warm smile.

The dark eyes narrowed and the lined features hardened, if that were possible, but nothing grim could survive in the face of Charlotte's unwavering charm. Slowly, the lips lost their malign certainty, dismissal was replaced by acceptance and finally something that might have been welcome. 'Very well,' she said. 'Please, wait while I change my shoes.' She disappeared round the corner and a few moments later they heard the sound of bolts being drawn before the door opened.

Jamie made the introductions as Inge Lauterbacher led them through a bare hallway into a large bay-windowed room with equally bare walls and heavy antique furniture devoid of any ornament. The furniture and a small, old-fashioned TV apart, her every possession appeared to be contained in eight or nine large brown cardboard boxes arranged neatly in the centre of the carpeted floor.

'Please, sit.' She indicated a worn cloth sofa. '*Kaffe*?'

'*Danke*,' Jamie replied for them both.

She placed a small table in front of them and vanished through a doorway into what must have been the kitchen, giving them the opportunity to study their surroundings more closely.

'It must have been very elegant once,' Charlotte whispered.

'Mm,' the art dealer grunted. Seedy and run down were the words that came to mind. Symmetrical patches marked the walls where paintings and photographs had obviously hung for many years. The paper itself was peeling in places, the paintwork cracked and flaking, and the furniture had seen better days. Jamie's eyes were drawn to the flickering, barely discernible images on the television. There was no sound, but they appeared to show the aftermath of some kind of accident, with blue flashing lights and people rushing around in panic.

Before he could work out what was happening on the screen, Inge Lauterbacher returned bearing two cups, which she placed carefully on the table. She flicked an annoyed glance at the television. 'Some kind of bomb, in Cologne, of all places.' She grimaced. 'Apparently there are many children dead.' She switched it off and took her seat opposite the two visitors, smoothing her dress over her knees and placing wrinkled, claw-like hands together in her lap.

'You said you wished to talk to me about my father?'

'Yes, Fräulein.' Jamie nodded. 'We had hoped to speak with him personally, but obviously that will not be possible . . .' He left the sentence unfinished, hoping to draw her into the conversation, but Inge Lauterbacher would not be drawn.

'Perhaps you might enlighten me as to the reason for this interest?'

He had been prepared to make Lauterbacher a straightforward offer for any information he could provide about the sword called Excalibur and the ritual, but his manifestly embittered daughter was an entirely different proposition. What to say? One wrong word and the interview would be over before it had begun. He felt Charlotte shift beside him, but the responsibility was his. Reluctantly, he took a first step into the minefield.

'Your father had an unusual war, and perhaps an even more unusual peace . . .' The thin lips twitched into an unlikely ghost of a smile at this cryptic excuse for a question. 'We are interested in certain areas of his war service. Did he ever speak about particular aspects of his career? He mixed with some very high-ranking members of the, ah, German hierarchy.'

'If you mean the Nazi party, Herr Saintclair, why don't you say so? My father never talked about the war and I never asked him about it. Let us be frank. I despised my father for what he had been and what he had done to us, his family. He married my mother on the day Adolf Hitler invaded Russia and she did not see him again for

164

more than six years. His position in the party allowed him to put her up in an apartment in Berlin and that was where she stayed until the end of the war.'

Jamie listened as a voice that had begun flat and emotionless, like a soldier giving a report, became shriller and more bitter as her story unfolded. He noticed idly, that though Charlotte raised her cup to her mouth, she was so hypnotized by Inge Lauterbacher's tale that the coffee never touched her lips.

'How she survived when the Russians came I never knew, because she would not speak of it. Not a single word. One day she piled her belongings in a small cart and walked all the way from Berlin to the Harz, in the British zone. She thought my father was dead, but at the end of nineteen forty-seven he appeared at her door demanding food. He stayed for a single night and left again, leaving me as the only evidence of his existence. In the next six years my mother had two postcards to confirm he was still alive, one from South America and the other from Egypt, but he did not send a single *pfennig* to support her or her child. He must have become desperate, because he reappeared for a month when I was eight, then vanished again for good. My mother died of neglect in nineteen seventy-six still loving him. Do you wonder that I should despise him? Yet when a worn-out husk of a man sought me out in the summer of nineteen eighty-eight, claiming that I was his only kin and offering to treat me like a princess if I would come and live with him in Spain, I was flattered enough to accept.' The memory made her face twitch with suppressed fury and the wrinkled hands twisted in her lap as if they were strangling something. 'Twenty years. Not as a princess, but as a prisoner in this gilded cage. Oh, I see you look at our tattered walls, but then it was very different; beautiful. But Rolf Lauterbacher, in addition to his many other faults, was a miser, who would spend nothing on food, or clothes or any luxuries, not even on wallpaper. For twenty years nothing was replaced. Not a painting, or a sheet, or a stick of furniture. I hate this place, I hate these arrogant, selfish people I am forced to live among and I hate their greasy food and their garlic and their sour wine.'

'Why didn't—'

'Why didn't I leave?' Her flat chest heaved with emotion. 'I could not. He kept my passport locked away.' She reached into her pocket and with a malicious gleam in her eyes brandished the maroon rectangle of a German passport. 'But I have it now and I have done with the old *schwein* for good.' Her voice rose an octave. 'I found it in the wardrobe in a safe I never even knew existed. And do you know what I found in that safe, lady and gentleman, when I finally discovered the key where he had hidden it beneath the floorboards?' She stood up and marched to a sideboard, bending stiffly to recover something heavy that turned out to be a leather satchel. She opened it and poured the contents at their feet, a cascade of loose coins, tubes of coins, rolls of notes and among it, the unmistakable glitter of cut diamonds. 'Almost half a million euros, the lawyer says,' she almost choked on the words, 'and for twenty years he treated me, his own daughter, as a servant, and refused to buy me a dress or a pair of shoes. I would have been naked and barefoot if it had not been for the pittance I made from my sewing.' She fought for composure and eventually the fury subsided. 'So now you know why I do not mourn my father. I was a teacher, Herr Saintclair, I had the love of my children and that was enough. But he took it away from me. You should also know that the only reason I am speaking to you is because I am done with him. I will walk out of this house tomorrow and never look back. I will answer your questions and then you will leave me alone, so that I never need think of him again. Do you understand?' Jamie nodded. 'Then ask your questions.'

'You say your father never talked about the war. Yet you also said you despised him for what he'd done. Forgive me, but there seems to be some contradiction in those two statements?'

Her frown deepened and Jamie imagined her taking a question in class, studying it from every angle, to ensure she had considered every nuance before answering. Eventually, she nodded.

'My mother kept pictures of my father in the house until the end of her days. He was a handsome man, I think, though there was a cruelty in those pictures that always disturbed me. Sometimes he would be in civilian clothes, sometimes in uniform. But always with the

JAMES DOUGLAS

same symbol on his arm. Later I would come to know what the symbol and the uniform signified.'

'So you know he was in the SS.'

'I knew that he had been in the SS and that he had served in the East. I was a great reader, sir, until I came here and he denied me even my books, and the things I read about what happened in the Soviet Union convinced me he was a monster.'

'Yet you still agreed to look after him.'

'He was my only blood relative, Herr Saintclair.' A bitter smile swept like a passing cloud across her worn features. 'And he was a great charmer. My mother used to say he could talk the birds from the trees if he wished. I paint a picture of an ogre, but he was different with other people. He could not have survived after the war without friends. In the early days, when we first came to Madrid, they would visit him, and they would talk and drink schnapps. And afterwards, he would sit in this chair and boast about the great people he knew. The Old *Kameraden* who ruled Germany now, the new friends he had made in Washington and New York and something he called "The Pullach Boys". He made occasional trips to America at the invitation of his friends up till the early nineties, and they sometimes came here. There had not been so many visitors in recent years, but one of them saw him a few days before he died.'

Jamie exchanged glances with Charlotte. 'You haven't said how he died.'

'Yes, of course.' She hesitated and he thought she

was composing herself, but she was only taking time to think. 'It was two weeks ago. A Friday. I'd been out at the market as usual trying to make the few euros he had given me buy enough food to make a meal for two. The trip took longer than usual because I had to haggle with that *schwarzer* bitch Maria at the fruit stall over the price she charged for her rotten peaches. When I opened the door on my return he was lying at the bottom of the stairs. His eyes were open and he looked peaceful, even serene, but he was quite dead.' Jamie felt a chill run through him at the memory of another old man's death. He had found his own grandfather in similar circumstances only two years earlier. 'The police said he had broken his neck and would have been killed instantly,' Inge Lauterbacher continued. 'They looked at the stair carpet. Near the top there's a worn patch and they said he must have been coming down, and tripped. When they said it, they were looking at me, and I knew they thought it was my fault. But they left, and the mortuary car came and took him away, and I heard no more. I thought it was strange.'

'That they didn't come back?'

'No, that he was coming downstairs. You see,' she met his eyes and there was something unfathomable in her expression, 'he had never left the bedroom once in eight years. Not once. I fed him and I washed him. I dressed him and emptied his necessaries. Eight years and never a word of thanks.'

'Are you saying it may not have been an accident?'

Charlotte's voice mirrored the puzzlement on her face.

Inge Lauterbacher shrugged. 'He had friends, but he also had enemies. He used to talk in his sleep. Sometimes it was the Russians who were coming for him. Sometimes the Israelis. There were others, but they were just names. He kept a gun by his bed, an ugly great black thing, but I put it out with the rubbish before the police came. I didn't want any trouble.'

'But surely—'

'I didn't want any trouble,' she repeated. 'He is gone and I am free and that is all that matters, Herr Saintclair.'

Jamie stared at her, waiting for more. He'd discovered his grandfather, a man a little older than Rolf Lauterbacher, at the bottom of the stairs at his house in Welwyn Garden City with his neck broken. The police had called that an accident too. Six months later, Jamie had tracked down the two men who had murdered Matthew Sinclair. He was certain that Inge Lauterbacher knew more than she was telling, but she met his gaze with a challenge and he knew it wasn't worth pushing her further. He changed course. 'You mentioned a gun. I wondered if your father had any other mementoes of the war – photographs, papers, perhaps a diary?' He said it without much hope of a positive response.

But the question was followed by a stillness in the woman opposite and a gleam somewhere deep in the wide-set eyes that convinced him this was the point of the interview she had been waiting for. As if she could read his mind she rose from the seat without a word and walked from the room, returning a moment later with another large cardboard box.

'I don't know whether it's about the war, but I was just going to burn them with the rest. This was in the safe beside all the money he kept from me. Nothing but gibberish, but you might as well have it.' She drew out a slim volume and Jamie had to hide his disappointment as he saw it was a relatively modern desk diary, or something similar. But when he opened the book there was a moment when his hands shook and he felt excitement welling up inside him.

'Was there a book that he was really fond of?' The words emerged as a croak.

Without a word she produced another four or five volumes from the box and placed them on the table for his inspection. Most of the books were old, but one stood out because it was so battered. It was obviously second-hand or well used, and the gold-embossed words on the spine were in English. Jamie's breath turned solid in his chest when he read them.

Sir Thomas Malory's Tales of King Arthur.

'Where did he keep this?'

'In his room with the rest of his books. I got the feeling that one was special to him.'

Jamie was overwhelmed by a feeling of being drawn into events beyond his wildest imaginings. Was it possible? His mind told him not, but something deep at the very centre of him screamed that he was on the verge of a find even greater than the Raphael or the Crown of Isis.

'May I . . .?' He offered her the book, but she waved it away.

'Take it. I don't want anything to do with him.' She saw him reach for his pocket. 'No. Keep your money. There's more in that satchel than I will ever need. All that matters is that I'm free of him and free of this place.'

She showed them to the door, formally shaking their hands. 'Wait.' She ducked back inside and appeared a second later with a pale-blue envelope. 'You might as well have these.'

'What is it?' Jamie weighed the envelope in his hand. Something metallic?

'His medals.'

XVI

Jamie hunched over the desk in the Madrid hotel suite, peering at the first lines of the diary as if the harder he stared the more likely they were to give up their secret. At first glance it was in an impenetrable code . . .

XH CLIQYAQL OBIONBQO BXOIOKRXBLNXJ DILKB XGQ XO KAE VILS HBXOBE RSLJBEBTNTBO EE SVJLPCLBL YSEBC KXBTLXGQ JBLICBO XGQ ESWWTB XQO AIC BXOB JBQBXHB HXEEXSO RSO JLSEETBL VBJWBXTBO – but . . .

Gault and Charlotte joined him in his room before dinner. The SBS man had recovered his humour after being left out of the interview with Lauterbacher's daughter. Jamie was more convinced than ever that it would have been a mistake to take him and he tried to explain his reasoning, but Gault just shrugged. 'Water under the bridge, old son.'

Charlotte was still excited about the discovery of the

coded journal, but sceptical about its significance. 'I don't see what you're so excited about,' she complained. 'It could be his laundry list.'

'You don't put your laundry list in code. I think Rolf Lauterbacher was killed for this . . .'

Gault sniffed. 'There's no solid evidence that he was murdered and the book is no good to anybody with-out the code to decipher it. That information died with Rolf Lauterbacher, so what was the point of killing him?'

'All right,' Jamie conceded, 'not killed *for*, killed *because* of. There are too many coincidences about Lauterbacher's death. What are the odds of some old friend turning up out of nowhere to see him before he died? Or of him being killed the week before we arrived to talk to him about a secret lost almost seventy years ago? It just doesn't add up, especially when the old man hadn't stirred from his bed for eight years and dies when he suddenly has an urge to see downstairs just one more time.'

Gault nodded slowly, conceding the possibility, at least. 'We should get the book back to Steele. He'll be able to lay his hands on a cypher expert who'll crack it in no time.'

But Jamie didn't feel like giving up the prize just yet.

'Let me take a look at it first. In the meantime, you can try to identify these.'

He spilled the contents of the blue envelope Inge Lauterbacher had handed him on the bed. 'Easy,' Gault grinned, picking up a dark Maltese cross. 'Das Iron Cross.'

'Yes,' Jamie said patiently. 'But what are the others and is it First or Second Class? Is it the Iron Cross or is it a Knight's Cross, which from memory is very similar? Remember that in the codex, Ziegler says Lauterbacher told him something about a Knight's Cross . . .' He retrieved the copy of the letter Adam Steele had entrusted him with. 'Here it is: *Beneath the Knight's Cross, one round table, five swords formed in the shape of a pentagram, twelve Knights of the Black Order – and one other element of which I will not speak.* The key to the first part of the Excalibur ceremony could be somewhere in those medals.'

'I'll take them back to my room and work on them there. So what happens tomorrow?'

'There's not much point in moving on until we have somewhere to go.' Jamie looked around the palatial room Charlotte had booked him into. 'There are worse places to hang about for a few days. I'll work on the code tonight and I plan to take look at the galleries in the morning.'

'Galleries?'

'The Prado, you Philistine,' Jamie laughed. 'Then the Reina Sophia to feast my eyes on old Pablo's most famous daub.'

'Ooh, can I come?' Charlotte chirped. 'I've never seen it before and I've heard it's incredible.'

'Sure, we can all go if you like. What about it, Gault,

jump on the underground after breakfast and head down to Atocha? The galleries are right next door.'

The former soldier frowned and shook his head. Was it his imagination or did Gault go a little paler at the thought of being introduced to a bit of culture?

With Gault gone, Jamie turned back to the code, acutely aware that he was alone in the room with a woman, and an attractive one at that. To compound his unease, Charlotte sat disconcertingly close to his shoulder so his head was filled with her perfume and something else, an underlying earthy, human scent.

'What are we looking for?'

'Patterns.' He edged away a little, but she moved with him. 'There are lots of different kinds of codes, and some of them would be impossible to break without getting one of Steele's experts involved. During the war, British SOE agents used what were called one-time pads where every message sent was in a different individual code, which was then burned. You could only read the message if you had a duplicate of the original pad. The Germans created a machine called Enigma – you must have heard of it – that automatically generated a code with billions of possible letter combinations. That code was only broken because the Allies were able to get hold of one of the machines and a bunch of geniuses at Bletchley Park figured out how to use it to break the codes.'

'It looks impossible.'

'Maybe.' He studied the diary's pages. 'But I have a feeling this one might be simpler. Look at the pattern of letters in the first line. If this was a sophisticated code the letters would probably be in blocks or groups of, say, five. But they're not. We have one group of two, two eights and a thirteen. That indicates the groups correspond to actual words, which makes the code so much easier to break. One of the three letter groups is very likely to be "the" and the two letters at the start will be "if" or "as" or "it". This wasn't written to stop someone like us reading it. It was written to keep prying eyes away. Specifically, his daughter's. And it wasn't written during the war or even shortly after it when Rolf Lauterbacher, undoubtedly a very resourceful man, was at the height of his powers. It looks as if it's only a couple of years old. When he wrote this Lauterbacher was an old man, and old men get forgetful. Could you hand me the King Arthur book, please.' Charlotte got up to fetch the battered volume and returned to his side. He leafed through the yellowing pages, but found it difficult to concentrate because of her presence. When he resumed his voice sounded unnatural and he felt himself blushing. 'The main point of my fascinating little lecture,' he swallowed, 'is that every code has a key. And I have a feeling Lauterbacher would have kept the key close by. One kind of code is a substitution code, where the code maker chooses a phrase, sometimes from a handy book, and uses it to replace the letters of the alphabet. We'll start with that.'

Charlotte leaned closer to get a better view of the book and he felt the curve of her breast against his arm.

'Er, why don't you go to your room and fetch a pencil and paper?'

'That's not necessary.' Her voice was almost in his ear and he could feel her breath on the back of his neck. 'I have one here.'

Abbie's face came into his head and he found it difficult to breathe. Had it really been just over a month? Charlotte had made it plain she was attracted to him, and any man would be attracted to her, but it felt wrong even to consider the possibility. He stood up and took a step away. 'Good.' He gave her an unconvincing smile. 'I'll take the first line of the book.' He scribbled the words in a pad and gave her back the Malory. 'You take a look through it for any memorable phrases he might have used. They'll need a minimum of twenty-six characters.'

He turned away and studied the words in front of him. *It befell in the days of Uther Pendragon, when he was king of all England . . .*

With a frown of concentration, he began writing. I (A) T (B) B (C) E (D) F (E) forget the second E, L (F) N (G) H (H), unlikely but not impossible, D (I) A (J) Y (K) S (L) O (M) U (N) R (O) P (P). He pursed his lips at the second unlikely coincidence of the letters synchronizing. This was looking less promising by the minute. Still, it would get his mind in the right gear. G (Q) W (R) K (S). Not bad, nineteen out of the twenty-six letters of the alphabet, and the two coincidences might actually make it more confusing for anyone trying to break the code. A double bluff that Lauterbacher, the intelligence officer, would have been familiar enough with. He checked the letters that weren't in the sentence – CJMQVXZ – and substituted them for those he hadn't reached in the alphabet – TUVWXYZ. Now he was ready.

He took the first three groups of letters of the coded diary. *XH CLIQYAQL OBIONBQO*. So, in this cypher, *XH* became VH, which wasn't a great start, and *CLIQYAQL* translated as BSDGXIGS, which didn't work in any language he knew and seemed an unlikely acronym. Just to be certain he tried the third group with a similar lack of success and sat back to rethink his strategy. He looked up to find Charlotte staring at him.

He shrugged. 'It would have been too much to ask to break it at the first go.'

'So it definitely isn't the first sentence in the book?'

He shook his head. 'It's not that simple. The first sentence may still be the foundation of the code, but Lauterbacher could have added another twist to it – a sort of combination code. The simplest way would be to add a shift.' He saw her look of bemusement. 'At the moment ABCDEF translates as ITBEFL in this cypher, but add a shift of one and A becomes Z, not I, B becomes I and so on through the alphabet. Add a shift of two and it changes again. We need to test all those possibilities before we discard the first line. It will be quicker if we both do it.' He handed her a piece of paper and pulled the room's other chair up to the desk so that they could both see the original course code. 'I'll take the odd shifts. You take the even. Don't worry about the whole message, the first three or four words will tell you.' He frowned. 'Unless he's been really clever and made the first three or four words of the journal gibberish.'

'You really think he might have done that?'

'I bloody well hope not,' he laughed.

An hour later, Gault came to the door. He took in the pile of crumpled paper on the desk with a look that said: *I told you so.*

Jamie smiled. 'Nobody said it was going to be easy.'

'You planning to come down for dinner?'

'I don't think so. Get them to send up some room service, would you?'

'What about your ladyship?'

'Oh, I'm having much too much fun here.'

The former soldier's face split in a sly smile. 'Who'd have thought . . .' And before either could react he slipped out of the room, his laughter echoing along the hall.

They looked at each other and Charlotte grinned. 'Filthy beast.'

It was close to midnight by the time they exhausted the possibilities of the first sentence. 'Maybe we should call it a day,' Jamie suggested.

'I'm not tired. Let's give it one more try.'

'All right. Did you have any luck finding a memorable sentence?'

She frowned. 'I got so involved in what we were doing that I completely forgot.' She reached for *Tales of King Arthur* and flicked through the pages until she found the passage she was looking for. Here it is. What do you think?'

His heart beat a little faster as he read the words. *Whoso pulleth out this sword from this stone anvil, is rightwise king of all England.* 'I like it and it's definitely worth a try.'

He found a new sheet of paper and began to transcribe the code. W (A), H (B), O (C) . . . The first attempt produced *TF UGCEIWEG,* but he wasn't dismayed. 'Same as before. I'll take the odd shifts. You take the even.'

They worked steadily and as combination after combination was cast aside his optimism began to fade. Before long they'd run out of pieces of paper and he picked up a crumpled note that Charlotte had been working on earlier, meaning to recycle it, when something caught his eye. 'What shift was this?'

She caught the excitement in his voice and looked up sharply. 'It should be on there. Yes, it says the twelfth.'

Jamie studied the letters, chewing his lip. *IM FRUHJAHR.* 'Idiot, of course it would be the twelfth.' Charlotte gave him a look of alarm. 'Not you. I'm the bloody idiot. *Twelve Knights of the Black Order.* Look, all this time we've been looking at that first two-letter word and thinking "is" or "if" or "as". *English* words, because *Tales of King Arthur* is an *English* book. But Rolf Lauterbacher was German. Of course he'd write in German. What does the next group say?'

'*NEUNZEHN.*'

'*Neunzen*. Nineteen.' He felt like grabbing her by the waist and kissing her, but that might have given her the wrong signal, so he contented himself with a fatherly pat on the shoulder, which produced a puzzled smile. 'And the next one?'

'*EINUNDVIERZIG.*'

'*Im Frühjahr neunzehn einundvierzig* . . . In the spring of nineteen forty-one . . .'

Quickly they worked their way through the rest of the first few lines.

'*Im Frühjahr neunzehn einundvierzig wurde ich in das Büro meines Vorgesetzten, SS Obgrpfrer Josef Dietrich gerufen. Ich sollte ihn auf eine geheime Mission von größter begleiten* . . .'

Jamie translated. '*In the spring of nineteen forty-one I was summoned to the office of my superior, SS Obergruppenführer Josef Dietrich. I was to accompany him on a secret mission of the utmost* . . .'

It was almost daylight when they reached the final part of the journal. As she read the passage, Charlotte let out a gasp and put a hand to her mouth. Jamie came to the same sentence and an icy hand gripped his heart. *The element of which I will not speak.*

'I think we need to get Gault in here.'

While she went off to fetch the former soldier, he picked up the journal and flicked idly through the pages. He froze as he spotted a tiny anomaly. Could it be?

XVII

*In the spring of nineteen-forty one I was summoned
to the office of my superior, SS Obergruppenführer
Josef Dietrich. I was to accompany him on a secret
mission of the utmost importance to the future of
the Reich. Poland no longer existed, mighty France
had been neutered, Belgium, Holland, Norway and
Denmark were ours by right of conquest. England
was an irrelevance. Now the Führer's thoughts
turned East to the destruction of the ungodly horde
that was the only threat to our domination of
Europe, and the annihilation of Stalin and the Jews
who kept him in power. My task was to command
a security detachment of the Liebstandarte, which
would provide a guard for the consignment carried
by my general, and, once we reached our destination, to provide security for the meeting that would
be held there. Only the general knew our route
and we followed his staff car in eight lorries, each*

carrying fifteen men, with the unmarked armoured truck containing the consignment in the centre of the column. Three men in SS uniform, but without identifying patches, shared the armoured truck driving duties and we had been warned that any man, including officers, attempting to communicate with them would be transferred to a punishment battalion. We drove for five days, often stuck in long jams of troops and supplies even though we had priority over other traffic. The further east we travelled the more crowded the roads became with troops and armour, as we passed through elements of the Second, Third and Ninth armies, past vast camouflaged tank and artillery parks. On the evening of the fifth day we reached a small town and turned onto a newly built road that ran alongside a railway line, and as night fell we were halted by military police opposite a construction site. Thirty minutes after they allowed us to proceed we reached our destination, a village beside a lake dominated by an ancient walled castle. The residents of the village had been temporarily evacuated and replaced by three companies of SS who surrounded the approaches to the castle with barbed wire and machine-gun nests.

We drove past the sentry posts and through the gate into the cobbled courtyard. While my men were allocated their billets in the village I supervised the unloading of the consignment and accompanied my general into the castle. We were welcomed by an over-excited officer with narrow features and restless shifting eyes who introduced himself as Standarten-führer Wolfram Sievers. He wore the black uniform of the Allgemeine SS, but with an odd badge that consisted of a sword entwined by a ribbon and surrounded by runes. I didn't recognize the name, but I saw my general's face twitch with a mixture of amusement and contempt.

'You are the first and the most welcome,' Sievers said. 'You have them with you? Excellent. They will be safe in the treasury until the others arrive.'

'I want two men in there with them at all times,' my general said. 'See to it, Lauterbacher.'

'Sir.'

He lowered his voice so the other man couldn't hear. 'Once Heydrich arrives they become his responsibility, thank Christ, and we can get this farce over with and back to the real war, eh?'

The interior of the castle was a shrine to the Schutzstaffel, and the order that had preceded them and whose power base it had once been. Banners with the symbols of the Totenkopf and the swastika hung everywhere, interspersed with the holy Knight's Cross and paintings of Germanic heroes of old. I escorted the consignment, which was enclosed in a coffin-shaped casket nearly two metres long, to an oak-lined cellar in the centre of the castle and relayed the orders for a permanent guard to my Scharführer. Then we waited.

Over the next twenty-four hours the High Priests of the SS arrived one by one, each with his own entourage. Some, like Dietrich and Daluege, were hard men who had broken heads in Munich beer halls and pulled triggers during the Night of the Long Knives when Hitler had taken revenge on Ernst Rohm and his Brownshirts. By contrast, Darré and Hildebrandt were intellectuals, men who advised the Reichsführer on racial policy. Von Woyrsch was a personal friend of Himmler's from the old days. Darré's views had shaped the Reichsführer's eastern policy; von Eberstein had introduced Heydrich and Himmler in the thirties. Bach-Zelewski, of Prussian aristocratic stock, had empty pockets but the bloodline Himmler craved. Berger, Jeckeln, Wolff and Pohl had all been with the Reichsführer from the start. Sievers directed them to their rooms in the castle, but sooner or later they all drifted back to the main hall in anticipation of the arrival of the man responsible for bringing them here. At precisely eight p.m. Reinhard Heydrich swept into the hall like a Crown Prince entering his own palace.

'Heil Hitler.' He raised a languid arm in salute before throwing his greatcoat to his aide, a shrewd-looking young Sturmbannführer named Schellenberg, with the black diamond of the SD, the SS intelligence section, on his tunic. In theory, Heydrich was outranked by every man in the room, in practice the power of Hitler's Hangman, as these tribunes of the

Nazi Party called him – but only behind his back – eclipsed them all and they knew it. The General accepted a glass of wine and stood by the great open fire. 'Gentlemen, success and victory.' A dozen voices echoed the toast before the cold, executioner's eyes surveyed the room. 'You all know why we are here?'

'I understand and fully agree with the purpose of this meeting,' the speaker was Daluege, the Ordnungspolizei commander, 'but surely it would have been more appropriate, not to say secure, to hold it at Wewelsburg. I do not think I'm alone in resenting being dragged halfway across Europe through a country filled with bandits.'

'I will pass on your complaint to the Reichsführer.' Heydrich's voice was like silk being drawn over a razor blade and Daluege's lips twitched. 'It was his express wish, for reasons practical, historical, ideological and geographical, that the ceremony should be held here on the very doorstep of our enemies, less than twenty kilometres from where the Führer will direct the coming attack.'

'I have made my reservations known to both the Führer and Reichsführer,' Dietrich growled, glaring from beneath beetle brows.

Heydrich nodded gravely. 'And yet you are here, General Dietrich? You are here because you took an oath to the Führer and a blood oath to the Order. Will you fulfil that oath?'

'I have never broken an oath in my life, I—'

Heydrich raised a cultured hand. 'Very soon our Führer will be sending millions of men to carry out a task of titanic proportions that will require a hardness and a merciless resolve that is unprecedented in history. Can our resolve be any less? Nostradamus spoke of the threat from the East that would descend like fire from the sky. That threat is the unthinking scourge of Bolshevism driven by the unbridled greed of Soviet Jewry. It is our Führer's destiny to eliminate these twin evils and the Reichsführer is prepared to explore any avenue that will aid him in his goal.' Once more he met each eye in turn. 'His wishes will be fulfilled. Each of us must put aside his doubts, forget his old beliefs and embrace the new. We have gathered here a weapon of enormous potential and it is time to release that power. The individual elements have been consecrated at Wewelsburg, now we will bring them together. Hildebrandt? You have been able to fulfil our requirements?'

A tall, balding figure clicked his heels. 'Of course. You could have had a hundred had you wished it. They were being held under Aktion T4.'

'Five will be sufficient,' Heydrich assured him. 'Just make sure they are ready.' He pulled back the sleeve of his uniform and glanced at his wristwatch. 'The time is now 8.25 p.m. We will gather in the Great Hall at midnight for the ceremony.'

Three and a half hours later I waited in the shadows beneath the enormous vaulted ceiling of the castle hall. Directly opposite me, perhaps ten metres away, Schellenberg stood equally motionless, his intense dark eyes just visible beneath the gleaming peak of his uniform cap. Between us lay an enormous round table covered with white cloth and circled at precise intervals by twelve throne-like chairs. A candle burned in front of each chair, providing the room's only light, and each was draped with a cloth embossed with a distinctive coat of arms. These were replicated by twelve banners suspended from the ceiling. In the centre hung the symbol of the Knight's Cross. Why did I have to be present, along with Schellenberg and the other SS aides? Sievers had explained it earlier.

'For the ceremony to be successful, there must be a circle within a circle. You, the Black Guard, will form the outer circle. You will not speak, you will not move, no matter what you see or hear. What occurs here will change all our lives,' His eyes had shone with an almost demonic excitement. 'None of us will ever be the same again.'

Did we breathe? Does a statue breathe? The silence was so dense and filled with anticipation that at times it made me want to scream. I thought of the millions of men in their great encampments throughout East Prussia and Poland, the millions more who waited unknowing on the far side of the border. My Führer. lying in his lonely bed, his mind bent on the destruction of the barbarians. The candle in front of me flickered and I was back in France.

*A kneeling figure in a khaki uniform pleading for
his life until the moment the rifle bullet pierced his
raised hands and entered his skull. Hardness and
resolve. Hardness and resolve. The end of my nose
itched infuriatingly, but there was no question of
scratching it. I felt Schellenberg's eyes on me and I
knew that he knew; was mocking my weakness. I
fixed my eyes on a point on the wall beyond his left
shoulder. Hardness and resolve. Like the long wait
before an attack, where a single movement will bring
the enemy guns down on you.*

*At last, the sound of approaching footsteps and
the low murmur of chanting voices. The urge to
look round was almost irresistible, but not a man
even twitched. Closer, until we could hear a soft,
swishing sound. I saw Schellenberg's eyes widen and
a dark figure passed to my right, cloaked in black
from head to foot and with a cowl covering his
features. To my astonishment he held a long sword
raised in front of him. He took his place in front of
me and I knew from his position and his bulk that
it was Dietrich. More cloaked figures appeared at
the periphery of my vision. Of these, seven took
their seats and placed their hands face down on the
table in front of them, but Dietrich and four others,
all sword-bearers, remained standing. Behind me a
voice chanted an eerie incantation in a harsh alien
language and when it ended the man at the eastern
end of the circle announced in powerful tones: 'I lay*

before you Joyeuse, mighty sword of Charlemagne, defender of the faith.' Erich von dem Bach-Zelewski placed the blade diagonally across the white linen coverlet, with the point towards one of the four other sword bearers. It was a beautiful weapon, the sword of kings, with a golden hilt and a cross guard formed in the shape of two winged dragons, and a long, slim blade that shone like fire in the candlelight.

'Zerstorer, sword of Frederick Barbarossa, defier of the Eastern hordes,' the second man said. I shuddered at the mention of Barbarossa – Red Beard – who legend said slept beneath his mountain at Kyffhäuser awaiting the call to rise again and save his nation from peril. The words belonged to Walter Darré, chief of the Race and Resettlement Office of the SS, and he in turn laid his sword diagonally across the table, creating a sharp angle with the first, where point and the lion's head pommel of the sword lay together. Zerstorer's point was aimed directly at the midriff of a third sword bearer.

'Durendal, imperious blade of Roland, hero of old.' The weapon placed by SS-Obergruppenführer Richard Hildebrandt across the centre of the table was of similar pedigree to the first, but with a less elaborate hilt. This time the point was directed at the man in front of me and I heard Josef Dietrich, commander of the Liebstandarte, proclaim: 'Gottes-werkzeug, the sword of Werner von Orseln, greatest of all the Teutonic Knights.'

This was a much more functional blade, the blade of a soldier, with a round pommel embossed with a Maltese cross. A new acute angle was formed, with the point of the sword aimed at the final bearer. As each sword had been placed, the tension in the room grew and the electricity in the air reminded me of the moments before a terrible thunderstorm. The castle was a gloomy, chill place, but sweat ran in rivulets down my back. I studied the blades for some clue to the ceremony's purpose, but they created an odd symmetrical pattern that didn't seem to have any form. Now the incantations began again – the voice, I realized, belonged to Sievers – and the men at the table joined in the harsh, grating chant. All but one.

The last man had stood ready while the other swords were placed, his heavy blade held unwavering in front of his face. His was a sword of the most ancient lineage, a broad-bladed, battle-notched iron man-killer. Without a tremor, Reinhard Heydrich allowed the blade to slowly fall, until its tip touched the hilt of the first sword and made the final connection. 'I lay before you Excalibur, the sword of Arthur, may his strength and the strength of all these great champions aid our cause and use their power to smite our enemies and the enemies of our beloved Führer.' At the word Excalibur I heard someone gasp. Who had not heard the story of King Arthur and his knights? The others were kings and heroes; Arthur was a legend whose fame had spread beyond his native land and beyond the boundaries of his time. If Arthur was with us we could not fail.

I was so mesmerized by this revelation that I hadn't recognized the symbol created by the final sword. At first I struggled to hide my astonishment: a Star of David?

'The five-pointed star of the pentagram is the most potent of all occult symbols,' Sievers answered my unspoken question as he took his place beside von dem Bach-Zelewski at the eastern point of the star. He wore a black robe with a silver pentagram embroidered on the chest. In the centre of the pentagram was a swastika. 'The connection of the five blades will channel the power of the men who wielded them, all that is required now is to propitiate the old Gods to ensure that power is ours to wield.' He paused, allowing the significance of the statement to carry to each of the men at the table. 'Bring forward the gifts.'

I heard the cry of a child and my blood turned to ice.

I dared not turn my head, but I witnessed them walk into the circle one by one. I have seen the face of war in all its terrible guises, but of them all, this was the most cold-blooded and the most ruthless. Small and naked, the babe was carried almost reverently in the arms of one of the men who had driven the truck and handed gently to Wolfram Sievers. He took the squirming bundle in one arm and withdrew something I could not see from the folds of his robe.

The twelve men around the table began to sing in a low monotone. Moving to the north side of the table, Sievers manoeuvred the child so that the head was above the blade of the first sword. It was crying loudly and I could see its angry, wrinkled pink face. In an instant, the cries were cut off as Sievers drew his right hand sharply across the exposed throat and a cascade of dark liquid spurted across the gleaming steel and the virgin white of the table's cloth. Without a change of expression, he placed the still-twitching body in the centre of the star. 'May the spirit of Charlemagne accept this gift.' A second child was brought forward. I turned my eyes away and found myself staring into those of Walter Schellenberg. I have never seen such hatred before or since. It took a second before I realized his loathing wasn't directed at me. He was looking at Reinhard Heydrich.

At the completion of the ceremony, with the five tiny bodies piled in the centre of the table, Sievers invited the sword bearers to pick up their blood-stained weapons. I saw Erich von dem Bach-Zelewski's hand shake as he reached for the hilt of Joyeuse and heard his cry of astonishment as he discovered Charlemagne's sword was as fixed to the table as if it were welded there. Dietrich, Daluege and Hildebrandt followed suit, and found the same. Heydrich reached towards Excalibur, hesitated, then withdrew his hand.

'The future of the Third Reich lies in your hands.'

Sievers' voice held a promise and a threat. 'As long as you, the paramount knights of the Schutzstaffel keep your honour and your faith, the spell will remain in place and the power of the swords and the men who wielded them will carry the armies of Adolf Hitler to victory. Draw strength from what you have seen and done here. Use that strength to advance the cause of National Socialism and in the execution of the difficult and glorious task that lies ahead. Weaken, and that power will turn against you.'

In the morning I wondered if I had dreamed it all, but as we were leaving the castle Dietrich turned to me. His tone was almost kindly. 'I am sorry you had to see what you did, Lauterbacher. You must forget everything and get on with your life.' My eyes were drawn to a column of smoke in the woods behind the castle. He shrugged. 'They were idiot mischlings who did not exist in the eyes of the law. You could say that at least they died for a purpose.'

His eyes told me he didn't believe that, and he knew I didn't either.

Two days later I was transferred to an assault group of the 1st SS infantry battalion and within a week I was fighting in the front line of the invasion of Greece.

There was more on Lauterbacher's war career, which ended on the Seelow Heights and included some questionable and self-serving justification of certain postings to the East. His capture and recruitment by the Allies to infiltrate the 'rat lines' that allowed the top Nazis like Mengele and Eichmann to escape to South America and the Middle East. The 'suggestion' from American intelligence that he volunteer to work with the Egyptians to create an ant-Israeli guerrilla force. His return to a divided Germany where the reward was protection and a job with the Gehlen Organization, which had turned out to be a smokescreen for fleecing his American employers.

And then the tiny imperfection Jamie had noticed earlier and was puzzling unless you were familiar with the signs.

Once again, Jamie Saintclair could barely believe what he was seeing.

XVIII

'Are you winding me up?' Gault's voice was heavy with derision as he laid down the decoded text. Lack of sleep made Jamie feel slightly detached from proceedings and it seemed almost unreal that, in the street outside the hotel window, the bubbling song of a lone blackbird soared and dipped in celebration of the new day.

'You think it's unlikely?'

'Pagan rituals? Human sacrifice? I think either it's a fairytale or the person who wrote it was deranged. Even for the Nazis it's unbelievable.'

'Almost as unbelievable as building death factories to exterminate an entire race of people? Six million is the last count, as I recall. What are the lives of five children compared to the Final Solution?'

'But there's evidence for that—'

'Wolfram Sievers existed,' Jamie interrupted. 'He was the general secretary of the *Ahnenerbe*, the SS research and ancestral heritage society that was a front for Himmler's obsession with the occult. Walter Darré was another of its leaders. The twelve men who took part in the ritual described here are all real and were key members of Himmler's inner circle. Charlemagne's sword Joyeuse is real. I could take you to see it in the Louvre, only it wouldn't be the real thing. Because the real thing went missing during the German occupation of Paris.'

Charlotte looked up from her computer. Her reaction to the revelations in the coded journal had been one of such shocked outrage that in anyone else Jamie might have thought it almost theatrical, which surprised him, because she gave the impression of always being in control. 'I've checked the reference to *Aktion T4*. It existed too. At the start of the war Hitler decided that anyone with a severe birth defect like Down's syndrome or with serious mental problems was a burden on the state and didn't deserve to live. They began the euthanasia programme in nineteen thirty-nine and the last killings took place a week after the war ended. It says here that at least two hundred thousand physically and mentally handicapped men, women and children were killed. Some of Germany's most eminent doctors were involved. One of its most enthusiastic supporters was *SS-Obergruppenführer* Richard Hildebrandt, who was later convicted of kidnapping or forcibly removing the children of Eastern workers. If anyone could *fulfil* Reinhard Heydrich's *requirements* it was Hildebrandt. God, I feel sick. They used five babies like sacrificial lambs to carry out some deranged Nazi's sick fucking fantasy?'

'They're dead,' Gault said brutally. 'And every man in that room is dead with them. Some of them were shot and some of them finished up at the end of a rope. Maybe you think the others should have suffered more. I doubt Heydrich would have agreed as he was lying there with a handful of grenade fragments covered in the contents of a Prague sewer in his belly. All that matters to us is finding that sword.'

'So now you believe?' Jamie demanded.

'You said it yourself. The elements existed and they were all in place. Only it didn't work, because in the long term the Red Army kicked their Nazi arses, Hitler put a bullet in his own brain and Heinrich Himmler ate a cyanide pill for breakfast. The question is, where does it take us?'

Jamie looked at his watch. It was almost eight o'clock and he experienced a curious mix of exhaustion and elation. His damaged rib throbbed and his brain whirled with new theories and possibilities, but for the moment he'd had enough of codes and Nazi atrocities. He needed something to clear his mind. 'It takes me to breakfast, then the Prado. Too late to sleep and I need a bit of time to think about all this. I usually find the best place for thinking is in an art gallery. There's a certain peace that soothes the mind, don't you think?' He ignored Gault's look of disbelief. 'Anyone fancy coming along?'

Charlotte smiled and headed for the door. 'I'll get my coat.'

'Mr Steele isn't going to like you swanning around Madrid like a tourist,' the former soldier grumbled at Jamie.

'Think of it as taking back a bit of overtime, old chum. And don't worry, there are a few things stirring in the old noggin. If I come up with anything concrete I'll give Adam a call and let him know.'

'I wouldn't do that,' the other man said hastily. 'I know for a fact he's in meetings all morning. He asked for an update in the early afternoon. Be back by one and we can have a chance to talk it over, yes?'

Jamie stifled a yawn. 'Why not?'

The young man hitched the rucksack on his back and studied himself in the mirror. Short hair, mirror sunglasses partially disguising his identity, Levi's jeans and a T-shirt advertising some heavy metal rock band. Just another student backpacker of indeterminate origin, looking for somewhere to stay in one of the many rooming houses and hostels that made Madrid a magnet for such people. The bomb was quite a small one, but he had been assured the type of explosives would do the greatest amount of damage in the confined space where it would detonate. One would have thought security would be much tighter given the events of four years earlier, but he had made three practice runs – assuming a different identity each time – and it appeared to have made no difference. The many signs urged people to report any baggage left unattended, but in such places human nature seemed to dictate that everyone must pay no mind to each other's business. He'd been able to leave the rucksack alone for fifteen minutes at a time without anyone even giving it a glance. Well, they would pay for their complacency. Perhaps he was doing them a favour.

The hotel on the Calle Velàzquez was only a short walk from the Metro station at Principe. The train took a few minutes to arrive, but when it did Jamie and Charlotte found a pair of seats together in one of the centre carriages. He could tell something was bothering her and he thought he knew what it was.

'Look.' He did his best to keep his voice neutral. 'Last night was a bit awkward, but we shouldn't let it get in the way of what we're doing. Just give me a bit of time.'

It was all of ten seconds before the light of understanding flickered in the blue eyes. 'It's not that at all,' she snorted. 'I was a little bored and a little attracted and I flirted with you, so what? If it makes you feel better, it didn't mean anything.'

Belatedly, he realized he'd completely misread her and prayed silently for the world to swallow him up. 'You seemed, er . . . preoccupied.'

'Oh, I was just thinking about Gault.' Her face twisted into a grimace. 'Sometimes he really creeps me out. Have you noticed the way he looks at me, as if I'm just a piece of meat? And you never know how he's going to react. One minute he doesn't think the sword exists, the next he's more eager to find it than any of us.'

Jamie thought Gault could be boorish and introverted, but apart from a few mildly close-to-the-bone jokes that were hardly surprising from a former soldier, he'd never noticed anything wrong in his attitude to Charlotte. But then maybe you have to see it from a woman's point of view. 'I can have a word with him if you like,' he suggested.

'That's all right,' she laughed. 'I can look after myself, but you did ask . . .' She frowned. 'It's just that he's so bloody calculating, and cold. He didn't turn a hair when he read about the murdered babies. I wanted to be sick. It's difficult to believe that any human being could be part of such a thing.'

Jamie kept his voice down. They were talking in English, but that didn't mean the people around them on the packed carriage couldn't understand what they were saying. 'You're wrong, Charlotte. When I started researching these things I rather naively believed only a few people were involved in the very worst of it, concentration camp guards and that sort of thing. But the deeper I dug, the more it became clear that every time you turned over a stone in World War Two you'd find another atrocity, maybe involving only a few people, but still sickening in its own right. You don't kill millions upon millions of people, Jews, Slavs, Poles and Russians, without getting your hands dirty, and Germany got its hands dirty.'

202

Charlotte chewed her lip with perfect white teeth. 'Yes, I can see that. What I don't understand is how those men – Himmler's Black Knights – could be taken in by all the mumbo-jumbo of the ritual. It was the twentieth century, for God's sake. One or two, yes, but not twelve. They were monsters, but they must have been intelligent monsters to reach the positions they held. Any fool can see that you won't change the world by sticking five pieces of metal together, no matter what those pieces of metal are, who held them or what they represent.'

'The answer is simple enough.' Jamie pushed his rucksack between his feet to allow an elderly woman to reach the exit. 'Heinrich Himmler believed, and every man who sat at the round table that day owed his status and his power to Himmler. Think of the SS as a kind of Freemasonry. There are thousands of Masonic meetings in Britain every week, attended by hundreds of thousands of ordinary men. All of them have undergone certain initiation rituals to gain membership or to advance in the organization. How many of them truly believe in those rituals? Probably very few. They are there for the influence and the power the membership of a select, secretive organization gives them. Of the men who attended the Excalibur ritual, Sievers and probably Darré were believers, Heydrich was doing his master's bidding, two or three were there because they feared the consequences of non-attendance, and the rest, like Josef Dietrich, were pragmatists who knew their place at the

Nazi top table depended on Himmler. They did what had to be done, just as they did what they were ordered to do later in the war, no matter how sickening it was. I doubt if more than three or four would have known about the children in advance.'

'That doesn't absolve them.' Charlotte rose from her seat as they reached their stop.

'No, it doesn't,' Jamie joined her at the door. 'And I'm not suggesting we do. By the end of the war every man in that room had the blood of hundreds, if not thousands, of children on his hands.'

They left the train at Retiro and emerged into what felt like the cleansing sunshine on the Calle de Alcala, with the constant rush of traffic in their ears. 'This is why I love this city,' Jamie said as he led Charlotte up a tree-lined avenue into a park that seemed to go on for ever. 'I thought we could walk through Retiro to the gallery. It's not too far.'

Fifty paces behind, a man in a short-sleeved shirt and jeans waited until they were out of sight before following in their footsteps. Oblivious to his presence, they walked for a while, enjoying the mid-morning sunshine, overtaken by lycra-clad joggers and weaving through crowds of families with children. Charlotte broke the silence.

'You must miss her so much.'

Jamie faltered at the unexpected question, uncertain how much Abbie's memory should allow him to reveal.

'We . . . we were at that stage where we couldn't get enough of each other.' He managed a tight, bitter-sweet smile. 'Both trying to play it cool but resenting every minute we had to spend apart. She'd been away for the weekend, but I persuaded her to come back a day early, and, well, that's why she was where she was.'

Charlotte's eyes filled with compassion. 'You can't blame yourself, Jamie. Nothing you could have done would have saved Abeba.'

'She was carrying our child.'

'Oh . . . I didn't know.'

'Neither did I.'

There seemed nothing else to say and they walked on in silence, both suddenly feeling the effects of twenty-four hours without sleep. Eventually, they reached a large boating lake, with sun-dappled green waters and dominated by an enormous monument on the far side. A food stall was selling snacks and Jamie fumbled in his pocket. 'How would you like to taste the best *churros con chocolate* in Madrid?'

She smiled her thanks, glad the melancholy she'd created had disappeared. He came back with two cups and a white paper bag. Their mood quickly altered, tired minds somehow invigorated by sips of the rich, dark brew as they nibbled the deep-fried dough sticks from the bag after dipping them into the liquid chocolate. 'I'm honoured you brought me here specially to eat the best *churros con chocolate* in Madrid.'

He grinned. 'Every cafe, chocolateria and stall in the

city sells the best *churros con chocolate* in Madrid. I hope you're not disappointed?'

'No,' she laughed. 'Just a little worried about the effect on my waistline.'

They reached a fountain with a winged figure in bronze on a plinth in the centre and Jamie turned right. 'This should bring us down to the rear of the Prado.'

The Prado was as close to heaven on earth as Jamie thought he could ever come. Paintings were his life, and he was intimately acquainted with several thousand of them, but room after room filled with artistic wonders still took his breath away. Velazquez and Goya, Titian, Rubens and Raphael, vast biblical scenes, miniature portraits, the colour, the depth, the majesty and the beauty captured by the geniuses of their age. What primal urges had first made man lay down images on a cave wall to be admired and remembered? Where had the combination of coordination, commitment, vision and patience come from to create this level of perfection? He discovered to his delight that Charlotte had a passion for the works almost as great as his own. She devoured every piece of information he dredged from his memory about the masterpieces that passed all too quickly as they flitted from chamber to chamber like butterflies in a garden full of nectar-filled flowers. At last they reached a room dominated by a huge painting more than six metres long and three high.

'I hadn't realized this was here,' Jamie laughed. An ornate temple of golden stone dominated the painting, but the focus was on the reclining figure of a medieval knight in the centre, surrounded by women in attitudes of either shock or grieving. Not a great painting, Jamie would have said: too fussy with its prissy little flower-filled garden and the not-too-well-imagined friezes, and too busy with people hanging around looking sad, but not really contributing very much to the overall vision. He turned to Charlotte. 'You are looking at King Arthur, as imagined by the English painter Edward Burne-Jones. *The Last Sleep of Arthur in Avalon* is as good an example of obsession as you'll find on a gallery wall. He started painting this monstrosity in eighteen eighty-one and didn't finish it until seventeen years later, at which point he cheerfully dropped down dead believing his life's work done.' He shook his head, smiling. 'Poor old Edward. They say he started to think he *was* Arthur and slept every night in that very same pose.'

'That must have been a bit of a bind for Mrs Jones. The lady whose lap his head is in doesn't look too comfortable.' They exchanged grins. 'No sword,' she pointed out.

'No, by the time Arthur reached Avalon, Excalibur had been safely returned to the Lady in the Lake.'

'So how did it come to be hidden away in an English mansion house in nineteen thirty-seven?'

'That, my dear, is what we are going to find out.' With a last look at the painting he turned away. 'But first I'm going to show you a real masterpiece.'

They were delayed in the steel-and-glass entrance hall

of the Reina Sophia by an altercation between the blue-shirted security guards and a young tourist who didn't want to give up his rucksack. Jamie stood patiently in line behind the man, waiting to hand over his own bag. His unease grew as the confrontation became louder. Almost in slow motion he watched the visitor's hand creep towards the toggle holding the neck of the rucksack. Jamie opened his mouth to shout a warning, but one of the guards was already making a grab for his holster. Too late. The young man tugged at a cord connected to something inside the bag. Jamie stepped back out of the line of fire as the cord came clear and pushed himself between Charlotte and the threat, horribly aware this might be his last moment. In the same second the guard pulled his pistol and aimed it at the suspect's chest, prompting screams of terror from those around who hadn't noticed the movement, but could see the gun. The young man froze, the rucksack in his left hand and the cord, with some kind of diplomatic pass, in the right. '*Ruso. Padre. Embajada,*' he protested weakly. Still shaking, Jamie led the way up the metal stairway as he was being escorted away.

'Just for a minute there, I thought . . .' Charlotte breathed.

'Yes, me too. My legs are weak.'

'Still, that was very brave.' She reached across to kiss his cheek.

He could still feel the warmth of it as they climbed to the second floor and through a stone walkway to the main gallery. A doorway to the left led to a series of open rooms where obscure artworks stood out stark against the bare white walls. As they entered a large central chamber Charlotte was drawn to a series of small drawings that were unmistakably familiar, but infuriatingly mysterious. Jamie drew her through another opening to the left.

'Wow.'

'Wow, indeed.'

The painting on the far wall was even larger and more complex than *The Last Sleep of Arthur,* and a hundred times more powerful. At over eleven feet tall and almost twenty-six feet wide, it dominated the room, dwarfing the crowd of tourists, mainly Japanese, it seemed to Jamie, who stood back enthralled to study its message. He led Charlotte forward through the couples and family groups until they stood directly in front of the picture. For anyone who had only seen it in a magazine or a book, the effect of Pablo Picasso's *Guernica* was astonishing. The painting had a magnetic quality that drew the viewer in to be part of the terrible drama unfolding on the enormous canvas. In the wake of the bombing of Guernica by planes of the Condor Legion, piloted by Germans sent by Adolf Hitler to trial a new, merciless brand of conflict, Picasso had been driven to embody the awfulness of war in a single painting. To do so he had eschewed the crimson of gushing blood, the sunburst at the centre of the explosion, or the obscene pink of torn flesh, for a monochrome blandness that depended on the stark agony of his images to carry its message. Here was death and dismemberment, a mother weeping over her child's limp body, a gaping mouth that would never speak again, a severed arm, the fingers still holding the stump of a broken sword, a horse pierced through by a spear of wood and at the mercy of a rampaging bull. In the centre, a chaos of stylized symbolism. To the right a man, or a woman, writhing in agony at the heart of an inferno.

'It's breathtaking.' Charlotte broke the hushed silence with an almost reverential whisper. 'A work of true genius.'

'Yes.' Jamie smiled at her reaction. 'But old Pablo worked hard to be a genius. For every one of his paintings there are a hundred examples of ideas he tried and discarded. Those pictures you saw out there are details of the painting, reworked until they were perfect. Only then did he start on the canvas. He completed it in the summer of nineteen thirty-seven.'

'When Wulf Ziegler stole Excalibur from an English country house.'

'Exactly.' Jamie moved aside to allow a party of Spanish schoolchildren through to the front of the crowd, pondering how well-behaved they were compared to their English counterparts he'd seen in museums and galleries. When they were past he moved to Charlotte's side and dropped his voice to a whisper. 'The raid on Guernica was a trial run for the planes and pilots who would pave the way for the Blitzkrieg and Hitler's early

victories in Poland and France. It didn't matter to the
Nazis that fifteen hundred innocents died to prove the
experiment worked. Why should we be surprised that
Himmler and his acolytes were prepared to kill five
children in an attempt to ally themselves with the forces
of darkness? The more we discover, the more convinced
I am that the ceremony happened and the sword existed.'

'You said we needed a description of Excalibur before
you would know whether it was worth pursuing?'

'Exactly and Rolf Lauterbacher has given us one. He
recited a line from the coded journal. *His was a sword
of the most ancient lineage, a broad-bladed, battle-
notched iron man-killer.*'

'What does that tell you?'

'It tells me it's worth continuing. Excalibur, if this
is Excalibur, would be a much older sword than the
others used in the ceremony, which were all medieval.
In design it would have been cruder, simple, heavy and
double-edged, and if the Arthur tales have a foundation
in truth, it would have been tested in war. The reference
to iron is also significant, because it would have been
forged in an age before the production of steel became
more than an accident of the smith's choice of ore. *A
broad-bladed, battle-notched iron man-killer* would
describe it very well.'

'So we're ready to take the next step?'

He nodded, his eyes still on the picture. 'Sometimes
you have to look beyond what you can see, because the
message is in what you sense. The message that painting

sends is more than that war is terrible. It's about mortality and the inherent inhumanity in men, and it's conveyed in the images you can't see, unless you know what to look for; the skulls formed by parts of different figures, the second bull goring the horse, lost in the carnage. I have a feeling Rolf Lauterbacher's journal is like that, and if we can look beyond the horror of the ceremony we'll discover the missing fact that will guide us to the next clue.'

'Then why are we standing here?'

'Because I have another mystery to solve first. And I'm not sure I want Mr Gault to know about it.'

They took a cab back to the hotel, but Jamie surprised Charlotte by asking the driver to turn off the Calle de Alcala and back into the area they'd visited the previous day.

'This won't take long,' Jamie assured her as they stopped outside the Lauterbacher apartment.

He rang the doorbell and Inge Lauterbacher appeared a moment later, a frown of puzzlement on her face that was instantly displaced by resentment. 'I told—'

'I apologize for the intrusion, Fräulein, but there is one more question I must ask you.' He pulled the journal from inside his jacket. 'I wondered if there was any reason why your father would have gone to a great deal of trouble to remove a single sheet from his journal?'

XIX

'You're late,' Gault growled as they walked into the hotel room. 'The boss is expecting your call in ten minutes.'

'I thought you wanted to talk over where we are?'

'We don't have time and there's no point in going over it twice. I faxed him a description of the sword. He's very excited.'

Jamie suppressed a rush of annoyance. He'd wanted to gauge Adam Steele's reaction to the breakthrough himself. Then again, there was no reason why Gault shouldn't tell Steele about the details in the coded book. He pulled out the sat-phone.

'No! He was very specific about the time. One thirty on the dot.'

A knock on the door heralded Charlotte's return. 'I've booked the tickets,' she said brightly.

Gault glared at her, managing to look simultaneously mystified and furious at not being consulted about whatever scheme they'd concocted on their trip to the galleries. Jamie ignored him, glanced at his watch and pressed 2 as the minute hand hit the half-hour mark. Again there was the frustrating delay as the first call rang out and he had to repeat the process.

The urbane Adam Steele sounded like a schoolboy who'd opened his birthday card to find the last Cup Final ticket. 'So you've confirmed it? Bloody fine job, Jamie. I confess that even with the Ziegler testimony I was still doubtful. Christ, Excalibur, the sword of Arthur, and it exists. It really exists.' Jamie tried to interrupt, but Adam Steele in full flow was like a burst dam: unstoppable. 'What a fool. I'd always visualized the sword as one of those gilded monstrosities you find in the Royal collections, a sort of deadly ornament. But it wouldn't be like that at all. A *sword of the most ancient lineage, a broad-bladed, battle-notched iron man-killer.*' He chuckled as he quoted the words. 'A proper fighting weapon from the Dark Ages. A warrior's sword that held back the Saxon hordes. And it was there, in that castle in nineteen forty-one. Yes, I know, you bloody pessimist, you'll tell me that just because it existed then doesn't mean it's still in one piece now. But I *know*, Jamie, I feel it in these old bones of mine. Find it for me, and offer whoever has it however much they want for it, within reason. And if that doesn't work, Gault will come up with a solution. Remember that. When it comes to any negotiations Gault is your ace in the hole. Just find it for me.' He waited for a response, but Jamie let him stew, exchanging a grin with Charlotte as the seconds passed. 'Jamie? Are you still there? What have you got? You're holding out on me, you bastard. You know something.'

'I've been taking another look at the codex and the Lauterbacher journal,' Jamie admitted. 'Lauterbacher gives us much more detail about the location and how he reached there, but I think the main clue is in the codex. *A place not far from where the Führer charted the course of the Thousand Year Reich.* Hitler was forever planning his legacy, and on the face of it, that could mean any of the places associated with him, like Berchtesgaden or the *Reichskanzlei* in Berlin. But when you take it with the information in the Lauterbacher journal, we're able to narrow it down significantly. Lauterbacher talks about the long journey east into what was then East Prussia and is now eastern Poland.' Gault moved a little closer so he wouldn't miss any of the conversation and Jamie could almost feel the anticipation at the other end of the line. 'The most famous site in East Prussia associated with Adolf Hitler is the one where he plotted Operation Barbarossa, the invasion of Russia, and from where he directed the war in the East. The place where, on July the twentieth, Claus von Stauffenberg and the plotters of the *Wehrmacht* high command attempted to blow the Führer to high heaven . . .'

'The Wolf's Lair,' Steele whispered. 'Of course the castle would be at the Wolf's Lair.'

'There's only one problem, Adam. The Wolf's Lair

sounds terribly romantic, but it wasn't a castle, it was a bunker complex in the Masurian woods, and the Germans blew up most of the place when they retreated in late nineteen forty-four or early 'forty-five. But the Wolf's Lair gives us our target. Somewhere within a few miles of the Wolf's Lair is the castle where the ritual took place and with a little luck I think we'll be able to locate it.'

'How?'

Jamie hesitated while he ran through his mind the theory that had come to him as he stood in front of the Picasso. Just as there were layers of symbolism in the painting, he felt certain they also existed in Rolf Lauterbacher's journal. The missing page was one mystery, but for the moment, and for reasons he'd have found it hard to explain, he had decided not to share that.

'Lauterbacher has always been very careful not to reveal the exact location of the castle, not even to Wulf Ziegler. Yet he's given us a description and a general location. That means he wanted someone to find it. I'm certain the secret is somewhere in the journal. It's just a matter of working it out. Charlotte's booked us on a flight to Warsaw and from there we can hire a car to take us east.'

They talked for a few minutes more. Steele mused on the possibility of chartering a helicopter to take them from Warsaw to the bunker complex, but Jamie had an aversion to sitting in something that was basically a million pieces of metal trying to tear themselves apart.

When he dialled off, he noticed the battery on the phone was low and instead of replacing it in his rucksack he hooked it up to its charger.

'So we're going to the Wolf's Lair.' Charlotte's voice held a shiver of anticipation. 'It sounds a bit like going into the lion's den.'

Jamie and Gault exchanged glances. 'Don't tempt fate, love,' the SBS man said.

They flew into Warsaw on a Swiss Air flight via Zurich, and spent the night in an airport hotel. While Gault worked out the next day's route, Jamie and Charlotte went through the journal again, studying maps of the area around the *Wolfsschanze*. 'The description Lauterbacher gives is of a walled castle beside a lake,' Charlotte pointed out. 'That should at least provide us with a starting point.'

'True,' Jamie agreed. 'But it would be helpful if the Wolf's Lair wasn't situated quite so close to an area called the Masurian Lakes, which, according to my online guidebook, is home to approximately two thousand rather scenic stretches of water. It also says here there are at least a hundred castles worth visiting in what was formerly East Prussia. Still, he hints that they reached the castle fairly soon after passing the bunker complex, so we can narrow it down to within, say, twelve and twenty miles?'

She nodded and nibbled her lip, a habit that reminded Jamie of his old friend and one-time partner Sarah Grant.

'Yes, that give us about seventy of the two thousand.'

'Progress,' Jamie smiled. 'At least we're looking for a needle in a haystack instead of a needle in a field of haystacks.'

'Do we know if Heydrich or any of the others had estates in East Prussia?'

Jamie leafed through the biographies she'd put together. 'Silesia, Bavaria, Westphalia. Only one East Prussian and that's Bach-Zelewski, but his family had long since lost their ancestral lands and he was the son of an insurance clerk.'

'There's one reference I don't understand.' Charlotte frowned. 'The Knight's Cross appears in both the Excalibur codex and the Lauterbacher journal. Could that be significant?'

Jamie studied the documents – *Beneath the Knight's Cross – Interspersed with the holy Knight's Cross – In the centre hung the symbol of the Knight's Cross.* 'The Knight's Cross was one of the highest military decorations in Nazi Germany, created by Hitler himself for extreme bravery on the battlefield. It was a sort of classier version of the Iron Cross, but it turned out German warriors were so brave the Knight's Cross wasn't reward enough, so they added golden oak leaves, then oak leaves and swords, and oak leaves, swords and diamonds, which made it more or less the equivalent of our Victoria Cross.'

Gault looked up from his map, the first time he'd deigned to become involved in the conversation. 'She might have a point, though. I've been around enough war heroes, but I've never heard of a medal referred to as holy.' He shrugged – they could take it or leave it. 'If I've got this right we should be at the Wolf's Lair by around one if we leave by ten tomorrow.'

Jamal al Hamza bowed his head low over the table in the coffee house in a back street of Peshawar, near the Afghan border. He might have been praying, but in fact he was listening to the whispered words of the young man seated opposite. The establishment was owned by one of the many subsidiaries run by his family and he might have held this meeting in one of the upstairs rooms, yet he always felt safer doing business in plain sight. 'You are certain of this?'

'Our friend in Washington was most confident. The phone is the same one used in the London attack. He has passed on the current location and arranged for our team to have the use of a scanning device, which will allow them to track it.'

Al Hamza frowned. The source in Washington was a white Muslim convert who had been inserted into the lower ranks of the CIA as a sleeper agent. Naturally, given his background, he had been treated with some suspicion, but his intelligence from within the enemy's computer section had been tested many times and had never failed. Yet . . . 'Perhaps our friend is becoming overconfident?'

The young man pondered the question. 'We are not

dead or wearing orange jumpsuits at Guantanamo Bay,' he said eventually, though they both knew that situation could change at any moment if Allah willed it. 'Do you wish me to abort the operation?'

'No. Tell them to continue. The orders are the same. They are to be taken quietly. Whoever is using the phone is to be held and persuaded to provide a confession and an apology on video. Once the apology is complete they will be subject to Islamic justice. Make sure the security team understands.'

'Of course.' The young man certainly understood. A ritual beheading would send a very forceful message to those who were tempted to usurp the Leader's authority. He bowed. 'I will personally bring you a copy.'

XX

'If you aren't capable of finding these people then perhaps I should find a Head of the Security Service who is?'

The DG's nose wrinkled with distaste and his aides kept their eyes on the table. She wasn't the first politician to threaten him – no, not by a long way – but at least the others had made a pretence of subtlety. She had a point, of course. More than six weeks after the M25 attack they were no closer to discovering the identity of the perpetrators than on the day it happened. It wasn't as if they weren't trying. His operatives were working round the clock. He'd hoped for some sort of breakthrough, on either the communications or the guns, or even on the transport they'd used, but despite using every resource at his disposal – nothing. And then there was the other problem, which was becoming increasingly complex. He sighed. Perhaps she was right. But no, he would not be forced out by these upstarts. He would go in his own bloody time, and not before.

'I can assure you, Minister,' diplomacy came naturally to him, it had to in his position, 'that everything that can be done is being done. We are focusing our efforts on the weaponry. Those guns and rockets must have come into the country somewhere. They were stored and they were distributed. My people continue the search for the warehouse where the lorry was kept—'

'Not bloody good enough.' Her fist slammed the table with each word. 'Don't you understand the pressure the Prime Minister is under? That *I* am under? His own backbenchers are turning against him, threatening a coalition with the opposition unless *strong* action is taken. That odious little shit Franklin is talking about sweeping the threat from the streets, as if all you had to do was run around with a broom and the problem would go away. They're calling for the immediate detention without trial of all known Islamic extremists and anyone who supports them. Identity cards to be carried at all times and that would affect the bearer's right to state employment and benefits, even a driving licence. Screening centres and immediate expulsion of those who prove suspect, regardless of place of origin. We've already increased police stop-and-search powers, and you've seen the backlash we've had from the Asian community. I've had to introduce a quota system of one white face for every four black or brown to prove we're not racist.' She took a deep breath. 'The Prime

Minister is actively considering a free vote on the return of the death penalty for murders involving terrorism or paedophilia in the hope that it will unite the party. It would certainly be popular in the country.'

The DG frowned. What she meant was that it would be popular with the voters who had put her where she was and who she hoped would put her there again. He had his own views on the death penalty, but he was damned if he was going to get into a debate with this bloody woman. Still, he couldn't just sit back.

'Of course, such a move would require the utmost analysis and consideration.'

'Of course it bloody would. I'm not a fool and, believe me, I do not wish to be remembered as the Home Secretary who returned the United Kingdom to the Dark Ages.'

Perhaps he'd misunderstood her. 'I'm sure you will come to the correct conclusion, Minister. And you have our every support.'

'I don't need your support,' she snapped peevishly. 'I need progress. What I said earlier is not an idle threat. I would not take the decision lightly, but I may be left with no choice.' The DG smiled. The cards were on the table now. If heads must roll she would sacrifice him to save hers. Ah, well. He felt her eyes on him. 'We cannot let the terrorists win, Director General, because if we do we unleash the forces of the worst kind of extremism. We have already seen the results in the capital, the Midlands and the north, but I fear that is just the spark.

One more atrocity may trigger a bloodbath and nothing you or I can do will stop it.'

'Minister, you should see this.' An aide switched on the television set at the far end of the room. 'A large explosion on the Madrid underground.'

She walked up and peered at the screen. 'Atocha again,' she groaned. 'Don't they ever learn?'

The Director General said nothing. His organization had stopped four attacks just like this the public knew about and another six they never would. All the terrorists had to do was succeed once more and this powder-keg of a country would go up in flames.

And the bombs in Cologne and Madrid proved it wasn't only Britain that was at war, it was the whole of Europe.

They set off after breakfast the next day in a sleek black BMW 5-series Gault had hired for the trip. Jamie offered to drive part of the way, but he was glad the ex soldier turned him down when he realized that Polish drivers were worse than the Italians, never happier than when they were playing 'chicken' with an eight-wheeler truck. Instead, he studied the journal and glanced through the notes Charlotte had put together about the area they were approaching. Hitler's *Wolfsschanze*, his theatrically named Wolf's Lair, lay to the east of Ketrzyn, formerly Rastenburg, in the centre of what, prior to 1945, had been the German province of East Prussia. It now lay just a few miles south of the border of the Kaliningrad Oblast, which was effectively part of Russia, but hemmed in by Poland to the south and Lithuania to the north and east. He knew that this had been the scene of some of the most vicious fighting of the Second World War, with the SS and the *Wehrmacht* battling to keep the vengeful Red Army from German soil. Kaliningrad, then called Konigsberg, endured a three-month siege before it surrendered in April 1945, leaving twenty thousand dead and at least five times as many captives of the Red Army. When the war ended, East Prussia had been carved up between Russia and Poland. What worried him was that, even if they did manage to find *the* castle in a land full of castles, there was no telling what might be left of it after the devastation of 1945.

'Then why are we here?' Charlotte asked.

He blinked as he realized he'd voiced the thought aloud, a lifelong habit that was going to get him in trouble one day.

'We're here because the boss wants us here,' Gault interrupted like an attack dog defending its master. 'This is where the sword was in nineteen forty-five and this is where we'll get the next clue to where it is now, isn't that right, your lordship?'

Jamie ignored reference to the manufactured up-market drawl his mother had insisted he cultivate for Cambridge and which he'd never quite been able to lose. 'All we know for certain is that this is where the Excalibur codex says the sword was last seen,' he said. 'It's not only the obvious place to come, it's the only place. Logically, there are two options. If it was here, either it's still here or it was taken somewhere else during the war. In the first case, there's a possibility some local, or someone involved with the castle, will have information, even if it's only an old folk tale about a buried hoard. We check it out, report back to Adam and walk away to give the treasure hunters a chance.'

'And if it was taken away?' Charlotte persisted.

'That would depend on who took it. If it was front-line troops of the Red Army, we have a problem. Excalibur could have ended up chopping kindling for some Siberian peasant. But it would be dangerous for a private to try to hold onto something of real value like that. Stalin was surprisingly discerning in his approach to loot. The *frontovik* could have his fancy carpet or an electric stove to impress his wife in their non-electric cabin, but the good stuff went to the Boss. He set up special Trophy Brigades that did to Germany exactly what Goring's Rosenberg Foundation did to France. At least two and a half million artworks and ten million books ended up in Soviet museums, or, more often, their basements, and most of them are still there.' He smiled at the thought. 'If Adam has the financial clout, I'd be happy to spend six months trawling through the cellars of the Hermitage in St Petersburg and the Pushkin in Moscow.

'The more likely possibility, though, is that the Nazis

evacuated it either during the war or at the end, when the Russians were closing in. Most of the Third Reich's treasures, including its gold reserves and the loot they collected in the Occupied Territories, ended up in places like the Kaiseroda salt mine at Merkers in Austria. It's possible there are other Kaiserodas still waiting to be found.'

He hesitated as he noticed that Gault appeared to be spending as much time looking in the mirrors at what was behind them on the two-lane highway as at what was in front.

'Do we have a problem, Mr Gault?'

Gault shrugged and twitched the wheel as an on-coming lorry threatened to ram them. 'All the cars behind us have their lights on, but they're identifiable by the beams. It looks to me as if a couple of them are in no hurry to get past us, which is unusual judging by some of the driving we've seen this morning. I slowed down a while ago and they kept their distance.'

'The only two law-abiding drivers in Poland.' Jamie laughed, but there was no humour in it. This was a forbidding landscape. Big-sky country where the over-hang of leaden cloud threatened to squash you into the ground. The terrain alternated between moderate-sized patches of cultivated land, each attended by a small farm, dark-green, impenetrable forest and, the further north they travelled, lakes large and small. Not the kind of place you wanted to stop and pass the time of day with someone.

'I'll keep an eye on them and maybe stop in one of the towns up ahead,' Gault said.

Twenty minutes later they pulled off the motorway and drove into the town square of a lakeside settlement that announced itself as Mragowo. For a few minutes they sat in the car while Gault studied the traffic entering the square behind them, but either he didn't see anything suspicious or he wasn't saying.

'I'm going to stretch my legs,' Jamie announced.

Gault made as if to veto the idea, but he relented with a begrudging: 'Don't get into any fucking bother.'

Charlotte suggested she join him and Jamie smiled. 'Er, you're welcome, but "stretch my legs" was actually a bit of a euphemism for "look for somewhere to have a pee".' Her face turned pink and she settled back into her seat. 'I'll let you know if I find anywhere,' he promised.

He was wandering round the centre of the town looking for somewhere favourable when he noticed a slim young woman walk into a nearby grocer's shop. Something about her made his heart quicken for no apparent reason, and he followed in her wake. By the time he entered the store she'd already disappeared. Puzzled, he searched among the long aisles of carelessly stacked boxes and sacks until he came to a magazine rack.

'Don't turn and look at me. Don't do anything. You're searching for a newspaper.'

The voice came from behind him in a low whisper, and the intensity in the words made the hairs on his neck stand on end. He hadn't heard that voice for more than two years, since she'd walked out on him to 'find herself' back home in the States. Which begged the question why Sarah Grant, late, or perhaps not so late, of some shady offshoot of Mossad, was doing in a one-horse town in northern Poland?

He was about to ask when she cut across him like a whiplash. 'Do you trust these people? Don't answer; it wasn't that kind of question. Just hear me out and we'll go our separate ways. You got that?' He supposed he was allowed to nod. 'You're way out of your league on this one, Jamie boy. This makes the Sun Stone look like a kid's parlour game. Take my advice and get yourself on the first train back to Warsaw.' Jamie forced himself to concentrate on the newspapers and magazines in front of him, though his mind whirled with any number of questions. The Sun Stone had been an ancient artefact that the Nazis had hoped would bring them the Holy Grail of unlimited energy, and the search for it had almost cost Jamie and Sarah their lives. They'd become lovers along the way, but he'd never been completely certain whether it had been the real thing for her, or just part of the job. Before he could speak she slipped something into his hand. 'My number's on there. Call me if you need help to get out.' He turned to reply, but the shop door was already closing behind her. The object in his hand was a simple strip of card embossed with a twelve-digit number.

He walked back to the car trying to come to terms

with the bizarre meeting. What the hell was Sarah doing here and what did it mean for him? It seemed clear enough that when she'd left him to go to 'find herself' in America, she'd instead found her way back to the Mossad agents who had originally recruited her and partnered her with him in the search for the Sun Stone. But how did Mossad know about the hunt for Excalibur? And if they did, why would they be interested in some madcap, probably doomed quest to find an ancient sword that nobody was sure even existed? One thing was certain, it wasn't just to warn Jamie Saintclair he was out of his depth – as if he needed to be told. What was it she'd said? *Do you trust these people?* If she meant Gault and Charlotte, or Steele and his people, the answer was probably a qualified no. In the last few years he'd learned to trust only his closest friends. The problem was he didn't have many left. Gault was too clever for his own good, and a shifty bastard at that, but that was probably why Steele employed him in the first place. Charlotte appeared what she seemed, a competent enough organizer, who was brighter than the little-girl-lost act she sometimes put on. Yet she'd come away with all that high-kicking, unarmed combat stuff that had saved his neck and left Otto Ziegler with a broken jaw. As for Steele, a status-obsessed banker with a liking for edged weapons and humiliating his employees, you could never trust his motives even if you could understand his ambition. But did that mean he would walk away? He knew the answer to that. Steele had challenged him as deliberately as if he'd thrown down a gauntlet or slapped him in the face. Jamie had never walked away from a challenge.

And then there was Excalibur. Myth or not, Arthur's sword was the embodiment of good against evil. He wanted it to exist and he wanted Jamie Saintclair to find it. For Abbie.

When he got back to the car Charlotte and Gault were chatting. He threw the paper he'd bought in the back and took his seat in the front. Charlotte's giggle made him look round. She was peering at the newspaper. 'Jamie, you idiot. You know none of us can read Polish.'

XXI

They got lost twice in Ketrzyn, the pretty little Polish town closest to the *Wolfsschanze*. Gault stopped to ask for directions, but it took them three attempts before they found someone who could speak enough English to put them on the right road. Eventually they reached the eastern outskirts and wound their way through two smaller villages until they reached what was little more than a track that followed the railway line through open country. A few minutes later a dense forest of evergreens seemed to wrap itself around the car and they found themselves in almost pitch darkness with the headlights creating a tunnel in front. Gaps in the trees revealed an occasional glimpse of ancient railway line with the rusting steel tracks laid direct on a layer of ash.

'Christ,' Gault complained. 'It's like somebody switched off the sun.'

As they drove on, the gloom of their surroundings seemed to be fighting its way into the car and it was a relief when they saw the sign for the Wolfsschanze Hotel and Gault turned off to the left. A hundred yards ahead they came to a clearing and the former SBS man slowed to a halt.

They studied their surroundings with varying degrees of bewilderment. 'Did somebody turn the clock back?' Jamie asked. 'We appear to be in nineteen forty-five.'

'I booked us into the nearest hotel,' Gault said defensively. 'The website said it used to be Hitler's former security bunker, but I thought they might have done it up a little since he was in residence. At least it's got atmosphere.'

'Sure, atmosphere as in all the ambiance of a concentration camp.'

'Look on the bright side,' Charlotte pointed out. 'Your concentration camp has a beer garden.'

The hotel looked what it was, a relic of the Second World War that had been given a coat of green paint. Fortunately the interior, though equally gloomy because of the small windows, turned out to be modern, if functionally basic in a way that reminded Jamie of his school canteen. They were met at the check-in by a cheerful, slim young man in a white shirt and dark trousers who thankfully spoke German, and broke into passable English when they produced their passports.

'Let me know when you want see Wolf's Lair,' he suggested. 'You need guide to get best of site, but official guides only speak Polish. Hermann gives good rates for English peoples. Shows you everything.'

He handed them a leaflet boasting the highlights of the complex, with pictures of enormous bunkers cloaked in green ivy, intimidating subterranean tunnels and huge chunks of nameless concrete. 'Just the place to come for a cheery relaxing holiday,' Gault chuckled. 'And that's without an introduction to the former residents. Anybody fancy a trip to the shooting range in General Jodl's staff bunker?'

Hermann's face split into a grin. 'You like? Try Mauser sniper's rifle, MP40?'

'What about a *Panzerfaust*?' Gault asked innocently.

'You joke with me, right? I get you discount. We talk later, I serve in restaurant.'

He walked away with a shy smile at Charlotte. Gault said he'd check in with Adam Steele. Jamie and Charlotte decided to take a walk in the grounds around the hotel to familiarize themselves with their surroundings. They moved silently in the dim light beneath the towering pines and beeches, passing a memorial cross topped by a crowned eagle. The writing was Polish, but a German translation commemorated the Polish engineers killed and injured in these woods during the ten years it took to clear 54,000 mines laid by the Nazis. Jamie shivered and not just from the raw chill that ate into his bones. This was a place of ghosts. He half expected a spectral SS general to walk out of the gloom. Huge shadowy bunkers loomed among the trees and his imagination created the mighty fortresses they had once been. Many looked as if they'd been tossed high in the air and crashed back to earth in giant pieces, some of them the size of a small house. Everything was overgrown with the creepers and moss that thrived in the damp atmosphere. He wondered how Hitler, the hypochondriac, had fared here.

'I see it's your turn to be preoccupied.'

'I'm sorry.' His mind took a little time to clear. He'd almost forgotten Charlotte was with him. She studied him, the blue eyes appraising, but the moment he looked up, she turned away, as if she couldn't bear him to read the message in them. Tall and slim in tight blue jeans and a jacket of shiny black leather, he suddenly realized just how achingly beautiful she was. 'I was just thinking that the very earth of this place is tainted by the Nazis, even after all these years.'

'I've been thinking, too,' she said seriously. 'Remember we were talking about Lauterbacher's description: a walled castle beside a lake?'

He nodded. 'We decided it wasn't much help because there are thousands of lakes.'

'And hundreds of castles.'

'Sure,' he agreed.

'What kind of people build castles?'

He wondered what this was all about, but decided to play along. 'Kings, princes, dukes, barons . . .'

'And knights.'

He stopped. 'Yes, and knights.'

She laughed, pleased with herself for surprising him. 'I did some research and I discovered that East Prussia is the creation of an order called the Teutonic Knights. They have their roots in the Crusades – Richard the Lionheart, the Saracens, and all that – a bit like the Knights Templar, but later they turned their sights closer to home. They drove the pagan Prussians out of their lands and established themselves here, building castles left, right and centre. Their hereditary enemies were the Lithuanians, and, like someone we know, the Poles and the Russians. The emblem of the order was a . . .'

Jamie dredged a memory from somewhere. 'A black Maltese cross. The holy Knight's Cross.'

'I know it doesn't take us much further forward, but it—'

'Hang on a second.' He delved in the rucksack for the journal. 'I should have seen this before. There's always been a name that doesn't quite fit. *Joyeuse, the sword of Charlemagne; Durendal, the sword of his lieutenant, Roland; Gotteswerkzeug, the sword of Werner von Orseln, defier of the Eastern hordes; Zerstorer, the sword of Barbarossa; and your sword, the most powerful of them all, the sword of Arthur: Excalibur.* Charlemagne, Barbarossa and Arthur were all kings in their own right. Roland was, at worst, a prince, and in any case his holdings were in France. The question is: who was Werner von Orseln, the man who carried a sword called God's Instrument?'

They walked back to the hotel, passing the beer garden. The route took them through the car park and Jamie noticed a large black car with mirrored windows, what the Americans called an SUV and the Brits a 4x4. He didn't realize it was occupied until the driver gunned the engine and drove away as they came up behind it. He glanced at Charlotte, but his companion didn't react. Hermann was polishing the glass panels in the hotel's front door, and as they passed him Jamie asked how long the car had been standing there.

'Maybe twenty minutes.' He shrugged. 'Looks like they didn't want to stay after all.'

XXII

'Werner von Orseln lived in the fourteenth century and was the seventeenth Grand Master of the Teutonic Order,' Charlotte read from a lined notebook as she sat with Jamie and Gault in the bunker restaurant of the Wolf's Lair hotel. 'He's credited with revitalizing the fight against Poland, Lithuania and Russia and is one of the great heroes of the Teutonic Order because he led from the front, wielding his great sword *Gotteswerkzeug* – God's Instrument. His family originally came from Frankfurt but as Grand Master he ruled Prussia from the great Teutonic fortress at Malbork, which is west of here and on a river, not a lake.'

'And doesn't help us much,' Gault pointed out gracelessly.

'That's true,' she admitted. 'But I managed to trace records of his holdings. It's not known when he joined the Order, but by thirteen twelve he'd been appointed *komtur*, which is commander, of Ragnit, now Neman, then in Lithuania, but now in the Kaliningrad Oblast, which makes it Russian.' She looked up. 'The geography of this part of the world is jolly confusing.'

Hermann hovered by the table and they placed their orders.

'I'm not sure where this is getting us,' Jamie said.

'Neither am I,' Charlotte admitted. 'But we have to start somewhere. By thirteen fourteen he was *grand komtur* at Malbork, which presumably means his career was on the up. A couple of years later he backed the wrong man in some dispute and ended up in exile. When he returned in thirteen nineteen, he was given command of a relatively minor castle, somewhere called Altburg.'

Jamie cleared a space among the cutlery and glasses and spread a large-scale map across the table. He studied the scattered communities among the lakes around the *Wolfsschanze*. 'I can't see anything that comes close.'

She frowned and scrolled through the document on her screen. 'Try Nortstein: that seems to be a more recent name.'

Jamie looked up as a shadow loomed over him. Did he imagine it, or did Hermann's face freeze for a split second? Certainly, the German's expression changed the instant he felt Jamie's eyes on him, but not before the art dealer recognized something intriguing. After a moment's hesitation the young man produced a fixed smile. 'You ordered the beetroot soup, sir?'

Nortstein proved as elusive as Altburg and dinner ended disappointingly. Charlotte and Gault moved away towards the bar and Jamie waited until the waiter returned to clear the table.

'You said you could take us on a tour of the Wolf's Lair.' He took out a wad of notes that made Hermann's eyes open and counted fifty euros onto the table. 'It looks as if we're going to have some time on our hands tomorrow. Would that be suitable?'

Hermann grinned. 'Sure, I get day off. You just let me know time. Best take warm clothes. I show you place where Hitler nearly *kaput*, but many other good things too. We got seventy bunkers, shelters, maybe some tank traps. Martin Bormann's house. Hermann show you tunnels nobody ever see before, not even Russkis, maybe he still living down there, huh?'

'Then again, old son,' Jamie counted another fifty onto the worn table top, 'maybe you can just take us to Nortstein?'

The smile faded to be replaced by a look of weary resignation. 'Sure.'

'In nineteen forty-five, Nortstein became Radznort.' Jamie pointed to a fly speck on the map as they waited in the hired BMW for Hermann. 'It's about ten miles from here as the crow flies, but probably a bit more by road because this is swamp and lake country. It looks as if there are two possible routes, both of them a bit complicated.'

'Why are we taking the Hun?' Gault demanded. 'Suddenly I can't drive this thing?'

'Because he knows the area and I think there's some kind of link between him and Radznort,' Jamie explained. 'When he heard the word Nortstein he reacted as if someone had stuck him with an electric cattle prod.'

'Do you want me to pump him on the way?' Charlotte suggested without any apparent irony.

'I'm sure there's nothing he'd like better.' Jamie caught Gault's grin. 'But let's just play it as it comes. I want to see the look on his face when we get there. If he volunteers something that's fine, but . . .'

Hermann, dressed in a combat jacket and jeans, bundled his way into the rear seats beside the English girl. 'You take Radzieje road, yes? Maybe you get lost without Hermann.'

'That's the other reason,' Jamie said, laughing at Gault's irritated growl.

Despite the incessant drizzle and the oppressiveness of the flat, open country, the journey felt like the final stages of a school trip. The excitement in the car grew with every passing mile on a narrow road that quickly turned into little more than a farm track. Though they fought the feeling, it was difficult not to think of this as an end in itself. Gault drove with a grim half smile and Charlotte grinned every time her eyes met Jamie's. Even Hermann caught the mood. He sat a little closer to Charlotte than was necessary and every few minutes he'd turn to stare artlessly at her, volunteering an occasional

241

direction as Gault approached a cross roads. 'Radzieje,' he said as they passed through a tiny settlement. 'You go right here, then take first left round lake. Not far now.'

Suddenly, to their right, lay an enormous expanse of water. *A castle beside a lake.* Jamie felt his heart beat a little faster. In the distance, beyond a second, smaller lake, he could see a cluster of houses. Radznort, was, if anything, smaller than Radzieje, perhaps home to less than a hundred people. Only the concrete road was evidence it had once been a place of some consequence. But something was missing. As they approached the hamlet his eyes desperately searched the trees beyond for some sign of what they were seeking.

Gault said it first. 'There's no fucking castle.' He turned in his seat and glared accusingly at Hermann. 'There's no fucking castle.'

They drove to the far side of the town and stopped where the buildings ended. Jamie got out of the car and walked to where the concrete paving crumbled and a jumble of low, grass-covered earthwork banks and ditches stretched into the distance, the only indication that there had once been a substantial building here. They were too late. Decades too late. There was no castle.

The others were standing by the car, Gault and Charlotte looking lost and defeated, Hermann's face a cracked mirror of confusion. As Jamie approached them, Gault turned on Hermann. 'Why didn't you tell us there was no castle?'

'You didn't ask about castle,' the young German spat back. He shot Gault a sulky glance and wandered off towards a clump of trees on the far side of the disturbed ground.

'Leave him alone, Gault,' Jamie said. 'It's not his bloody fault there's no castle. We need to spread out and knock on a few doors. Find out if anyone knows what happened here during the war. Throw some of Steele's money around. It looks like the only way we're going to get anything out of this place.'

The first two houses he tried were empty, but at the third door a young woman stared at him blankly as he tried German and English. When he asked the question in Russian she turned and called to someone inside and an elderly man appeared in the doorway behind her.

'*Dzien dobry, dziadek.*' Jamie greeted the old man politely in his rudimentary Polish, before returning to Russian. He explained that he was a representative of an English television company planning to film a documentary of East Prussia during the war years. Was it possible there was someone in the village who could tell him about Nortstein and the castle? The company was happy to pay.

The old man sniffed and something in his eyes hardened, showing the much more formidable person he had once been. 'You can keep your money, sir. They are all gone.'

'Gone?'

'The Russians,' he said with a dismissive shrug,

meaning the Russians had sent them away. 'All gone, and if they were here they would not want to talk about what happened then, may the Lord forgive us.'

He began to shut the door, but Jamie smiled and stood his ground. 'Surely . . .'

The hardness in the eyes was replaced by real threat that made Jamie take a step back. 'Keep your money and leave us alone.'

When Jamie returned to the car, Charlotte and Gault were already there. They met his look and shook their heads. 'Nobody,' Gault said. 'Not one of them was here during the war. It's as if the place only existed since the Germans were kicked out.'

'The old man I spoke to said they were all gone. Something about the Russians.'

'Of course they are all gone.' Hermann's sudden cry, in German and jagged-edged with bitterness and rage, made them jump. 'This was our Holocaust, don't you understand? Everyone talks about the Jews, but no one about the Prussians.' He waved a frantic hand towards the fields they'd driven through. 'This was my family's land before they stole it. This is where the bones of my ancestors were buried until they ploughed up the cemetery. We had done nothing wrong, but Stalin took it away from us.'

'Your family owned the castle?' Jamie demanded.

Hermann shook his head. 'They had a farm and supplied the estate of Graf von Reinhardt, who lived in castle. They were not rich, not Nazis, but they were

German and that was enough. You have heard of ethnic cleansing, yes? Of what happened in Bosnia and Kosovo? What happened to my people was a thousand times worse. I came here in hope that one day I will be able to reclaim my family's heritage.'

'I'm sorry,' Charlotte said.

'Sorry?' He turned on her. 'Sorry will not bring back the old and the sick who were driven from their homes in the freezing winter and herded hundreds of miles like animals to Germany with only what they could carry on their backs. It will not unrape the women the Russians raped. And they were the fortunate ones. They speak of Auschwitz and Treblinka, but do they ever speak of Nemmersdorf and the women who were raped, then crucified, before they were shot or had their throats cut? Or the babies bayoneted to death? Does anyone ever denounce the tens of thousands of civilian refugees crushed under the tracks as they fled Russian tanks? Or the sinking of the *Wilhelm Gustloff*, which was the greatest individual naval tragedy of all time? Almost ten thousand men, women and children. When my grandfather came back from Konigsberg—'

'Your grandfather was here during the war?' Jamie felt a resurgence of hope. Perhaps the story didn't end here after all. 'Is he still alive?'

Hermann's eyes flared. 'He died five years ago, but the war killed him. He was a flak helper on an 88mm gun, but near the end of the war they sent him to the front. He was wounded in the fighting around Konigsberg and returned to his home, the ruined farm you see there.' He pointed to a single blackened chimney that stood at the centre of a scattered pile of rubble in the middle of the field. 'The Russians would have shot him, but he was very young and the family destroyed all the pictures of him in uniform and dressed him up in a child's clothes. When the fighting passed, they were relieved. They could get on with their lives, they were farmers, they grew food. Why would the Soviets want to harm such people?' Hermann shook his head and tears stained the dust at his feet. 'But very soon they were pulled out of their houses and marched in a column that grew and grew until they were thousands strong when they reached the new German border.'

'What about nineteen forty-one, before the invasion of Russia?' Gault demanded, his tone saying that he wasn't interested in what happened to a few German refugees. 'Did he say anything about a gathering of high-ranking SS officers?'

For a moment Hermann looked as if he wanted to strangle the Englishman, but gradually his anger subsided. 'He was twelve years old, a *Hitler Jugend*, such an event would have excited him, but I don't remember him saying anything. All he told me about that time is the village was often evacuated if Von Ribbentrop came to stay with the Graf when he visited the *Wolfsschanze*.'

Jamie remembered that Joachim Von Ribbentrop had been the Third Reich Foreign Minister hanged for war crimes after the Nuremberg trials. He would have been a regular visitor to Hitler's headquarters but he was a politician and it was doubtful whether he had anything to do with the events chronicled in the Excalibur codex. 'You said he was here at the end,' he persisted. 'Did he say what happened when the Red Army came?'

'He was here,' Hermann admitted. He marched out into the centre of what must have been the square in front of the castle, now surrounded on three sides by a scatter of modern houses. 'He told me he hid in the woods over there. There was a den, his favourite place as a boy, where he had a view of the comings and goings from the castle. But it was not the Red Army, not at first. He called them brigands, but I think he meant partisans. It would have been about the time the Nazis evacuated the Wolf's Lair, and were withdrawing to a new defence line, I think, and Nortstein would have been in the no man's land between the Red Army and the *Wehrmacht*. They rode in on small horses, a dozen of them, their feet almost touching the ground and weighed down with weapons.'

Jamie matched the description to old newsreels he'd seen of Russian and Yugoslav partisans operating behind the Nazi lines. He knew they'd made entire regions no-go zones for the *Wehrmacht* and the SS, but the reprisals taken against them had been terrible. Captured fighters would be shown no mercy and any village suspected of supplying or supporting them faced being wiped off the map and its people slaughtered. It meant they would be equally pitiless towards their enemies or those who didn't offer help.

Hermann saw his look and nodded. 'They must have been watching the town, because they found the hiding places of the few people who had stayed in their homes and did terrible things to them. When they'd searched the houses they stood looking at the castle, before the leader, a big man in a bearskin coat, ordered them forward.' He hesitated for a second and when he resumed Jamie knew the young German was describing the scene exactly as the old man had told him. 'My grandfather thought the castle had been evacuated with the Wolf's Lair, but soon there came shooting from inside and he saw a man in SS uniform stagger from the door and try to escape before he was cut down by bullets. A little later the partisans forced more men from the castle at gunpoint and lined them up by the gate. There seemed to be a conversation between the leader and one of the men, and, almost in a friendly way, the partisan commander led him back into the castle. As soon as they were out of sight the remaining partisans turned their guns on the prisoners, killing them all, before standing among the dead men smoking cigarettes. They seemed to be waiting for something. Then it came.' The young German's eyes turned bleak. 'The screaming. Screaming such as my grandfather never forgot for the rest of his life. He tried to shut his ears, but the screaming would not stop. How long it lasted he didn't know, but eventually the leader, who my grandfather now called The Bear, emerged from the castle with his arms red to the elbows and called his men together. He lined them up with their weapons slung and made a speech. It must have been a good speech because my father could hear their cheers.' He paused, suddenly frowning at the memory of the old man's astonishing revelation. 'When he was finished he saluted them, turned away and then swivelled to cut down his own comrades with bursts from a sub-machine gun. They were so surprised they didn't even try to run. As they lay dead or dying, just about where we are standing now, he pulled out a pistol and put a bullet through each of their heads.'

Hermann looked from face to face, studying the reaction to his tale, but only Charlotte's showed any emotion.

'My God, Jamie, what does it mean?'

Jamie was still trying to work out the implications of what he'd heard. The swords, it had to be about the swords. Why else would the Russian commander kill his own men? Unless von Orseln's castle contained some other secret they weren't aware of. 'I don't know, I—'

'Trouble.' Gault's warning held an edge that said *big trouble*.

Four men emerged from between the houses and walked towards them in the kind of open, gunfighter formation that told Jamie they were probably armed and that at least two of them were former soldiers. In fact, walk was the wrong word, they had the kind of wary, swivel-headed swagger of a pack of hunting lions.

'I don't suppose you happen to have that *Panzerfaust* with you, Hermann?' Jamie glanced at the German and saw something he didn't like his eyes. 'Jesus, you set this up. Who the hell are they?'

Hermann looked as if he were about to run. 'You didn't say was secret. They ask. I tell.'

'Good morning, Mr Saintclair,' a voice speaking Russian cut across the square. The owner was the slight young man in the centre pairing of the four. He wore an expensive leather bomber jacket over a white shirt, tan cowboy boots and, despite his lack of physical stature, had a natural authority that made the others defer to him. If he was the velvet glove, his companions were the iron fist; narrow-eyed, unsmiling and with hard muscles bulging beneath jackets professionally cut to disguise shoulder holsters. Professionals. But what kind of professionals?

'Charlotte, get behind the car. Gault, if this gets rough do what you're being paid to do. Hermann? You and I will have words.'

Charlotte edged towards the BMW, and Gault took a step right, which coincidentally put him at a favourable angle to the two men opposite him and closer to the driver's door of the car. He gave Jamie an imperceptible nod. The young Russian raised his hand. 'Please stay where you are,' he said in perfect English. 'I am here to deliver a social invitation to Mr Saintclair to visit our lovely city of Kaliningrad, and if his companions should wish to accompany him, they will experience the best of our famous Russian hospitality.'

Jamie kept his confusion to himself. He'd thought this was about the swords. But why would anyone want him to go to Kaliningrad? The four men in front of him reeked of the Russian mafia. Had they somehow got wind of the Excalibur codex? It was possible. Maybe Rolf Ziegler, or more likely Otto, had had more than one copy and had tried to sell the contents. Whatever the explanation, Jamie wasn't planning to go anywhere near Kaliningrad. He stood, ready to fight or flee as the circumstances dictated. The car lay eight feet to his left and if Charlotte had been two steps closer he would have been tempted to opt for the latter. In their present situation, he saw no chance of the four of them getting into the car before the Russians made their move. Still, nobody had pulled a gun. It wasn't time to fight yet.

'Perhaps if you explained the specific attractions of your lovely city?' he suggested. 'I might consider your offer.'

'We,' the Russian smiled and waved a hand at his marble-visaged comrades, 'represent a gentleman who is travelling all the way from Moscow to our fair city. He "heard you were in the neighbourhood", as I believe our American friends put it, and because he is very keen to make your acquaintance, jumped on the first available plane. That plane, I might say, is one of several he owns, so the hardship is not so great as you might imagine.'

Jamie tried to think of a Russian he might have annoyed, but could only come up with one, and Oleg Samsonov, the former owner of the fabled Eye of Isis, was dead, a psychopath's bullet in his throat. Still, the Russian billionaire might have friends and some of them could well blame Jamie Saintclair for his demise, along with his wife and several bodyguards. The young man's smile broadened as he saw understanding dawn. 'I see we are already "on the same wavelength", as they say. Yes, my . . . client is interested in the circumstances of the late and dearly lamented Oleg Samsonov's death, particularly from one of the last people to see him alive.'

'He was already dead,' Jamie pointed out. Sometimes a situation required brutal honesty.

The Russian pursed his lips and nodded. 'Yes, that may be the case, but nevertheless you have a certain knowledge of his apartments at the time of his demise, yes?' Jamie blinked. He remembered a sunburst of colour as the only version of Van Gogh's *Sunflowers* in private hands slipped into view as he checked Samsonov's safe room. The man shrugged. 'There is a question of certain assets unaccounted for . . . unpaid debts, business liabilities . . . and my client would be willing to pay handsomely for information about their possible whereabouts.'

'I don't think I can help your client,' Jamie said evenly. 'As you see, we have some . . . birdwatching to do, and the migrants don't stay still for long.' He noticed the three heavies stiffen and their fingers moved a little closer to their chests. The young man waved a calming hand.

'Perhaps—'

The Russian was interrupted as two large black Mercedes SUVs drew into the square and drove slowly between the two groups to stand idling near the houses on the far side, their mirrored windows glittering menacingly in the low sun that had fought its way through the drizzle. They were stationary for only a moment, before the engine note picked up and equally slowly, they made their way back out of the square.

Both sides of the little confrontation stood not quite certain how to react to the intrusion. From the look on the Russian faces, Jamie was certain the cars didn't belong to their reinforcements, not that they needed them. That seemed to indicate only one thing and Jamie was still pondering the perfect timing of Sarah Grant and her team when he noticed the Russian approaching cautiously across the Tarmac. 'It seems you are not the only birdwatchers, Mr Saintclair, but please don't think this is over. My card.' The young man handed over a cardboard rectangle. 'Be certain to get in touch when the . . . birds are less elusive.' He put out his hand and Jamie took it to find his fingers in the grip of an iron vice. 'My client can be an impatient man and any future invitations may be more forceful.'

'Is that a threat, Mr . . . ' he glanced at the name on the card, '. . . Vatutin?'

'Oh, I believe it is, Mr Saintclair. Good day.' He turned and walked back the way he'd come with his comrades in his wake. Jamie waited until he heard the sound of a car's engine before he moved.

'Let's get the hell out of here. And Gault? Find a different route back to the hotel. I don't want to drive a mile up the road and find those bastards waiting for us.' Gault started to unfold the map. 'We haven't got time for that. Hermann, get in the front.'

Jamie slipped into the back seat beside Charlotte. 'What was all that about?'

'Some business that wasn't as unfinished as I thought.' He saw Gault's eyes on him in the rear-view mirror. 'Just drive.'

XXIII

'They came to the bar last—'

'It's done. Hermann; there's nothing we can do about it now.'

'Who the fuck were our guardian angels in the up-market hearses?' Gault demanded.

Jamie shrugged. 'Does it matter?'

'I'm a thousand miles from anybody I trust, I want to know all the angles.'

'Friends, I think.'

He felt the ex SBS man staring at him in the car mirror. 'That's fucking helpful.'

They drove for an hour, following Hermann's directions along a circuitous route using single roads and farm tracks, past lakes and through forests. Eventually they reached a junction with a sign directing them to Ketrzyn. The road it pointed to had the familiar railway line that ran past the *Wolfsschanze* to their right side.

'Thank Christ,' Gault muttered.

'What do we do, Jamie?' Charlotte asked. 'We can't give up now.'

'I don't know,' he admitted. 'Nortstein isn't quite a dead end. Somebody will know the identity of the partisan leader. There'll be records. But the chances are he's long dead, and even if he's not he's unlikely to want to chat about the day he butchered his men. It would tarnish the memory of his glorious war record. Still, it might be worth a try. Otherwise, it's back to the archives. Deep down in some box file in Moscow or Berlin or Washington there may be a piece of paper that lists *Five swords of unknown origin*. It's a long shot.'

'It's a fucking waste of time, and you know it.'

'I'm not psychic, Gault. When the Red Army destroyed Nortstein castle and forced the local residents out to Christ knows where, all the evidence went with it. We could have been standing within twenty feet of the bloody thing, but we'd never know.'

Hermann turned in his seat with a look of puzzlement. 'Red Army not destroy Nortstein Castle.'

'What?'

'Nortstein Castle is not destroyed. It is dismantled one stone at a time and taken away in trucks.'

'Why would anyone . . . ?' Jamie's head reeled at this new and utterly surreal turn. 'You mean they knocked it down and took the rubble away?'

'No. Not knocked down. Tadiusz who works in hotel was labourer. They very careful with everything.

Window glass. Wood panels. Roof tiles. Everything in back of trucks.'

'What would the Russians want with a Polish castle?'

'Not Russians.' Hermann grinned. 'Man who told Tadiusz what to do was English, like you.'

'Our friends are back,' Gault interrupted.

Jamie looked back to find one of the Mercedes SUVs approaching fast behind them.

'Do you want me to let them past?'

'I don't know,' he snapped.

'Well, make up your mind.'

'Maybe . . .'

'Friends my arse.' Gault threw the big BMW into a screaming turn as another of the black Mercs drove from a forest track to block the road in front of them. Jamie's head hit the padded roof as the car bounced over the verge to straddle the rail track. 'Put your bloody belts on.' The three-litre engine roared as Gault accelerated the bucketing car in an attempt to bypass the roadblock, but the Mercedes easily kept pace with them. 'I hope to fuck the two o'clock Bialystok express isn't due.' Gault's eyes darted between the tracks ahead, the first Mercedes barrelling along to their left and the second, which had now joined them on the track, was catching up fast.

Charlotte screamed as they hit a crossing point and the car leapt in the air, crashing back to earth a millisecond later. The impact made Jamie wince as a spear of agony lanced through his chest, confirming his ribs weren't as well healed as he'd thought. He glanced left to see the Mercedes slightly above and a few feet away on the road. What in the name of Christ was going on? He'd been certain the cars belonged to the Israelis, but if Sarah Grant wanted to get in touch she had his phone number. The Russians? The passenger side window of the Mercedes dropped slowly to answer his question. A hard brown face stared at him and motioned with his hand to slow down. In case Jamie hadn't got the message his other hand appeared showing what looked like a Glock 9mm.

He turned to Gault. 'I think they want us to stop.'

'Do tell.' The SBS man kept his eyes on the track ahead.

'The chap who suggested it looked like an Asian or an Arab.'

'Well, fuck you, Abdul.' Gault put his foot to the floor and the BMW surged ahead, but only for a moment before the Mercedes came level again, overtook and bumped across the verge on to the track ahead, immediately hitting the brakes.

'Shit.' The trunk of a tree flashed past Jamie's window as Gault hauled the wheel to the right and the car rocketed out of the railbed and into the forest, swerving between the trees and bucketing over the uneven ground at breakneck speed.

'Where in the name of Christ did you learn to drive like this?' Jamie shouted, when it became clear he wasn't going to die just yet.

'Close protection course. Hereford. Nineteen ninety-three. Ouch.' Gault grimaced as a fallen branch scraped along the car's metalwork. 'It was fun, especially when you had a celeb crapping themselves in the back. Are the bastards still with us?'

The bastards were, but they weren't quite so confident among the trees and the SUVs were falling back. 'I think we're losing them.'

'Great,' the SBS man said through gritted teeth as a bunker loomed up in front of the car and he spun the wheel to take the BMW past with an inch to spare. The front tyre hit something solid with a horrible whack and suddenly Gault was fighting the wheel much harder.

'I know where we are,' Hermann screamed. 'Go right and you will reach a track.'

'Will it take us back to the hotel?' Charlotte asked breathlessly.

'No, but it will take us away from these people.'

'That'll have to do,' Gault grunted. 'This fucking thing only wants to go right anyway.'

Two hundred yards ahead, they hit the track and the bucketing motion eased. Everyone relaxed a little, except Gault who kept one eye on the mirror. 'Where does this lead us?'

'Out to General Jodl's bunker,' Hermann said. 'From there you will find a way back to the hotel.'

'They might be waiting for us,' Jamie pointed out.

'We have to go somewhere,' Gault snapped. 'And

better among other people than out here in the sticks where nobody hears you scream. Oh, fuck.'

Gault hit the accelerator and Jamie didn't have to look to know that the Mercedes was back. 'Just stay ahead of them. They're not going to start a war.' He regretted the words the moment they were out of his mouth. Muzzle flashes rippled in the passenger mirror before he heard the chainsaw rasp of a burst of automatic fire that ripped white chips from the bark of a tree ahead and to their right. 'Get your heads down,' he shouted.

The second burst was short or wide, but the third must have hit something because the rear of the BMW swung right and left.

'The tyres,' Gault said unnecessarily. 'Now we're really fucked.' He kept the car on the track, but the Mercedes closed up and it was clear the next burst would be through the back window. 'Hold on tight.' He spun the wheel left and the car shot between two trees and down a tree-filled gully, bouncing across rocks and fallen branches until it slid to a halt, engine roaring, beside a small stream.

'Out.' Jamie ignored the pain from his ribs and ripped open the door. As he emerged, Hermann burst from the front passenger door, his eyes wild with fright. Between them they hauled Charlotte clear and crawled away from the car.

'Where's Gault?' Charlotte hissed.

Jamie glanced desperately round. 'He must have gone the other way. He'll have to take his chance.'

He froze at the sound of a branch snapping some-where not far away.

'Come out with your hands up.' The demand was in English, but with a thick accent. 'You will not be harmed.'

Jamie looked around for any sort of protection from the marksman above, but the gully was a death trap. He sighed wearily and was about to stand up when Hermann placed a hand on his arm.

'I know a way,' he whispered.

XXIV

Hermann wriggled slowly backwards through the undergrowth, leaving Jamie and Charlotte to follow as best they could. With every movement Jamie waited for the crack of dry twig that would draw the fire of their pursuers. He had no doubt now that these men, whoever they proved to be, were killers. You didn't carry that kind of firepower without being prepared to use it for the purpose for which it was designed. He froze as something touched his leg. When he looked up, Hermann was peering from what appeared to be a bramble-covered storm drain that entered the gully from the right. The young German nodded encouragement for first Charlotte, then Jamie to follow. They made their way through the leaf mould and sludge for fifty yards and Jamie realized it wasn't a drain at all but some kind of reinforced trench, perhaps a rudimentary bomb shelter.

When he reached the limit of the trench, Hermann raised his head a few inches – and froze. Jamie could hear the sound of a whispered conversation and feet rustling through damp leaves.

Eventually, Hermann hissed that whoever had been making the noise was gone and they slipped over the end of the trench into the open, in the shadow of a massive, moss-covered concrete emplacement. Hermann led them through a doorway and pointed upwards to a square of light in the roof. 'You climb now. Wait until I come back.'

'What?' Charlotte whispered incredulously.

'Climb.' The German indicated a rusting steel ladder anchored to the wall. A burst of fire somewhere close made him shrink back into the shadows. 'Climb, please.'

Charlotte scrambled up with all the athleticism of a trained acrobat and Jamie followed as she slipped through a jagged-edged hole into the fresh air. 'Stay low,' he hissed. They crawled across the rough concrete to what looked like a sunken pond set into the roof.

'Jacuzzi,' she mouthed.

He smiled at the attempt to lighten the mood. Up here their situation seemed less perilous, but he knew that was an illusion. 'Flak emplacement,' he explained in a low voice. 'There would have been an anti-aircraft gun. Hitler was paranoid about being bombed.'

More shots rang through the forest, slightly more distant than the first. Maybe Gault was leading them away? Jamie risked a look down at the clearing they'd crossed, instantly withdrawing his head in response to what he saw. Four men, each armed with a machine gun, were just being joined by a fifth. They were in their late twenties to early thirties and dark haired, two of them wore beards. He could hear them talking in what might have been Pashto, or one of the other languages from around the Khyber Pass. It sounded as if one was making his point more forcefully than the rest. Abruptly, the talking stopped and from the opening at the top of the ladder they heard the clink of metal below.

Jamie squirmed his way to the hole and, with one eye, attempted to work an angle where he could see without being seen. He froze. Two of them: one with his foot on the lower rungs of the ladder and ready to climb. The other apparently arguing that they had better things to do. Jamie looked round frantically for something he could use as a weapon, but the only objects to hand were a few old branches that had fallen from the tree canopy above. He searched for a piece of concrete loose enough to prise away, but quickly realized why no one had managed to blow up this particular bunker. The mortar was as solid now as the day it dried in the spring of 1941. Charlotte watched wide-eyed as he moved to the opposite side of the opening to a position where he'd be behind the gunman when he reached the top. She picked up a slim branch and crawled to his side. The argument below ended and they held their breath and waited. Had they left? No, there it was again, the soft chink of feet on rusting metal. Jamie tensed, and Charlotte raised the branch.

A head crowned with dark hair appeared in the opening, some kind of machine gun slung by the strap over his khaki combat jacket. Charlotte's face contorted with effort and she brought the branch down two-handed towards the exposed head.

'No,' Jamie hissed, grabbing her arm.

Hermann turned to grin at them. 'You think I'm not coming back, huh? You must come with me, it is safe for now.' He began to descend the ladder again. When they were on the ground, the young German proudly showed Jamie the gun he'd brought from the shooting range. 'I have key,' he explained. 'Sometimes we party there.'

'It's a bloody antique,' Jamie said incredulously. 'I've only ever seen them in war films.' It was a matt-black sub-machine gun with a pistol grip and a skeletal metal stock. The magazine looked too long for the rest of the weapon.

'*Schmeisser MP40*. It shoot good. I show you when we meet these bastards.'

'No you bloody won't.' Jamie prised the machine pistol from his reluctant hands. 'Does it even fire real bullets?' He pressed a button below the barrel and removed the long magazine, which proved to be full of 9mm cartridges. The gun was cocked and ready to fire, although the cocking handle sat in a notch that seemed to act as a safety catch. It was much heavier than the more modern machine pistols he'd fired during his OTC course at Cambridge, but it seemed to be well maintained. With any luck it wouldn't blow up in his face.

Hermann reached into his jacket and pulled out a second magazine. He handed it to Jamie, who took it and shoved it into the inside pocket of his jacket. 'This boss's gun. He lets special guests use. Lech Walesa shoot this gun,' he said proudly.

Jamie tested the weapon against his shoulder. He didn't particularly want to shoot anyone, but the knowledge that if anybody tried to kill him he'd be able to shoot back gave him a warm glow

'Can you get us back to the hotel?' he asked the German.

'They might be waiting for us,' Charlotte pointed out. 'Wouldn't it be safer to stay here until they give up and go away? We could hide on the roof again?'

Jamie studied their surroundings. 'I don't think they're the type to give up. This is the perfect place to do whatever it is they've come to do. Our best chance is to get back to civilization. Poor old Gault could be lying out there somewhere bleeding to death. If we can't go to the hotel, we still have to get out of here. Hermann? This is your territory.'

The young man's face creased into a frown. 'Maybe we go other hotel. Księżycowy Dworek on far side of the forest. Is where Eva Braun stay when she is fucking Hitler.'

Jamie almost laughed out loud at the outraged expression on Charlotte's face. 'We don't have a lot of choice,' he shrugged. 'And it sounds as good a place to hide out as any.'

Hermann grinned. 'Hermann knows good way. I show, but first need to get to air raid shelter.'

He checked the path was clear and led them swiftly through the trees and bushes, unerringly guiding them past ankle-breaking trenches and pits hidden by grass and brambles. The heavy undergrowth limited visibility to less than ten paces and every step felt as if it could be taking them into an ambush. In the rear, Jamie scanned the greenery for any sign of danger, his fingers in a death grip on the pressed steel of the machine pistol. Hermann turned and indicated an almost intact bunker. 'This Martin Bormann's air raid shelter.'

Jamie relaxed a little as they approached the lichen-covered concrete ruin and it almost cost him his life. A shadowy figure seemed to grow from the bushes to his right. He sensed the man's finger on the trigger and fired as he pirouetted, the machine pistol stuttering his hands and almost deafening him with its staccato growl. The MP40 had only one setting, fully automatic, and the recoil pulled the barrel upwards and to the right, so that a burst that had been aimed at the legs stitched a line of bullets from groin to shoulder and his target went down screaming. He cursed himself for an idiot as he realized he'd fired half the 32-round magazine.

'Jamie!' He heard Charlotte's screamed warning and sprinted for the bunker entrance as another figure erupted from the undergrowth behind him. A rasping burst of fire fizzed by his ear from somewhere to his left. His body cringed at the near miss and he heard the zing of bullets ricocheting from the concrete. Charlotte had been standing by the doorway, but when he looked again she was gone. His mind screamed at him that the bunker wasn't a refuge, but a trap. On the other hand, they weren't going anywhere and six feet of concrete backed up by the MP40 was a pretty useful deterrent unless the enemy were suicidally brave. He told himself that they could hold out until help arrived, but a little voice cursed him as an optimistic fool.

Inside the bunker his heart stopped. Charlotte lay on her back with a face as pale as death. Her eyes were closed and blood leaked from a wound on her forehead. Hermann stooped over her, dabbing ineffectively at the injury with a handkerchief.

'Oh Christ . . .'

The German looked up, his face stricken, but his next words filled Jamie with hope.

'I think she is hurt by concrete from when bullet hit bunker.'

Jamie crouched beside Charlotte and she gave a soft groan as he carefully checked the wound with his fingers. With an almost physical surge of relief he realized Hermann was right. Whatever had hit her hadn't penetrated the skull, but had torn a nasty two-inch gash just below the hairline. 'Look after her,' he ordered the German, then he ran back to the door, staying in the shadows where he couldn't be seen from outside.

Nothing moved, but that didn't mean anything. He loosed a short burst from the *Schmeisser*, reckoning that it would buy them another few minutes. What he really needed was a clear shot. As his tactics instructor had once said, there is nothing like a man down screaming with a bullet in his belly to make the enemy think twice about his next move. By the time he rejoined Hermann, the hotel worker had moved Charlotte to the back of the bunker and was shifting rubble from a rusting piece of iron that lay flat on the concrete floor.

'I thought I told you to look after her.'

Hermann didn't answer. With a grunt he pushed one last big lump of concrete aside. 'Help me,' he urged, easing his fingers under the four-foot iron plate. Without waiting for an answer he heaved upwards, raising it a few inches. Jamie laid the MP40 on the floor and went to his side. Together they managed to haul the heavy plate upright, revealing a dark cavity in the floor.

'All the big bosses' bunkers linked by tunnels,' Hermann explained breathlessly. 'You hold.'

While Jamie kept the plate steady, the young German took Charlotte's semi-conscious body under the arms and dragged her to the edge of the tunnel entrance. From somewhere he produced a small torch and Jamie saw that a set of concrete stairs led downwards for about five yards. Hermann descended until his chest was at floor level and took Charlotte in his arms.

'Now you come,' he said, before disappearing into the darkness.

Jamie had the choice of dropping the iron plate away from the entrance, ensuring their hunters would discover the tunnel the minute they were brave enough to enter the bunker, or finding a way to drop it back in place as he made his exit. He solved the problem by using the MP40, which was close enough to retrieve, as a support to prop up the plate. Once he had slithered backwards into the tunnel, he removed the gun and allowed the iron to settle into place, using his back to slow its descent. He knew it wouldn't fool the ambushers for long without the camouflage of the rubble, but it was better than nothing.

When the metal plate had sunk into position he slung the *Schmeisser* over his shoulder and followed the light of the torch to where Hermann waited. Charlotte was slumped at his feet with her hands over her face, which at least meant she was conscious. Between them they got her to her feet and supported her along the dank tunnel, which Jamie now saw was about eight foot high and the same wide. Dripping with damp and the wires for the lighting still hanging in loops from the ceiling, the passages must have been built to ensure the work of the High Command could continue even if the complex was attacked. Naturally, Hitler wouldn't want his quest for world domination to be interrupted by anything as minor as a few Russian bombs.

They stopped to rest every few minutes and Jamie used the intervals to listen for sounds of pursuit. He heard nothing. Maybe the hunters were afraid of the dark, but he doubted it. As they stumbled through the twisting labyrinth, Charlotte kept repeating how sorry she was and she'd be all right soon, while Hermann muttered to himself constantly in German. The reason for his nervousness was revealed when he stopped abruptly and probed with the torch until he found a side tunnel a few paces ahead. 'Main tunnel blocked,' he said. 'Nazis, Russkis, who knows? Many tunnels blocked. This way take us to guest shelter. Not far from there to Księżycowy hotel, yes? We get help there.'

After what seemed like an eternity they saw a speck of natural light in the distance. At the same moment Charlotte's legs went out from under her and Jamie struggled with her limp body until Hermann was able to help support her. When they were a few yards from the end of the tunnel, the two men staggered to a halt and laid their burden gently to the floor. The source of the light turned out to be a curtain of ivy growing beneath the collapsed roof of a demolished bunker. Jamie unslung the MP40 and crawled through beneath the overhanging slab until he could get some notion of his surroundings.

And found disaster.

Hurriedly, he slithered backwards into the mouth of the tunnel, where Hermann sat holding Charlotte's hand. 'There are more of them,' he whispered. 'I don't know how many, but three at least, and they're being methodical. They might find us, and they might not, but I don't think we can take the chance. If Charlotte was up to it, I'd try to slip past them, but we don't have that option. You're going to have to stay with her until she revives. I'll lead them away. Try to get her to the other hotel. Okay?' Hermann nodded, but his eyes were filled with fear. 'You'll be fine.' Jamie squeezed the young German's arm. 'Your grandfather would be proud of you.'

He replaced the half-empty magazine of the MP40 with the full one from his jacket. Plenty of ammo to make a demonstration, but if he got into a firefight he was in trouble. He noticed Charlotte shivering and he took off his jacket and covered her with it.

Hermann shook his hand. '*Viel Glück*, my friend.'

Jamie licked his lips and crawled to the tunnel mouth.

XXV

From his viewpoint beneath the concrete slab, Jamie had a clear view of two men armed with assault rifles clambering over the rubble of another demolished bunker away to his right. As he watched, two more appeared, searching the adjacent woodland and checking anything that would hide a man.

He wanted to be seen, but couldn't afford to be caught leaving the hiding place, so he leopard-crawled to his left until he was out of sight of the hunters, using his elbows and knees and cradling the MP40 across his arms. Regulating his breathing, he checked his surroundings. Thankfully the heavy woodland would conceal him as he crossed their rear to the far side of the clearing. When he was ready he jogged through the trees, keeping low for about a hundred yards, then straightening as he changed direction to leave the protection of the woods and cross the far corner of the clearing. He'd ensured the angle of his approach would make it appear he had

come from well to the west of the tunnel where he'd left
Hermann and Charlotte. He was now on the left flank
of the four gunmen. They would have spotted him in
the end, but just to make certain he fired a sharp three-
round burst in the general direction of the searchers.

With shouts of dismay and alarm the men dropped
to the ground and someone had definitely seen him
because a second later the air above his head buzzed
with the sound of passing bullets. Crouching again,
Jamie jogged in the opposite direction. He took his
time, firing another short volley as he went in the hope
that wariness of the MP40 would ensure there'd be no
reckless charge in his wake. If they were combat-trained
– and he had no doubt they were – they'd work a position
where they could flank him. As he ran, he scanned the
woods to left and right. There was no sign of immediate
danger, but even now two of them would probably be
in the trees sprinting in a wide arc to cut him off ready
for the others to come up behind and drive him into the
killing zone created by their comrades. Ahead, a large
oak offered good cover and he stopped behind it to rest
and listen for a few seconds. Nothing yet. The muzzle
of the machine pistol came up as his mind registered
a flash of russet in the middle distance. With relief he
recognized a big old dog fox that trotted across his path,
stopped, sniffed the air and looked back the way it had
come, before continuing its progress.

That settled it. Breaking into a run, he changed
direction, following the fox's path on a diagonal route

that would take him hopefully beyond the radius of the killing ground ahead. It was a decent enough plan, but it didn't take into account the third flank runner.

They saw each other in the same instant between the stately columns of a stand of beech trees. Jamie threw himself to his right just as a row of bullets kicked up the earth where he'd been standing. In this part of the woods the broad tree canopies allowed little light to reach the forest floor. It meant the undergrowth was low and stunted, providing only sparse cover. Hugging the earth, he loosed a hopeful burst in the general direction of the enemy and squirmed backwards and to his left as the reply scythed over his head, ripping chunks of bark and leaving naked white scars on the trees behind. As he moved, the dynamics of his dilemma flickered through his head like images on a computer screen. The enemy possessed more firepower and a seemingly unlimited supply of ammunition. All the other man had to do was keep him pinned down and allow his compatriots, out there somewhere among the trees, to close in for the kill. Jamie's only advantages were the ancient *Schmeisser*, the relatively few rounds he had left, and the fact that his opponent couldn't be certain of his position. A short length of branch caught his shirt. He pulled it free and tossed the stick low and to his right where it landed with a rustle that instantly attracted another burst of fire and confirmed his last thought. Still moving left he went through his options and realized he only had one. He stopped and waited, allowing the seconds to pass and his mind to clear. Fire and manoeuvre, that was what they'd drummed into him at the Cambridge OTC. Keep your enemy guessing. If his hunter had any field sense he'd be on the move now, but either he was a very good woodsman or he'd decided his position was so dominant that all he had to do was sit tight. There was no way Jamie could be entirely certain, but he had to do something. He started crawling forward to where his enemy waited.

The gunman's caution gave him hope. It meant he would have taken up a safe position, probably behind a tree. It would protect him from the *Schmeisser* bullets, but would also restrict his vision. Jamie chose an angle that would hopefully bring him in on his enemy's flank and he took all the care of a man who knew that the sound of a breaking twig would be his death warrant. Working his way stealthily through the ferns and the leaf mould, he called on the skills he'd been taught during combat training at the university OTU. Don't put your weight down until you're certain what's underneath you. Don't look at your target: the chances are that if you can see him, he'll see you. No matter how well you're concealed, the subconscious is programmed to home in on faces and eyes. The soft rustle as he eased his way through the undergrowth sounded like hail on a window to his overstrained ears. The tree he'd chosen as his aiming point hadn't seemed far away, but getting there took an age and every second of the journey his body tensed waiting for the agonizing punch of copper-jacketed steel. When he reached the aged oak he had to use a low branch to help him to his feet and his legs shook as if he'd just run a marathon.

Jamie waited till his breathing subsided, then squatted so his head was lower than a watcher would naturally expect it to be. One glance to fix the tree his ambusher had chosen and he stood again with his back to the oak and his eyes closed as he went over the plan for the last time. There was no subtle way to do this. No second chances. If his enemy happened to look in the wrong direction at the wrong time Jamie Saintclair would be a sitting duck. He took a deep breath and launched into a headlong charge across the ground separating them.

Ten paces. The undergrowth snapped and hissed beneath his feet, but there was no helping that. Twenty. Almost there. The trees a blur as he sprinted hard and low towards his target, the *Schmeisser* cocked and ready in his hands. A shout away to his right, and another from behind, before the inevitable burst of fire shredded the leaves in front of him and confirmed that his other pursuers were closer than he thought. He waited for the muzzle flashes from the tree ahead that would be the last thing he would ever see. When they didn't come he felt a flare of triumph even as his spine cringed in anticipation of the bullets striking. Of course, his target would be as surprised by the firing as he was. He rounded the tree at a run and a crouching figure looked up, the Uzi in his hands coming round to

JAMES DOUGLAS

meet the new threat. But Jamie was already on him and he swung the butt of the MP40 into the bearded face with all his weight behind it. It landed with a satisfying crunch, but he had no time to assess the damage. No time even to stoop and pick up the Uzi with its big magazine and greater firepower. Instead, he maintained his pace and his line, keeping the tree between him and the hunters. If he was lucky, they'd hesitate and help their friend. But even as the thought formed he knew it wouldn't happen. These men exhibited a ruthless professionalism that didn't include compassionate aid for stragglers. Which begged a question that had been niggling at his brain since the first bullets had flown . . . Before he could answer it another burst of fire churned the ground in front of him and he swerved right. Christ, how could he have forgotten the beater? He half turned on the run and fired a volley in the general direction of the gunman. More gunfire from his right and he winced as a splinter from a nearby tree sliced across his cheek. In the same heartbeat something smashed into his left knee and he was down, his leg momentarily useless. He wrestled the MP40 round and pulled the trigger as two men ran towards him. The gun bucked in his hands and one of them collapsed with a despairing cry before the bolt clicked on empty. Jamie threw the MP40 aside in disgust and checked his knee for damage, discovering to his relief that the impact had been a fallen branch and not a bullet. Not that it would matter in the end.

He sat for a moment with the dampness of the earth seeping through his clothing and waiting for the bullet that would finish it. A large figure loomed over him, his breath coming in short gasps, dark eyes glaring a mix of hatred and triumph from a swarthy, pockmarked face. Jamie ignored the man and focused on the gun muzzle that looked like a railway tunnel from his angle. The barrel twitched, ordering him to get to his feet, and he managed to struggle upright. He raised his arms in surrender, although he had a feeling it wouldn't do him much good. From behind competent hands patted him down, checking for hidden weapons, and he remembered the question that had been eating at him from the start. If these people were so fucking professional why wasn't he dead by now? He was still pondering the answer when his head exploded in a ball of agony and the lights went out.

He came to with his scalp on fire and someone hauling so hard on his hair that it felt as if his face was going to come off. His first instinct was to claw at the offending hand, but that wasn't possible because his arms were behind his back and didn't seem to want to move. It took a moment before he realized they were securely tied and his lower stomach turned to ice water at the possible implications. He opened his eyes to find that he was on his knees with a man standing in front of him holding a mobile phone at eye level. With a grunt of defiance, he heaved and lashed against his bonds until something large and metallic slapped against the side of his head with enough force to make him forget the pain in his scalp.

'It will be much easier on you if you do not fight it.' The voice, in heavily accented English, had an almost seductive quality. 'Soon it will be all over, but first Hassan here will film your confession.'

Confession?

Gradually the identity of his captors dawned on Jamie. The obvious questions flashed through his mind – the how and the why – but they were quickly consumed in the white hot flare of rage that erupted inside him. 'If you're going to kill me get on with it.' He resumed his futile struggle with his bonds. 'You filthy bastards killed Abbie and my child and four hundred other innocent people. I don't have anything to confess except the fact that I wished I'd killed a few more of you.'

The phone dropped away from Hassan's eye-line at the mention of the massacre and Jamie saw puzzlement on the dark face. 'But you—'

'Hassan!'

The other man obediently raised the phone and began filming again.

'Of course, you would say that, a liar and a faithless infidel, and if we had time I'm sure we could have a long and fruitful discussion, but since we do not I must insist.' Jamie winced as something stabbed into his palm. 'I will ask you once and if you do not answer, I will cut off the fingers of your right hand one by one.

If that does not stir your memory, I will take out your eyes. Do you understand?'

'I don't know what you're fucking—' The soft sting of a razor edge froze the words in Jamie's mouth. This couldn't be happening, but now the knife – oh Christ, it was a big knife, a fucking cleaver – was at his throat.

'This is your last chance.' A burst of fire echoed in the distance, quickly answered by a second.

'Rashid, we do not have time for this,' Hassan insisted urgently.

'You will confess that you are the infidel who has usurped the authority of the Lion of the Prophet, who has besmirched the name of the Chosen Ones and masqueraded as a Son of Islam . . .'

Jamie wriggled desperately to free himself, but the man Rashid held him in a grip of iron. 'Christ, please, I don't know what—'

'Rashid!' the cameraman pleaded.

Jamie felt his head pulled back to expose his throat still further. He could see the great blade in front of his eyes ready to sweep round and take out the big veins in his neck. 'Very well.' Rashid's voice turned solemn. 'I sentence you to death in the name of Abu Ayoub al-Iraqi. *Allahu Akbar*. God is Great.' Jesus, they were going to cut his head off. Jamie opened his mouth to scream louder than he had ever screamed before.

The twin crack of the shots merged with the butcher's block smack of metal against muscle, but the hand that held the blade retained its menace until the third bullet struck. Suddenly the knife was gone and Jamie felt a great weight on his shoulders. As he fell forward under the bulk of his executioner he saw Hassan turn to run, only for part of his skull to detach itself and fly into the air. Simultaneously, the cameraman's legs gave way beneath him and he fell without a sound.

Jamie lay trapped as footsteps rustled warily through the leaf mould. Someone removed the dead weight from his back, but he couldn't find the strength to raise his head to bring the world into focus. A hand picked up the big knife and he shuddered at what might come next. Only when the blade began to work at whatever was tying his hands and arms did he realize he was safe.

'Dear God.' The words emerged as a babbled sob. 'From this day forward I will only do good in the world. If you want I'll take Holy Orders and—'

'Jesus, don't be such a big baby, Saintclair.' Sarah Grant helped him to his feet and he had to resist the urge to hug her. They'd been lovers once, but that time was past. More to the point she had saved his life. The man with the pockmarked, angry face lay back in the leaves with two patches of scarlet on his chest and a neat 9mm hole below his left eye. Sarah bent down to search him, removing a pair of mobile phones and a wallet from his inside pocket, then walked across to the other man and repeated the process after first checking him for a pulse. 'I doubt the IDs will be much good, but whoever cleans up here will get their prints. I assume one of these is yours?' She held out the two phones and Jamie took the high-tech mobile Adam Steele had provided.

'You don't know who they are, then why . . . ?'

'They flew into Warsaw the same day you did, all on separate flights, but one of them appeared on the radar and we picked him up. He led us to the others. Some kind of Al-Qaida hit squad, we think. Someone must have wanted you bad to set these guys on you, Jamie.'

It was a statement, but with a question buried in there somewhere.

Jamie suppressed a shudder. 'Butcher boy here wanted me to confess to something, but I've no idea what he was talking about. Something about *usurping the Lion of the Prophet* and *masquerading as a son of Islam*. There was more, but I was too busy being frightened to death to catch it.'

She gave a little whistle and studied him seriously. 'The Lion of the Prophet is the title traditionally given to Islam's greatest warrior. Saladin, who won back the kingdom of Jerusalem from the Crusaders, took it. It's what Osama Bin Laden called himself and the man who holds it now is hiding in a cave somewhere on the border between Afghanistan and Pakistan.' She produced a sudden grin. 'You should take it as a compliment. Not many people can say they personally pissed off the man who replaced Bin Laden.'

'Thanks, I'll bear that in mind next time someone's about to cut my head off.'

'The question is why?'

'I've been thinking about that, but I just can't see why it should have anything to do with the sword.'

'Sword?'

'You mean you don't know about Excalibur?' Her face answered his question and his voice faltered. If not the sword, then why was she here? He tried to distil some sensible explanation from the confusion and the shock, but his mind wasn't up to it. 'But you said I was out of my depth?' He gave her the short version of the Excalibur story and the clues that had brought them to the *Wolfsschanze*. 'I thought Heydrich and the ritual might have something to do with you being here,' he ended lamely.

She shook her head. 'I meant the people you're dealing with, idiot.' A hint of the affection of their earlier relationship took the sting from the word. 'The kind of people who can call on the security services of a foreign power for a favour. The people,' she nudged the corpse with her toe, 'who attract this kind of attention. Whatever your friend Steele is up to, it isn't just about money or an old sword.'

'Then what?'

'My bosses are only interested in two things, Jamie. Politics and power.'

The firing had died down and Jamie wondered what had happened to Gault and Charlotte and muttered, almost to himself, 'I hope the good guys are winning.'

She stopped and turned to face him. 'Who are the good guys?'

'Your people, I thought—'

'Get this straight, Jamie. I am violating every rule in the book by being here. Our orders were to take a watching brief only.'

'Then how . . . ? Why?'

'As for the how, that business card I slipped you has a tiny strip of foil in it that acts as a very basic tracking device. After your little brush with these guys on the road, I was able to keep an eye on your movements. You can sure move fast through the woods when you need to.' He returned her grin, remembering that she'd had a fair turn of pace herself in the Harz Mountains. The smile faded and he felt a sudden rush of nausea at the thought of what would have happened if he'd kept the card in the pocket of the jacket he'd given to Charlotte, instead of his jeans. 'And as to the why,' she continued. 'I wasn't about to let an old boyfriend have his head chopped off by some lunatic Jihadi, no matter how annoying he'd been in the past.' They came to a crossroads. 'I go this way.' She pointed to the right. 'That one should lead you back to your friends.'

'I haven't said thanks.' He took her hands and looked into her eyes. He'd forgotten how brown they were. For the first time he realized that she was no longer the mercurial, doll-like girl he had loved. The fiery streaks in the raven hair were long gone, along with the hard edge and the diamond nose stud. This was a mature, sophisticated woman who'd put her career on the line for him. Her expression softened.

'No thanks required, lover boy,' she whispered as she kissed him on the cheek.

They parted, Jamie with something close to regret, but unable to read what the Mossad agent was thinking.

He'd walked a dozen paces when her voice reached him. 'And Jamie . . . ?'

He turned. She was almost out of sight among the trees. 'Yes?'

'I was sorry about your friend.'

He nodded. 'You would have liked her.'

The next time he looked she was gone.

Sarah Grant walked back to what looked like being an uncertain future. She had no regrets, she'd done what was right, and that was all that mattered. One thing bothered her, though. When they'd discovered the identity of the suspected Al-Qaida operative, her chiefs had passed on the information to the CIA as a matter of courtesy. They'd been surprised when all they received from the Americans was a terse acknowledgement and a . . . not quite an order, more a suggestion, that it would be a good idea to stay at arm's length.

Perhaps she should have told Jamie Saintclair that somebody was using him as the sacrificial goat tethered to attract a tiger. Or maybe – her mind pictured a bearded figure in a gloomy cavern half a world away – a lion?

She smiled and dismissed the thought. From now on Jamie Saintclair would have to look after himself.

Sarah Grant was still smiling when the watching

figure stepped out onto the path behind her and very deliberately pumped two bullets in her back with a silenced pistol. As the Israeli agent lay with the blood filling her lungs a slim shadow loomed over her and put a third bullet in her brain.

XXVI

'Where the hell have you been?' Jamie 's head felt as if it had been put through a gravel crusher and the fact that Gault was nursing a nasty gash on his cheek didn't inspire any sympathy. The former SBS man appeared from the trees close to where they'd crashed into the gully, accompanied by the Russian who'd been at Nortstein.

'I could ask you the same question,' Gault grunted. 'I got out of the car and took off expecting you to follow. What do I find? I'm on my own and there are three of the bastards up my backside yelling in Pashto. The only reason I'm still in the land of the living is because your Russki mate and his pals appeared and gave me the chance to find a bolthole.'

Vatutin approached with a solemn look on his pale face. 'Such a shame, eh, but when we saw you were in trouble we felt we had to help.'

'Yes?' Jamie didn't hide his suspicion.

'Sure.' The Russian shrugged. 'My client would be

upset if I mislaid you. Don't worry about this,' he gestured to where his men were loading bodies into the back of a white van. 'We make it all go away.' He grinned. 'It is what we do.'

Jamie had a feeling that the proper thing to do would probably be to call the authorities, but Vatutin was very certain and since he couldn't hear the sound of sirens it was probably for the best. He could still feel the knife blade at his throat. 'There are another two, possibly three, back there in the trees,' he said.

The Russian nodded and called something to one of the men. He turned and his face changed as he looked over Jamie's shoulder. 'I think maybe you have a problem.'

Jamie followed his gaze as Charlotte staggered from the trees close by. She was still bleeding heavily from her forehead and when he caught her in his arms, her body went limp.

'They killed him,' she sobbed. 'They killed Hermann.'

Jamie closed his eyes.

'What is it you English say? It never rain but it pours.' Vatutin's voice dropped to a whisper. 'Just remember, Mr Saintclair. You owe Kaliningrad a favour, yes?'

More than a thousand miles west of the Wolf's Lair, the chairman of the Committee for a Greater Britain raised his eyes from the papers on his desk. Beyond the windows of the London mansion the first fresh buds of spring were making an appearance and sunlight streamed into the room, but the three men were indifferent to the pleasures of their environment. 'How is the planning proceeding for the detention centres?'

'My people have identified suitable sites in the ten districts we'll create, each with first-class road or rail access to a port. As you suggested, we used the Polish models as our starting point, but with some added refinements to increase security. It helps that the adult males will be separated from the families.'

The chairman nodded. Keeping the families apart would allow the new authority to use them as carrot and stick against each other. Any threat of trouble from the most likely source, what might be called those of military age, and they would be denied contact of any kind with their families, with the implied threat that those families might suffer further hardship. On the other hand, good conduct and cooperation would be met by promises that they would be reunited at some unspecified point in the future. Whether that promise was ever met only time would tell.

'And the guards?'

The bland features altered into a grim smile and the chairman mused that it was like watching candle wax set. Still, he was the type who would always get the job done. Every new regime needed someone like that. 'I doubt we'll have any trouble recruiting them given the climate that will undoubtedly prevail. We already have lists of suitable candidates from our friends in the Met and elsewhere. We'll need more, of course, so we'll target former army NCOs and police officers, plus certain members of the lower classes, who tend to be ideal for this type of work – pre-brutalized, if you like.' The smile turned into a smirk. 'We've created a security company that is already screening applications, identifying possible NCO material and admin types.'

'Thank you, that is most satisfactory.' The chairman turned to the tall man in the dark suit. 'Are we satisfied with the military aspect of the operation?' He'd been tempted to recruit the general on to the central committee, and the old soldier had seemed keen, but some instinct had made the chairman decide otherwise. The larger the committee, the greater the chance of a leak, and they couldn't risk that now. But there was something else. Not a squeamishness, quite, but a suppressed sense of tainted honour in the military man that made him hesitate. With the decision made, he was happy to leave the liaison to the tall man, himself a former soldier with an SAS background. Well placed, with the best of access and contacts, and entirely without scruples, like the earlier speaker he could be trusted to do what was right, whatever the cost.

'The general assures me everything will be in place. Four regiments based in London and commanded by officers sympathetic to our cause, another regiment in the Midlands and a further two in the north, each fully armed and equipped with heavy weapons. As far as the junior officers and rank and file are concerned, it will be just another realistic anti-terror exercise. When the code word is issued they will take control of key transport links, TV and radio stations and other communications hubs, they'll also guard power stations and refineries. All mobile phone signals and Internet links will be severed, apart from a shadow service that will be operated and utilized by our people. In effect, we will control any and all information the country will receive. When everything is in place the Duke will solemnly inform the nation what has occurred via selected television channels. At the completion of the broadcast he will summon the emergency committee. Once the scale and enormity of the atrocity becomes clear we envisage that the country will immediately rally to our cause and back the new regime.'

The chairman suppressed a shiver as he reflected the power such control of events would give him. To the two other men in the room, he seemed to grow in stature, his hands flat on the oak table in front of him as he raised himself to his feet. He might have been about to make a speech and his eyes had a distant look as he considered the steps he had set in motion. Strong leadership could only be provided by those with the power to enforce it. The army would ensure a peaceful change of leadership in the capital, secure the centre of the country and provide an unassailable show of force in the north, where most opposition was expected. Initially, only carefully selected information would be released. First, they would parade the bodies of the terrorists who had planned and carried out the attack. Then they would provide evidence of links to key individuals who would be detained in the first hours of the changeover and create a wave of revulsion against those they represented and those who had given them succour. As the noose tightened on the non-indigenous community, a few more minor atrocities would no doubt occur to generate doubt in the minds of those most likely to protest against the crackdown. Mass arrests of individuals deemed a threat, while the misguided liberals would be held incommunicado for their own safety. Secret internment camps in remote parts of the country would already be in place to house the most dangerous detainees under a regime that would be correspondingly severe, and any dissent punished by lethal force. Detention centres to hold the majority of the male population until they could be repatriated. In the meantime, the regime would have introduced a rigidly enforced identity card system. The holder's card would allow access to certain categories of food and levels of employment. Naturally, that access would be controlled by the new government and dependent on the cooperation of the holder. Non-indigenous subjects would no longer be allowed to own factories or run shops that could provide support and logistics for the terrorists. Their property rights would be restricted. As they could no longer work they would be forced to turn to the state for support, which would be provided in the form of government-allocated housing and food from state-controlled stores. Accommodation and supplies would only be available in designated areas and, once established, these areas would be subject to restricted access, successfully completing Phase One of the operation: containing the threat from the suspect population.

Phase Two would follow when he was ready.

Strong, decisive leadership. Clarity of thought allied to purity of purpose. The first step to a Greater Britain.

But before that faltering step could be taken the way must be cleared.

The tall man interrupted his thoughts. 'Our man reports that the Duke was drunk yesterday. Drunk and talkative.'

An involuntary sigh escaped the chairman's lips. 'Did he say anything indiscreet?'

'It seems he is on the cusp of a change of circumstances. A change that makes him nervous, but for one thing—'

'He didn't name it?'

'No.' A moment of hesitation. 'You said there had been a setback?'

'It was not something we could have predicted. Our international connection should have prevented the attack. I remonstrated with them, but they weren't in the mood for discussion. It seems they lost someone.'

The former SAS man raised an eyebrow. 'You should have let me arrange the security.'

'Perhaps, Gerald, but, as you're aware, that would have created its own problems.'

'Should we be concerned about the Russians?'

'They appear to be an unfortunate relic of Saintclair's

past and they did us a favour in cleaning up the mess.'

'I would feel better if I knew who they represent.'

'Very well, see what you can do.'

'We have less than a month.'

The chairman stared hard. 'I don't need reminding, thank you. A new avenue of investigation has opened up. Our people are on it now. I want you to check it out and be ready to exploit any opportunities it provides.'

'His name is *Marmaduke* Porter.' Charlotte's lips twisted to avoid smirking as she read the name from her notes. Thin Warsaw sunlight highlighted the flesh-toned plaster and carefully applied make-up that disguised the injury to her forehead. 'He's English and what used to be called a fixer, but now prefers to be known as an international communications consultant.'

'Bully for him.'

She ignored Gault's interjection. 'They wouldn't have found the name if it wasn't for a letter from the Friends of the Teutonic Knights, would you believe, to one of the English-language newspapers in Warsaw. Outraged of Elblag wrote demanding an investigation into the loss of Nortstein Castle. The letter mentioned a development company that may or may not have paid kickbacks to the Communist state governor of the time. Adam's people tracked down the company to somewhere in Jersey and with the application of a little financial *force majeure* a name was forthcoming.'

'Do we have an address?' Jamie asked.

'We do.' She looked triumphantly at Gault. 'He lives on the sun-kissed Greek Island of Corfu. Adam is arranging for the charter of a private jet to fly us direct from Warsaw. By us, I mean Jamie and me. While we are topping up our suntans, Mr Gault is to return to England to give Adam a briefing.'

The former soldier grimaced. 'I'll call him. He needs to know that you two lovebirds shouldn't be let out on your own.'

'You weren't much help at the Wolf's Lair,' she pointed out tartly.

'I—'

'Whatever Adam decides is fine with me,' Jamie interrupted. 'We'd better get packed. If Steele is sending us a private jet, he must be getting impatient.' He threw his satellite phone on the bed beside Gault. 'Use this, it'll save time.'

'I prefer to use my own – in private.' The SBS man got up and stalked from the room.

'What was that about?' Charlotte demanded.

'I don't think he appreciated being reminded that he hung us out to dry.'

'Well, bugger him,' she sniffed. 'He'll do what he's told like the rest of us. The whole point of having him along was to prevent something like that happening. Don't you think it's a bit suspicious that he walked away more or less without a scratch?'

'So did I,' Jamie pointed out.

'Yes, but you saved my life and you were lucky. Maybe there was more than luck to Gault's great escape?'

He wondered what she was implying, but decided that for the moment it didn't matter now that they were parting company with the former SBS man. Something to worry about later.

They left Gault in the international departure lounge at Warsaw Chopin while a guide escorted them to the airport's general aviation terminal where the Beechcraft private jet waited. Two hours later they were approaching Corfu airport at a height so low they seemed to be skimming the sun-dappled wave tops and when they landed people were looking from their hotel balconies down onto the plane. A waiting limousine carried them to the hotel, an elegant wedding-cake-shaped edifice overlooking the anchored yachts in Garitsa Bay. Charlotte dealt with reception and returned with an arch look and a single key. 'After what happened in Poland, I thought it would be more secure if we shared a room. You're not shy, are you?'

'Secure?' He turned away to hide his confusion. What could he say? No was the first thing that came to mind, but that wouldn't be gentlemanly. It implied that she was . . . Anyway, he was too tired to argue. Of course he was attracted to her, but that didn't mean anything would happen. He tried to laugh it off with a lame joke. 'I always sleep on the left.'

'Don't get any ideas.' She grinned. 'It's a twin room. We're here on business.'

In the room on the third floor there was the usual awkward moment after their luggage arrived deciding whose clothes went where. Charlotte took the chance to freshen up while Jamie opened the curtains to the balcony. He'd been vaguely aware of the view as they'd arrived, but now, from his elevated position, it was truly spectacular. The bay curved in a shallow crescent, from a magnificent towering castle on the left to a tree-shrouded headland a mile distant on the right. In front of him a band of aquamarine a hundred yards wide hugged the shore, before gradually turning to a deeper, more intense cobalt scattered with shiny floating gin palaces that must have cost a million apiece and more. In the far distance, softened by a slight haze, lay the coast of Greece – or possibly Albania? He formed a map of the island in his head. According to Adam Steele's sources, Marmaduke Porter lived on the west coast in a villa close to the tourist resort of Paleokastritsa. The 'consultant' would undoubtedly have the information they needed, but, given his profession, was unlikely to be willing to give it up freely. As an incentive, Jamie had Steele's authorization to draw a substantial sum from a bank in Corfu Town. If that didn't work he'd need to find his own way to get the information.

He felt Charlotte at his shoulder. She placed a cold glass in his hand and he took a sip. 'Cheers.'

'It's beautiful,' she said, so close he could feel her breath on his ear.

'Mmm.'

'We can't do anything today. We might as well make the most of it.'

He shuddered at the touch of her lips on the back of his neck.

'I thought we were here on business.'

Her hands reached over his shoulders and he could feel the firm roundness of her breasts against his back as she began to unbutton his shirt. 'Hotel rooms bring out in the worst in me.'

'That's odd.' He slipped round to face her, so their lips were an inch apart. 'I always think they bring out the best in me.'

She drew him hard against her. 'Good,' she said.

And it was.

The shadows of the yacht masts were lengthening on the waters of Garitsa Bay as Jamie sat on the balcony, still not quite certain how what had happened had happened, or how it made him feel about himself. He could hear Charlotte shifting under the covers of the bed they'd shared and he tried to rationalize his feelings for her without any particular success. His mobile phone twittered on the table beside him and he picked it up, automatically going to the far end of the balcony so as not to disturb the English girl.

'Saintclair,' he answered.

'Did you kill her?'

The raw fury in the voice froze the blood in Jamie's

veins and his heart began to pound as if it were trying to escape his rib cage.

'I said, did you kill her?'

A male voice, and something familiar about it, English with a slight inflection. He looked in on Charlotte. What the hell was going on? 'I don't know what you're talking about.'

'You were the last person to see her alive.'

'This convers— What did you say?' A realization was dawning, but he couldn't – wouldn't – allow it to fully form.

'I don't think you understand your situation. Look down at your chest. Slowly.'

Jamie allowed his eyes to drift down to the front of his shirt and the red spot of the laser sited directly over his heart.

'It would be wise not to move.'

'I wasn't planning to.' Jamie understood perfectly that out there on one of the boats a sniper had him in his sights. A pro, armed with something like a Barrett M98 chambered for a 33.8mm magnum round that would blow a hole in him the size of a dinner plate.

'Give me one good reason why I shouldn't kill you.'

'I didn't . . . No, I won't believe it.' He remembered their last moments together. The soft touch of her lips. The slim figure disappearing into the trees, so vibrant and alive and invulnerable. But of course, this wouldn't be happening if it wasn't true. Grief threatened to overwhelm him the way it had when he heard of Abbie's murder. 'She saved my life.'

'They found her face down in the wood with three pistol bullets in her. She was executed.'

'I didn't kill her.'

'Maybe that doesn't matter.' The voice was very familiar now, but harsher than he'd ever heard it. 'Maybe all that matters is that she died because of you.'

The red spot seemed to brighten and he tensed for the strike of the bullet. 'That's for you to decide, David. I'd rather—'

'Do not demean yourself by suggesting you would rather have died in her place, Mr Saintclair. She was worth ten of you.'

Suddenly anger overwhelmed sorrow; a great up-swell of heat and fire that started in the guts and filled his entire body. 'Don't fucking lecture me, *old boy*. I loved her, and she'd still be with me if you hadn't lured her back with whatever lies you came up with. You deceive people for a living, but don't think you can deceive yourself. Your organization pimped itself out to a politically connected multi-millionaire, or she wouldn't have been there. You *knew* those men were following me, yet you still let her walk into that forest alone . . .'

'That was a mistake.'

'Some mistakes cause harm.' He spat the words into the phone. 'Your mistakes kill people.'

'Jamie?' The drowsy voice came from beyond the sliding windows behind him.

He lowered his voice. 'I can't bring her back. Tell me what you want?'

'You owe us, Mr Saintclair. You already owed us, but now you owe us a life. Remember that. If on your travels you encounter anything that might be of interest to the State of Israel, you will contact me directly.'

'And if I were to tell you to fuck off?' Even as he said it, he knew how pathetic the threat was. Their fates had become entwined during the quest for the Sun Stone, and the Mossad spy knew there was an Estonian art dealer and Nazi war criminal whose death in London wouldn't bear close investigation.

Without warning David's tone lost its threat and became businesslike. 'Tomorrow you will speak to a man called Marmaduke Porter?'

'Perhaps. Why?'

'You will ask him about a shipment of canned goods originating in Volgograd on 24 May 2008 and destined for the port of Baku in Azerbaijan, but which made an unscheduled detour in the Caspian Sea, which took it further south. We wish, among other things, to know the final destination of this shipment.'

'And why should he tell me?'

'I doubt he will, but you will further ask him how the facilitation of this shipment would be seen by his former business partners in the light of certain items of information channelled through the CIA Head of Station in

Kuwait City. Again, he will prevaricate and dissemble, but all you need to do is tell him his *new* partners will be in touch.'

'That's all?'

'That is all.'

'You really are a bastard, David.'

'Tell me that the next time your country is fighting for its survival, Mr Saintclair. And one other thing you should know . . . If I discover you had anything to do with her death I will hunt you down to the ends of the earth and you will not escape me, whatever stone you attempt to hide under.'

He rang off before Jamie could reply. When he returned to the room, Charlotte sat up naked in bed rubbing her eyes. 'Who was that?'

'An old friend.'

XXVII

Next morning, they headed north in their hire car. For the first few miles, Jamie kept to the coast, but after the tourist hotspot of Gouvia he turned off into the less populated interior and a road that crossed the mountainous spine of the island. The narrow highway twisted through endless groves of olive trees and villages too tiny to be worth a name, where leather-featured men and women sat in the shade outside their houses selling home-grown oil, oranges, lemons and peaches. Eventually, they reached a towering height where they could view the sea again and began to descend in ever more precipitous turns. As he drove, Jamie attempted to keep one eye on the rear-view mirror, but the constant braking at every corner and the way the local truck drivers treated the narrow roads as if they were the sole proprietors made it impossible. He contented himself by pulling in two or three times where the road permitted and allowing the traffic behind to overtake. David's threat was reason enough to be careful. The Mossad agent was out there somewhere and Jamie wanted him to know he knew. But there was more. Whoever killed Sarah Grant was out there too: a deadly threat without face or form.

He glanced at Charlotte, lying back in the passenger seat with her face to the sun, mirrored sunglasses covering her eyes. Should he have told her? The scar on her forehead was still visible beneath the make-up. Safer for her not to know, he'd decided. There were things he didn't yet understand, niggling questions that needed answers. Adam Steele's aide had unbuttoned her shirt to allow the sun to reach the soft curve of her breasts and they brought back a memory of the day before. Jamie felt a wave of affection for the English girl until a supermarket truck almost forced him off the road and into the ditch. He shook his head ruefully. Keep an eye on the road, you silly bastard, haven't you got trouble enough?

Around noon they reached a magnificent clover-leaf bay, a symphony in blue and green that must once have been achingly beautiful, but was now cluttered with hotels, bars and apartments, and overlooked by villas that perched on every cliff-top site capable of construction. Jamie asked at a souvenir shop for the address he had been given and the young woman and the man who appeared to be the owner exchanged shrugs before directing him south, with the suggestion that he try Liapades. Here the roads clung to the hillsides like ivy roots on a south-facing wall and a similar instruction took him to Giannades, a hill-top village where fewer people seemed to have the Corfiot facility for the English language, but where a woman kindly drew him a map.

'Has it occurred to you we may not be very welcome?' Jamie steered the hire car round another twisting bend among the olive trees.

Charlotte thought it over. 'At least he's agreed to see us.'

'Great. "Will you walk into my parlour? said the spider to the fly."'

She tilted her sunglasses back. 'It can't be any worse than Poland, and we survived that.'

'All the same, and much though it pains me, I wish we had Gault along for the ride.'

'Too late now.' She pointed to an electric security gate set into a tall drystone wall. 'I think this is it.'

Jamie pressed the access button and waited. In an olive tree to one side of the gate he noticed a small security camera scanning the road before the gate swung open without any form of acknowledgement from the householder. Inside, an unmade track cut into the cliff led them to a magnificent villa perched above the sea like a fish eagle watching for prey. From the front terrace the ground dropped sheer past five or six hundred feet of grey rock and bushy outcrops to a narrow strip of sand that must only have been accessible by boat. This was a man who liked his privacy.

They parked the car beside a garage filled with a Range Rover and a large Bentley, and a tanned youth wearing only a pair of shorts bounded from the house and opened the door for Charlotte. '*Kalimera.*' He gave them the traditional Greek greeting with a short bow. 'Please follow me.'

Charlotte studied the polished muscles and honed legs as he walked away. She felt Jamie's gaze and turned to meet it with a sardonic half-smile. 'Don't worry, darling. He's *very* pretty, but I like my men to be the real thing.'

They followed the young Adonis inside to a large, well-lit room where the owner of the house lounged comfortably in a chair with a towel covering his waist. The walls were lined with paintings and ordinarily Jamie would have taken pleasure in studying them, instead his eyes were automatically drawn to the remarkable figure in the centre. Marmaduke Porter might have been anywhere between forty and sixty, but it was difficult to tell. He had a curiously small face, which seemed out of place on his large, quite round head, a head that perched directly on the shoulders of the largest body Jamie had ever seen. Drooping folds of flesh overwhelmed the chair beneath him and each of his enormous thighs encompassed the width of Charlotte's waist. Thick curls that were a little too pristinely black fell to his shoulders, but otherwise his smooth skin appeared entirely devoid of hair. The young man took his place behind a pair of blubbery shoulders and, pouring oil on his fingers, plunged them deep into the flesh, kneading and grinding until Porter sighed with satisfaction.

'You must forgive me if I continue my daily routine, but my doctor insists.' He smiled. The voice was pure English public school and languorous, as if the speaker was half asleep, but the deep-set dark eyes that studied them were filled with a combination of shrewd intelligence and wary suspicion. Porter picked up a wine glass half filled with golden liquid and took a deep draught. 'Too much reliance on the finer things in life, he says. But how could one live without the finer things in life, I ask you?'

Jamie smiled acknowledgement. 'I admire your good taste. Unless I miss my guess, your collection includes at least two Cezannes and a Chagall, and the large nude dominating the far wall would appear to be one of Herr Gustav Klimt's later works. Some people think him a little fussy, but I rather admire his worship of the female form.'

Marmaduke Porter laughed, making his great jowls quiver. 'You know your art, but please don't tell my insurers, Mr . . .'

'Jamie Saintclair, and this is my . . . assistant . . . Miss Charlotte Wellesley. I hope this is a convenient time for us to talk?'

Porter's eyes appraised Charlotte with new interest. 'Related to the old Iron Duke, I trust,' he chuckled. 'Of course, you're most welcome, as long as you're prepared to take us as we are. We're rather set in our ways, Spiros and I.' He raised a hand and stroked the young man's cheek, ending with what looked like a painful pinch that only made its victim smile. He whispered something and Spiros backed away, giving him space to heave himself to his feet. The towel on his lap dropped to one side, and Charlotte turned her eyes away from a symbol of manhood that matched the scale of Marmaduke Porter's girth. Within a second Spiros had enveloped him in a voluminous white robe and Porter led the way to the balcony, where another bedewed bottle of wine and a single glass waited at a parasol-shaded table set with three chairs. The fat man took the chair facing the glittering expanse of the Ionian Sea and waved Jamie and Charlotte to the other seats. Spiros removed the cork and smirked at Jamie as he poured a generous glass of fine Meursault and turned away.

'Mind your manners, little pig.' Porter slapped the younger man on the rump. Spiros ran off laughing and returned with two more glasses. 'Just our little game,' the fat man assured them as he poured. His voice took on a more serious quality. 'You said you wanted to talk to me about a lucrative business deal, but you were not particularly forthcoming about the detail.'

Jamie nodded, meeting the other man's challenging stare. 'Deal as in the past tense, but lucrative in the present, depending on the arrangements we agree and the information you provide.'

'Naughty,' Porter admonished with a wag of a plump finger. A twinkle of light advertised the presence of a gold ring with a large diamond buried somewhere deep in the fleshy digit. 'Of course, there's no guarantee I'll agree to anything. Firstly, I have to know what's in it for Dukey to even consider speaking to you. As you've noticed, my time is precious . . . and expensive.'

'Our client has authorized a goodwill payment as a symbol of our good faith.' Jamie reached into his jacket and placed a well-filled envelope on the table. Marmaduke Porter didn't even look at it.

'My sources at the airport tell me you arrived on a private jet,' he said patiently. Jamie produced another identical envelope and placed it beside the first. The fat hands reached out and weighed the two packages, before slipping the flaps and running a finger across the edge of the notes inside.

'Swiss francs.' He nodded gravely. 'I'm so glad to be dealing with a man who understands economics. All around you on this island you will see nothing but beauty, but it is like a peach rotting from the inside. Bite into it and you will find only corruption. Shortages and blackouts, boycotts and strikes. Even Spiros threatened to come out in solidarity with the workers and I had to chastise the little pig. The Greeks have fallen out of love with the euro. For the moment, the dollar is king, but this,' he took out one of the crisp new notes and held it up to the light, 'is a most acceptable substitute.'

'Our client has also authorized payment of the sum of fifty thousand euros in the currency of your choice, dependent on the outcome of our negotiations.'

'Fifty thousand pounds?'

'Of course.' Jamie smiled. 'You must have misheard me.'

Marmaduke Porter swept the envelopes into the pocket of his robe. 'Then you have earned the right to ask your question.'

Before Jamie could speak, Spiros returned with a tray filled with dishes of immaculately presented local delicacies: whitebait lightly coated in batter; fat langoustines glowing pink in their shells; juice-filled baby tomatoes; thick, grainy hummus; peppers, yellow and scarlet; grilled morsels of meat and chicken pierced with skewers.

'You must try Spiros' deep-fried zucchini,' Porter insisted, pointing to a pile of thin slices of emerald-edged gold. 'It is the best on the island.' His hands scooped the discs onto a plate and hovered over a pyramid of stuffed sardines. 'Please,' he indicated to Jamie, 'no business is so urgent that it cannot wait for food.'

'Of course.' Charlotte beamed. She took Jamie's plate and filled it, before repeating the exercise with her own. Marmaduke Porter looked on approvingly as Spiros selected him a gargantuan pile of appetizers.

'A toast.' He smiled. 'To the finer things in life.'

The food was wonderful, but Jamie's patience was wearing thin by the time Spiros cleared the table. Porter had drunk the better part of a second bottle of the Meursault. Now he announced that he couldn't possibly talk business so soon after lunch. It was his habit to retire for a nap during the heat of the day. They could relax by the pool. Perhaps have a swim. They shouldn't be shy. No one worried about bathing costumes in this house. He made it obvious there could be no argument and walked from the terrace with Spiros, his hand caressing the back of the younger man's neck.

Jamie and Charlotte exchanged glances.

'What now?' she asked.

'I suppose we do what the man says.'

Her nose wrinkled. 'It's a long time since I've been skinny-dipping.'

'Not that,' he laughed. 'No matter how appealing the idea is. We relax and enjoy the view, which is, you'll acknowledge, spectacular.' He walked to the balcony and looked over, his head spinning for a moment as it took in the vertiginous six-hundred-foot drop. The coast stretched away to north and south, a saw-toothed barrier between mountain and sea, between a medley of name-less blues and a mottled patchwork of grey and green. 'I could do with a rest after Dortmund and Madrid . . .'

'And Poland.'

'Especially after Poland.'

He felt her hands around his waist and her head on his shoulder.

'But not too much of a rest.'

He grinned. 'No, I think I'll have made a dramatic recovery by tonight.'

They walked across to the sun loungers by the mirrored surface of the infinity pool.

'So, we don't search the place while they're doing . . . whatever it is they're doing?'

'There's no point. If there was anything to find Marmaduke Porter wouldn't have given us the run of his house.'

She lay back on one of the loungers and unbuttoned her blouse to the waist, revealing a flat, tanned stomach. 'What do you think of him?'

Jamie tried to ignore the golden flesh and the curves emphasized by her black silk bra. 'Arrogant, intelligent, sophisticated. An unscrupulous rogue, though that doesn't make him any worse than the bankers who've put the world in its present spot.'

'I quite like him.' She smiled. 'I'd been prepared for some greasy fast-talking little spiv. Marmaduke Porter has a certain charm. I may not approve of his lifestyle – Spiros can't be any older than eighteen and he must be well past fifty – but for someone who deals in the type of business he does, he seems refreshingly honest. A man who is very comfortable in his own skin, given that there's so much of it.'

Jamie looked over the villa, pondering what David had told him and suspecting the luxurious retreat might not be the product of years of refreshing honesty. 'Of course, it could all be a front, and Marmaduke could be in there plotting to take us to the cleaners or sell us down the river, rather than doing whatever it is we think he's doing.'

'I suppose we'll find out when they're finished.'

XXVIII

'We'd like to know what happened to Nortstein Castle,'
Jamie said when Marmaduke Porter reappeared on the
terrace dressed in a silk kimono designed for one of the
Japanese sumo wrestlers he so resembled. The big man
frowned as he took his seat, his eyes almost disappearing
into the folds of his face. He noticed Charlotte taking a
moleskin notebook from her bag and raised a plump
hand. 'No notes, please.'

'Don't you want to search us for recording equipment?' Jamie suggested playfully.

'I can assure you I would already know, Mr Saintclair,
unless the equipment was so sophisticated my machines
could not trace it, in which case I'd be unlikely to find
it on your person. I prefer to trust to your honesty.'
He laughed at the unlikely thought. 'You understand
that my reputation, such as it is, has been built on a
penchant for discretion as much as my ability to bring
people together and make things happen in difficult

and unlikely circumstances. My clients trust me to keep their secrets. However, sometimes certain facts can be disclosed without abusing their trust, and your earlier generosity deserves some reward. The question is where to start and what to tell?'

'I always find it simpler to start at the beginning.'

'Indeed.' The fat man stared out to sea for a few moments, apparently mesmerized by what he saw there. 'I bought this place for the view, you know, and of course the privacy, but I have never been near the balcony, partially because I suffer from vertigo, but also because I am not a man who takes risks. You must bear that in mind as we continue. Information is not dead material. It is a living thing that changes shape and value depending on who has it and who wants it. It can have a positive influence, or a negative. It can be beneficial to whoever has it, yet in other circumstances it may be fatal.'

'Are you threatening us, Mr Porter?' Jamie asked mildly.

'You misunderstand me, Mr Saintclair. I am a creator, not a destroyer.' He paused and the odd little face creased in concentration. 'It began, if memory serves me, in the summer of nineteen eighty-seven. I was a young man and ambitious. I'd had dealings with the Polish government for a few years, mainly in the area of asset sales likely to accrue foreign currency, which they badly needed at the time.' Porter nodded sagely, reflecting on a job well done. 'You must remember that the so-called iron grip the Communists had on the country was never really much more than a weak man's grip on the collar of a large and frisky dog. It was always on the verge of breaking free. In nineteen eighty-seven they were under pressure on several fronts. Pope John Paul the Second's visit had emboldened the Catholic majority and galvanized the priesthood to become involved socially and politically. Walesa's Solidarity movement had been forced underground, but was threatening to break out into the open rather in the manner of an erupting volcano. General Jaruzelski's grip on power was weakening—'

'I'm sorry,' Jamie interrupted. 'But we didn't come here for a history lesson.'

'Of course,' Porter acknowledged airily with a smile towards Charlotte, who sat back with her legs crossed, sipping at a glass of iced water. 'I am merely setting the scene in the manner of the gentleman who introduces one of Shakespeare's plays at the Globe. You are offering a great deal of money, you deserve a little entertainment. So, in nineteen eighty-seven the men who ran Poland and Poland's administrative regions were nervous and already looking to the future; a Communist-free future. In the August of that year I was approached by a certain party by way of another certain party. The certain party was a foundation, endowed with considerable means, which had an interest in Polish culture and heritage. Its benefactors feared for the well-being of certain aspects of that heritage under the current, and possibly future,

Polish regime and wished to purchase for shipment to its home country an example that could be protected and studied at leisure.'

'A castle?'

'Indeed. I'm sure you'll understand, Mr Saintclair, that I am a man who is often asked to provide unusual items and unusual services, but even I was surprised at this request. More so when I was told that they wished to purchase a *specific* castle, and, dare I say rather fortunately, an insignificant one. The export permit was surprisingly easy to arrange. Not many people in Warsaw were interested in a small German castle up near the Kaliningrad border where they have castles to spare. The good citizens of the Olzstyn region were another matter. German or not, the castle was part of their heritage.' A rumble heralded the departure of a jet from Corfu Town and it crossed the mountains behind the house with its afterburners straining. Jamie looked up to see the white underbelly etched against a sky of pristine blue and as Marmaduke Porter waited for silence, Spiros appeared with a third – or possibly fourth – bottle of the Meursault. The consultant took a long drink before continuing his story.

'Fortunately for me, the party chairman of the administrative region was a man of the old school, a dictator in all but name. He was also one of those preparing for their future I mentioned earlier. I was able to ensure he could look forward to a long and happy retirement with regular holidays in Switzerland, where most of his money is now held. As for the good burgers of Olzstyn, thanks to a hefty injection of zlotys to build a new school and a hospital in Ketrzyn, they discovered their feelings for the castle were not quite as passionate as they thought. The goodwill this bought also allowed me to use a local labour force, which might not have been possible had there been significant community opposition.' He sat back in his chair with a satisfied smile and a soft burp. 'We trucked the entire castle, right down to the curtains and hangings, to Gdansk and shipped it in containers to its eventual destination.'

'And that destination was?'

'Client confidentiality.'

'And the client's name?'

Porter didn't even deign to answer the question and in the silence that followed Jamie pondered what he'd been told, and the implications it raised.

'The client must have given you very specific instructions if you were paying attention to the curtains and wall hangings of a six-hundred-year-old castle – the window glass and wood panelling too, I'm sure – that must have been looted when the Russians over-ran East Prussia?'

For the first time a defensive note crept into Marmaduke Porter's voice. 'I think your question answers itself.'

'All I'm trying to elicit from you is the level of detail involved.' Jamie smiled. 'For instance, I believe the hangings may have included certain items related to a former occupier of the building from the time of the Teutonic Knights? You were aware of the association with the Teutonic Knights?'

'I'm not a student of the history of the Baltic regions, Mr Saintclair,' Porter said dismissively. 'And now I think we must bring this interview to a close. I may have said more than I intended.' He sniffed. 'I'm aware that your client is unlikely to be satisfied with what I have been able to divulge, but I believe I have given enough quite specific information to have earned, let us say, half of the agreed amount?'

'I'll have to discuss that with my client.'

The fat man's face relaxed. 'Of course, but I'm sure he will see my point of view.' He sat with the smile fixed on his fleshy features, waiting for them to rise from their seats. Jamie didn't move and Charlotte, though she wasn't certain she understood the undercurrents of what was happening, took her lead from him.

'I have one further question about the castle.' Jamie broke the silence. 'Were you given specific instructions about the safeguarding of certain artefacts that may not have been in their natural position in the castle, but were nevertheless part of its fabric, or that of its out-buildings?'

He had to admire Marmaduke Porter. His expression didn't alter. Only the slightest flicker of panic in the deep-set eyes signalled that the next words he would say were going to be a lie.

'No. Now I really must insist, Spi—'

Jamie raised a hand. 'That really wouldn't be wise, Marmaduke, not for a man who doesn't take risks.'

Porter heaved himself out of his chair, his whole body quivering with outraged dignity. 'I will not be threatened in my own house. I really must ask—'

'A shipment of canned goods left Volgograd on 24 May 2008,' Jamie quoted. 'It was destined for the port of Baku in Azerbaijan, but it made an unscheduled detour in the Caspian Sea, which took it further south. Some friends of mine wish, among other things, to know the final destination of this shipment.'

The blood drained from the big man's face and he slumped back in the chair, his features a mask of dismay. 'I don't know what you're talking about.'

'I think you do, Marmaduke. And I have to insist that you answer my questions. What was the destination of the castle and who was your client?'

'You know I can't tell you that. My reputation would be destroyed.'

'The only people who will ever know are the people at this table.'

'And my client.'

'Your client is a foundation – a faceless entity carrying out an act of laudable cultural preservation. The people who run it would have no incentive to broadcast who had provided us with its name.'

'You don't understand,' Porter choked. 'It is more than my life is worth to tell you.'

He was pleading now and Jamie had to suppress a

twinge of compassion that wasn't helped by the glare of disappointment Charlotte directed at him. He took a deep breath and twisted the knife.

'My friend said to ask you how the facilitation of the Volgograd shipment would be seen by your former business partners in the light of certain information channelled through the CIA Head of Station in Kuwait City?'

Marmaduke Porter groaned and began to shake as if he was having a seizure. 'No, Christ, no. You can't, they'll—'

'Give me the name, Marmaduke. The name and the destination and we'll be on our way.'

'Please, no.'

'Do you want to know what else my friend said?'

A few mumbled words spilled from the fleshy lips. Jamie signalled Charlotte to get her notebook ready. 'Could you repeat that please?'

Charlotte scribbled the name and darted a puzzled look at Jamie.

Jamie rose to his feet. 'I know you won't believe it, Marmaduke, but I'm truly sorry it had to be like this. If it's any consolation, fifty thousand pounds in Swiss francs will be couriered to you in the next few days.'

It appeared the money didn't mean much to Marmaduke Porter, because he didn't even look up as they left. Jamie hesitated at the door and looked back with a pang of regret at the broken man sitting with his head cradled in his big hands. 'Er, there's just one more thing, old chum. Your new partners will be in touch soon. Do you understand that, Marmaduke? Your new partners will be in touch soon. I'd be a bit more forthcoming with them.'

They left the room to the sound of frantic, chest-tearing sobbing.

XXIX

'Why would something called the Bialystok Foundation transport a demolished Polish castle to New York?'

'I don't know,' Jamie admitted. Back in the hotel he still felt guilty about what he'd done to Marmaduke Porter. Maybe he could justify it by telling himself that if he hadn't passed on the message, the Israelis would have got someone else to do it, but he knew that was lily-livered hogwash. On the one hand he wished he'd never got involved with Adam Steele, but on the other was the tantalizing possibility that it was true. That Excalibur existed and he, Jamie Saintclair, hitherto purveyor of other people's second-rate daubs, was the man who might discover it. He thrust the thought from his head and tried to concentrate. 'I'm certain the five swords were part of the shipment, but there are easier and less expensive ways to smuggle them to the States. Maybe this isn't about the swords at all. The answer could be something to do with the castle itself. Remember that the Teutonic Knights based themselves on the Templars. When the Order was disbanded and Philip of France had their leader Jacques de Molay burned at the stake, they were said to have gathered a great treasure that later vanished. Who's to say they didn't hand it over to their brother knights in the East for safe keeping? Perhaps Nortstein Castle was the repository of that treasure? I think we need to go back to London to talk to Adam.'

Charlotte nodded. 'I'll let him know once I've checked out the foundation.'

'That's all right. I'll call him now.' Jamie reached for the sat-phone, but she laid her hand on his.

'Leave it until we reach the airport. We have better things to do with our time.'

David Van Buren III closed his eyes as he lay back in the Jacuzzi on the after deck of the MV *Diana*, a beautiful classic motor yacht, the loan of which was the three-week gift of a grateful Italian industrialist to the United States ambassador to NATO. A satisfied smile wreathed his face as the squeals of his children drifted up from the bathing platform where they played at the port side. He knew he needn't worry about their safety because the au pair and one of his five bodyguards would be with them. His ever-beautiful wife, Maryanne, was reading as usual up on the sun deck.

Christ, he'd needed this break, and the offer of the yacht had come just at the right time. Things had gone quiet in Afghanistan, or as quiet as they ever did in that benighted country, after a start to the year that had stretched him to the limit with multiple IED casualties, helicopter crashes and the usual European pissing contests and threats to pull out their military contingents. He'd managed to calm things, but it had worn him down to the point where he felt fifty going on ninety. Later in the year there'd be the running sore of Kosovo to consider and the negotiations over missile defence. But, for now, he could relax, even if his cell phone was never more than two feet away.

They'd flown down from Brussels to Venice and boarded the yacht after two wonderful nights at the Cipriani. MV *Diana* could carry up to twenty-six passengers in complete luxury, but her crew of twenty-four were having it easy with only eleven on board. She sure was a beauty, a real Sophia Loren of the seas, all sophistication and sleek lines, with the polished brass and glowing mahogany that came with her pedigree. She'd been launched way back in the twenties, before the Crash had given her kind of extravagance a bad name, but she'd been refitted in the last decade and kitted out with the kind of modern amenities no self-respecting super-yacht would be without: the pool, the cinema, the sauna and the gym. Two hundred and sixty feet long, with a beam of thirty-nine and a top speed of ten knots from her quadruple steam engines, she was a floating home from home, with the added benefit that the sun was guaranteed to shine every day. Not that they'd only spent their time sunbathing. On the way south they'd marvelled at the opulence of the Roman Emperor Diocletian's Palace in Split, walked the walls of ancient Dubrovnik and only yesterday they'd wandered the narrow streets of Corfu Town, visiting the New Fortress while the *Diana* was resupplying. To cap a perfect day, the kids had been able to watch a crazy cricket match in the park from a restaurant on the Liston Arcade.

Later, there'd be reports to read – you couldn't totally escape the job. But for now he was happy to enjoy the tranquillity of Agni Bay after a lunch enlivened by the proximity at the next table of the crew of the Russian oligarch's yacht moored about two hundred yards off the starboard bow. The way they'd eyed up his security detail reminded him of stags at the beginning of a rut, but a round of drinks and a few toasts had ended that particular Cold War.

He was still smiling at the memory when he noticed a curious phenomenon. The world turned first red, then blue and he seemed to be spinning above what had once been the yacht, but was now a spreading ball of fire. A dream, surely? The reality only became clear when gravity regained its grip on the body of David Van Buren III, minus both legs and one arm, and he plunged back into the flaming wreck of the *Diana* with a scream that the waiters at the Taverna Agni would have nightmares about for a very long time.

Even before the echo of the explosion died, Stefano, who ran the boat taxi business from the jetty, had cast off. He gunned the boat out towards the pool of flame surrounding the sinking boat and plucked three children and the nanny from the waters. The tender of the Russian billionaire's yacht picked up most of the crew, but it would be days before divers from the Greek navy recovered what was left of the ambassador and his wife.

Two hours later Al-Qaida claimed responsibility for the attack for its Albanian wing in a phone call to an Athens news agency. They cited brotherhood with the Taliban and justice for the indiscriminate slaughter of Afghan civilians by NATO forces.

'This will harden attitudes in the United States against Islamic extremists,' Adam Steele predicted, waving the rolled-up newspaper as if it was a conductor's baton. Jamie and Charlotte had flown in from Corfu the previous evening and the banker had insisted they come to a breakfast meeting in the vast dining room of the Mayfair house. 'The Senate is already calling on the President to authorize drone strikes in Albania and extend those against Al-Qaida targets in Somalia and the Yemen to camps in Uganda and even Kenya—'

'I doubt his Kenyan relatives would be too impressed.' Nobody laughed and Gault's grin faded under his employer's glare. Adam Steele didn't like to be interrupted.

'The world's fault lines are becoming more defined and deeper,' he continued. 'We've had America and the Twin Towers, and now this. Russia and the Moscow tube bombings. The Bali bombings aimed at Australian tourists. The Mumbai terror attacks in India. Explosions across the European mainland and the M25 massacre in the United Kingdom. China, too, has its own problems with Islamic extremists, but it does not advertise them and has an effective and very permanent way of dealing with them.' Jamie looked up and found Steele's eyes on him. 'Perhaps we could learn from them.'

The art dealer shook his head. 'All you'd do is create martyrs for the cause. Abbie wouldn't have wanted to see any more blood spilled.'

'As it happens, I agree.' Steele nodded. 'But what I'm trying to say is that we are reaching a tipping point, and not just in Britain, when, if Governments do not act, the people will.'

'I was wondering if there's a link between Al-Qaida and the sword,' Jamie frowned. 'Or the search for the sword. It's as if they're shadowing us wherever we go. Madrid, Poland, and now Corfu.' Steele laid the newspaper down on the mahogany table beside the evidence they'd gathered: the codex, the envelope containing the medals Inge Lauterbacher had given Jamie, the Lauterbacher journal, and Charlotte's slim file on Heinrich Himmler's Knights of the Round Table. Jamie wondered if the collection had been put there to embarrass them. It was such a paltry return for all the time and money Steele had invested. 'I suppose you can explain Madrid and Corfu as unlikely coincidences, but what about Poland?'

He saw Steele and Gault exchange glances. The former SBS man nodded. 'It is not widely known,' Adam Steele said carefully, 'but Mr Gault was involved in certain operations in Afghanistan that resulted in terminal damage to the higher echelons of the Al-Qaida leadership. He was even given a shiny piece of silverware for his efforts, which unfortunately he is not allowed to wear in public. Not the highest level of terrorist leadership, but high enough to make him a target for revenge. That would go some way to explaining their pursuit of you and the attack in Poland.'

'It's one explanation,' Jamie conceded, but he wondered, if that were the case, why Rashid and Hassan had been so keen to remove his head, but had never even mentioned Gault.

'It is the only explanation. Come, we're being side-tracked.' Steele must have made some kind of signal, because Charlotte produced a handful of printed reports, which she distributed to the three men, keeping the last for herself. 'Your theory about a possible Templar treasure is fascinating, Jamie,' the banker smiled, 'but immaterial. My only interest is in Excalibur.'

He nodded to Charlotte and she turned to the first page of the report with a nervous smile at Jamie. 'The Bialystok Foundation was set up in the early nineteen seventies to strengthen cultural links between Poland and the United States in the wake of the Communist takeover,' she said, her voice becoming more confident with each word. 'It makes sense because Polish Americans make up the largest ethnic group of Slavic origin in the United States and at the last count there were at least ten million of them. The foundation sponsored exchanges between arts groups, sporting organizations, Polish-language classes, and that sort of thing. Its offices were in a rather prestigious area of Washington, not far from Langley. At one point there were rumours it was a CIA front, but that's never been proved. The fact that the Ministry of Public Security allowed it to operate and the Polish government actively encouraged its activities is evidence the authorities there certainly believed it was clean. The reason for those suspicions may be the accounts, which are a little murky and involve a number of offshore banks, but again nothing illegal has ever been proved.' She frowned. 'For that reason we have no insight into the incomings and outgoings in and around the summer of nineteen eighty-seven when Mr Porter was doing business with them.'

'Who was behind it?' Jamie asked.

Charlotte consulted her notes. 'The trustees have included a number of eminent Polish Americans and ex-patriates. Businessmen, scientists, professors of the arts and philanthropists . . .'

'Any war heroes?'

'We're having their backgrounds checked,' she assured him. 'There are no public records of the meetings, but we have uncovered one thing that might be of interest. At some point in nineteen eighty-seven three of the six directors either resigned or retired.'

'Doesn't prove anything,' Gault growled.

'No, it doesn't, but the timing is interesting, don't you think?' She looked to Jamie for support, but he was frowning at the piece of paper in front of him.

'An organization like this would normally have a patron or a founder?'

She checked her notes again. 'Sorry, I should have thought of that. Give me five minutes.'

When she'd left the room Steele turned to Jamie. 'What do you think?'

'Charlotte's right, the timing of the board changes is interesting, but it doesn't really take us anywhere. Maybe we could have someone interview them to find out why they quit? Say some magazine is thinking of doing an article on the foundation's good work. Maybe the fact that the Bialystok Foundation is so secretive is a clue in itself. An organization like that would normally be much more transparent – trumpeting their good works to the world.'

'Unless those good works included stealing Polish castles?'

'Exactly,' Jamie said.

'Then—'

Charlotte swept back into the room before Steele could answer. 'The current patron of the organization is Lukasz Pisarek, a fifty-four-year-old Professor of Eastern European Studies at Harvard University.'

Jamie shook his head. 'Too young.'

'He took over eight years ago from the previous

patron, Mr Harold Webster, an industrialist of Reno, Nevada.'

Adam Steele banged his fist on the table in frustration. 'This is getting us nowhere. We're running out of time.'

Jamie stared at him. This was the first time he'd heard of a timescale. 'I . . .' Something Charlotte said flicked a switch in his head. 'Wait a minute. What did you say?'

'Harold Webster, an industrialist?'

'No, the other part.'

'Reno, Nevada.'

Steele frowned as Jamie went to the table and emptied Rolf Lauterbacher's medals onto the polished surface. The art dealer studied the postmark on the empty envelope. 'What do you know.' He smiled. 'Whoever was corresponding with our Nazi friend was doing it from Reno, Nevada.'

Adam Steele's face split into a shark-toothed grin and he turned to Charlotte. 'I think you should book flights to the States.'

When the others had left to make their preparations, Adam Steele flicked through the pages of the newspaper. The item, on the International page, was so small, only a single paragraph not even worthy of a headline, that he almost missed it.

Corfu, Greece. Police are investigating the death of an English ex-patriot and his nurse at a villa on the island. Marmaduke Porter, 54, and Spiros Dimopoulou, 19, are believed to have fallen from the balcony of the house near Paleokastritsa on the island's west coast.

He wondered for a moment whether to tell them, but decided not. He didn't want Jamie Saintclair side-tracked at this stage of the operation. Otherwise, his only reaction was curiosity. Whoever was responsible had saved him a great deal of trouble.

XXX

'We're here.' Gault's voice woke Jamie from a nervy, jet-lagged slumber where he'd been dreaming of being chased by enormous knives with a life of their own. He hoped it wasn't a portent for the next few hours. Fortunately, when he forced his eyes open he was greeted by a breathtaking Sierra Nevada vista of snow-draped mountain and steel-blue lake, the slopes below carpeted by a dense covering of pines and the glittering waters stretching into the distance. But while his eyes feasted on the scene, his mind struggled to catch up. He remembered that Charlotte had stayed in New York, putting together some kind of exit strategy in the event they actually did find anything they needed to get out of the United States without the authorities knowing about it. Then he and Gault had flown west to Reno.

'Where exactly is here?'

'Lake Tahoe. We're about an hour out of Reno. Incline Village is on the bay in front of us, but the

334

place we're looking for is somewhere in the hills off Highway Thirty-eight.' He nodded to the left, where a road hugged the Nevada shore. 'But given that the lake is more than twenty miles long and our man doesn't encourage visitors, I could do with another pair of eyes.'

Jamie picked up the file Adam Steele had put together on Harold Webster. For such a successful businessman Webster had kept a surprisingly low profile even before the age of the TV star entrepreneurs like Donald Trump, Warren Buffett and Bill Gates. He'd made his first fortune manufacturing electrical batteries after the war, where he'd served as a flight engineer in the US Eighth Air Force, then identified the potential of television before any of his rivals. But the real money had come when he'd branched out into computers at just the right time. The few pictures of him had all been taken in the fifties and he'd disappeared from public view entirely after the death of his son and successor in less than clear circumstances about a decade earlier. Since then he'd lived as a recluse on his ranch in the mountains. What linked an American multi-millionaire with a dismantled Polish castle? Jamie still wasn't sure of the what, but he was certain the link existed. Harold 'Hal' Webster had been the original patron of the Bialystok Foundation long before it had attracted its respectable veneer of distinguished Polish board members. The foundation was Hal's baby. And the envelope containing the late Rolf Lauterbacher's medals and addressed to the former SS man had a Reno, Nevada, postmark. Coincidence?

Maybe, but as an old friend had told him, there was no such thing as a coincidence when you had a dead body at your feet.

Equally interesting was the fact that Hal Webster hadn't answered any of Adam Steele's enquiries. All right, a recluse was hardly going to welcome a request for a meeting, but you'd think he'd be curious enough to ask what it was about, especially when it was accompanied by the offer of a substantial donation to his pet foundation. In Jamie's experience, historical artefacts and rich men went together like the proverbial apple pie and ice cream. Excalibur was nearby. As Adam Steele would say, he could feel it in his bones.

And that was why Mr Hal Webster was about to get a surprise visit: if they ever found the ranch.

They took the winding road down through the village past substantial mansions and condos hidden amongst the trees. When they reached an intersection by the lake, Gault turned the big SUV on to Tahoe Boulevard and followed the shoreline at the foot of towering mountain peaks that seemed to hang over them like a gigantic Sword of Damocles.

'Gold Rush country,' Jamie said to Gault as they passed the rusting skeleton of some kind of heavy equipment. 'Fortunes made and lost in a day.' The former SBS man only grunted. 'You don't like me much do you, Mr Gault?'

'It's not a question of liking. You're an amateur. Amateurs get people killed.'

Sarah Grant's face appeared in Jamie's head and he went very still. Just for a moment he wondered if Gault was mocking him about her death. Someone had killed Sarah, and he had spent the days since David's concentration-enhancing phone call on the Corfu balcony trying to work out who. The most likely explanation was that she'd been murdered by the lone Al-Qaida assassin who'd escaped from the forest, but there was another possibility. Gault had been AWOL at the Wolf's Lair for the whole shooting match. What if the SBS man had been lying? What if, instead of running the other way, he'd followed them? He'd no doubt Gault had access to weapons. It would have given him ample time to put three bullets in Sarah Grant and then get back to the crash site at the same time as Jamie. Then there were the hints that Charlotte had dropped before they flew to Corfu. *Maybe there was more than luck to Gault's great escape.* 'Remind me where you got to while I was so busy being an amateur at the Wolf's Lair?' he said.

Gault stared at his companion as if he'd sensed the change in atmosphere. 'Now don't get me wrong, your lordship. You didn't do too badly. How many was it? Three? Four? And all with a Second World War pop gun. Proper little Rambo we are.' His voice turned sly. 'Maybe if you'd dumped your little squeeze Charlotte a bit sooner, we wouldn't have needed help from your Russki mates. Still, it must have taken some doing. All those trigger-happy ragheads after your blood and you managed to outfight them.'

Jamie turned to him. 'Everybody needs a little luck, Mr Gault. Even you.'

'Why are you getting so worked up all of a sudden?' Gault felt the cold eyes on him and his fingers fumbled for the radio, filling the car with the sound of a wailing country-and-western crooner. 'We can't be far away now.'

'I lost a friend back there and I wondered if you had anything to do with it.'

'Hermann?' Gault looked at him as if he'd gone crazy. 'Hermann wasn't a friend, he was a Kraut hustler. Hermann, a friend.' He chuckled. Jamie sank back in his seat. If Gault had anything to do with Sarah Grant's murder he was hiding it very well. He closed his eyes as the SBS man darted another puzzled glance at him. 'What you need is a good night's sleep, your lordship. Now where is this fucking place?'

'You mus' be thinkin' of Thunderbird Lodge – fancy place by the shore just along apiece,' the young man running the coffee booth in a roadside picnic area suggested. Jamie said no, he was certain the Webster ranch lay in the mountains between Carson City and Lake Tahoe. The boy's brow puckered beneath his dark-blue Reno Aces baseball cap. 'Hell,' he laughed. 'You must mean that outfit way out by Marlette Lake. Nobody goes there, on account of there's no road.' Jamie exchanged a pained glance with Gault and the young man caught the look. 'Ain't no road, but thar's what you might call a trail takes you so far before it'll tear the axles out of your truck, then you hitch on your pack and keep climbing till you can't climb no more. Once you hit the top of that old hill, you see the lake laid out below you, maybe a mile wide and three long. On the far shore you'll see a jetty, maybe with a Twin Beaver tied up there.' He grinned. 'That's the sensible folk's way of visiting. The ranch house is somewhere in the trees beyond. Man, that fella likes his privacy; I hope you guys got an invite. Not too popular with the folks round here, though. This here's an eco-management area. No development, period. My daddy told me that about twenty odd years ago these here trucks just started rolling up the old sluice way and they started building. Didn't even use one local pair of hands. Whadya' think of that?'

Well, they didn't think much of that, but they had business with the gentleman in question and they weren't going to let a little old mountain stand in their way. Jamie hadn't expected it to be easy, but equally he hadn't expected to do any mountain climbing. Fortunately, they'd come prepared for a hike and when they surveyed the hill as Gault parked the car off the road at the end of the trail, it looked more of a steep walk than an alpine ascent. They pulled on anoraks of camouflage green and sturdy walking boots.

'Here.' Gault handed Jamie a rucksack and the younger man grunted at the weight.

'Hand grenades or mortar bombs?'

339

'You'll thank me when we get wherever it is we're going,' the former soldier said as he hitched an identical bag onto his shoulders.

They followed the course of a stream up through the scattered trees and multi-coloured patches of wild flowers with Gault setting a thigh-burning pace that left Jamie gasping in his wake. He considered himself fit, but hiking in the Sierra Nevada was a world away from his morning jog around the park. A few hundred feet higher and his lungs were burning and his head began to spin. The sensation was similar to an experience he'd once had in the Himalayas and it was only when Gault helpfully pointed out they were probably at around seven thousand feet that he realized just how high these mountains were. At this height they were tramping through a dusting of snow that crunched beneath their feet and made the walking even harder on the thigh and calf muscles, but Gault was relentless. Jamie gritted his teeth and put one foot in front of the other, determined not to be outdone.

Once they reached the crest the former soldier stopped among the thin cover of the trees and shrugged off his rucksack. Sweat coursed down his face and his breath rasped from his lungs, but he was still grinning. 'Like the Brecons, but without the mud and the sleet.' Far below, a lake shaped vaguely like a hump-back whale stretched away diagonally northwards in a narrow cleft between the mountains. The wider part lay closest to them and it narrowed the further north it went. Gault hauled out a pair of binoculars and sighted the lenses on the far side. After a few moments he handed them to Jamie.

'You can see the jetty just to the north-east at the top end of the lake, but I don't see any sign of a float plane.'

Jamie found the wooden pontoons in his lenses. 'Hopefully that means he's alone, like a good recluse, or maybe just with a couple of staff.' He studied the area behind the jetty, but the trees were denser in the valley than on the slopes and it was difficult to make anything out. Unless . . . 'I think I can just see a tile roof among the trees, but it's difficult to tell because it's hidden by the contour of the hill.' He scanned the rest of the lake, looking for the best way to approach the Webster property. He followed the line of what looked like a track to the south end of the lake. 'Bastard.'

Gault looked up round in alarm. 'What can you see?'

'A road. A road that the little prick at the coffee stand didn't tell us about. We could have driven most of the way.'

The SBS man took the glasses and laughed. 'A Yank with a sense of humour? You don't meet one of those every day.' He shrugged. 'It's hardly a surprise. If they were supplying the place by float plane, there'd be one here permanently. Never mind, your lordship. We've had a bracing stroll and now we're about to have another. It might be for the best. Harold Webster may be a recluse, but he's a reclusive millionaire, and I've never met a millionaire yet who didn't want his security as watertight as a duck's arsehole. I'm betting our man will have the road watched and every car that stops checked out and there'll be a few juicy surprises in those woods.'

Jamie took the binoculars again. 'If the security is that tight, how the hell are we going to get in?'

The other man grinned. 'Leave that to your Uncle Gault. The house hasn't been built that I couldn't get inside. Once you're in, it's up to you.'

'What do you mean?'

'If you can persuade the old man to part with the sword, that's fine. Pay him what he wants. If not, you're going to have to steal Excalibur.'

XXXI

'So we're talking fences, cameras, motion sensors and microphones.' Gault rattled out the dangers like a haiku poem. 'Any or all of the above, in whatever combination. And we won't know we missed them until the bastards are on top of us. So we take it slow and you do everything – and I mean ev-er-y-thing – that Gault does. I drop, you drop. I run, you run. If I stop for a piss, you get your John Thomas out, understand?'

It had taken them another hour to reach the east side of the lake where they lay among the trees about a mile from the Webster property. Jamie's gut churned with nerves, but he smiled. 'You didn't tell me you wanted to scare them away.'

Gault grabbed his wrist and looked into his eyes. 'Just do as you're fucking told, okay?'

'All right,' Jamie snapped, already regretting his attempt to be friendly. 'What happens in the unlikely event I get hold of the sword?'

'I told you. When you have it, press one on the sat-phone. That will alert me and I'll call down the float plane from Reno that will be patrolling overhead just waiting for the word. When I set this up I thought he'd be picking us up from Lake Tahoe, but this is even better. He'll take us on at the jetty. The guards might be a problem, but there don't seem to be too many of them and we'll deal with that as it comes. We fly straight back to Reno, then on to New York, where Charlotte will be waiting for us and will hopefully have arranged the export of the sword—'

'How . . . ?'

'Probably better you don't know that. I think they call it accessory after the fact over here. We'll hole up for a few days and enjoy the sights and then head home.'

'It sounds simple.'

'It is simple, your lordship. The only difficult part is finding the sword and getting out of here. Let's go.'

They moved slowly through the trees, keeping low to make best use of the cover of tall ferns that sprouted in flares of emerald green from the mossy ground. Gault's eyes moved continually between the earth in front of him and the trees around. Jamie's never left the man in front. Twice they froze at the sound of animals, the first probably a raccoon or a squirrel, but the second most definitely a deer of some kind that sniffed the air before trotting across their front, a fleeting, dusty shadow among the pines. The ground undulated and sudden outcrops appeared in front of them, but Gault insisted on climbing the obstacles rather than being diverted from their path. From time to time he consulted a compass, but Jamie was certain he didn't need it. The access road lay somewhere about a hundred yards to their left, and to the right the mountains formed a more or less insurmountable barrier. It meant they always knew where they were, but also that they had only one line of escape. For a time Jamie relaxed and the spectre of Gault's security guards faded as the forest became less threatening. But that was before they came to the fence. It loomed in front of them like a razor-wire wall, ten feet high and running to right and left as far as they could see. Jamie reached out to touch it, prompted by some foolish instinct to see if it was real or the product of his fevered imagination, but drew his hand back when Gault hissed, 'Idiot.'

He signalled right and they soon came to a metal sign with an unmistakable zigzag symbol and the words, in bright red, DANGER – 10,000 VOLTS. KEEP OUT. PRIVATE PROPERTY.

Gault bent his mouth to Jamie's ear. 'Told you you're a fucking amateur,' he whispered, fumbling at the younger man's rucksack.

Jamie sat back, staring at the sign. Well, that was that. They'd have to try the gate. But Gault had other ideas.

'The chances are it's just something to keep nosy hikers out. Too many animals in this forest. They'd be resetting the command box every five minutes. Still,' he stared at the wire, 'no point in taking any risks.' He withdrew

JAMES DOUGLAS

three lengths of cable from the rucksack, each four feet long and tipped with a large crocodile clip at either end, with the lugs of the clip covered in thick rubber. Very carefully he placed the first clips three feet apart on the bottom wire, before repeating the process on the second and third. Once he was satisfied, he reached back into the sack and drew out a pair of heavy-duty wire cutters. 'I told you to trust your Uncle Gault, eh?'

When the wires were cut he'd created an opening three feet wide and the same high. He replaced the wire cutters in Jamie's rucksack and pushed it under the wire. 'You first.'

Jamie squirmed through, making sure he kept to the centre of the hole, and watched as Gault followed. 'Now,' the former SBS man said, 'I want you to remember every tree we pass, so that you'll know how to get back here.'

'I thought you said we'd be going out by the jetty?'

'We had an old saying in the army son. SNAFU. Situation normal: all fucked up. You hope for the best and plan for the worst. Let's go.'

They continued through the trees for another hundred yards and Jamie became conscious they were being forced closer to the lake shore by the terrain. Everything ahead was cloaked by the shoulder of the mountain overlooking the jetty and Gault wriggled upwards through the sparse bushes and well-spaced trees on the outcrop.

'Jesus Christ.'

Jamie joined him, his astonishment at the incredible

sight before them marginally reduced by the fact his suspicions had been growing ever since he'd spoken to Marmaduke Porter. 'Nortstein Castle.'

'It's quite a place.'

'It's not a patch on Wewelsburg.'

'But nobody shipped that from Germany and rebuilt it in cowboy country,' Gault said.

'Point taken, old chum.' Jamie whistled softly. 'Every bolt and every nail. Every brick and every tile. You'll note how the orientation with the lake and the north–south axis are exactly as they were at Nortstein. Our man looked long and hard before he found Marlette Lake.'

'Why in the name of God would he do that?'

'It's possible he's just fascinated by the Teutonic Knights.' Jamie studied the massive building on the far side of the meadow. 'I'd say it's not because he enjoys the aesthetic beauty of their creations.' As castles go, it was one of the least handsome he'd ever set eyes upon: more medieval Hitler's bunker than Louis XIVth chateau and in a jigsaw puzzle of styles. The squat main block reminded him of a Norman keep, but in red brick, with added wing extensions and a roof clad in tiles of bright orange. A large doorway dominated the façade and at some point an octagonal tower had been added to the west wing. It drew his eye and he borrowed Gault's binoculars to study the flagstaff.

'The holy Knight's Cross.' Jamie confirmed the black Maltese cross against a white background. 'If we were playing blind man's buff I'd say we were getting warm.'

Gault ignored him and rummaged in the bottom of the rucksack. 'You go first and I'll cover you.'

'Cover me with what?'

A big black Ruger automatic appeared in the former SBS man's fist. He saw Jamie's startled look and grinned sourly. 'This is the States, son; they give them out with the groceries. Go.'

Reluctantly, Jamie left the cover of the trees and made a diagonal run for the angle of the east wing. It came to him that he and Gault were unconsciously following the tactics Wulf Ziegler and his *Hitler Jugend* had used when they'd stolen Excalibur from the mansion in the north of England. He wondered if there was some kind of karmic circle that had brought him here. But Wulf Ziegler had had darkness for cover, while Jamie felt completely naked as he crossed a meadow as wide as two cricket pitches in broad daylight. No sign of the guards, thank God, but given the size of the fence they must be around somewhere. He could hear the sound of the grass rustling in his footsteps and prayed it was Gault and not some hulking great ex Navy Seal. He reached the wall and stopped to get his bearings. To his right, the castle's frontage stretched away with the main door in the centre. No point in breaking in to the ranch then knocking on the front door to ask for directions. It was a castle. It would once have been surrounded by a wall, or even by a series of walls. They were long gone, but the entrances to the kitchens and the servants' quarters might still exist. He made his decision and weaved his way through a labyrinth of outhouses until he reached the rear of the building and looked round the corner.

'Don't move.' The order was superfluous because the cold touch of steel on his forehead froze him to the spot. The owner of the steel, which by the lettering on the barrel an inch from his nose was part of a Glock 9mm, was a tall, rangy man with close-cropped hair, dressed in the kind of outlandish camouflage gear Americans used for deer hunting. A communications set hung from a hook beside one of the outhouses and Jamie realized he must have just returned from a patrol before some buffalo-hoofed English idiot alerted him. 'Do you have a weapon?'

'No.'

'If I find you have a weapon I'm going to make you swallow it and then rip it out your asshole.'

'I don't have a weapon.' Jamie let the anger flow into his voice. 'I got lost in the woods.'

'Yeah? And I'm George Washington. Now, very, very slowly, turn round and face the wall. You got that?' Jamie did as he was told and rotated his body, keeping his head as steady as possible, with the barrel of the Glock scoring his skull as he moved until it was resting in the indent above his neck. 'Now tell me again why you're here?'

'I told you—' The barrel of the Glock rattled against his skull.

'Every time I think you're not telling the truth I'm

going to hit you with my personal weapon, which you'd be advised to understand has a hair trigger. Now, why are you here?'

'I came to talk to Harold Webster.'

'Well, crawling through the woods seems a mite un-neighbourly, which leads me to suspect that you already know Mr Webster don't welcome no visitors. Which brings me to my next question: did you come alone?'

'I—'

'Don't answer that.' The voice lost its edge and the fierce pressure on the back of his skull eased. Jamie heard the unmistakable crack of metal against bone and the sound of a falling body as the presence behind him vanished.

Gault ran his hands swiftly through the fallen guard's camo jacket and trousers, coming up with a set of keys and what looked like a plastic bank card. When he completed the search he handed what he'd found to Jamie and dragged the unconscious man to the outhouse and, from somewhere, produced a set of plastic ties to bind his wrists.

'What are you waiting for? Take his gun and get going. If my guess is right the card will get you through that door.' He pointed to a doorway with a swipe machine attached to the jamb. 'Old technology, but by the looks of thing they've been here long enough to feel pretty secure.'

Jamie picked up the Glock and weighed it in his hand before laying it down again. 'I don't think I will, Gault.

I'm not sure I'm ready to shoot somebody just at this very moment.'

The former SBS man glared at him, his mouth working. 'You really are a fucking amateur. If you screw this up I might shoot you myself.'

Jamie ignored the threat. 'What will you be doing while I'm risking my neck inside?'

'What I do best,' Gault produced a fierce grin. 'Causing bloody mayhem. As soon as you hear them charging from the front door make your move.'

For the moment Jamie had no inkling what that move would be, but he licked his lips and nodded. Gault rechecked the bound man's ties, dragged him into the outhouse and closed the door from the outside. With a wink at Jamie, he was gone.

Jamie hesitated by the doorway to the house, but there was no option really. He hadn't come all this way to turn back just when things got a little tough. Of course, he was going to look silly, if not worse, if he was found wandering the hallways of the old man's house and there was nothing to find. But he remembered the effort that had gone into bringing this ugly piece of East Prussia here and he knew in his heart Hal Webster was hiding something. Whether it was Excalibur or not, the only way to find out was to get inside. He slipped the card into the swipe slot and pulled sharply down, triggering a soft buzz and a click. With the other hand he pushed the heavy door open and stepped into the last refuge of the Teutonic Knights.

A short corridor with what seemed to be staff quarters
and kitchens to left and right led to a door at the far end.
He pushed the door an inch and his heart quickened
as he recognized the banners of a dozen SS divisions
hanging from the high ceiling of a large entrance hall.
They were all there. The silver key on a black shield
that was Sepp Dietrich's lucky charm and the symbol
of his 1st *Liebstandarte*. The Death's Head skull of the
3rd *Totenkopf* hung alongside it. The inverted Z of *Das
Reich* and four or five more divisions he could name.
Many of them had lost their entire strength four or five
times before finally being annihilated on the vast Russian
steppes, the narrow lanes of Normandy or the ruins of
Berlin in April and May 1945. The banners appeared
dusty and frayed; in fact, the whole atmosphere was one
of progressive decay, cold and dank with a raw chill
that seemed to flow from the floor of grey flagstone. Yet
these black strips of fading silk cloth were very likely
the ones that had hung there in 1941 when Reinhard
Heydrich had marched into the hall of Nortstein Castle.
Jamie shivered. Somehow, they still carried the same
malignant power they had when the young men of the
Schutzstaffel had marched behind them more than
sixty years earlier. To his right and left a great double
stairway curved up on either side of the room, linking
it to the upper floors of the east and west wings. As he
retreated back to the empty kitchen he caught sight of
himself in a mirror and almost laughed at the piratical
bearded figure staring back. A shave and a haircut were

definitely on the cards at the end of all this. But first he had a job to do.

Twenty seconds passed before the sound of an alarm bell filled the building. He heard doors open a few feet away and prayed no one wanted to grab a quick snack before dealing with whatever emergency Gault had cooked up. The sound was followed by the swift tramp of running feet heading away from him and he waited until it had cleared before returning to the door into the hall. When he reached it, he hesitated and waited again, and was rewarded by the sound of at least two men racing down the stairs to the west wing. When the door slammed behind them he ventured warily into the hall, every sense seeking out the man who had been delayed, or deliberately left to deal with just this scenario, but there was nothing. The men had come from the west wing, which meant presumably that was where Hal Webster had his quarters. Logic said search the east wing first, but logic and instinct fought a short sharp battle and instinct won. The octagonal tower on the west wing was where the owner of this monstrosity had chosen to flaunt the symbol of the Teutonic Knights as if it was his personal banner.

Images from Wulf Ziegler's journal transposed themselves on the scene in front of him.

Over the next twenty-four hours the High Priests of the SS arrived . . . Dietrich and Daluege, were hard men who had broken heads in Munich beer halls and

353

*pulled triggers during the Night of the Long Knives
. . . Darré and Hildebrandt were intellectuals . . . von
Eberstein had introduced Heydrich and Himmler . . .
Bach-Zelewski, of Prussian aristocratic stock, had
empty pockets . . . Berger, Jeckeln, Wolff and Pohl . . .
At precisely eight p.m. Reinhard Heydrich swept into
the hall like a Crown Prince entering his own palace.*

For a heartbeat Jamie felt as if the surrounding chill had
pierced his heart. The Third Reich's merchants of death
had all stood together in this room, the architects of
the Holocaust and the *einsatzgruppen*, and their taint
still marked it now like the scent of blood. All logic
was forgotten as some force beyond nature drew him
to the right where a darkened doorway loomed like the
entrance to a tomb. He did not want to go there, but his
feet moved of their own volition until the shadow engulfed him. Gradually the details of the room emerged
as his eyes adjusted to the gloom.

*An enormous round table covered with white cloth
and circled at precise intervals by twelve throne-like
chairs . . . each draped with a cloth embossed with
a distinctive coat of arms . . . replicated by twelve
banners suspended from the ceiling. In the centre
hung the symbol of the Knight's Cross . . .*

This was what he had come here for, but he found himself gripped by a sort of mental paralysis. Only now,

with every detail laid out in front of him, did the full horror of that night truly register. Around him twelve dark figures stood deathly still, cloaked in black robes lined with white silk. Below the robes they wore the black and silver uniform of the SS and the oak leaf collar patches of their rank. Only the dead eyes were wrong. Suddenly it was difficult to breathe, as if some unseen hand gripped his throat. Hot bile crept up from his stomach into his chest and he retched, his face grimacing in pain as more visions forced their way into his brain.

'I lay before you Joyeuse, mighty sword of Charlemagne, defender of the faith.' . . . *a beautiful weapon, the sword of kings, with a golden hilt and a cross guard formed in the shape of two winged dragons* . . . *'Zerstorer, sword of Frederick Barbarossa, defier of the Eastern hordes,'* . . . *'Durendal, imperious blade of Roland, hero of old.'* . . . *'Gotteswerkzeug, the sword of Werner von Orseln, greatest of all the Teutonic Knights.'* . . . *The blades* . . . *created an odd symmetrical pattern* . . . *The last man had stood ready* . . . *his heavy blade held unwavering in front of his face. His was a sword of the most ancient lineage* . . . *a broad-bladed, battle-notched iron mankiller* . . . *Reinhard Heydrich allowed the blade to slowly fall, until its tip touched the hilt of the first sword and made the final connection. 'I lay before you Excalibur, the sword of Arthur, may his strength*

*and the strength of all these great champions, aid our
cause and use their power to smite our enemies and
the enemies of our beloved Führer.'*

'No, please no.' The cry came from somewhere inside
his head, but still he couldn't move.

'Bring forward the gifts.'

'No.'

In his mind it was a shout of defiance as he stepped
forward to lay his hands on Excalibur, the sword of
Arthur and remove it from the pentagram of blades.
The reality was a strangled squeak from the doorway
behind him. He turned very carefully and found himself
staring into what appeared to be the barrel of a nine-
inch howitzer, but maybe that was just a matter of
perspective. On further appraisal it was probably only
a .45 pistol – one of those old-fashioned revolvers Clint
Eastwood used so successfully to make holes in the bad
guys – which wasn't a great deal of comfort. At this
range the effect would be much the same. Jamie tried
to remember if these guns fired on first pressure, or if
they needed a bit more effort. He sincerely hoped it was
the second. The shock was compounded by the heavy-
set man who confronted him from the wheelchair. Two
different people stared from the face of the silver-haired
patrician with the .45 waving shakily in his right hand.
Something had happened to his left side that seemed to

have melted his features and twisted his hand and arm into a hooked claw. The flesh of his forehead drooped over his eyelid, which gravity in turn drew down to meet his lip, which seemed to be trying to slip from the bottom of his jaw. If anything, the effect was made all the more bizarre, almost schizophrenic, by the fine-boned features and cold-eyed certainty studying him from the right half of the face.

That single cold eye told him he needed to talk his way out of this, and fast.

'Mr Webster, I—'

The shaking arm extended and the gun barrel homed on to Jamie's chest and held steady. All of a sudden the chances of negotiating a ceasefire seemed a lot slimmer. The options flashed through his mind. Ten feet. Rush him to put off his aim and he might miss. No, he couldn't miss at that range and a .45 round would take off his arm or blow a hole in him the size of a man's fist. The knuckle of the trigger finger went a little whiter and he tensed to throw himself at Harold Webster's feet, praying the American couldn't bring the gun to bear before he upended the chair.

He was so focused on the old man he didn't notice the third person enter the room.

'I've told you often enough you're not allowed to shoot trespassers, Gramps.' A flash of silver flicked out to knock the barrel to one side.

Jamie risked a glance at his saviour – at least he hoped she was his saviour. Slim and blonde, she must have been close to his own age, and the tight-fitting black bodysuit she wore emphasized the curves of a body that combined the strength of an athlete with the poise of a supermodel. Surprisingly, given that Gramps had just been about to commit murder, she was smiling: the sort of cold-eyed, knowing smile that made Jamie suspect his presence here wasn't all that unexpected and she'd quite enjoyed watching him squirm in the sights of a one-man firing squad. Even more surprisingly, she was holding a fencing foil.

XXXII

Hal Webster snarled and sputtered, saliva drooling from his twisted mouth and a single tear trickling from the damaged eye as he tried to bring the big gun back to bear. The woman effortlessly maintained the pressure on his wrist with the foil and reached down with her free hand to take the pistol from his fingers. Just for a second Jamie noted that the barrel hovered over his chest and he took a deep breath, before their eyes met and with a short laugh she moved it aside. She reminded him of a very dangerous version of a woman he vaguely remembered from an old British TV series called *The Avengers*: Emma Peel with a splash of Lauren Bacall and more than a touch of cornered black widow spider. Her next words seemed to confirm it.

'You have an interest in swords, Mr Saintclair?' Why wasn't he surprised she knew his name? 'I also hear you can use them. Carl?' A black man in fencing gear appeared in the doorway and Jamie realized he and Webster's granddaughter must have been sparring somewhere in the house. 'Give him the sword.'

The man approached with a grin. 'You know the meaning of the phrase "greased lightnin'", sir? Well, you're about to find out.'

'Don't you want to know why I'm here?' Jamie played for time as he studied the sword, which was one of the old-fashioned Italian types with a button point. The blade felt comfortable in his hand, but he had a feeling this was unlikely to turn out well.

'Oh, we've plenty of time for that, Mr Saintclair,' the woman said with airy confidence. 'You aren't going anywhere soon. Your friend is being entertained by some of our staff who don't take too kindly to people who are guilty of trespass, arson and pistol-whipping their comrades. You think that's amusing?'

'No.' He glanced at the old man in the wheelchair. 'I think it's probably a recipe for starting World War Three.'

Her smile was as cold as her ice-blue eyes. 'Don't mind Gramps. He's never been the same since he had his stroke. Maybe a little crankier, but that would be difficult to tell. We just keep him locked up here in his little Nazi fantasy world waiting to die.'

She saw Jamie's startled glance and laughed. 'Clearly you don't know my grandfather, Mr Saintclair. He is not a likeable man. You have no idea how much pleasure it gives me to be able to stand here and heap the kind of humiliation on him he heaped on my daddy and then me for all those years. In fact, every day he lives is a blessing, trapped in that broken, rotting body and knowing there is not one thing he can do about it.'

'I've heard of dysfunctional families, but—'

'*En garde.*' The sword snapped up and froze in place. 'Shouldn't we at least be introduced?'

She frowned for a second. 'Sure, why not? I'm Helena Webster, and I am chairman and chief executive of the Webster Corporation. Miss Helena Webster, if you care to know, because that vegetable in the wheelchair would never let a worthwhile man come near me. And you are Mr James Saintclair, art dealer of London, England. Locator of items of interest that changed ownership in World War Two without the consent of their owners. Would that be correct?'

'You seem to know a lot about me.'

'Oh, I do, Mr Saintclair. I became curious when I discovered you were dabbling in areas where I have a mutual interest. For instance, I know that you recently lost someone very close to you.' She noticed him flinch and shook her head. 'I apologize. Cruelty is in danger of becoming a habit. However, I also know that you have an unfortunate predilection for attracting some rather dangerous enemies, and, dare I say, curious friends. Do you gamble, Mr Saintclair?' she asked before he could ask any one of the several questions that came to mind.

'Since you know everything else about me, I'm sure you already know the answer to that.'

'Well, I do like to gamble, or perhaps that should be,

place my faith in my own skills. If you're willing, we shall have a small wager on our bout. If you touch me you may walk away from here and we will say no more about aggravated assault, trespass and fire-raising, which you may not be aware can carry a life sentence in this state. If I touch you, we will honestly discuss the reason you are here and you will consider doing a service for me.'

'It would be unwise of me to agree without knowing what the service was,' Jamie pointed out.

'True,' she smiled, 'but all I am asking is that you consider it. If you find it distasteful you have every right to say no.'

'In that case, why not? Where are the masks and the vests?'

'Oh, we don't bother with little formalities like that here, Mr Saintclair. Swords have always been a way of life in my household. We trust in God and the expertise of our opponents to keep us safe.'

Jamie managed a rueful smile as he remembered the day Adam Steele had persuaded him to fight without a mask. Why do these bloody people always choose me? Still, what choice did he have? 'Then God help us,' he said, not altogether ironically.

'Indeed. *En garde*.'

He'd planned to launch the first attack and finish it quickly, preferably in his favour, but the instant their swords touched he discovered just how good she was. Good and fast. She met his attack with a perfectly timed defence and counter that rocked him back on his heels and had him frantically trying to protect shoulder and breast where her relentless attack threatened. Just when he knew she had him, Helena Webster stepped back and resumed the *garde* position with an amused smile.

'Not bad, Mr Saintclair. Not bad at all. I assume you know my grandfather flew with the Eighth Air Force? What you possibly do not know is that on 18 September 1944, during a mission to support the rising of the Home Army in Warsaw, his plane was shot down on the way to its Russian landing place. This was the only time in the war that Marshal Stalin had sanctioned the landing of Allied planes on Russian soil. Not surprisingly, given the distances involved and the casualty rate among the squadrons who'd previously flown to Poland, the crews regarded it as a suicide mission.' Without warning she renewed her attack, but this time Jamie was ready and he managed to hold his own for a few seconds before she again took command. He tried to concentrate on the glittering blade as she continued the conversation. 'His was one of nine planes lost.' Christ. The point flashed before his left eye. 'It was forced north and came down in the Byelorussian forest.' He just got his foil in place to parry a lunge and dance out of range. And again. 'Gramps was the only survivor and he joined the local partisans.' She stepped back and Jamie took the chance to recover his breath and try to calm his thumping heart. Helena Webster was better than good. She was world class and she was playing with him.

'Or that is the story,' the American continued, her breathing as regular as when they'd begun. 'My investigations, albeit impossible to verify, indicate that the "partisan" band he joined was actually a gang of bandits who terrorized the Polish villages between Byelorussia and what was then East Prussia, but took part in very little fighting against the Nazis. When the Red Army advanced into Germany, Gramps' merry band roamed the no man's land between the two sides, preying on the weak and stealing everything they could lay their hands on.' She smiled at the man in the wheelchair. Hal Webster fixed her with his single eye and whined like a caged animal. 'Isn't that right, Gramps? A thief and a murderer, even before.'

Before what? Jamie's attention drifted between the astonishing story he was being told and the point of Helena Webster's foil, which he now discovered had somehow lost its protective button during the fight. Accident or design? He didn't have time to ponder the question, because she came at him again and this time he knew he was fighting for his life. Time after time, he only just managed to get the edge of his foil in position to parry a thrust. Again and again, that point came back at him with lethal intent. His arm began to ache and the breath tore at his chest and throat. He could feel himself slowing and knew she could feel it too.

She fended off his counter-attack too easily and he knew it must end soon. He had one last chance. Using sheer power he pushed her blade up and away in an *attack au fer*, positioning himself for an angled strike that would have taken her in the left breast, but Helena Webster pre-empted the move with one of her own and he found himself breast to breast with his opponent. 'The only question, Mr Saintclair, is how much you know about what comes after. And, more important, what will you tell?'

With a piece of footwork that would have pleased a prima ballerina she disengaged and came at him again, the relentless steel seeking out his eyes and throat. But the red rage that had been building up inside came to his rescue, fuelling his speed and the desire not to be beaten by this beautiful, infuriating, dangerous woman. Gradually it took over his movements. Now she was on the retreat, parrying right and left to stay in the fight. He saw his chance and lunged at her chest. A whir of light and a searing pain in his wrist. A pinprick at his throat.

'Never underestimate the opportunity to *envelope*, Mr Saintclair. It is a little flashy, some would say a little too Errol Flynn, but it has its uses.' He looked along the three feet of high carbon steel into eyes as hard and unyielding as the sword at his throat. 'You see, in many ways I am my grandfather's daughter. So let me ask again. How much do you know about what comes after?'

Sometimes not answering a question is an answer in itself, but he doubted Helena Webster would care for that option. He felt a tiny trickle that might be blood run down over his Adam's apple and into the little hollow below.

'All right.' He nodded carefully. 'A Byelorussian partisan group visited Nortstein Castle before the Germans had time to evacuate it in nineteen forty-five. They killed what was left of the garrison, while their leader had a, let us say, conversation, with the officer in charge. When he'd finished with the German, he lined his men up and shot them.'

The sword point slipped from his neck and Jamie relaxed. 'Yes, their *leader*, as I'm sure you have surmised, was none other than my grandfather and he had his little chat with the SS officer on that very table,' she pointed with the sword, 'which is symbolic, if you like.' She looked up at the banners hanging from the ceiling and smiled in a way that sent a shiver through him. He remembered Hermann's description of a man red to the elbows and he didn't feel like smiling back. Helena Webster read his look as she handed her blade to Carl, the guard. 'The villagers had to bury what was left of the poor man. They couldn't leave a whole heap of dead Germans and Russians lying around, so they hid them away in the woods.'

'Do you mind telling me how you know all this?'

'Oh, I was always curious about this – let's call it a house, shall we? – and why my grandfather was the way he was.' Her gaze drifted to the old man in the wheelchair and Hal Webster must have felt her eyes on him, because he lifted his head and now the expression on the untouched side of his face was one of sheer terror. 'So when I got the opportunity to do some research I used all the resources at my disposal to find out, and those resources are considerable, Mr Saintclair. In this age of instant information and high-speed global communication all things are possible. A few people from Nortstein survived the war and the forced evacuation, and even those who did not left their stories. It was only a matter of tracking them down.' Her voice took on an edge that hadn't been there earlier. 'Whatever happened in this room that day changed my grandfather, Mr Saintclair. He was never what you would call a good man, but . . . Are you aware of the story of Faust?'

An involuntary shudder ran through Jamie as he remembered a long day in the depths of the Harz Mountains *where Goethe met his demon* and a man sold his soul to the devil. 'I'm acquainted with it.'

'Then you understand. His obsession with Nortstein Castle led to where we are today, trapped, for want of a better word, inside this monstrosity; a temple to a culture of death. I by family responsibilities I cannot escape and you by circumstances currently beyond your control,' she frowned and stared at him, 'and perhaps even by a sense of duty?'

'I thought you hated him.'

She turned to the man in the wheelchair with a look of loathing. 'Oh, not my responsibility to my grandfather, Mr Saintclair; never that.'

'Why?'

The question surprised her. 'My family affairs are my own, please understand that.'

'No.' Jamie indicated the twelve shop dummies elaborately dressed in cloaks and SS uniforms, the Teutonic Knights' banners, the round table and the iron pentagram of heroes' swords. 'I meant why all this?'

The blonde head tilted a little to one side and the over-bright blue eyes studied him quizzically. Eventually Helena Webster smiled.

'Before I answer that question I must decide whether I'm going to kill you.'

XXXIII

They locked him in the wine cellar, but at least they brought him food and nobody said anything about the condemned man's last meal. He wondered how Gault was enjoying his captivity, but decided the former SBS man was quite capable of looking after himself and, anyway, there was little chance of doing anything about it. A strip light illuminated his makeshift dungeon and as he searched in vain for a way out he looked over the contents. Would it be wise to use his last few hours comparing Harold Webster's Château Margaux '66 with the '68, or the '72 Gevrey-Chambertin with the Nuits Saint Georges of the same year? Probably not, and, if his luck so far was anything to go by, there wouldn't be a bloody corkscrew.

I must decide whether I'm going to kill you.

Was she serious? He touched the scratch on his throat and remembered the ice-blue eyes at the end of that long sliver of steel. That depended on what she had to gain and how much she had to lose: credits and debits judged as they would be on the corporation balance sheet. Was there more profit to be had by keeping the rather awkwardly persistent Mr James Saintclair alive, or sending him for a swim in the lake with a concrete block tied to his leg for ballast? On initial appraisal, the second option seemed more likely and he felt a little flutter of panic in his stomach. If she knew so much about him, she knew he was here for the sword. Ergo, if she wanted to keep the sword, it would be best to be rid of the inconvenient Saintclair. On the other hand, and now he felt a contrasting and unlikely stirring of what might be called hope, she had suggested he could do her a service and she had seemed quite serious about it. What that service could be, he had no idea. He recalled the figure-hugging bodysuit and one or two thoughts sprang to mind, but the chances of turning them into reality seemed slim in his current situation. All of which left him none the wiser. There'd been almost a twinkle in her eye when he'd asked that final question, and he had a feeling that, whatever the outcome of her deliberations, she wouldn't be able to resist giving him the answer.

The question now was what to do while she made up her mind?

In the end he couldn't pass up the '66.

'Mr Saintclair?' Jamie groaned and opened his eyes, blinking at the bright light. 'Miss Webster will see you now, sir.'

His back ached from lying on the hard floor with his jacket as a pillow, but on the plus side the early morning call didn't have the feel of an invitation to a firing squad. He followed the guard to a large room in the west wing, with a polished wooden banqueting table – rectangular, not round – at the centre, and walls lined with bookcases that reminded him of the day Adam Steele had revealed the contents of the Excalibur codex. Jamie allowed his eyes to drift over the titles as the guard took his place by the door with one hand poised disconcertingly over the butt of one of the omnipresent Glock 9mms. They seemed to consist mainly of American literary classics, but Harold Webster's collection also contained a few British books. There was a section on Dickens, another containing the complete works of Shakespeare, and a shelf of leather-clad titles by Sir Walter Scott. One wall was devoted to what looked like every book ever written on the Arthur legends, ranging from the eighteenth century to the latest modern works. He randomly picked one called *Arthur and the Lost Kingdoms* and had just opened it when Carl, the guard who had watched the fencing bout, entered the room. Curiously, the black man carried a long sword across two outstretched hands, almost as if he were taking part in some kind of solemn ceremony. Jamie felt as if an electric shock ran through him, his heart quickened and the breath caught in his throat as he realized what he was seeing. It didn't seem possible even now, but there it was, finally, within touching distance. *A broad-bladed, battle-notched iron man-killer.* How well it fitted the description. Almost four feet of dull, crow-black, rust-pitted metal, the edges worn thin by relentless honing and nicked where they'd once clashed with other blades. Yet for all its utilitarian appearance it took on a curious, almost awesome beauty in his eyes. This was a sword that had been revered, for how else had it been protected and cared for, for more than a thousand years? Carl laid it carefully in the centre of the table. And yet . . .

'Thank you for your patience, Mr Saintclair.' Today she wore an immaculately cut suit of slate-grey silk over a simple turquoise blouse open at the neck and offset by a necklace of thick gold links. Another of the guards followed her, pushing Harold Webster in his chair, twisted and glaring, like a malignant land crab.

'Does this mean you're not going to kill me?'

Helena Webster ignored the question. 'When I heard of your interest in Nortstein Castle, I had a choice to make. I could have tried to stop you, and believe me when I say that I would have succeeded. Or I could watch and judge the mettle of the people I faced. Fortunately for you, I chose the second option. When you found your way here, I was impressed by your perseverance and your ingenuity, but it left me with another choice. My only interest in all this is to protect the good name of my family and my company. You are patently a man of honesty and integrity.' Jamie blinked. If the description was accurate, he was in the wrong line of business. 'But you are also a man of great curiosity. The first I can use.

The second I must eliminate.' There it was, the shiver down the spine again. 'I have decided that the best way to proceed is to be entirely candid with you. All I ask is your word that nothing you hear today will be repeated outside these four walls. Do you agree?'

Jamie met her stare as he considered the question. 'You're very trusting.'

'No, Mr Saintclair, I am a very good judge of character. For instance, I would not make the same offer to your companion.'

'Then I agree.'

She greeted the words with a smile and turned to Harold Webster with what might have been a look of triumph. The old man wriggled in his chair and snarled like a caged beast, his single eye glowing with suppressed rage and hatred. Helena walked to the table and laid a hand on the great sword.

'What my grandfather learned from the man he tortured and murdered at Nortstein Castle drove him quite mad. You decoded Rolf Lauterbacher's journal, so you are aware of what took place in the castle in nineteen forty-one?' Jamie nodded. 'But there was more. Much more. My grandfather's victim was an aide to Wolfram Sievers, Himmler's black magician. He told him every detail of the ceremony and the lineage of the five swords Reinhard Heydrich had brought together to make it happen. All the elements had been in place, he said, but the human element had proved false. They were weak men who did not believe. Sievers had his doubts from the first, but Heydrich insisted the ceremony go ahead to please Himmler. It would have worked. It still could. Harold Webster had always been interested in the occult. You've heard of a man called Aleister Crowley?'

'The crazy mystic with the Scottish castle? Of course.'

'Black magician and occultist. Some people considered him the Antichrist, others the potential saviour of the world. My grandfather fell into the second category. He was in correspondence with Crowley before the war and until his death in nineteen forty-seven.'

'So all this was like the Holy Grail to him?'

'An interesting analogy,' she admitted. 'But probably an apt one. He would always say that a great force had led him to Nortstein Castle and the treasures it contained. The swords were only part of it. The German showed him occult texts dating back to Ancient Egyptian times giving details of ceremonies to draw on the powers of the Dark Gods and containing words of power to bring death and disaster to the enemies of those who uttered them. He believed he was bartering the information for his life. He was wrong.'

Jamie studied the hunched figure in the chair. What was he thinking, trapped in that broken, useless body? Did he ever wonder if it was retribution for the men he'd killed? 'So,' he challenged, 'Harold Webster – your grandfather – has just made the most important discovery of his life. What does he do now? He can't take the swords and the manuscripts back to the partisan camp, because they'll probably be stolen from him. Once he's killed his men, he could strap the swords to a pony and try to ride west, towards the Allies, but the chances of him making it would be very slim.'

Helena nodded gravely. 'He can't take them, so he decides to hide them, along with most of the Nazi paraphernalia you saw yesterday. The castle was full of potential hiding places, but none offered guaranteed security. Eventually, he chose somewhere, probably a small cellar, found a local man who had the skills to brick it up, and, when he was satisfied, he got rid of the evidence – all the evidence – and does as you suggest. He rides west. He kept to the woods and the marshes, avoided contact with anyone who looked threatening, stole what he needed from the weak and the fearful . . .' Her eyes hardened. 'He was very good at that by now. By good fortune he had chosen a route between two Soviet army groups, but eventually events forced him onto a main highway where he joined a column of refugees being screened by the Russians. When they questioned him, he revealed his true identity and was placed with a group of former prisoners of war. They repatriated him to the United States a month later.'

'What I can't understand,' Jamie's voice reflected his confusion, 'is why it took him so long to retrieve the swords. If he was so obsessed, surely there was a way he could have gone back for them earlier, and without bringing the whole castle with him?'

She produced an unexpected smile. 'You don't know my grandfather, Mr Saintclair. He'd already formed his plan by the time he returned to the States. The ritual had to be carried out in perfect conditions, in its original form and its original setting. At first he planned to return just after the war, but within a few years Poland had become a Soviet satellite state and pretty much closed to westerners. There was also the small matter of certain crimes committed against the Polish population by the Byelorussian partisans, who could be very cruel to the people they lived amongst.'

She paused to allow the reality behind those words to sink in. Carl stood behind Harold Webster's wheelchair, but the black man might have been deaf for all the interest his face displayed. By contrast, the mobile part of the old man's face was a mirror of his emotions; a twitching arena of fear and anticipation. A dribble of saliva escaped his drooping lip as Helena Webster resumed her story in a flat, almost uninterested voice. 'My grandfather could never be certain his part in those crimes wasn't known. Circumstances forced him to bide his time, and he used the interval to begin gathering the essential commodity he needed to make it happen: money. Before the war he had been an electrical engineer. When he returned, he foresaw the growth of the automotive industry and focused his attentions on components shared by all automobiles. He eventually settled on the battery. Relatively simple, cheap and easy to make. The fortune he made in the following ten years allowed him to invest in television technology, and later computers. The Webster Corporation is now one of the largest providers of security software in the world. Along the way he created the Bialystok Foundation, and began building relationships in Poland. When the time was right he used the foundation to employ the services of a rather brash young man called Marmaduke Porter. Porter paved the way for the purchase of the castle, its dismantling and export to the United States. My grandfather had already identified this site and greased whatever palms were required, and here we are. For ten years he attempted to replicate the ritual that took place in Nortstein in April nineteen forty-one,' her lips wrinkled with distaste, 'recruiting like-minded people to take the place of the twelve Nazis. If one combination didn't work, he would try another. When he had harnessed the power of the swords he planned to run for president. Harold Webster would create a new America that would wipe away the shame of Korea and Vietnam. He had already decided Russia was not the United States' greatest enemy. Once in the White House he planned to focus all this country's energy on defeating Communist China, first economically, but if that did not work he was prepared to use every means at his disposal.' The words tumbled free, her breathing quickened and the pain she patently experienced was almost enough to make Jamie feel sorry for her. But he knew Helena Webster wouldn't thank him for his sympathy. As he watched, something curious happened. The expression on her face didn't change, but the effect of it altered, as if some classical Medusa was lurking behind the beautiful mask. 'My grandfather's obsession killed my father and robbed me of my childhood. The day I received the call telling me he had had a stroke was probably the happiest of my life.' She went to the old man and stroked his hair. The gesture might have been affectionate, but the atmosphere seemed to take on a new chill and Jamie saw fear in the single bright eye. 'I can feel his hatred and his loathing. What I am about to do will destroy him still further, but not, I hope, kill him.' She returned to the table and picked up the sword. Harold Webster groaned and struggled in his chair so much he might have tipped it if the guard Carl hadn't pushed him back. 'That is the service I ask of you. I want you to return this to the person it was stolen from.'

Jamie took the sword in his hands, the ancient iron rough and cool against his flesh, instantly feeling the power that emanated from the battle-scarred blade and the life force of the kings who had wielded it. The grip was bone, worked smooth by countless generations of use, and only the pommel, a two-headed dragon worked in gold, gave any indication of its lineage. What had Adam Steele said? *A sword is the child of earth, air and fire. Look closely at this blade and you can see the ghosts of the tree roots that bind the earth to the Otherworld.* And he was right; the dark metal still retained the magic of the smith who had created it, the jealously guarded secrets of its manufacture and the shadow of the eight glowing bars of specially selected metal that had been used in its forging. Excalibur.

'You understand . . . ?' Her voice faltered.

Jamie met her gaze. 'Yes.'

'I told him, but he would never listen. So you will return it?'

'I will try, where . . . ?'

She smiled. 'You're a clever guy, Jamie Saintclair. You'll work it out.'

XXXIV

'We have the sword.' A rumble of congratulations greeted the news and Adam Steele saw the thrill of excitement
run through the five members of the inner committee.

'Then we can proceed?'

Steele nodded. 'Initiate the countdown. Everything
must be in place for the State Opening of Parliament in
two weeks.'

When they were gone he stared out of the window,
surprised at how calm he felt and how easy it had been to
issue the final, irrevocable order. This had always been
part of the plan, but he'd hoped that the M25 massacre
and the inevitable upsurge of anger against the Muslim
population would make it unnecessary. The people of
this country – the real people – should have taken to
the streets in their hundreds of thousands and forced
on the Government the kind of changes the committee
had been demanding. The rest, a quiet, non-violent shift
of power, would have followed inevitably. A few had

acted as he had forecast, but the masses had stayed in front of their televisions and their computer screens, had lounged at the bars of their smelly pubs and kept attending their silly football matches – and done nothing.

He felt his rage grow at the decision they had forced on him. It was all for them. All this risk and sacrifice. Didn't they realize the cancer that was spreading among them? Tribal enclaves, transplanted from their foreign homelands, growing and pulsing in every city, taking over whole streets, then whole districts, driving out the native species by their very numbers and their insidious financial strength. He shuddered at the thought of the alien culture and barbaric religion taking over his beloved Great Britain. The black and brown and yellow faces that tormented him every time he left the sanctuary of his home. The babel of unnatural languages that assaulted his ears. No, they had to be stopped. Dead. There was only one way to remove an alien breed, and that was to cut it out at the roots. But he couldn't do it alone. So Adam Steele had made the first tentative approaches and was surprised at how many of his class had similar concerns.

It had begun quietly. They didn't advertise their presence, but used their collective influence to try to make the changes that were so obviously needed. But those in power hadn't listened. It had taken many months before he understood that the political system he believed was ruining the country was nothing but a sham. A cowardly, neo-Liberal conspiracy with a shadowy all-party core that ensured the status quo at all costs. After that, the way ahead had been clear. There could be no change without sweeping away the existing order.

After 9/11 and 7/7 another great atrocity was only a matter of time. The people who had died in the M25 massacre were the price that had to be paid for bringing the country to its senses. They had died for Britain, and it didn't matter who had killed them, as long as the right people were blamed. But it hadn't been enough, and now one more great blow must be struck to ensure the backlash that was needed to sweep away the old regime, create a new Britain, and at the same time ensure a speedy and efficient change of power. It would happen on the only day Parliament was sure to be packed with politicians of all persuasions. The Queen's Speech brought all but the most sedentary out to cram the velvet benches and show their over-fed faces for the TV news cameras.

They would all be there, the ambitious and the slothful, the greedy and the God-fearing, the thieves and the liars, Franklin among them, unaware that he was no longer required. A pity about Her Majesty, but she had done her job and now it was time to move on. Not her fault that she had ruled such a cabal of spineless failures. And since this was a special year, she would be conveniently accompanied by her entire brood. All but the Duke, who would be laid out by a last-minute indisposition.

The Duke would be as shocked as the nation when it transpired that Al-Qaida, in an outrage unheard of even in terrorist warfare, had somehow managed to conceal a container of hydrogen cyanide in the Commons chamber. He had gone along with the lesser conspiracy in good faith, flattered to believe that he could be Britain's saviour. When the doors shut behind the royal entourage, a high-pressure stream of lethal gas would fill the great hall, killing everyone inside in less than a minute. Despite his grief, the Duke would be persuaded to step forward to head a committee of national solidarity, and, by the time it met, the army and police would already be in control of all communications, transport and security.

Then it would begin.

But first there were a few loose ends to tie up.

Gault still couldn't believe it. 'So they kept me sweating in a stone dungeon for two days while you were drinking the old bastard's wine cellar dry?'

'More or less.'

'And you got the sword. You actually found Excalibur.' He shook his head in wonder and Jamie was struck by the effect the blade could have on even the most cynical and hardened soul. At Helena Webster's request he'd waited until they were back in New York before he revealed that the mission had been a success.

'I told you, she wanted me to have it.' Jamie glanced back to where the sword was concealed in a stubby green tube, of a type normally used to transport what the Yanks called fishing poles. It lay anonymously across the rearmost seats of the seven-seater Mercedes taxi van as they stuttered their way through the traffic of 7th Avenue.

'Well, you might look a bit cheerier about it. You've done it, your lordship. I didn't think you had it in you, but our master is wetting himself with excitement and the money is in the bank. Who knows, Charlotte might even let you have your wicked way with her.' He nudged the younger man in the ribs and Jamie managed a tired smile and rubbed a hand over the several days' stubble that had accumulated on his cheeks.

'Actually, old chum, all I want to do is have a shave and a shower and a bit of kip, and not even Charlotte could wake me up. Where is she, anyway? I thought she'd be at the airport to meet us?'

'She's putting the final touches to the export arrangements. The boss doesn't want any loose ends and his precious sword stuck in customs for six months. We do this by the book, just like we agreed.'

When they reached their hotel, Jamie carried the tube containing the sword up to the fourth-floor room Charlotte had booked for them, while Gault handed over their passports at the desk. Before he reached the check-in the former soldier switched one of the passports in his hand with another in his pocket. Just why Adam Steele wanted the young art dealer checked in under a different name wasn't clear, but Gault had learned not to argue with his employer.

Three hours later he shook Jamie awake. 'It's all set up. I have to meet Charlotte, I take the sword to her and she'll deal with it from there.' He laid a slim metal briefcase that had been waiting for them in the room on the bed. 'Don't let this out of your sight.'

'What's in it?'

'My laundry, what do you think? It's a laptop and a few other electronic gizmos I asked Steele to send along for the trip in case they were needed. The problem is they're not exactly legal and if anybody else gets hold of them we could end up in jail. What time to do you have?'

Jamie looked at his watch and yawned. 'Around five forty-five.'

'I mean exactly.'

'Five forty . . . six p.m.'

'Good. Unless you hear otherwise, at precisely six thirty you will call Adam on the satellite phone and tell him the deal is done. Got that? Normal procedure. Speed dial two.'

Jamie felt the hair bristle on the back of his neck. 'I'm not an idiot, Gault. Stop treating me like one.'

'Keep your shirt on.' The other man shrugged. 'I'm only passing on the instructions. One way or the other it'll soon be over and we don't ever have to see each other again.'

The tube lay by the window and Jamie picked it up, reluctant for a moment to part with the contents. But this had been the whole point of the mission: to get the sword to Adam Steele. Gault noticed the hesitation and looked at him curiously as they carried out a gentle tug of war. Eventually, he persuaded the stubby green cylinder from Jamie's hands and pulled on his jacket. He shook his head. 'This thing drives people crazy. I hope it was worth all the effort,' he said before the door closed behind him.

Jamie waited till he was gone before picking up the briefcase and studying the combination lock. His fingers hovered over the dials for almost a minute before he placed it beside the sat-phone and lay back on the bed. It would wait.

Their hotel was just off Washington Square in Greenwich Village, and Gault walked through the park and along 5th Avenue before taking a right into East 9th Street. He was entirely unselfconscious about the burden he carried. He'd been in New York often enough to know that nothing surprised the inhabitants. As long as you minded your own business you could wear what you liked and do what you liked. He'd once seen two men carrying a stuffed horse, for Christ's sake. The building he sought was another small hotel set slightly back from the street of high-rise apartment blocks. He walked past it once and carried on for another hundred paces before turning back abruptly, checking for any unnatural reactions in his fellow pedestrians. Retracing his steps, he tried the side door to the block's underground garage and found it unlocked as he'd been told. With a last scan to make sure he was alone, he slipped inside and closed the metal door behind him.

The garage was a place of shadows, with dimly lit bays alternating with patches of darkness, but nothing in the air said he should be nervous. Besides, this wasn't the first time he'd been here. He walked slowly down the centre of the concrete roadway between the bays, checking each one as he went, his hand close to his waistband and the butt of the pistol he carried. Reaching the end of the row, he took the slipway down to the lower level. He caught a whiff of a familiar perfume and smiled. Charlotte was waiting where she said she'd be, in the fifth bay down, the slim figure silhouetted against the light and standing by the open trunk of the anonymous hired Ford. He walked towards her.

Two sharp puffs of disturbed air broke the silence, followed by the sound of a body falling to the ground. A pair of shadows detached themselves from the deeper darkness of one of the unlit bays twenty paces away and manhandled the still warm body into the trunk of a second car.

'Hello?' The hand that gripped the mobile phone was slightly damp, and there might have been a hint of regret in the voice. 'He's here. You will find him in room 408 of the Washington Park Greenwich Hotel.' The words were in Pashto, the language of Afghanistan and northern Pakistan. When the message had been confirmed, the speaker programmed the Ford's satnav for JFK and moved the car into gear.

Jamie Saintclair lay fully dressed on the bed. He looked from his watch to the satellite phone for the twentieth time and felt the adrenalin coursing through his veins like pure heroin. It had all begun to come together in his mind on the way back from Reno. Tiny snippets of conversation, a scrambled detail from a news bulletin, a few words out of place while a man had been trying to kill him, and all the odd little coincidences that seemed to follow them around Europe and the USA. He reached for the briefcase, then changed his mind yet again. His suspicion that something wasn't right had hardened earlier, while he'd been pretending to doze, when Gault had left the room for more than an hour. Instinct told him the SBS man had been replacing the gun he'd lost at Marlette Lake. Why? All right, men like Gault didn't take any chances and it was patently clear he felt naked without a weapon, but all he had to do was deliver the tube. Why would Gault need a gun to walk four blocks? Was he right? He couldn't be sure, but he had to make a decision. He looked at the watch again: six eighteen. Twelve minutes.

He got up and marched to the window, studying the traffic on the street below. How long could he wait? The door drew his eyes. What if Gault walked back through that door now? Would that change anything? His brain urged him to relax because everything was fine and Gault knew what he was doing. The SBS man's travel case was still in the wardrobe where he had placed it, alongside Charlotte's. The plane tickets were on the table beside the phone. Three First Class flights from JFK to Heathrow at ten the next morning. Hell, they'd be drinking champagne for breakfast. Six twenty-two. His fingers twitched and he reached out and drew the satellite phone and the case to where he could comfortably reach them. The street outside was bathed in shadow. He picked up the bottle of water beside the bed and took another drink, but his mouth seemed to absorb the liquid like a patch of desert and he felt no benefit. He thought of Abbie, and her last cryptic message, and Sarah Grant in the dank East Prussian forest – *Whatever your friend Steele is up to it isn't just about money or an old sword*. Six twenty-four. He closed his eyes, counting the seconds in his head. Not yet. Not yet. Six twenty-five. How in the name of Christ had he got into this? His hand closed on the sat-phone and he looked at the face. The 2 button seemed to scream at him. Still five minutes to go. No, four minutes.

It was as if a series of tiny levers inside his head clicked into place. *Too many coincidences*. He scooped up the briefcase on the way to the door, which he opened slowly, checking the corridor beyond. Christ, hurry. He could feel the seconds ticking in his head as he rounded the corner to the lift area. The stairs were situated beyond the lift and he made his way quickly towards them, not quite running. Ahead of him a maid's trolley sat outside one of the rooms, blocking half the corridor and covered in sheets and pillows. The lift was to his left and as he passed it the soft double beep of the car arriving at his floor almost gave him a heart attack. Behind him the doors began to open and he dropped softly behind the maid's cart, his heart pounding in his chest. He'd look an idiot if he was wrong and some tourist couple walked past on the way to their rooms. But he knew he wasn't wrong.

Three or four sets of feet on the carpeted floor. A whispered conversation that his imagination told him was not in English. He waited, certain the harsh scream of his breathing would give him away. Now. Without looking back he made a dive for the stairs and descended, taking two at a time. When he reached the ground-floor entrance to the lobby he slowed to compose himself and checked his watch. Fifty seconds. Still time. He opened the door and walked briskly across the lobby. As he headed for the hotel entrance he noticed a nervous-looking brown-skinned man sitting on a chair to his left studying him with startled eyes. Then he was in the street.

Upstairs, outside Room 408, the leader of the four-man hit team nodded to his comrade with the pass key and the man slipped it into the lock and turned the handle. Drawing their pistols, they burst into the room. At the same moment, in the hotel lobby below, the dark man reached for his phone.

Jamie took ten paces up Washington Place and at

exactly six thirty pressed the 2 button and put the phone to his ear.

He wasn't sure what to expect, but he was looking directly at the hotel window when the explosion punched the front of Room 408 into the street, a bright blossom of flame with a flat-screen TV and a blackened truncated starfish shape that had once been human at its centre. The blast almost knocked him off his feet and he hunched down, partially deafened, as windows shattered all around and a hail of burning wreckage tumbled onto the people and cars below. As his hearing returned, a woman's hysterical screams split the unnatural silence and a hubbub of disbelieving voices grew and spread even as the sound of the first sirens reached them.

Men and women ran past towards the hotel to help the casualties, but Jamie didn't join them. Instead, he carefully removed the SIM card from the sat-phone, placed the phone on the ground and crushed it under his foot. When he was satisfied, he picked up the smashed casing and crammed it into his pocket before walking away in the opposite direction.

XXXV

Still stunned by what he'd witnessed, Jamie walked in a daze for what seemed like hours before his survival instinct kicked in and he found a public telephone booth on the corner of 17th and Broadway just past Union Square. Panicked fingers dug into his pockets for the card that just might save his neck, discovered another that made him pause, then settled on the initial card and dialled the number. He allowed it to ring for almost a minute without an answer. Eventually, he closed his eyes in frustration and hung up. A sour-looking Hispanic woman eyed him through the perspex and he reluctantly stepped away, giving her access to the phone. She took his place without saying thank you, which he found surprisingly irritating in the circumstances.

While he waited he tried to evaluate what had happened. He knew he was still in shock, but he must clear his mind. Whoever planted the bomb in the hotel could still be looking for him. Maybe it had been the men he'd heard coming from the lift? What they called an own goal. But it had happened at precisely – he remembered Gault's sneer: 'I'm only passing on instructions' – *precisely* six thirty p.m. Coincidence? There had been too many coincidences. Everywhere he went they seemed to follow him. He relived the blackened starfish cartwheeling across the street and a wave of nausea threatened to overwhelm him.

Gault had set him up. There was be no another explanation. And if Gault had set him up, that meant Adam Steele had set him up. His legs went suddenly weak and he staggered onto the pavement. 'Hey, pal,' someone said, and he realized he'd walked into their path. They were all around him. People. Anonymous faces of brown and black and white and every shade in between. Uncaring eyes of brown and green and black and blue. Potential enemies. He clutched the briefcase to his chest. Any one of them could blow him away and there wasn't one thing he could do about it. He was alone in an alien city. He had no weapon and no friends. A passport and a few hundred dollars in his pocket were his only link to the world he had formerly inhabited.

The woman was still talking, a hundred-mile-an-hour one-sided conversation in Spanish; something about her son needing to find a job. Who in the name of Christ used pay phones these days? Desperate people. He battered on the perspex and met her glare with one of his own. 'Excuse me, ma'am, but I don't have all day.' Her eyes narrowed, but she uttered a few words into the

handset and handed it over with a poisonous glance.
When he put it to his face he could smell her sour breath.
He hesitated before dialling the number on the card. It
was the last thing she'd given him before he'd left the
castle. *If there's anything else you need just call.* But
why should she help him? The sword was gone. He'd
failed. But there was something about her that made it
worth a try. He punched in the number.

'I hadn't expected to see you quite so soon, Mr Saintclair.' The tone was businesslike, but not unsympathetic.
Jamie wearily raised his head and found Helena Webster
looming over him, with Carl hovering protectively a
few paces in the background. Jamie had spent the night
moving about the city, trying to stay out of the way of
the cops who'd by now know the name of the room's
occupiers and at the same time in constant fear that
he might be being followed. By the time he returned
at dawn to the rendezvous she'd specified he was cold,
hungry, exhausted and irritable. Would she help him or
not? That's all he needed to know. But her next words
held only faint promise.

'You're fortunate I left for New York not long after
you and your friend did.' She joined him on the bench
and studied him for a few moments. 'Carl? I think Mr
Saintclair might benefit from a cup of coffee from the
booth over by the lake. I'll have one too.' She waited
until the guard had left. 'You said you needed my help,

but I'm a little perplexed. I gave you what you came for. What more can you expect of me?'

'Someone tried to kill me. I think it was because of the sword.'

'Which you no longer have,' she pointed out.

'I can still get it back to the original owners.'

She studied him, taking in every weary line on his face and evidently coming to a decision. 'Tell me.'

Exhaustion and relief almost overwhelmed him, but somehow he found the strength to relate his story. He told her about the bomb and his suspicions about Gault and Steele. 'He was very keen that I had this with me when I was blown to bits.' He placed the briefcase between them. 'There's a laptop in it. I think what was left of it was supposed to be found with what was left of me. That makes me suspicious that there may be something on it that links me to other things.'

'Things?'

Carl returned with the coffees and Jamie sipped his appreciatively, feeling the warmth seep into his bones and for the first time becoming aware of the vibrancy of his surroundings; the contrast between the dazzling green of the park and the pink glow of the surrounding high rises in the morning sun, between the sleek roller-bladers and the smart business types and the drab figures snuffling and scratching like animals as they emerged from the bushes that had sheltered them for the night. 'I don't know for certain,' he admitted eventually. 'But you were the only person I could think of who might be able to help me.'

She looked around. 'I do like Central Park on a spring day, don't you? Come.' He rose shakily to his feet and they walked through the grass and the early spring flowers past the softball fields and onto the Mall. Eventually she stopped by a larger-than-life bronze statue. 'You look very tired, Mr Saintclair. Do you need somewhere to hole up?'

He shook his head. 'I can manage.' It was only as he spoke that he realized she'd put out her hand for the briefcase. He passed it over and she studied the combination. 'Five digits; I think we can handle that.'

'Try one nine two one nine. It might save you a bit of time.' She stared at him and he shrugged. 'Just a hunch.'

'Perhaps we'll leave it until we're in a more secure environment.' She passed the case to Carl, whose face didn't move a muscle. 'You realize this could take two hours or two days? Possibly even two weeks.'

'I'll wait.'

She nodded slowly and turned away. 'Oh, I almost forgot. You'll need this, pay phones are too public. When – if – I discover what you want to know, I'll be in touch. We'll meet again here.' She handed over a slim South Korean-made mobile phone. 'It's pre-paid and untraceable. I will text you a time. Use it to contact me if necessary.'

Jamie watched the slim figure walk down the broad avenue of giant elm trees, followed by the watchful Carl, and realized he had never felt so utterly alone. Sooner or later the NYPD or the CIA were going to link him to the bombing at the Washington Park Hotel. When they did that they'd use all their resources to uncover the series of coincidences that had brought him there. Once that happened every law enforcement agency in the United States and Europe would be looking for Jamie Saintclair. The SIM card from the sat-phone felt as if it was burning a hole in his pocket. He'd no doubt the sat-phone records and the timings of the bombings in Madrid, Corfu and New York would match up. And how many more had there been in Germany and Poland? Someone had used him. All the evidence pointed to Gault and Adam Steele. He couldn't understand why, but he was going to find out.

But that meant he had to get out of the States and back to Britain, and how the hell was he going to do that?

He turned his eyes skywards for inspiration and found himself staring into the face of a familiar-looking young man. Oddly, the bronze figure was doing something very similar as he sat with his quill pen poised to record his latest piece of genius. Time had given the statue a patina of pale green, which, if anything, added dignity to the subject. The memory of excruciating nights in his grandfather's kitchen listening to indecipherable doggerel in a heathen tongue and being forced to eat what had tasted like spicy sawdust made Jamie smile despite the desperate circumstances. Old Matthew

Sinclair had been a great Burns man, and here he was, Robert Burns, another lad stranded a long way from home. *The best laid schemes o' mice an' men gang aft agley.* The line from an oft-heard poem seemed to perfectly sum up Jamie's current predicament.

But if Rabbie Burns had a message it was one of perseverance and hope, and Jamie took comfort from it now. All he needed was some of that inspiration. Did he have any favours he could call in? Not exactly – the balance sheet was all on the debit side – but maybe that didn't matter.

He pulled out the mobile phone Helena Webster had given him and dialled a number that was etched on his brain. The ring tone sounded twice.

His voice was surprisingly steady when he spoke. 'I'm in trouble and I'm going to need some help getting home . . . Yes, I understand that. But I have something to trade. Get back to me when you know what's possible and I'll tell you what I have.'

He rang off with all the care of a man who had just prodded a large cobra with a short stick.

By late afternoon Helena still hadn't got back to him and he considered buying a sleeping bag in preparation for another night in the park. He was walking towards the stores when the phone buzzed to announce the arrival of a text. An hour later he stood by the Burns statue, staring across at its companion, another Scottish literary giant, when he noticed a certain pattern of movement. Large men in jeans, wearing designer sunglasses and jackets cut to conceal a certain kind of weaponry, took up strategic positions at all points of the compass around him, cutting off every avenue of escape.

He didn't feel any fear. There'd always been the possibility of this outcome. But it surprised him. It was difficult to believe she'd betray him.

Helena Webster marched up the avenue with a sense of purpose that matched the military dispositions she'd put in place. Only one thing didn't quite fit, and that was the silver case in Carl's hand as he walked behind her. When she reached him, her face was so pale he could see the marbling of the veins beneath her skin. 'Give me one reason why I shouldn't hand you in.'

He didn't flinch as he met her cold stare. 'If you've looked at the material in there, and you need a reason, I doubt I'm going to convince you. Either you trust me or you don't, Helena.'

'My sources in the FBI say they have a passport picture of the man who rented the hotel room. A man with an Islamic name. They plan to put it out later today. You are a dangerous man to know, Mr Saintclair.'

He nodded, there was no disputing that. 'Someone needed a sacrificial goat and I was volunteered.'

'You know what's in here?'

'Not the specifics,' he admitted. 'But, in general, I think I can guess.'

'We are talking about mass murder. If what is contained on the hard disk of this computer is true, the kind of detail involved could only have come from the terrorists themselves. Detail of timings and logistics, types of explosives, even estimates of casualties. Dozens of attacks all over the world. The only thing that stops me handing you over to the authorities is the fact that it has been fragmented and repeated all over the disk in a way that's designed to ensure at least some of it would have survived the explosion in the hotel.'

'Doesn't that suggest I'm telling the truth?' He could hear the weariness in his own voice and it sounded like defeat.

'Perhaps.' It wasn't quite an acceptance. 'But there are other things on here. A kind of information timebomb designed to stay hidden for weeks before any normal technician would reach them. Information about things that haven't *happened* yet. And those things scare the hell out of me. I need to know what you're going to do with it.'

'I'm going to use it to buy my life.'

She took a deep breath and walked past him up the Mall towards the intersection with Center Drive. For a moment he thought he'd lost her and waited for the security detail to close in, but she stopped abruptly and turned back towards him.

'How?'

So he told her.

Later, when the ring of guards was gone and only Carl remained, ostentatiously examining the statue on the far side of the paved road, she studied the briefcase with puzzled disgust. 'You took a chance giving me this. The information it contains could be very valuable to certain people I know in the CIA.'

'I trusted you.'

'Still, I might have been tempted.'

'You would have been sentencing me to death.' He shrugged. 'Or at least several lifetimes in one of your lovely state penitentiaries. I didn't think you'd do that.'

Her eyes hardened and he knew he was back on dangerous ground. 'What made you think that, Mr Saintclair?'

'I'm a very good judge of character.'

She looked up sharply, but gradually her face relaxed into a smile at the reminder of her own boast.

'You could have made me disappear at the castle,' he pointed out, 'and it would have been much more convenient for you if you had. But you didn't. I think you've had enough of killing.' The smile froze and Helena Webster's eyes flashed with new menace. He knew he might be talking himself into a noose, but he'd gone too far to stop now. 'You spoke about your grandfather *replicating* the ceremonies, thinking I wouldn't know what that meant. But I do, right down to the last detail. And I understand *exactly* what it would have taken. That's what killed your father, wasn't it? The knowledge of what *his* father had done in his deranged quest to unleash the secret of the swords. There had to be blood and, more important, a source of that blood. Did Rolf Lauterbacher supply them? Is that what was on the page you cut from his journal? At first I didn't understand why you didn't just take the whole book, but then I realized you couldn't have known the daughter didn't have access to his safe. If she did, she would have noticed it missing and the German police would have investigated his "accident" a bit more thoroughly. So you ran your high-tech scanner over the pages, decoded the contents – that would have been simple enough for you with the decryption software you supply to your friends in the CIA – took the incriminating page and said a fond farewell to your father's old pal Rolf.'

A vein throbbed in her temple, and for a moment he thought he'd pushed her too far.

'I was right, Mr Saintclair, you are clever.' She glanced towards Carl. 'What do you intend to do with that information?'

He studied the pale face, noticing something he hadn't earlier, a resemblance to a martyred saint in a Caravaggio painting. 'Nothing. I think your family has suffered enough.'

After a moment's hesitation she signalled Carl and the black man approached with the case. Jamie took it and weighed it in his hands. He delved in his pocket until he found what he was looking for. The combination was as he'd guessed – 19 2 19 – the numbers in the alphabet that matched SBS. He popped it open and dropped the SIM card inside, before closing it and whirling the dials to relock it. Helena Webster gave him a questioning look as he handed it back to her.

'I'd like you to send it to this address, please.'

He produced a piece of paper and she took it with a puzzled frown. 'Will it be safe there?'

'As safe as anywhere.'

They walked to the end of the road. 'Are you sure I can't help you get back home?'

He managed a tired smile. 'You've done enough.' The truth was that he doubted whether Helena Webster's gratitude for him keeping his mouth shut would last long. She was beautiful, a bit too intelligent, and there was always that buried element of black widow spider.

Anyway, he had plans of his own.

Jamal al Hamza took the news with his usual equanimity. The target would be dead if Allah had willed it. There was nothing to do but pass on the information to his master. He left the coffee shop in Peshawar through the back entrance and directly into the garage that took up the entire rear of the building. At random he chose a beige Toyota, one of the six different SUVs parked there, and flicked the switch for the electronic doors. As he drove through the familiar chaos of the busy streets he was unaware that his progress had been picked up by one of several satellites programmed to monitor the particular pattern sprayed on the vehicle's roof by one of hundreds of ground operatives recruited to help monitor the movements of the many doubtful vehicles that moved through the area in and around the border between Pakistan and Afghanistan. The dye used to mark the car was invisible to anyone on the ground and the SUV was one of four that the satellites had tracked between the street behind the cafe and a residential complex in the centre of Kohat, one of the less likely terrorist strongholds in the region. It would take several months before the significance of the movement was identified, and at that point it would become a priority for high-ranking officials of a country several thousands of kilometres away. The results would be spectacular.

XXXVI

'Can you accompany me, please, sir?'

Jamie had seen them watching him as he approached passport control at Heathrow after his more or less straightforward return to London by way of a meat truck into Canada and a scheduled flight from Montreal. The passport he'd used was identical to his own apart from a slightly modified number and with the name he'd been born with – SINCLAIR – instead of the supposedly aristocratic version his mother had believed would help him ascend the social heights at Cambridge. A cursory glance from the passport officer seemed slight recompense for an hour in the snaking line through the security gates, but it turned out to be for confirmation rather than identification.

He followed two suited young men with identical close-cropped sandy hair through an unmarked door, conscious of the matched pair of armed cops watching in the background, their trigger fingers twitching. Out of the public eye any pretence of politeness disappeared and the men removed the shoulder bag he was carrying, took an arm each and propelled him along a corridor until they reached another anonymous door.

'May I ask what this is all about?' he said as politely as the circumstances merited. 'I do have certain rights, you know.'

'No.' The man on his right in the grey suit twisted his arm painfully and pushed him so his head hit the door, fortunately as his partner was opening it. Once inside they sat him at a table facing a blank wall of opaque grey glass that no doubt allowed people to see in, but not the prisoner to see out.

'Can you place the contents of your pockets on the table, please?' Grey suit gave the order in a monotone that gave nothing away as he rummaged through Jamie's flight bag.

Jamie fumbled for a few moments, eventually producing his passport, mobile phone and wallet, his house keys, loose change in a mixture of four currencies, and a pile of boiled sweets. He laid them on the surface in front of him.

'They're for my ears,' he explained as he spread the sweets in a mosaic pattern, green to the right and orange to the left. 'They don't like the pressure changes.'

Grey suit immediately homed in on the mobile phone, which he placed in an evidence bag and took to the door, where it was whisked away by an unseen hand. The second man – Jamie was fairly certain they were from the Met's anti-terror branch – separated out the pile on the table, pushing the sweets haphazardly into another evidence bag. He picked up one of the coins and examined it with a look of suspicion. 'A Polish *piatka*, can I assume you've been in Poland recently?'

'Relatively recently.'

'Only I don't see a stamp in your passport.'

'That would be because, as you see, it's quite a new passport – I had to have mine replaced because it was stolen recently in New York – and they don't tend to stamp your passport at Polish airports the way they used to do. I rather miss it. Now can you *please* tell me what's going on?'

Blue suit glanced at grey suit, who in turn glanced at the opaque wall.

'You are being held under Schedule Seven of the Terrorism Act 2000. You should be aware that this entitles us to take DNA samples and carry out a strip search.' He paused to allow the words to sink in. 'Also that it is a criminal offence not to answer our questions.'

'Fire away, old chum.' Jamie produced an unlikely smile that reflected a confidence he didn't feel. 'I'm perfectly happy to answer your questions. Nothing to hide at all. I'm sure it'll all iron itself out when you find out you have the wrong chap, but don't worry, I won't sue.'

As it turned out, they didn't ask him anything. With a final perplexed look from blue suit they left him alone with a uniformed constable who seemed to be a deaf mute and whose eyes never left the far wall. Jamie knew this was where he was supposed to be unnerved into confessing all his sins, but as he went over his strategy for the fifteenth time, he still couldn't improve on playing every bouncer with a straight bat until the opening he hoped he'd carved for himself arrived. If it didn't, he was probably going to jail for a very long time, but there wasn't a bloody thing he could do about it. He was also glad he'd had a pee when he left the plane.

Ninety minutes after he'd disappeared, blue suit returned with an older man who took his seat on the opposite side of the table and slapped down a thick orange file as the uniformed officer left the room. The older man, bulky in a dark suit and with the pinched angry features that so often herald a heart attack, hunched over the maroon oblong of Jamie's passport, studying it with the intimate care of a coin dealer. Eventually, he threw it dismissively on the table between them.

'What do you know about a man called Mohammed al-Awali?' They must have handed out flat, emotionless voices at Scotland Yard special casting.

'I've never heard the name. As I told your colleague, I have no idea why I'm being held here and I'd very much like to call my lawyer.'

The man – in Jamie's mind he'd become *The Chief Inspector* – ignored the suggestion, pulled out a photograph and placed it beside the passport. 'Do you recognize him?'

Jamie picked up the picture, a grainy head-and-shoulders photo, and squinted. 'It does look a bit like me,' he admitted, 'though a few years older. That explains what I was saying to your colleague about mistaken identity.'

The Chief Inspector's head lifted and Jamie found himself the focus of two drill-bit eyes. 'Please don't underestimate the seriousness of your position, sir. The man in the picture, *who looks a bit like you*, has been linked to terrorist offences all over the world. Until twenty-four hours ago the FBI believed Mr al-Awali, a Muslim convert of British origin, had died in an explosion in New York along with other named Al-Qaida operatives, but he is obviously a gentleman of some resource because he escaped with moments to spare. He is currently whereabouts unknown,' the cold eyes bored into Jamie, 'or at least he was. United Kingdom, Germany, Spain, Greece and the United States. Does that list of countries ring any bells with you, Mr Sinclair? Or the deaths of over a hundred innocent people, including the US ambassador to NATO and his wife?' Jamie didn't say anything, because he sensed there was nothing he could say. Without warning the other man changed tack. 'Is this your mobile telephone?' From the folder, he slid the slim pre-paid mobile phone Helena Webster had handed over another lifetime ago in Central Park.

'Yes, it looks like it.'

'The one you normally use?'

'I've had it since New York.'

'And before that?'

'The old one was stolen.'

'In New York?'

'Yes.'

'How very convenient.'

Jamie let his shoulders sag. 'Look, I'm sorry I can't help you . . . Inspector? I really don't know what this is all about. My girlfriend died in—'

The Chief Inspector leaned across the table. 'I've just told you what this is all about, Mr Sinclair, or Mr al-Awali. If you have anything to give us, now is the time before it's too late.'

'What do you mean too late? I hope that's not a threat?'

'Oh, you can be as defensive as you like, son, but don't try to be too clever. Right at this very moment a team of lawyers is putting together a case against Mohammed al-Awali in New York on charges of inciting terrorism, causing an explosion and multiple counts of murder. Once they're in place they will be asking for the extradition of the suspect to the United States of America, which the British government will undoubtedly fast-track. There al-Awali will go on trial in a state that currently favours the death penalty. What do you fancy, son, lethal injection or the chair?' He pushed his face into Jamie's, close enough that the younger man could smell the mint on his breath. 'This is your one chance. If you give us enough evidence to build a case in this country and on the European mainland against the men who ordered the attack, the bombers and their quartermasters, then the likelihood is you'll be tried in this country. You didn't act alone. Maybe you don't know it all, but you know something and that something could save your life. But you have to give me it now, or it's out of my hands.'

Jamie swallowed to ease the noose tightening around his neck. Suddenly the room seemed infinitely smaller and it was as if he was in the bottom portion of an egg timer with the sand pouring over his head. Right now, it had reached his chin, but in a few more minutes it would be a lot less comfortable.

'Inspector, I—'

The door swung open and the Chief Inspector turned with a shout of fury. 'Get the—' The words died in his throat as he recognized the grey-haired man in the camel coat who filled the doorway.

'I think we'll be taking it from here, Inspector,' the Director General of the Security Services announced.

'Sir, I have to protest . . . protocol . . . this isn't right.'

But the DGSS was above protocol and he didn't give a damn whether it was right or not. 'Close the door on your way out.' His bodyguards were already ushering the Chief Inspector and blue suit from the room. 'And make sure the office next door is cleared.'

The door closed behind them and the two men were left in silence. The DGSS's eyes ranged over Jamie with a hint of mild distaste, as if he'd just found greenfly on one of his roses. 'Now, Mr Saintclair, perhaps you can explain what this is all about.'

For a moment, Jamie felt like collapsing. The first stage of his unlikely plan had worked. Now came the difficult bit. 'I thought you were never going to bloody get here.'

XXXVII

The Scotland Yard anti-terrorist surveillance team assigned to Jamie Saintclair/Sinclair/al-Awali reported him getting into a taxi outside his Knightsbridge flat and followed it to his fourth-floor matchbox of an office in Old Bond Street, where he emerged from the cab and entered the building. The lights went on in said office exactly seventy-five seconds later and the surveillance team settled in for a long day. It was only when the lights went out at five p.m. and nobody left the building that the alarm bells began to ring.

'We've lost him.'

The Chief Inspector's rage was legendary and entirely predictable. 'Well, bloody well find him again, and don't come back until you do, or you'll end up back on the beat in bloody Brixton.'

Several hours earlier, Jamie had crouched in the rear of the taxi as the lookalike substitute wearing his clothes got out and walked into his office building. He stayed with the cab until the driver was certain they were no longer being tailed and dropped him outside King's Cross Station. There he bought a ticket to Welwyn, where he still had his grandfather's house, but left the train five stops early and picked up the hire car he'd arranged to have left at Potters Bar. The route was fixed in his head, even if the destination was uncertain. All he was missing was the Baedeker map Wulf Ziegler and his *Hitler Jugend* troop had used to guide their way north.

Before he started he had one more thing to do. He picked up the slim Nokia phone from the passenger seat. It seemed a long time since Gault had given him it as part of Adam Steele's package for hunting down Excalibur. He'd left it behind in the flat by mistake during the rush to get ready for the New York flight and it seemed a shame to waste it. The number he dialled came easily to his fingertips and the call was picked up on the second ring.

'Hello, Adam.' He'd vowed to stay detached and the cold menace so apparent in his voice came as a surprise to him. Still, it was perfectly understandable. The man on the other end of the phone had tried to destroy him and might yet succeed. The silence stretched out like a high-tension wire and for a long moment he wondered if Adam Steele was going to hang up.

'Jamie?'

'I thought you'd be surprised, *old chum*. After all, you've already got me dead and buried, or at least what wasn't scattered across half of New York.' He heard the splutter of false indignation and the beginning of a denial, but he cut the businessman short and continued swiftly, making no attempt to conceal his contempt. 'Let's not waste our time, shall we? The bottom line is that, whether you like it or not, I'm still in the land of the living, and by now you know about the sword. That was a bloody shock, I can tell you. A lovely piece of early medieval workmanship, but about two hundred years too late to be Excalibur. It would have served you right if I'd offered the Websters the million quid you boasted about at the start. But I wasn't certain then, and you'd have found a way to wriggle out of it, because you're a real slippery bastard, Adam. In fact, you're so slippery you give slippery bastards a bad name. You might even have got away with it, but you were too clever for your own good. The laptop computer you hoped would be blown to bits with me wasn't as secure as you thought. If anyone was to link the computer to you all those succulent titbits of information you planted to blacken my name would condemn you before you could say Jack the Ripper.'

'Naturally, I deny all this,' Steele replied, all the false bonhomie gone from his voice. 'But why don't I humour you, for old times' sake? What do you want, Saint-clair?'

'I want that million quid you promised me, Adam. For that you get the computer and all that juicy information that, with a little help from me, could put you away for the rest of your life in a place with no servants or Chateau Lafite 'eighty-two, and where a good-looking chap like you would be very popular at shower time.'

'Not good enough, Saintclair.'

'It is if I tell you where to find the real Excalibur.'

Steele gave a snort of disgust. 'You must think I'm a fool.' He paused and Jamie could almost hear his mind working. 'Unless you switched swords before the flight from Reno.'

'Gault will tell you that wasn't possible. No, the sword you have is the sword from Nortstein Castle.'

'Then you're selling me a bigger fantasy than the Ziegler codex—'

'Think about it, Adam.' Jamie let him hear the urgency of a desperate man. 'Reinhard Heydrich went to a lot of trouble to acquire a specific sword. He would have known the moment he saw it that it wasn't the real thing, just as you did, but he managed to convince Himmler it was Excalibur. To do that, he must have had some pretty solid evidence. If I'm right, part of that evidence was the English country house it was stolen from. The codex isn't a fantasy, it's a trail that will lead me to the sword. Excalibur exists and I will find it, but I want a million pounds.'

'And what if I agree to this foolishness?'

'Get Gault to drive the pair of you north towards Newcastle and keep your phone charged. I'll be in touch and let you know where we'll make the exchange. And make sure you bring the sword. I promised someone I'd get it back to the former owners and, unlike you, I keep my promises.'

'You've never struck me as greedy, Saintclair.' Suspicion edged Steele's voice like a surgical saw. 'Why would you want a million pounds?'

'Because I know Excalibur's worth it to you and because, to be truthful, you haven't left me much choice. I've got half the police forces in Europe, not to say the States, looking for my Islamic alter ego. I need to disappear before they link him with Jamie Saintclair Esquire of this parish and a million quid will help me do it in a bit of style.'

'What guarantees do I have—'

'There are no guarantees.' The words came out as a snarl. 'Take it or leave it. All you need to know is you won't get blown up or shot at. If you want Excalibur and the computer a million is the price you have to pay. And if that's not incentive enough, maybe I'll throw in the chance to get even for making you look like a five-star clown on the fencing mat. No guards, no tips. Just you and me and two swords. An old-fashioned duel, though I doubt you've got the guts to meet me face to face.'

When he hung up, he discovered the sweat was running down his back and his hand was shaking.

He'd cast the lure, but would Adam Steele take it? He closed his eyes and a familiar face filled his mind. He would do it. He had to do it. For her.

Before he drove off he plugged the phone into the in-car charger and made sure it was switched on.

*

The two days spent more or less under house arrest had been useful for planning the journey and he had a print-out of the relevant section of the Excalibur codex to give him a rough guide. It had been a spying mission – albeit with a secret at its heart – and he reckoned on the German boys not doing much more than twenty miles a day over the hilly northern countryside. He studied the first section.

> *That summer . . . My eight-man section cycled east from Manchester and then north up the spine of the country. After just over a week we reached a range of low, bleak hills where seldom a tree grew. We camped with an armoured unit under training in the area and they made us welcome, almost treating us as comrades. They appeared to have no suspicion of the war we knew was coming and for which we had trained. We thought them . . . very naive.*

Jamie covered the two hundred miles between Potters Bar and Manchester in just under four hours, including a stop at a Little Chef for a meat pie that had pastry the consistency of cardboard, and was filled with a brown-grey sludge. At Manchester, he swapped the M6 for the M62 and headed over the Pennines towards Leeds. He was happy to stay on the motorway for the moment. The tricky part would come later.

His gaze fell on the mobile phone plugged into the

charger. Jamie was banking on the near certainty that its previous owner had installed some kind of tracking device and was even now trying to make up the miles between them. Steele's instinct would be to lash out with deadly force, but the question was whether he'd give Jamie time to find the true sword, or cut his losses. If he took the second option that would be unfortunate for Jamie, but something deep in his gut told him Adam Steele was as obsessed with Excalibur as Harold Webster, only for different reasons. And that meant he would wait. Of course, Steele wasn't the only potentially lethal fly in the ointment. There was always the possibility Al-Qaida were still on his tail, looking for payback and to make good their promise of a farewell video with an edge. And the cops who'd been watching him were unlikely to just sit back and accept his disappearance. By now he was probably on Britain's Most Wanted list. He glanced at the traffic behind him, looking for the dark 4x4s that seemed to be the discerning assassin's vehicle of choice, and finding more possibles than he liked. Maybe he should have taken the Chief Inspector's advice and stayed in jail.

He hit the main A1(M) at three in the afternoon and turned north again, hugging the east side of the hills, but conscious he would eventually be pushed ever closer to the North Sea. Soon there would be a decision to be made and he pulled into another service station to study the map. At first glance, the problem with the codex was the lack of detail, yet when he considered it, he wondered if, for him, that wasn't actually its greatest asset. *The spine of the country* – that was the key. There was no deviation to take in likely espionage targets like industrial Darlington and Middlesbrough, the population centre of Durham or the port of Newcastle. Wulf Ziegler and his *Hitler Jugend* boys had stayed with the Pennines because the hills were the arrow taking them straight to the heart of their true goal. The more he studied the map, the more certain he became. His finger followed the line of the hills right up to the border. Here in this crucible of broken country south of Hadrian's Wall lay the answer. And he would find it tomorrow.

Sensing that he'd soon need a breathing space, he switched off the phone before he reached Darlington and a few miles later he turned off the motorway. This was the gateway to the western reaches of County Durham, and took him across the Wear valley and into the sparsely populated moor and farmlands of the north Pennines. Here, among the rolling hills, he could finally picture the hardy, brown-shirted German boys on their heavy iron bikes gritting their teeth as they attacked each climb, before the whooping, exhilarating plunge into the valley beyond. They'd have sung their marching songs, the same songs they'd sing a few years later when they invaded Poland and France, Belgium and Holland, Denmark and Norway. And Russia, where most of them probably still lay in unmarked graves. When they rode these drystone wall flanked highways they were just children. Yet these children had been sent on a perilous mission by their country's highest leaders. It was almost impossible to imagine now, in this over-televised, Xbox, PlayStation age that sucked young people into the nearest screen. Yet he supposed there were boys not much older serving their country, and dying for it, arguably for a lot less reason, in the heat-fractured dust bowl of southern Afghanistan.

He shook the melancholy thought from his mind and concentrated on the countryside around, his eyes seeking anything that might resemble Ziegler's description of *low, bleak hills where seldom a tree grew*. His heart sank as he came to the conclusion that it fitted everything in the landscape for about twenty miles.

As dusk fell he approached the east–west axis between Carlisle and Newcastle that more or less followed the route of Hadrian's Wall. It also followed the line of the Tyne and he'd already identified Corbridge, a village on the north bank of the river, as a possible location for the *small town with an impressive ruin*.

Dog-tired he booked into a bed and breakfast just outside the town centre and after dinner at the local Italian restaurant fell into a fitful sleep where he was always chasing something that never came within his grasp. He hoped it wasn't an omen for tomorrow.

XXXVIII

'Can I help you?'

Jamie looked up from the leather-bound volume and returned the woman's smile. She was about fifty and reminded him of his mother; narrow, intense features and wavy silver-blond hair swept back from her forehead. It was just after eleven and Corbridge library had only been open for about five minutes. He sensed she was uneasy about a stranger's presence at this time of the day and felt he had to explain. 'I'm just trying to find out a few things about the local area.'

The smile lost a little of its sparkle. 'You'll be here for the Wall.' Her voice told him most people came here for the Wall and not much else. 'Well, if there's anything else just let me know.'

'There might be one thing.' He explained about the small town with the spectacular ruin.

The riddle piqued her interest. 'That doesn't sound

much like Corbridge. The only ruins we have here are a few Roman foundations and a couple of pillars. They're just outside the village: interesting, but nobody could describe them as spectacular. Hexham, along the way a bit, has an abbey. It's old, but it's no ruin.'

He thanked her and continued his research as she returned to her desk, staying for an hour until he ran out of patience with ancient tomes full of descriptions of local country houses, none of which remotely resembled the one described by Wulf Ziegler. As he was leaving the library a thought struck him. 'It's just a long shot, but would there be any hills around here with a very distinctive silhouette?'

'Plenty of hills round here, but none that you'd say were that distinctive.' She shook her head ruefully. 'I'm sorry. I'm not being much use to you.'

He smiled his thanks. 'It was worth a try . . . One last question. Would you know if there was some sort of army training camp around here during the war?'

'Och, the army's been using Otterburn since Pontius Pilate was a bairn.' The grizzled character at the bar of the Otterburn Arms had a distinctive accent that seemed to have little need for the letter r, so the words came out as 'Otta'bu'un' and 'bai'n'. He supped gravely on the pint Jamie had bought him. 'They took the place ova' before the First War, all sixty thousand ugly acres of it. Seen more bombs, shells and bullets than the Somme, a' reckon.'

'Would there have been tanks here before the Second World War?'

'No tanks now.' He shook his head. 'The muckle things they have these days is too heavy for the soft peat. But before the war they had these wee light boo-gas that could barely stop a bullet. There'd have been plenty of them.'

Jamie's anticipation had been growing since he left Corbridge and saw the long, low shadow of the Cheviot Hills in the distance. The librarian had laughed. 'That would be Otterburn Camp. It was here during the war and it still is. It's about twenty miles up the road. You'll see it away to your right, beyond the village.'

He left the old man with a second pint. As he drove north from Otterburn, the ground began to rise and soon he was among bleak hills clad in heather and rough grass that exactly fitted Wulf Ziegler's description, *where seldom a tree grew*. The road wound up a long cleft in the hillside before the sky opened up and he found himself at the top of a rise with the whole country laid out before him like a rumpled plaid carpet of grey, brown and green. He slowed and pulled into a layby by a big boulder bearing a sign that announced he was WELCOME TO SCOTLAND and got out of the car into the bite of a chill wind. With his heart in his throat he studied the great swathe of patchwork, captivated by the shadows of individual clouds that scudded across the land from right to left. Finally he understood. Wulf Ziegler's target hadn't been in the north of England.

It was the south of Scotland. At first he didn't see it amongst the jumble of humps and hillocks stretching far to the north. Then, in the middle distance, there it was. Ziegler's signal post. Three hills standing shoulder to shoulder like warriors in a shield wall. A silhouette that was unique and utterly distinctive. He returned to the car with a feeling of growing awe and a sense that fate was leading him inexorably towards a prize beyond his comprehension.

A few miles ahead the road dropped into a winding river valley with cliffs of layered red sandstone occasionally peeping from the trees. Eventually the valley opened out and on the far side of a long green meadow lay the next marker – *a small town with an impressive ruin*. The town was Jedburgh, and the spectacular ruin the remains of some great abbey with a square tower a hundred and fifty feet high. Intrigued, he turned off the main road and drove across a bridge towards the town centre. The way took him over the top of a rise, with the soaring walls of the abbey to his left. As he topped the rise he glanced casually to his right and his blood froze as two black 4X4s passed by in convoy on the main road below. Was he starting at shadows? He looked at the mobile on the passenger seat to make sure it was still switched off and broke into a cold sweat at the thought that he'd planned to turn it on after Otterburn. Coincidence? Adam Steele was no fool, he could follow the trail as easily as Jamie. The question was how much he knew? If Steele had the location of the *small schloss* there wasn't a lot Jamie could do about it. But it might cause danger to people he hadn't even met. Reluctantly, he resisted the temptation to follow the cars. Instead, he drew into a car park opposite the abbey that backed onto a low flat building advertising itself as a tourist information centre. Since information was precisely what he was looking for, he decided to take a look inside.

The walls were lined with posters and shelves filled with colourful guidebooks, fluffy knitwear and endless tartan scarves. A long counter took up most of one side of the interior and the floor was scattered with stands filled with more books, fliers for local businesses and maps.

He rummaged through a selection of Ordnance Survey maps on one of the stands and chose a large-scale chart for the approximate area of the hills he'd seen. As he approached the counter to pay, a display of books by local writers caught his attention. Several had the same name on the spine. One in particular made the breath catch in his throat. It couldn't be a coincidence that he'd last seen it in Hal Webster's library. On instinct, he added it to the map and took it to the sales assistant.

'This book looks very interesting. I was wondering if the author lived around here?'

The girl nodded. 'I believe he does, though I'm not exactly sure where, sir.' Oddly, her accent was entirely different from those on the far side of the imaginary border ten miles to the south. 'But you'll find him in the telephone directory.'

'Where can I get one?'

She smiled and reached below the counter. 'We don't do this for all our customers, but seeing as it's you . . .'

'It was good of you to meet me at such short notice.'

The older man nodded graciously. 'I was intrigued by your interest in Arthur. The subject is a passion of mine, as you'll know from *The Lost Kingdoms*.' He indicated the book Jamie was carrying. 'And also that you wanted to meet somewhere off the beaten track with this particular vista.' He waved a hand that encompassed the three hills looming on the far side of the Tweed Valley. Alistair Moffat was tall, but with the slight stoop tall men take on when they're not entirely comfortable with their height. Balding, with a neatly trimmed, fast greying beard, and shrewd, deep-set eyes in a face scattered with humour lines, there was something almost Pickwickian about the writer. The two men had arrived a few minutes earlier from opposite directions on the narrow minor road and parked side by side in the little car park overlooking the River Tweed. Moffat continued: 'The legends say these hills were a single mountain until the wizard Michael Scott, who hailed from these parts, split them into three.' He smiled as he regaled the unlikely myth. 'The truth is a wee bit more prosaic, the Eildons are probably the product of volcanic activity. Mind you, Scott was the very man for splitting mountains. He was

427

an alchemist and sorcerer, a figure of awe and fear who
had mixed with the greatest thinkers of the time. The
problem with the story is that he lived in the twelfth
century – he was an astrologer to Frederick the Second
in his court at Padua – and the Romans called these hills
Trimontium at least a thousand years earlier.' His grey
eyes took on a self-mocking twinkle. 'The clue is in the
name.'

Jamie didn't hide his puzzlement. 'In the book, you
link Trimontium and Arthur with the Romans, does
that mean you think *he* was a Roman? I thought the
Arthurian legends all had their origins in Wales or
Cornwall and Arthur was the archetypal Briton, fending
off the Saxons.'

The writer didn't take offence. 'Every legend is the
product of centuries,' he smiled, 'sometimes millennia,
of stories passed on by word of mouth, and occasionally,
away back in the mists of time, those stories are born
from a kernel of truth.' He shook his head gravely.
'I've never said Arthur was Roman, only that he may
have been a Roman officer, which isn't quite the same
thing. You can't see it from here, but on top of the
northernmost hill is an Iron Age township; the remains
of literally hundreds of mud and wattle houses. These
were the sacred hills of a tribe called the Votadini, and it
appears that the Votadini were what we call "clients" of
Rome; a sort of buffer state between the Empire and the
wild tribes of the north. To the north-east of the hills is
a platform above the river and the Romans built a fort

there, first in Agricola's time, and then later reused and refurbished it over almost two centuries—'

An almighty rush of sound drowned out the author's words and Jamie ducked, fearing they were under some kind of attack. Moffat didn't even blink. When he looked up, a warplane, flying unfeasibly low, was just disappearing over the shoulder of the hills.

The author smiled. 'It's not just the Romans who used the mountains as a signpost. You get a lot of low flying round here and the RAF – or NATO – lads like to use it as a reference point for turns during their exercises. It takes a bit of getting used to, as you've just found out.' He laughed. 'Anyway, sometimes Trimontium was garrisoned, sometimes abandoned, depending on the political mood of the day. But the Romans still ruled here, through their patrols from the Wall, diplomacy and the strength of their surrogates, the Votadini. We know from the historical sources that the Votadini were horse warriors – they were the same Gododdin who rode to Catraeth *though none was Arthur* – and the Romans often recruited native horse as auxiliary cavalry and valued them greatly. I think it entirely possible that Arthur was a war chief of the Votadini, possibly a *prefect*, a local commander of auxiliary horse, and as the Romans withdrew behind the Wall in the third or fourth centuries he and his men stemmed the tide of invasion from the north. He became a warrior commemorated in song and story, and his name rang through the ages as a testament of valour.'

Moffat's final words sent a shiver of almost super-stitious awe through Jamie, but they also begged a question. 'But how . . . ?'

The writer smiled. 'You're still sceptical, and you have every right to be. You mentioned that the Arthur legend had its genesis in Wales, but perhaps it would be more accurate to say *in Welsh*. Would it surprise you that the Votadini spoke a variant of Celtic that became Welsh? Or that the Saxon invasions of later centuries drove them west and then south away from their spiritual homelands and this place of secrets? The Men of the North were eventually absorbed into the *Cymri*, who became the Welsh. They took with them their songs and their stories, their legends – and their heroes. Perhaps Arthur is a combination of many of them, but this,' his long arm reached out to encompass the rolling hills around them, 'is where it began.'

As he said the words, Jamie looked at the brooding triple peaks and felt another shiver. 'It feels as if this is a land soaked in blood . . .'

The other man laughed. 'Aye, if you had time, the stories I could tell . . .'

'What do they call this place?'

'It's known as Scott's View.'

'After the wizard, Michael Scott.'

Moffat shook his head. 'No, you're wrong. It was named for another Scott who lived just downriver from here a couple of hundred years ago. Sir Walter Scott.'

XXXIX

'Sir Walter Scott.' It had all come together for Jamie in that single moment. The cryptic reference in the codex to *the gift of the Lady in the Lake*. The shelf of books in Harold Webster's library. The statue in Central Park. Helena Webster had sat with him on the steps below Robert Burns, but they'd been looking directly across the Mall to the grave figure of Scott. When Webster had tortured Wolfram Sievers' assistant in Nortstein Castle, he hadn't only given up the swords, but their origins: the castles, museums and houses they'd been stolen from. Helena Webster had laid it on a plate, but he'd missed it. *You're a clever guy, Jamie Saintclair. You'll work it out.* What did she know?

'There's a roundabout half a mile past the new hospital,' Moffat had said. 'Abbotsford House is just down the road from there. You can't miss it. Pillared entrance on your right-hand side and a big house with grey chimneys.'

He took it slowly down the narrow road, allowing the headlights to pick out the detail of the trees and ditches that lined the winding Tarmac. His first instinct had been to get to the house to pre-empt any move by Steele and whoever he had with him, but this was the start of the tourist season. He needed privacy for what he planned. Abbotsford closed for visitors at five-thirty p.m. So, at the writer's suggestion, he'd driven into the little town of Melrose for a coffee. And waited for darkness.

It was a different game now, so he left the mobile phone off. Instinct, intuition, call it what you like, but he *knew* the two sinister 4x4s he'd watched passing through Jedburgh were something to do with this. Whether it was Steele or not only mattered because it would be good to know whether he was the hunter or the hunted. If it was the sword collector there was only one answer. Adam Steele looked on his adversaries as prey whether it was on a pheasant drive, in the boardroom or on a fencing mat. It would be foolish to give him the advantage of knowing how close he was.

Excalibur. When this had started it had all been about Arthur's sword, or so it seemed. Now he wasn't so sure. Yet in the final reckoning it might be the bargaining chip that meant the difference between life and death, so he would find Excalibur if he could. Every instinct told him that if it existed, the sword was here.

Scott was a hoarder, Moffat had said. *Scott has hundreds of weapons in his collection. Rob Roy's claymore. Swords from Waterloo. Pistols and muskets from Culloden. Relics of Napoleon and Bonnie Prince Charlie.*

The sword Wulf Ziegler had stolen in 1937 had belonged to a warrior king in the twilight years after the Romans had left Britain, but it was not *Excalibur.* Yet that in itself was significant, because it was evidence of an unseen hand protecting the *true* sword. It had been left as a substitute by someone who knew that, some day, people were going to come looking for the real thing. If nothing else, that told Jamie Excalibur was close.

When he rounded the next bend a substantial wall of lichen-dotted grey stone replaced the trees and bushes. A sign with a gilt arrow appeared in the twin beams pointing to the Abbotsford visitors' entrance, but the gate was closed. He drove on, keeping the same pace and scanning his surroundings for any hint of danger. Up ahead on the right lay a derelict single-storey lodge or gatehouse and he guessed this was the original entrance to Sir Walter Scott's estate, leading to some sort of driveway through the trees to the house. Moffat had told him that the only permanent presence in the building out of visiting hours was an elderly housekeeper and her husband who lived in the accommodation wing. So why, as he passed the gatehouse, did he imagine he saw the faint gleam of black paint belonging to a car parked in the shadow of the building?

Because they were here.

He drove on for almost a mile before he found somewhere to turn and studied the very basic plan of the house and gardens in the brochure he'd picked up in Jedburgh. He was to the west of the house now, and a band of woodland screened this side of the estate. On the plus side, it would mask his approach, but the trees in the car's headlights were ancient hardwoods and that meant a forest floor strewn with rotten branches like a natural minefield. It might take him hours to work his way to the house. He didn't have the time and he couldn't risk a broken ankle. Which more or less made the decision for him. He retraced the route back to the entrance, again bypassing the lodge house, and continued until he reached the visitor car park. Steele was no fool. He had worked out the location of the house from the Ziegler codex and got there ahead of Jamie. But he thought Jamie had the computer and the skills to find the true sword, so the team waiting in the shadow of the lodge house weren't to stop him getting in, they were to stop him getting back out again.

What Steele didn't know was that the computer was with Abbie's parents and that Jamie intended it to stay there. His original plan had been simply to walk up to the door of the private apartments and knock, relying on the famous Jamie Saintclair charm to talk his way in. Then, when Steel arrived, events would take their course to the inevitable point when the good guys won the day. With Steele waiting for him that was no longer an option. He needed to know how many they were and exactly who was where in the house. Certainly more than four, or what was the point of coming in two cars? Excalibur and the computer were the main attractions, although he suspected Steele had a strong secondary motive: to see the inconvenient and annoyingly persistent Jamie Saintclair safely dead and buried. Silence was golden, and there wasn't anything more silent than a dead man.

As quietly as he was able, he opened the boot of the car and retrieved his rucksack. It contained a Sig-Sauer P226, weapon of choice of the British Special Air Service. He weighed the gun in his hand. This was the target shooting variant and a relic of his pistol competition days. That didn't make it any less deadly, only more accurate. He checked the fifteen-round magazine and clicked it home. Jamie wasn't planning to shoot anybody, but he reckoned that Adam Steele would expect him to be armed, and he didn't want to do anything that might make the businessman suspicious.

Shrugging the rucksack onto his shoulders, he jogged across the Tarmac to the other side of the road. The visitors' entrance was locked, but the six-foot wall didn't pose much of an obstacle to someone fit and able-bodied. He heaved himself up and slipped over onto the walkway behind, crouching in the darkness for a few moments to be certain of his surroundings. Ahead of him a path sloped away into the gloom, hemmed in on one side by an impenetrable beech hedge and on the other by a high wooden fence. While he assumed that none of this would have been here when Wulf Ziegler made his one and only visit in 1937, this was still the most likely route the German would have come. Jamie advanced cautiously down the path until it ran parallel to a high stone wall. He debated whether to climb it, but remembered the lines in the codex – *We followed the walls until we came to a gate, which took the work of only a few moments to open.* What was good enough for Wulf Ziegler was good enough for Jamie Saintclair and he reached the gate a few seconds later. He unshouldered the rucksack, removed an eighteen-inch crowbar and forced the narrow end into the gap beside the Yale lock. One sharp tug and it opened with a crack – he flinched at the sound, and decided that Ziegler's solution had probably been a little more elegant, but the effect was the same. On the far side of the cropped lawn he saw Abbotsford House properly for the first time, silhouetted against the night sky. Someone was home, because a subdued light glowed from windows in the centre of the building, but the gable facing him was in darkness. He had a feeling he'd need a jemmy more than the gun in the next few minutes, so he re-stowed the Sig-Sauer and carried the crowbar in his right fist. It must have been a hundred yards from the gate to the side of the house and he felt terribly vulnerable as he made his way furtively to the centre, adrenalin coursing through him and every sense pitched to an intensity he'd seldom experienced.

A tall shadow appeared in front of him and he ignored it, remembering Ziegler's encounter with the statue of the boy. But as it passed to his left the shadow moved inexplicably, separating into two distinct forms. One of them wrapped its arms around him with an enormous strength that punched the breath from his lungs. Instinctively he rammed his head backwards and felt the jar of bone on bone and a crunch as something less solid gave way under the impact. Still there was no lessening in the pressure on his ribs and chest, but his assailant's hold was high enough on the forearms that he could move his hands and he stabbed backwards with the crowbar into the other man's ribs. By luck it was the pointed end that connected. It wasn't sharp enough or the blow powerful enough to penetrate the flesh, but the man behind must have thought he'd been stabbed. He reeled away with a cry and the respite allowed Jamie to wheel and bring the crowbar round in a scything blow that took him across the jaw and cheek. The impact was solid enough to jar Jamie's wrist and the other man dropped like a stone.

Jamie stood for a few moments, his whole body shaking and on the verge of shutdown. He knew that if he didn't move quickly he might not have the nerve to continue, but somehow he couldn't get his feet to obey his brain.

A scream of mortal agony tore apart the fabric of the night. It was a woman's scream and it acted like an iron nail being run down the inside of his skull.

His first instinct was to sprint towards the source of the sound, but he knew he couldn't afford to leave a threat to his escape route. He dropped to one knee to check the man he'd hit and found a faint pulse. His attacker was bleeding from the nose and mouth, and it felt as if his jaw was broken. When he touched the side of his head he felt a distinct dent in the temple that didn't bode well for an early recovery.

Plan B had been to make some kind of covert entry through the private quarters, but the scream and its implications meant he had no time for the recce he'd banked on. It also brought the Sig-Sauer back into play. He ran towards the front of the house. What he'd thought was a continuous wall on the far side of the lawn fortunately turned out to be a series of open arches and he could see a gravel parking area beyond. He scrambled through one of the arches and stood with his back against the base of a hexagonal tower at the corner of the building. A second scream made his spine creep. It came from the far side of the car park, somewhere in the private area. He took a step forward and froze as a light came on in the window next to him. Instinctively, he dropped to the ground and squirmed slowly across the gravel. When he reached the far side he heard voices coming from a rectangle of light that marked an open door. With his heart in his mouth he made his way across the intervening ground and stood with his back to the wall, just to one side of the light. All he had to tell him what waited inside the door was a single male voice.

'You'll tell us eventually,' the man said. 'Better to give me it now than what the boss will do to you. I've seen him work on a woman before and it isn't pretty. You're a rare beauty, he'll use that against you. No? Well, that's a shame.'

The scream that followed a second later would have frozen Jamie to the spot if he hadn't been expecting it. Instead, he stepped into the doorway with the Sig-Sauer in front of him. He was in a relatively modern kitchen and a tall man with his back towards the door held the left hand of a partially bound girl he didn't recognize over the steam from a boiling kettle. The girl's face was contorted in agony, but her eyes were open and he saw the moment she registered the newcomer with the pistol. Somehow through the agony she found the focus for rational thought. A dozen possibilities flickered in those eyes and the result was an even louder and more prolonged shriek that gave Jamie the vital moments it took to cross the kitchen. With one movement he raised the Sig-Sauer and smashed the butt of the pistol into the base of her torturer's skull and the man collapsed on to the tiled floor.

Jamie made sure he was unconscious before turning his attention to the victim. The girl was hunched over and obviously close to collapse herself. She was small and dark haired with a pale, slim face and dark pain circles under wide electric-green eyes that in other circumstances might have been described as hypnotic. He helped her to a chair and she slumped forward with her head on the kitchen table, sobbing quietly. He felt a surge of compassion, and her blistered hand needed treatment, but he knew he didn't have time to play nurse.

'I'll need a knife,' he said.

She raised her head and blinked before nodding

towards a drawer next to an ancient Aga. Jamie laid the pistol on the table and rummaged in the drawer until he found what looked like a bread knife. He cut her free, using the cord to bind the hands of the unconscious man on the floor. When he looked up she was watching him.

'Thank you.' She shuddered. 'I think you might have saved my life. He said this was just the start. Who are you?' She had a very soft voice with a gentle Scottish lilt.

'That can wait.' He gave her a smile that was meant to be reassuring. 'Can you stand? It's time we got you out of here. How many of them are there?'

'Three that I've seen, apart from this one, but possibly more.' She groaned and tried to get to her feet. He went to help her, but she shook her head. 'Their leader is an older man. I think he's a little mad. He keeps talking about Excalibur. They're searching the house.'

He nodded. 'If I help you out to the trees, do you think you can find somewhere to hide out until the police get here?'

She frowned. 'What about you?'

'I have some business to finish with these people.' He picked up the pistol and checked that the magazine hadn't been dislodged by the impact on the man's skull. When he was happy, he held out an arm to support her.

'I'm not going anywhere without you.' Her voice was hoarse, but there was no mistaking the conviction there.

'Jesus . . .' The word burst from him.

'No,' she said, and he was astonished to see a twinkle of humour in the tired eyes. 'Fiona. Fiona Maxwell.'

She held out her right hand and he took it, wondering what in the name of God he was going to do with her. 'Look, you're still in shock—'

'He has one of those too,' she said, ignoring him and pointing at the Sig. 'I saw it under his coat.'

Jamie cursed himself for not searching the downed man. He checked under the black bomber jacket and came up with a Ruger automatic, the twin of the one Gault had carried in America. He saw Fiona Maxwell studying the gun. 'Do you know how to use it?'

She met his gaze and raised a cultured eyebrow. 'I assume you point it and pull the trigger.' He shook his head as he handed her the pistol, but he couldn't help smiling. Fiona Maxwell might be small in stature, but it was clear she had a giant heart. Five minutes ago she'd been having her hand broiled and her future promised nothing but a shallow grave. His mind rebelled against allowing her to risk her life again, but there was no fighting the determination in her eyes. The gun looked huge in her petite hand and she struggled to hold it straight, but she had long musician's fingers and her forefinger curled round the trigger. She glared as she looked along the barrel. 'Better with two hands, but one will have to do.'

'It has two pressures,' he explained. 'You take the first strain on the trigger, and it will fire as soon as you deliver the second.' He was looking towards the internal door on the far side of the room as he said the words. When he looked back the gun was pointed at his chest. His heart missed a beat.

'I'm asking you again. Who are you and why are you here?' Her face was deathly white, but the gun was steady enough now and there was iron in her voice that demanded a response.

It was a question Jamie had always known he'd have to answer, but the circumstances were a little different from what he'd imagined. Staring down the barrel of the Ruger there didn't seem any point in arguing, so he gave it to her straight. 'My name is Jamie Saintclair, I'm an art dealer who specializes in the return of stolen works and artefacts.' The intensity of the dark eyes deepened a fraction, but it was only later he would understand why. 'I came here to make sure some property that was taken from this house is returned to its rightful owner.' He met her gaze. 'I am also probably responsible for what's happened to you. I'm sorry, that wasn't part of the plan.'

The pistol drifted to the side. 'You mean the sword the man brought with him? You really shouldn't have bothered. We've more swords in this house than we know what to do with.' For a moment the dismissal of his efforts took Jamie's breath away, but before he could reply she said: 'In that case, perhaps we should be on our way.' She turned to the outside door, but hesitated when he didn't follow. 'Well?'

'There's another reason for staying. I owe it to a friend.'

'So it's a matter of honour?'

He shrugged.

'Well, why didn't you say so in the first place?'

XL

Fiona Maxwell wanted to lead the way, but Jamie refused on the grounds that whoever went first was also likely to stop the first bullet. Instead, he made her draw a rough map of the interior of the ground floor. A corridor led from the private rooms to the main house, through an ante room to the armoury. Beyond the armoury lay the entrance hall, which had doors connecting to the library and Scott's study. There was also a large dining room off the armoury.

'Where did you last see Adam Steele?' Her only reply was a look of puzzlement. 'The older man you mentioned,' he explained.

'He seemed very interested in the armoury and the weapons,' she whispered. 'There are hundreds of them: swords and pistols, suits of armour and spears. Sir Walter collected them from all over the world, including some from the field of Waterloo. He has Rob Roy's claymore, you know.'

'But not Excalibur?'

Her face went blank. 'If such a sword exists, Mr Saintclair, it will never leave this house. You have my word on it.' It was strange to hear the sentence spoken with utter conviction, but her eyes contained an element of doubt, as if she was uncertain whether she was telling the truth.

He considered the diagram. 'It's my intention to surprise Mr Steele if I can, but that doesn't look very likely if we go through the armoury. Is there another way into the main house?'

She thought for a few seconds. 'The spiral stair!' She hurried back through the house to the kitchen where Jamie's victim lay groaning on the tiled floor, still more unconscious than not, but for how long?

'Can I borrow your scarf?' He indicated the bright print at Fiona's neck.

'It was expensive.' It was a very female response and he smiled. 'It's Louis Vuitton.'

'If he damages it I'll buy you another,' Jamie promised as she reluctantly handed it over. He used the brightly coloured silk to gag the prone intruder. 'Hopefully he won't choke.'

'It would serve him right if he does. Here.' She led him through to the hallway of the private wing and pointed to a painted door. 'This leads to the cellars.'

'I thought you said we were taking a spiral stair?'

'You'll see,' she said mysteriously.

Jamie opened the door and hesitated. 'Just one last

thing. Do you think you can manage another scream?' She shot him a startled look. 'You've been awfully quiet for a while,' he explained. 'If they don't hear from you they'll be expecting our friend in the kitchen to report back that you've either fainted or given him what he wants.'

She disappeared for a few seconds and another agonized shriek filled the house before she reappeared. Jamie took his first step into the darkness.

'Watch out. The steps are worn. There should be a light switch on your left.'

'Thanks,' he said, recovering from his stumble.

The light clicked on and he found himself in a long, low cellar that seemed to stretch half the length of the house.

Fiona let out a hiss. 'They've been here.' She pointed to an antique chest of drawers that had been overturned, with the drawers emptied out and generations of anonymous bric-a-brac dumped on the floor. There were other signs, shelves tipped over to reveal the bare stone walls behind. Baskets and boxes were tossed aside, their contents strewn haphazardly around. 'The stair is there. In the far corner.'

They made their way carefully through the mess until they reached the far end. 'Stay here.' He held the pistol in front of him and slowly ascended the clockwise staircase.

Her voice followed him. 'You'll come to a little alcove halfway up. The door leads to the entrance hall.'

'Okay, it's clear. But I think you should stay here.'

'This house and everything in it is my responsibility, Mr Saintclair. I thought we agreed that.'

'Christ.' He noticed the blisters sagging like grapes from her left hand. 'You must be in agony. Please.'

'Pain is part of life,' she said. 'Just as death is. We cannot escape it; therefore we must learn to endure it. You may not think it, but this house has borne a great deal of pain.' She looked into his eyes and he felt as if she was searching his soul. 'Just as pain has marked you. She must have been very special to you, your friend?'

He halted abruptly and stared at her. How could she have known? But when he looked into those green eyes, he understood. 'She was.'

'Did they hurt her?'

'I . . . don't know. I think so.'

'Then we have to stop them.'

Reluctantly, he capitulated. 'All right, but stay behind me. Keep the gun pointing at the ceiling and don't shoot anything unless someone else starts shooting first.'

'I wouldn't dream of it.' A thought occurred to her. 'I hope you're not going to do any damage, Mr Saintclair. This house means a great deal to a great many people.'

It seemed an unlikely request, given the circumstances, but he bowed his head in acknowledgement. 'I'll do my best not to, Miss Maxwell, but Adam Steele and the people with him are very dangerous. As you've seen, they won't hesitate to hurt you.'

'I won't let them touch me again.' The words emerged

with an animal ferocity and he believed every word. 'I'd kill them first.'

Jamie edged open the door to reveal a large wood-panelled hall big enough to hold a medieval banquet in. To his right, at the far end of the hall, the subdued lighting illuminated two full suits of armour complete with massive broadswords. Scott had festooned the walls with the mounted heads and horns of unfortunate beasts of indeterminate origin as well as hundreds of lesser ornaments Jamie couldn't quite make out. An impatient upper-class voice that could only be Adam Steele echoed round the room, but, he guessed, not from within it. It seemed the sword collector was fascinated by the depth of the late Sir Walter's collection of weapons in the armoury next door, but frustrated by the sheer scale of it. From what Fiona Maxwell had said, there were so many swords of so many origins and so many periods it might take hours before Steele was satisfied that none of them was the one he sought. Jamie eased his way into the room and motioned the Scottish girl to follow him. With a little luck he could step into the armoury and get the drop on the financier and whoever was with him. He was momentarily distracted by the skull and horns of an aurochs, a breed of massive wild cattle that had been extinct for some four hundred years and almost missed the sound of footsteps marching purposefully towards the door. He looked round desperately for somewhere to hide, but there was nowhere close enough. At the edge of his vision he sensed Fiona Maxwell slipping back inside the stairway but he knew he'd never make it. A shadow appeared inside the doorway and he skipped right to take advantage of the only cover available, the narrow gap between the door and the wall.

The footsteps grew louder as they reached the tiled floor of the entrance hall and he waited with the pistol in both hands for the moment the door was pulled back and his sanctuary discovered. But the sound faded as the man – he was certain it was one of Steele's drivers – walked the length of the hall and out of the door at the far end. He let out a long, slow breath, willing his heart to slow, and by the time he emerged Fiona Maxwell was already waiting by the doorway. Their eyes met and Jamie nodded and stepped inside.

Adam Steele turned from the display of swords he'd been studying with an angry frown. 'Is he . . . ?' His eyes widened when he recognized the intruder. The guard behind the banker went for his gun, but Jamie pointed the Sig-Sauer at Steele's head.

'That wouldn't be wise. Finger and thumb and draw it out by the butt. Lay it on the floor and kick it towards me.' The bodyguard obeyed and a second later Jamie heard a soft movement as Fiona moved in behind him. 'You're losing your touch, Adam. I didn't think it would be this easy.'

Steele smiled and it wasn't a pleasant smile. 'That has yet to be proved, old boy. Why don't you drop the gun and take a look behind you?'

'You don't think I'm going to fall for that old trick, *old boy*?'

'Oh I do, old boy.'

'Do as he says, Jamie, or I may have to blow your pretty little friend's head off.'

Jamie flinched at the familiar voice from behind him. He bent and placed the Sig on the floor.

'Very sensible,' Steele said. 'Collins, take a look around and make sure there aren't any other nasty surprises about.' The guard picked up the two pistols and walked past Jamie with a look that said he'd like to use it to break his jaw.

'Trevor's in the kitchen with a sore head and a bad temper. I left him tied up.'

Jamie turned and looked into the familiar, classically beautiful face of Charlotte Wellesley. She stood by the door with her gun against Fiona Maxwell's head and a knowing smile on her lips.

'Surprised to see me?' She blew him a kiss. 'You're not the only one who knows where the basement is. Join your saviour, darling,' she pushed Fiona towards him, 'temporary though it's likely to be.'

'I was expecting someone else.' Jamie tried to keep the defeat from his voice, but he knew everyone in the armoury could hear it. They'd suckered him in like a mouse following a trail of crumbs. And now the trap was about to slam shut.

'Gault?' Adam Steele snorted incredulously. 'Poor old Gault didn't like you at all, Saintclair. Forever complaining there was something not quite kosher about you. Too many coincidences, he said. Always had the answers. Always some old mate from the past turning up just when you needed them. And, of course, he was right. Who were your old chums, Jamie?'

'Russian intelligence, Mossad, MI6 and the CIA. A chap can't have too many friends, Adam, you should know that.'

Steele laughed and selected a French cavalry sabre from the wall and slid it from its scabbard. Jamie moved protectively in front of Fiona Maxwell and Charlotte smiled. 'Ooh, how very chivalrous.'

The financier turned to Fiona. 'It's good to know that you preserve the proprieties, Miss ah . . . ?'

'Maxwell,' Fiona snapped.

'Honed to a reasonable fighting edge. It's the only way to keep them properly conserved. A few spots of rust don't matter at all as long as the blade is well waxed.' He tried a couple of practice swings, the heavy blade hissing ominously through the air as he approached the two people in the middle of the room. Jamie stood his ground as Steele brought the point of the sabre to his cheek so he could feel the edge against the skin. 'I think we have some business to discuss. Let's start with the computer, shall we?' Jamie raised his hands and slowly brought the right to the inside pocket of his jacket. The other man raised a warning eyebrow and Charlotte laughed as if she was having the most fun ever. Jamie pulled a card and a pen from his pocket. With the sabre still touching his flesh he wrote three or four words on the card. Adam Steele smiled and held out his hand, but the smile froze when Jamie slipped the card into the back pocket of his jeans.

'You can have it later.'

'What's to stop me cutting you into little pieces and taking it now?'

'Because that would mean you're too frightened to fight me, Adam, and you wouldn't like Charlotte to think that, would you? Anyway, it wouldn't be as much fun.'

'Oh, I don't know about that, old boy.' With a flick of the wrist the financier brought the point down across Jamie's shoulder and chest and the art dealer winced as he felt the razor edge score across his skin through the jacket and shirt. Steele smiled and walked back to the display to choose another sword.

'You were talking about Gault,' Jamie reminded him.

'Yes, too many coincidences. So many, in fact, that even a dull dog like Gault began to get suspicious. He was talking about having it out with you, man to man, as it were, and we couldn't have that. Charlotte took care of it. She enjoys that kind of thing, you see. Apparently, she didn't take kindly to Gault groping her or something. Strange girl.'

'Odious little man,' Charlotte laughed.

'Like you took care of Sarah Grant?'

Jamie's voice held a cold threat and Charlotte laughed

at the unlikelihood of him ever making it a reality. 'Sarah . . . ? Oh, you mean the girl in the woods.'

'Why? That was one thing I didn't understand. That and Hermann.'

'Well, I had to see what happened to you. We couldn't have you getting yourself killed just then . . .'

'Yeees,' Steele drawled. 'That was unfortunate. We had to use a phone linked to Al-Qaida. How were we supposed to know they'd be able to track the damned thing?'

'I almost saved you myself, but then Miss Perfect stepped in. I watched you talking together and when you parted with that chaste little kiss I saw the wheels going round and the moment she put two and two together. After that there was no option, really.'

Jamie barely restrained himself from charging across the room and taking her by the throat. But she smiled and lifted the pistol so it was lined up on his chest.

Steele finally selected a sabre that pleased him. 'In the hall, I think. More room and it wouldn't do to get blood on the carpet.'

Jamie followed him warily. Like Steele he removed his jacket and Fiona Maxwell gasped at the bloody stain across his shirt.

'No.'

He turned and shook his head. 'You don't have to watch this.'

'Oh, I think we do,' Charlotte laughed, pushing the barrel of her Ruger in the other girl's back.

'The other thing I don't understand,' Jamie continued, 'is why you killed hundreds of people all over Europe just to frame me. You already had your atrocity and a reason to carry out your little revolution.'

Steele's eyes hardened at the final two words, which were evidently less than welcome. 'It appears you know more about my business than you should. We'll discuss that in a few moments. Not *just* to frame you, Jamie. It was Charlotte's idea.'

'It was terribly kind of you to help out, Jamie,' Charlotte chimed in. 'Adam needed to be entirely certain no one in Europe would try to interfere with what we had to do after the takeover. The Europeans can be so stuffy sometimes, but when they were under attack themselves they'd have no option but to let events in the New Britain take their course. Of course, that meant once you had succeeded in getting us Excalibur you had to go. We couldn't have you running around denying everything and making people suspicious.'

'But I didn't get Excalibur for you.'

'No.' Steele's voice took on a new menace. 'And that is something I will be discussing with your new lady friend once I've trimmed you down to size. A pity you won't be around to watch. It could be quite entertaining. By the way, how did you know about our *little revolution*? I don't remember that being on the computer?'

'Poor old Gault. It turned out he talked in his sleep.'

Adam Steele's nostrils flared. 'I don't think so. Now, what did you say? Oh, yes. *No guards, no tips. Just you and me and two swords.* I'm going to take a huge amount of pleasure in killing you.'

He tossed the original sabre to Jamie and the moment it settled in his hand the art dealer understood the true nature of this contest. The competition sabres he'd fought with in the past weighed less than a pound, had blunt edges and no point. Against a French cavalry sabre that had been used at Waterloo, it was like comparing a grizzly bear with a sheep. Three pounds of solid steel with an edge that would take your arm off and a point that would go right through you, this was a genuine killing weapon. If he hadn't known before he was in a fight to the death he did now. He raised the sword to eye level, checking it for flaws.

'Excalibur for his life,' Fiona cried. 'Let him live and I'll give you Excalibur.'

'No!' Jamie said. 'You—' Steele's sword came up to his lips to silence him.

'Yes.' He smiled at Charlotte. 'I'm sure that would be an excellent bargain, but . . .' He whipped the blade to the right and Fiona shrieked as the edge split the skin of her burned hand. 'Now that I know for certain you actually *do* have Excalibur, there's really no need. And it would be such a pity to forego the satisfaction of killing Mr Saintclair.'

Fiona Maxwell slumped to the floor and Jamie was consumed by a red rage that would have launched him at the financier, but for the new voice from the doorway. Trevor, the guard Jamie had clubbed in the kitchen, stood with a look of pure hatred on his face and a pistol in his hand. 'If you don't, I will.'

For a millisecond all Jamie could hear was the sound of his own breathing. The pause allowed his anger to subside and he felt a coldness settling on his heart. It seemed that, win or lose, he was going to die. Oddly, he felt no fear, only a settled calm he recognized from the past and which boded ill for his opponent. One thing was for certain: if he was going to die, Adam Steele was going to die first.

The thought made him smile and Steele's grin faded when he saw the look on his face.

'*En garde.*'

XLI

It would be a messy death. Essentially the sabre is a giant meat cleaver and whoever first made the metal connect with the meat would win. Jamie had two options: play for time or go for the kill. Under the circumstances he decided on the second.

They stood ten feet apart on the hexagonal tiles of the entry hall, with Steele facing west and Jamie east, towards the tourist entrance where the two suits of armour decorated the wall. As Adam Steele brought his sabre up to his face in a formal salute Jamie launched into a jump lunge with his blade at full extension. The thrust would have skewered Steele through the middle if the financier hadn't somehow managed to get his blade down for a lightning parry that beat Jamie's point to one side. Steele followed up with a scything back-cut designed to take out his opponent's throat. Jamie preempted the move with a piece of fancy footwork that took him out of range, but he still felt the whisper of the blade as it hissed past his face. Steele stepped back, his eyes almost glowing with excitement despite the close call.

'That was a bit out of order, old boy.'

'It's not a fucking game, old boy.' To emphasize the point Jamie chopped at the grinning face, forcing Steele to parry, and then met the inevitable riposte with one of his own. They exchanged cuts, taking each other's measure and Jamie gradually became more familiar with the weight and balance of his sword. Every meeting of the blades was accompanied by a resounding clang that echoed round the panelled halls and vaulted ceiling. In an official bout, the referee would have called stop at the end of the inconclusive exchange and they would have retreated to their own ends of the mat. But this wasn't an official bout. And there were no rules. A parry pushed Jamie's sabre down to the left and Steele took advantage of the opening to dance to his own left, bringing his blade scything round in a terrible arc that should have severed Jamie's spine. The initial movement had been designed to force the younger man to circle right, following the attack, but Jamie Saintclair had a few tricks of his own. Instead, he let the momentum of his sword carry him left, in a pirouetting turn that allowed him to catch Steele's blade on his, almost behind his own back. By the time the financier had recovered Jamie was facing him. Again Steele danced left, looking for an opening, but Jamie's sabre point followed him all the way, and his eyes never left his opponent's. By now both men were breathing hard and sweat was running from Steele's thick, dark hair into his eyes and he dashed at them with the back of his hand to clear his vision. Steele's movement had taken him full circle for no advantage and Jamie had held the centre ground and expended less energy. Round One to the challenger.

As if by common assent each man took a step back, attempting to gauge the extent of the other's weakness. The anticipation in Steele's eyes had been replaced by a glaring, almost maniacal, hatred. Jamie met his stare with what he hoped was a look of implacable resolve, tinged with just the slightest hint of defeat. He saw the other man dart a glance towards Trevor at the door, and he knew that all it would take was a nod and he'd be fighting with a bullet in his back, which would make things tricky. He was depending on Adam Steele's need to look like a winner in front of Charlotte and his men. Having your opponent shot was effective, but it smacked of cheating, and winners didn't have to cheat. What he had to do was keep making Steele think he was going to win. Right up till the moment he lost.

A second later the first part of that strategy looked simple enough. Without warning Steele feinted to his left, drawing Jamie's guard with him. But the movement was a cover for the attack that had almost taken Jamie by surprise the last time they'd met on the fencing mat. The financier bounded forward with the sabre at full stretch and aimed directly at Jamie's heart. This time there was no time for any elaborate counter. He could almost feel the three feet of steel piercing his heart as his blade came up to meet the other man's. The sheer strength of his wrist forced the attack to his left, but not far enough because he felt as if a hot poker had been rammed into his side below the ribs. The agony was almost numbing, but instinct maintained his advance and he stepped inside the blade and ducked forward to butt Steele in the face. It wasn't the perfect blow, and Jamie's forehead struck just above and to the left of Steele's nose, but it stunned the businessman. He reeled back with his left hand against his eye and the sword swinging wildly to meet Jamie's counter. But the younger man's movement was slowed by the waves of pain coming from his side. He stepped back out of range and the hand he clutched to the wound came away dark red. When he looked up, Steele's eyes were wild and blood streamed from a cut on his right eyelid. Jamie shook his head to clear it and charged, all pretence of swordsmanship gone, the blade coming up to hack at his enemy's face. Steele caught the sword on his own and responded by ramming his point at Jamie's eyes.

For almost a minute, they matched each other blow for blow and strength for strength, each meeting of the curved blades an assault on the ears and accompanied by the animal grunts of the men wielding them. From another world, Jamie heard Charlotte's ringing laughter as a cut almost took the head from his shoulders, but she went quiet when he stepped inside with a lunge that sliced the flesh of Adam Steele's shoulder. Steele screamed in agony but he had the presence of mind to step forward and his sabre point sought Jamie out. By good fortune Jamie's momentum had already taken him inside the danger and he found himself chest to chest with the man who had tried to destroy him. Steele's body reeked of a bitter sweet *mélange* of expensive cologne, sweat and fear. His face was in Jamie's, lips drawn back from the teeth in a feral snarl, one eye already swollen almost shut, and the skin blood red with effort and fury. Unable to use the sword he wrapped his arms round Jamie and the art dealer felt himself lifted off his feet. Helpless, Jamie heard his enemy laugh as he fought the deadly embrace. He battered his head forward, but this time Steele was too clever for him and he'd already come in too close for the blow to be effective. They crashed against a table and something china smashed to the floor sending shards spinning under their feet. Steele's strength seemed unaffected by the wound in his shoulder and Jamie screamed as his enemy rammed him back against the massive stone fireplace, sending a lance of pain through his injured side. He began to fade and he knew if he didn't break the hold soon, Steele would throw him to the ground and he'd be too weak to defend himself. A piece of wooden furniture splintered under their combined weight and he felt his oppressor stagger. He attempted another feeble butt and Steele laughed again, but this time a warm piece of flesh brushed Jamie's lips and hung there tantalizingly.

In desperation he sank his teeth into the tender flesh of Adam Steele's ear. Now it was Steele's turn to shriek as Jamie worked at the ear like a hyena tearing the flesh from a dead antelope. Steele loosed his grip and tore himself away, leaving a hunk of his flesh in the other man's mouth. Jamie spat out the vile piece of meat and lurched after his opponent. By now there was no Fiona or Charlotte or Trevor, only the two men fighting for their lives. He swung and missed, the weight of the sword almost carrying him over as it passed Steele's shoulder to strike a marble statue of the house's owner with a terrible mistuned clang. His opponent saw his chance and tried to ram his point into Jamie's defenceless guts. Jamie saw the sword as if in slow motion, the bright streaks of the honed edge, the twinkle of reflected light on the point. He was exhausted, but so was Steele. Somehow his legs found the strength to sidestep the blow and as the sword slipped past he brought his own blade up to counter-attack. But there was no blade, only a jagged eight-inch stump.

He heard Steele's manic laughter at the knowledge his enemy was disarmed, Charlotte's scream of delight and Trevor's shout of, 'Finish him, boss.' But even as the words reached his ears he darted forward, knowing Steele was off balance and this was his only chance. With the last ounce of his strength he rammed the saw-toothed edge of broken metal two-handed up under Adam Steele's chin and felt the awful crunch as it broke through flesh and muscle and cartilage, scraped against bone, tore through palate. Steele gurgled and wriggled, his mouth pleading and eyes gaping with shock and terror. Jamie snarled like a dog as he forced the terrible spike upwards until it reached the brain and the eyes suddenly turned puzzled. Finally, Jamie hauled the stump of sword clear and blood pulsed from the wound as Adam Steele collapsed forward, taking the art dealer with him and covering him with gore.

As he struggled to free himself, he heard Charlotte scream and by the time he managed to get to his feet she had her pistol aimed at his head. Very deliberately, the muzzle dropped until it was pointed at his groin.

'You bastard,' she snarled.

A blur of movement from somewhere to her right distracted her and Trevor's shouted warning came too late for her to react to the mini-whirlwind of Fiona Maxwell, who launched herself screaming at the other girl. Charlotte went down, cursing under a hail of blows, and Jamie turned his attention to the final threat. Trevor was still by the door where he'd been throughout the fight and he had his pistol aimed unerringly at Jamie's head. He was a professional and the smile on his face said he wasn't going to miss.

Jamie knew he was dead, but still the fighter in him had to try. 'It's finished, Trevor,' he gasped. 'Without Adam Steele whatever you've been plotting is never going to happen. You can walk away now.'

Trevor's expression didn't even alter. 'I don't think so. There are plenty more where he came from. Anyway,' he touched the back of his neck, 'I owe you for this. No hard feelings, old son.'

Jamie recognized the moment thought turned to action. He knew he'd see the flash of the muzzle before he heard the sound and felt the bullet hit. But somehow Trevor's resolve faded, the gun dropped and the black droplet that had magically appeared below his eye became a well gushing blood. Without a sound his legs buckled and he dropped to the floor.

Jamie slowly swivelled to find Charlotte staring at him with a look of puzzlement and her pistol aimed at his head. It all seemed a bit unfair, really.

'I wouldn't do that if I were you, dear.' The words seemed to come from inside him, but it wasn't his voice, it was a commanding voice, more mellow and terribly upper class. His last thought before he collapsed was that maybe it belonged to God.

'You were hoping I'd kill him,' Jamie's voice emerged as a soft croak. 'Or that he'd kill me.'

The Director General of the Security Services' nose twitched like a suspicious rabbit as he looked down at the body of Adam Steele and prodded it with his foot.

'I'm afraid we're not that devious, Mr Saintclair. The reason for our untimely arrival was that we got lost, sometimes it's as simple as that.' He sniffed. 'Mind you, I'm not saying it's not convenient. Adam Steele will become the sixth victim of a terrorist atrocity that unfortunately consumes his house and five other upstanding members of society at ten o'clock this evening.'

'Is one allowed to ask who they are?'

'No, but I'm sure you'll read the obituary of the outspoken MP and former Defence Secretary Colin Franklin in the newspapers in the next few days. Unfortunately, there'll also be one of our own. A young man with a bright future. SAS hero and all that. Adam Steele managed to seduce him with his awful vision.' He sighed and his gaze wandered over the weapons and suits of armour until they settled on the skull of the unfortunate aurochs. 'His time was past, you see. All of their times were past. They'd never have done it.' He sounded as if he might have been trying to convince himself. 'The General they thought was their trump card came to us as soon as they approached him. That's when we put in Gault.' He looked up. 'You didn't know? Oh, yes, Gault was one of ours. The only problem was he couldn't penetrate the inner circle. So we had to bide our time.'

'And then the M25 happened.'

He nodded. 'We were under pressure to move. To make mass arrests. But Gault persuaded us to hold our hand. If he came back with Excalibur, Steele would give him access to the inner circle and we'd know everything.'

A figure appeared in the doorway. Dark haired, tanned and compact in his blue bomber jacket. 'Hello, David,' Jamie said quietly. 'I wondered when you'd turn up.'

'Is she here?'

The DGSS called to someone in the armoury and Charlotte Wellesley appeared in handcuffs between two men. She looked resentfully from Jamie to the Israeli and Jamie had a moment of, not quite doubt, but perhaps regret, which he swiftly brushed from his mind. She was responsible for the deaths of too many people to deserve his sympathy.

'We have a place out in the Negev,' the Mossad man said conversationally. 'An oven in summer, an icebox in winter. You will spend many happy hours there with the old ladies of Baader Meinhof and Hamas, and never see sunlight again.'

She started screaming as they led her away.

'Just out of interest,' the DG asked conversationally, 'when did you realize she was a bad 'un?'

'Not soon enough.' Jamie shook his head in dismay at his own blindness. 'I think Charlotte Wellesley is the most truly evil person I've ever met. Keeping me close was like a game for her. I was her trophy, to be used for her amusement. A constant reminder of what she'd made me suffer.' The memory of all her victims made him grimace. 'But she wasn't a good enough actress to carry it off and it was the fact that we were so close that betrayed her. I think I had my first suspicions when we were in Corfu. After that, it took a long time for everything to come together, but by the time we were in New York and the laptop was used to try to frame me for the M25 attack, I became certain she was linked to Abbie's last message.' He shrugged and the other man stared at him. '*febluis*. At first I thought it was code, then I understood it was much simpler than that. You see, she was trying to tell me that the person who killed her was female, and in a certain light I realized that Charlotte Wellesley had the most startling blue eyes.'

Epilogue

The house backed onto the south-east slope of the triple peak, mottled pink stone and grey slate set squat and low to fend off the winds that had battered their way down the valley for countless millennia. Judging by the hotchpotch of building styles and the outbuildings that clung haphazardly to either side, it might be only the most recent manifestation of at least three earlier structures.

'Home,' Fiona Maxwell announced, pushing back the door with her uninjured hand, the other held across her chest in a makeshift sling. 'This is my place. My mother and father usually look after Abbotsford, but fortunately they were away for the weekend. I was only standing in.'

She led the way through the house to a back room obviously used for storage. A painted door was set in the far left of the rear wall and she opened it to reveal a deep cupboard. Not for the first time, Jamie wondered if he was in a dream as Fiona reached up and pulled at the right hand wall until it slid aside with barely a squeak. 'My uncle's work,' she explained. 'He was a great one for the joinery.' The gap led into a short corridor that led in turn to another door. She stood in front of it and turned to him, her green eyes shining cat-like in the gloom. As she spoke the pain of his wounds seemed to fade.

'You have the right, twice over,' she said formally. 'The blood of kings runs through you. The St Clairs of Ravensneuk are descended through the matriarchal line from Lllachar, ruler of hosts, remembered in the Gododdin, and whose forefathers held this land for the High King of the Votadini. Yet you need not pass if you do not have the will.'

'You said twice.'

'And because you have been touched by the Lady. But you already know that.'

The Lady was Isis, paramount goddess of Ancient Egypt, and he had recovered her crown that had been lost for two millennia. Jamie felt a moment of utter certainty unlike any other in his life. 'Then I will pass.'

She pushed the door back and they were in a tight space between the house and the hills, hidden from above by an overhang and from the sides by outcrops that buttressed the rear of the building. In front of them lay an ominous cleft that looked to Jamie like the entrance to the Underworld.

'A great stone once covered this,' she explained in a

spectral voice that seemed to come from another age. 'It was a shrine through the centuries and men came with offerings though they knew not what they worshipped. Then, in the time of William, known as the Lion, a young man was found wandering these hills, his hair turned white as a mountain fox in a single night. He carried one gold piece and told of a dark cave, a great treasure and a terrible king who had woken and ordered him to begone or be swallowed by the mountain for ever. The townsfolk took the madman to Michael Scott, the wizard, who had ceased his wanderings for a time, but he never recovered his senses. It is said Scott placed a spell of concealment on the cave and appointed himself its Guardian. Scotts have been the Guardians ever since.'

'But you are a Maxwell.' Jamie was surprised at the tremor in his voice.

'My aunt was a Scott,' Fiona said simply, 'the last of that line, and someone must be chosen. Come.'

He shivered and would have hesitated before the dank, freezing tomb if Fiona Maxwell hadn't led the way unflinchingly inside. She produced two tall candles from some hidden void and lit them with a long match. In the flickering yellow light Jamie saw that the sloping six-foot-high passage beyond the entrance had been cut from the rock by men and widened so that two people could pass side by side. Fiona set a steady pace over the uneven surface and Jamie followed at a slight crouch to shield his head from the tunnel's rock ceiling. After

469

a few minutes they reached a horizontal stretch and somewhere far ahead Jamie had an illusion that the walls were rippling as if they were a molten river. It was only when they came closer he realized the effect was caused by an uneven line of gleaming two-foot bronze discs ingeniously set into each side of the passage. When Fiona reached the first of the polished metal plates she placed her candle in a holder so that the disc reflected the entire light of the flame. The effect was astonishing. The curvature and angle of the mirror-surfaced disc focused the light diagonally on to a similar disc on the opposite side of the tunnel, which repeated the exercise on to a third, and a fourth until twenty discs illuminated the space a hundred paces ahead. When she took Jamie's candle and inserted it in the disc on the opposite side of the passage the effect was almost as bright as day.

Oddly, the lights only increased Jamie's sense of fore-boding.

They continued down the passage and he noticed scorch marks on either side of the floor. A few paces later Fiona warned against a dark stream that cut across their path, appearing from one side of the tunnel and disappearing into the other, through a channel that had been cut by hand. Very gradually he began to work out where he was. The growing realization was reinforced by the dark oblong of a great pit ahead and his step faltered and his stomach seemed to drop as the full, quite literally awesome, reality threatened to overwhelm him. The emotion he experienced was as intense as when he first entered the Sistine Chapel or gazed upon the great paintings of the Louvre, but magnified a thousand times.

'We're in a Mithraeum?'

'Yes.'

Mithras, god of the East, the soldier's god, bull slayer and keeper of the mysteries. Jamie could imagine it now. The naked initiate escorted down the tunnel, his senses battered by sights and sounds and smells. The heat from the twin fires singeing his flesh, and then the bewildering drop into the freezing cold waters. Every step a test of courage. A single flinch or a foot backwards and the ceremony would be abandoned. Beyond the stream they would have lined the floor deep with cattle entrails and whispered in the man's ear that they were the remains of his family. Something soft and fleshy forms a barrier. A sword placed in his hand. 'Your eldest son. Thrust deep and sure, or Mithras rejects you.'

And finally the grave pit with your sword in your hand. The sound of the bull being brought and the terrified lowing as it scents the gore. And then you're drowning in blood, gallons of it pouring over you, hot and thick and oily from the beast's slashed throat, choking and blinding you and filling your nostrils with the stink of death.

And then you rise. Reborn.

Sweat poured from Jamie's body as if he'd personally suffered the ordeal. He was so focused on the pit that he almost didn't notice the skulls cut into niches in the walls, each of them topped by an exotic helmet of ancient origin: a distinctive Thracian cap with its griffin crest; the conical dome of a Scythian archer; the plumed headgear and fish-scale neck protector of a Parthian cataphract; a Celtic-era pot helmet from Gaul or Hispania decorated in gold. Even a jewelled head-dress that looked as if it might have originated from somewhere on the Russian steppe.

'These were the Sword Brethren,' Fiona said reverently. 'Enemies, but men who also worshipped the bull slayer. Warriors who fought well and died well and have been given their place in his halls for all eternity.'

Jamie stopped as he reached the gaping hole in the ground.

'No, do not hesitate.' Her voice was urgent. 'You are welcome here. You have not suffered the trials, but you have bathed in the blood of your enemies.' He remembered the awful crunch as the jagged fragment of sword had cut into Adam Steele's throat and the warm blood that had spurted slick and viscous onto his face and clothing. 'It is your right.' As she repeated the words she'd uttered at the cave entrance she pointed towards the end of the chamber. 'It has many names, but in our time it has always been Excalibur.'

He followed her gaze. There, on the far side of the pit, glowing in the combined spotlight of the final pair of discs as if at the bottom of a sea pool, was a sword. Excalibur, the sword of Arthur, lay encased in a bubble of almost clear aquamarine calcite. Only the hilt and pommel, a wonderful twin dragon head of pure gold, remained clear of the beautiful flowstone formed from the stalagmite hanging above. A *spatha,* Jamie realized in wonder. Of course it would be a *spatha.* The heavy sword carried by Roman auxiliary cavalry during their centuries in Britain. The sword of a great lord, but a warrior's sword, for all the fancy decoration. Awe filled him, as the eerie light from the centre of the bubble filled the chamber and made it feel like being at the centre of a sunburst or the gates of some strange blue Heaven.

Fiona waved him forward and he felt a liquid tremor as he realized the implications of what she'd said. It was his *right* to lay his hands on the sword of kings. It was his *right* to draw it from the embrace of the marvellous blue stone if he were able. But Jamie Saintclair knew it was not *right.* Nature had kept Excalibur safe for close on a hundred generations. Nature would keep her safe for another hundred. He shook his head wearily and slumped onto the stone bench carved into the tunnel wall by the pit, listening as Fiona Maxwell's footsteps faded down the passageway.

He closed his eyes and for the first time since he'd heard the news of Abbie's death he felt at peace. Here, he was surrounded by the spirits of departed warriors. Men who asked nothing of their friends but friendship in return. Men who had fought. Men who had gone to their deaths willingly and without complaint, their only concern that they should take their last breath with a sword in their hand. He stood up and said a silent prayer to their shades. Their God was long gone, he was sure, but the *syndexioi*, the faithful who had created this temple remained, loyal beyond death to the greatest hero of them all. For beyond the unnatural black veil that silhouetted the aquamarine rock that gripped Excalibur in its stony embrace lay a second chamber, and, he was certain, a secret more significant still. But that secret would stay with him till the end of his days.

As he made his way back through the honour guard of Sword Brethren he thought he heard a sound – not a whisper, more a shimmer in the still air . . .

Arthur.

Acknowledgements

.

As always I have to thank my wife Alison and children Kara, Nikki and Gregor for their unfailing support and encouragement. To Shirley and Kenny Allan for keeping my German right, and Siobhan Lennon for checking my codes. Special thanks to Alistair Moffat for allowing me to take his name in vain and for the enormous pleasure his books have given me. For a fresh and unique take on the Arthur legend, *Arthur and the Lost Kingdoms* is hard to beat. Finally, to my agent Stan, and, Simon, my editor at Transworld, and the fantastic team who do such great work on my books.

James Douglas is the pseudonym of a writer of popular historical adventure novels. This is the third novel to feature art recovery expert, Jamie Saintclair – the first two being *The Doomsday Testament* and *The Isis Covenant*. James Douglas lives in Scotland.

THE LABYRINTH OF OSIRIS
Paul Sussman

A journalist is murdered in Jerusalem's Armenian
Cathedral and Detective Arieh Ben-Roi is spoilt for
leads. But one seems out of place – a link to a
decades-old missing-persons case in Egypt. Baffled,
Ben-Roi turns to Inspector Yusuf Khalifa
of the Luxor Police, for help.

Although struggling with personal tragedy and
immersed in a case of his own – a series of mysterious
well poisonings in the Eastern Desert – Khalifa agrees
to do some digging. What he discovers will
change both men's lives for ever.

As their investigations intertwine, the detectives are
drawn ever deeper into a sinister web of violence,
abuse, corporate malpractice and international
terrorism. At its heart lies a three thousand-year-old
mystery that has already taken two lives, and
will soon be claiming more . . .

'A genuinely exciting read from a world-class
storyteller . . . a beautifully observed thriller'
FINANCIAL TIMES

'Sussman knew how to keep a complex plot bowling
along while constantly ratcheting up the tension . . .
this is top drawer popular fiction'
MAIL ON SUNDAY

THE DOOMSDAY TESTAMENT
James Douglas

1937, Hitler sent an expedition to Tibet in
search of the lost land of Thule.

1941, Heinrich Himmler spent a huge fortune,
and sacrificed the lives of hundreds of concentration
camp prisoners, to turn Wewelsburg Castle
in Germany into a shrine to the SS.

Art recovery expert Jamie Saintclair thought he knew
his grandfather, but when he stumbles upon the old
man's lost diary he's astonished to find that the gentle
Anglican clergyman was a decorated hero who had
served in the Special Air Service in the Second World
War. And his grandfather has one more surprise for
him. Sewn in to the endpaper of the journal is
a strange piece of Nazi symbolism.

This simple discovery will launch him on a breathless
chase across Europe and deep into Germany's dark
past. There are some who will kill to find that which
is lost, and although he doesn't know it, Saintclair
holds the key to its hiding place.

THE ISIS COVENANT
James Douglas

The Crown of Isis, once part of the treasure of Queen Dido of Carthage, was reputed to grant its wearer immortality. In AD 64 it was stolen from the Temple of Isis. It was believed lost forever. Until now.

Art recovery expert Jamie Saintclair receives an unexpected phone call from Brooklyn detective Danny Fisher. Two families have been brutally murdered, one in New York, the other in London. The only link is a shared name, that of a German art thief who disappeared at the end of the war.

Jamie's investigation will take them into the dark past of Nazi Germany, to a hidden world of the occult – where a carefully guarded secret reveals a legacy of bloodshed. As Jamie and Danny will discover, for the promise of eternal life there are those who would kill, and kill again.